About the author

Moyra Calde[...] [...] 1927, and
moved to Lond[...] [...] and raised
three children. [...] [...]hy and an
M.A. in English [...] [...]nces from
the spiritual and p[...] [...]sical dimensions – but
are also deeply roo[...] [...]ve historical and religious research.
She has a passionate interest in the meaning of myths and legends,
believing they form a code of universal symbolic significance.

Moyra now lives on the fringes of Bath.

Also by Moyra Caldecott

Fiction

The Tall Stones
The Temple of the Sun
Shadow on the Stones
The Silver Vortex
The Lily and the Bull
The Tower and the Emerald
Etheldreda
Child of the Dark Star
Daughter of Amun
The Son of the Sun
Daughter of Ra
The Winged Man
The Green Lady and the King of Shadows

Non-fiction/Myths and Legends

Women in Celtic Myth
Crystal Legends
Twins of the Tylwyth Teg
Taliesin and Avagdu
Bran, Son of Llyr
Myths of the Sacred Tree
Mythical Journeys: Legendary Quests

AQUAE SULIS

BATH
CIRCA 72 AD

A NOVEL BY
MOYRA CALDECOTT

Bladud Books
An Imprint of Mushroom Publishing

First published in 1997
By Bladud Books
An imprint of Mushroom Publishing,
156 Southlands, Bath, United Kingdom, BA1 4EB.

Painting of Minerva and illustration of Bladud's Head
by Helen Folkes.
Design by Martyn Thomas.

The gilded bronze head of Minerva and the carved
stone Gorgon's (or Bladud's) head from the Temple
pediment are on display at the Roman Baths Museum
in Bath, England.

ISBN 1-899142-20-7

Printed and Bound in Great Britain by
Cox & Wyman, Reading

For Florence Tullia
Because of her Etruscan connection…
And because she has brought me so much joy.
With love.

Contents

Contents

Introduction

Aquae Sulis is the Roman name for the City of Bath, in North East Somerset, England.

The story of this novel is set in the late first century (c.72 AD), mostly in the town of Bath and its surroundings, but briefly also in Glastonbury, Rome, Pompeii, Petra and Jerusalem.

By 72 AD the Roman invasion of Britain (in 43 AD) had settled down to an efficient occupation. Roads, temples and forums had been built, but the memory of Boudicca's bloody rebellion in 60 AD was still fresh in the mind, and there were still skirmishes between the Romans and the Celtic tribes.

The hot waters that gush out of the earth at Bath, a quarter of a million gallons a day, have done so for millennia. The earliest people marvelled at the mystery and worshipped the gods and goddesses they thought were responsible for the phenomenon.

A potent ancient legend, well known in the region, tells of a British King, Bladud, who founded a healing sanctuary in the steaming marshlands when he discovered that the hot mud had curative properties.

By the time the Romans came, it was already a famous sacred place, under the protection of the Celtic tribe, the Dobunni and their Goddess Sul. Pilgrims came from all over Europe to take the healing waters and pay homage to the local gods. With their usual efficiency, the Romans tamed the waters, diverting them in lead pipes and drains to form a magnificent complex of public baths. They tamed the local gods as well, building temples to them Roman-style, and giving them Roman names. The Celtic goddess Sul became Sulis Minerva and the town that grew up around the baths was called Aquae Sulis, the Waters of Sulis.

After the Romans left in the fourth century, their buildings fell into disrepair. An Anglo-Saxon poem of the eighth century describes the ruins:

"Roofs fallen, towers ruined;
Rime on the mortar,
Walls rent and broken,
Undermined by age.
As a hundred generations
Have passed away,
All who built and owned
Are perished and gone,
Held fast in Earth's embrace,
The relentless grip of the grave…"

For centuries, the Roman town was forgotten until gradually bits and pieces began to emerge. The wonderful gilded head of Minerva so strikingly displayed in the on-site museum today was unearthed in 1727 when workers were digging a sewer beneath Stall Street. However, it was not until 1878 that the extent of the Roman remains was fully appreciated.

Today many of the Roman buildings have been excavated and are on display, but many are still waiting to be discovered under the 17th, 18th and 19th century buildings of Bath.

As a resident of 20th century Bath I never tire of visiting the site of the ancient Roman baths. They have been preserved and restored most sensitively and the information given is continually being updated as archaeologists extend their knowledge. I enjoy the feeling I get of familiarity and continuity as I see people throw their coins into the sacred spring to mark a fervent wish, just as citizens and pilgrims did nearly 2000 years ago.

What thoughts are in the minds of those who watch the waters of Sul rushing out of the dark earth, staining it rust-red? Do they stir to the ancient mystery of the place? Why do they linger? What memories… what dreams…? Are they held by the long thread of Time to that which has never gone away…?

Moyra Caldecott, Bath, August 1997.

Chapter 1

Megan leapt forward and furiously punched the centurion in the chest. He seemed amused and stepped back, choosing not to return the blow.

She picked up a pewter jug and flung it at him with all her strength, but it glanced harmlessly off his shoulder and fell clattering to the floor. He stooped and picked it up and set it back on the table. Then he slowly moved towards the door. There, before he left, he turned to look back at them, his expression enigmatic.

Megan and her grandfather were both shaking. She could see the old man's eyes were brimming with tears.

"What did he say to you? Why was he here?"

"Never speak to me of him, granddaughter. Never let him in the house!"

"He is a centurion, grandfather. If we defy him – others will come. I know how you feel – but they have such power. We cannot hope to win alone. Shall I call Brendan and the others?"

Megan knew her grandfather belonged to a group of disaffected Dobunni who often met to plan secret resistance to the Romans. As the years had gone by and the mighty Celtic warriors they had once been grew old and feeble, their determination to oust the hated conquerors never grew less, though their ability to affect change diminished. The population as a whole had grown comfortable and rich under the Roman occupation and fewer and fewer people were inclined to support them. Two years before, the Roman army had attacked a hill fort to the south of the town, and killed or driven off the entire population after an unsuccessful insurrection. Brendan, the rebel's fiery young leader, had escaped and made his way to Aquae Sulis where he had soon associated himself with the disgruntled but impotent old veterans, led, up to that time, by Owein.

"You will say nothing to Brendan and the others," Owein snapped. "This is a personal matter. If you ever see that man again you are to treat him with silence and contempt."

"But grandfather..."

"Enough! That is enough, girl. Leave me alone."

"But..."

"Go!"

Roughly he pulled away from her and turned his back on her.

Megan had heard angry voices in the front room of her home and had gone to investigate. Her grandfather Owein was shouting furiously at a Roman centurion in full military uniform standing stiff and straight in front of him. The girl scarcely heard what the old man was saying so astonished was she that a Roman had even been allowed into the house. She could only think that her grandfather had committed some offence and was being arrested.

She had stormed into the room, eyes flashing, and demanded to know what was going on. Both men looked at her – the old man suddenly silent in mid-imprecation, the younger man – with disconcerting interest.

Megan could see that the Roman was in his early middle years – his skin browned by the sun of a climate hotter than their own, his features lean and sharp.

"Leave us!" Her grandfather had said tersely. "There is nothing to concern you here."

The girl looked from one to the other. There were veins standing out on her grandfather's neck. She had never seen him so angry – nor so determined to control his anger in front of her. The Roman was not angry. He was staring at her as though sizing her up. Not as a young man would look at a woman, but as a military man would look over a new recruit.

"Go girl!" snapped Owein.

"Not until I know what is going on, grandfather. Why are you here, sir?" She had asked haughtily. "Why do you harass an old man?"

"I harass no one," the Roman began, but before he could continue the old man had rushed at him and butted him with his head like a man using a battering ram on a door.

"Get out!" He screamed. "Get out of my house! Leave us alone you... you bastard... you traitor... you Roman excrement!"

Now, after hesitating for a moment, not wanting to leave him, yet knowing that he wanted to be left, she went to the door and stared down the narrow street. There was no sign of the centurion. It was strange the way he had looked at her, she thought. Strange the way he had let them push him around. Usually the Romans were quick to retaliate if their precious dignity was assailed. They ruled firmly, justly, uncompromisingly. The local population was never in any doubt who were the masters. Even those locals who had built villas in the Roman style knew they were only second class citizens in their own country, no matter how many wealthy and powerful Romans they entertained in their luxurious homes.

The twin's mother had not lived beyond their first day, and their father had turned away at his wife's last breath and left the town. They were brought up by their grandfather, who had fought the Romans, and their grandmother, who was from the tribe of the Ordovices who were still at war with the Romans. They were named Megan and Ethne, and it would be hard to find two girls who looked so alike but were so different in temperament.

Megan was told she was like her father – stubborn, rebellious, fiery. Ethne was quieter – not passive and docile as her sister sometimes accused her of being – but the possessor of an inner strength and independence of mind that allowed her to keep her own counsel and go her own way without rising to every provocation.

When they were children Megan took the lead in the games they played together. If a queen was to be crowned, it was always Megan. If a slave was to be chastised, it was always Ethne.

At sixteen the two young women were tall and slim, with long hair of deep auburn burnished with gold, eyes grey-green, noses small but straight, lips full enough to look generous, but not generous enough to be voluptuous.

Aquae Sulis was not a garrison town though there were always soldiers about. When the Romans came it was already a famous religious centre founded centuries before by the great King Bladud in honour of the Goddess Sul who presided over the mysterious hot waters that sprang from deep in the earth. The conquerors had respected what they had found but expanded and Romanized it. The hot spring sacred to Sul they had enclosed, and they dedicated the temple they built beside it to their own Goddess of wisdom and healing, Minerva. To placate the locals they had identified the two Goddesses, the local and the imported, and a new composite one now ruled the spring – Sulis Minerva. They had even honoured the ancient Goddess Sul in the name of the town, Aquae Sulis – "the place of the waters of Sul".

Since ancient times, even before the time of King Bladud, an oracle had spoken for the Goddess, and the Romans did no more at first than house her more comfortably and elaborately. An efficient staff of priestesses made appointments and controlled the crowd who came from far and wide to consult her.

It was said that her fame had already reached the ears of Julius Caesar years before the successful invasion of Britain by Claudius, and one of Caesar's greatest disappointments when he withdrew from these western islands was that he had not encountered the famous Oracle of Sul, nor had a chance to compare her with the celebrated Pythoness of Delphi and Sybil of Cumae.

The present Oracle of Sul was an old woman. No one knew how old, but she had not been a young woman when the Romans had arrived more than thirty years before. Recently there had been some concern about her. Pilgrims had been turned away several times during the past winter with no explanation from the stern priestesses who served her. It was rumoured that she was ill and that the Romans were anxious to replace her with someone of their own choosing.

Another thought struck Megan. Could the centurion have been asking about Ethne with this in mind? If another Oracle was to be chosen this summer many of the locals believed it would be Ethne.

Since an early age, Ethne had pleaded with her grandfather to allow her to join the priesthood of Sulis Minerva. He had refused because, he said, the Romans had polluted the spring and corrupted the Oracle.

"There is nothing of the old religion there," he insisted. "If you want to get close to the Goddess – the *real* Goddess – avoid anything touched by the Romans."

He told her about a little round hill that rose clear of the forests on the southern ridge overlooking the Roman town, yet far enough away to have escaped the attentions of the Romans.

"There Sul used to be worshipped and there she still is," he said.

Ethne had made this hill her sacred place and spent much time there.

It was there one day when she was still a child she had encountered the Oracle. And it was there that they still sometimes met in secret.

Megan knew about this hill, and now, wanting to find her sister to discuss the centurion's visit, she decided to seek her there.

She made her way through the forests that clothed the long, slow hill south of the town. The Romans had discouraged the use of the sacred hills outside the city limits and tried to concentrate all holy observances within the temples they provided, but the forests were still criss-crossed with paths linking the more ancient sites.

The hawthorn was in blossom everywhere like a white mist showing between the dark trunks of the taller trees. As she looked up, the sun flickered and sparkled through light green leaves like sunlight dazzling on rippling water.

She already felt calmer.

The Roman had not seemed angry. It was her grandfather who had raised his voice. Even after the shouted insults the Roman had smiled. Such an unusual reaction suggested an unusual situation – but not a threatening one.

She heard a twig crack and swung round to see who was following her.

A young man emerged from the shadows into the sunlight carrying a bundle of logs on his shoulders.

He greeted her cheerfully, his light hazel eyes taking in her beauty appreciatively.

She paused until he came level with her, gazing at him suspiciously. He wore the short white tunic of the Romans, embroidered at the hem as though he were a nobleman, and yet he was carrying logs like a slave.

"Venus herself?" he asked lightly, smiling, standing boldly before her and looking her straight in the eyes as no slave would have dared.

"Apollo?" she mocked at once, raising an eyebrow.

He laughed.

"Ah well," he said, "perhaps not." And then, after a pause: "Lucius Sabinus is my name, lady. At your service."

He waited expectantly for her reply.

"A Roman" she said scornfully.

"Sadly, not," he said. "But a man at your service nevertheless."

'Good day, sir,' she said coldly and turned away.

He gazed after her with admiration as she walked quickly away. What a woman! The sunlight caught her hair and turned it and his heart to flame...

But by the time Megan had reached the steep slopes of Sul's hill she had forgotten all about him. There was no sign of Ethne among the shimmering grasses and jewelled flowers of the summit. A rolling landscape of hills and valleys stretched out as far as she could see. On the northern banks of the river below her the neat and geometric pattern of the orderly Roman town lay. Elsewhere, wooden houses clustered in clearings in the forest. Further away, she could see the great fields of grain and the opulent villas of the landlord farmers who owned them. Tiny figures, bent almost double, worked in rows. "Always in rows!" Megan thought with a sneer. "Everything for the Romans has to be done in straight lines."

She was just wondering whether she should return to the town when she heard someone approaching and looked down the eastern slope towards the sound. She saw a woman carrying a child obviously too heavy for her. She toiled up the hill to a point just below where Megan was standing and put her child down. Then she fell on her knees. The child, a girl of about five, remained standing. She was very pale and thin and seemed to be having great difficulty in breathing. Megan could see her chest heaving with the effort.

"I beseech you, lady," the woman pleaded, looking into Megan's eyes, "reach out your healing power to my daughter as you did to my son."

Megan stared. Did the woman believe her to be the Goddess? Embarrassed, she cleared her throat.

"You are mistaken, woman, I cannot heal your child. Why do you not take her to the healing waters of Sulis Minerva in the town like everybody else?"

The woman looked shocked.

"But you healed my son..."

"Not I," Megan said brusquely. "I have no power to heal." But even as she said it, and saw the hurt and betrayed expression on the woman's face, she thought of her sister Ethne.

Without another word she turned away and started down the hill. She felt two pairs of eyes staring at her back – but she did not stop.

"If Ethne wants to play Goddess," she thought bitterly, "let her. But I cannot!"

Brambles scratched her legs as she began to run, but she scarcely noticed them. Something was beginning to stir, to move, to change. Suddenly, she felt as though she was out of her depth in a deep and swiftly flowing river.

18

Chapter 2

Ethne had left the town early that morning, but not to visit her sacred hill. She had walked westwards searching for herbs that grew along the riverbank. She was so absorbed in her task that she wandered further than she intended. Hunger and weariness at last made her turn for home. Just as she did so, she noticed the columns of a villa on the slopes above her, half hidden by orchard trees. She paused, wondering who lived there. Curiosity drew her up the slope. She could hear ducks and chickens and soon found herself wading through farmyard fowl. The villa itself appeared newly built in the elegant Roman manner, with a long colonnaded verandah running the whole width of the front. Men were still working on this, kneeling on the ground apparently laying mosaic. A smaller wooden house stood a short way away and beyond that lay various farm sheds and barns. The owners were clearly working farmers – not aristocratic foreigners – probably locals who had made a profit from the influx of pilgrims and settlers in the years since the Pax Romana had civilized the valley.

She was about to turn and leave as quietly as she had come when she was startled to find she was no longer alone. A woman stood behind her, watching her closely, sizing her up carefully from the top of her tangled and untidy auburn hair, to the muddy hem of her homespun skirt. Her gaze paused at the bulging pouch hanging at her side.

Ethne flushed. "They are herbs – wild herbs," she said hastily, and then added after a long pause in which the woman's gaze did not waver, "for healing." Did the woman think she had been stealing food from her farm?

She wished she could run away, but the stranger, haughty and stern, blocked the path.

"You know this is private property?" She spoke at last, coldly.

"I did not realize. I was at the river... and I saw..." Ethne's voice faded away feebly.

The woman's expression seemed to be softening.

"What is your name?" She asked at last, and her voice was a

shade less harsh. The girl was well spoken. She was muddy but her skin was fine and her features refined. It was unlikely after all that she was a thief or a slave.

Julia Sabinus was a lonely woman in her late twenties. Her mother was long dead and from a very early age she had been the matron of the household of her step-father and step-brother. There were female servants and slaves of course, but they were not suitable friends and companions. The town was just too far away for easy access to companionship there.

Ethne told her her name and lineage and described where she lived. Julia knew the area – and approved of it.

"You must be tired and thirsty," she said stiffly, but not unkindly. "If you come to the house I'm sure Sallus will find you a drink. It is a long walk back to your home."

Ethne thanked her at once, and gratefully followed as Julia led the way towards the smaller, older house.

"We cannot go into the new house," she explained. "The men are still working there. We are paying for the best mosaic team in the country, but they take their time and eat and drink like twenty men."

The kitchen they entered was all terracotta paving and scrubbed wood. Bundles of herbs hung from the ceiling, scenting the air. A male slave was chopping vegetables and throwing them into a large pot. He stopped at once when they entered and bowed to his mistress.

She commanded him to bring a drink for her guest. Ethne caught a look of surprise as he took in her muddy and dishevelled appearance, but it lasted only a flash. He served cool elderflower cordial from a jug of red Samian ware as the two women sat on a bench in the garden.

Fields of green wheat stirred in the breeze covering the rolling hills. Horses grazed in a paddock to the left. Birds sang. A boat rode quietly at tether beside the river bank.

"How peaceful it is here," Ethne remarked.

"Too peaceful," Julia sighed. "I envy you the town."

Ethne smiled. "I envy you the country."

"You would soon be bored," the older woman said and Ethne sensed her restlessness, *her* boredom.

"You are not so far from Aquae Sulis that you cannot visit," she suggested mildly.

Julia pursed her lips. "I go in sometimes. It is better than nothing. But one day I intend to go to Rome. I'm tired of small places and small people."

Ethne raised a quizzical eyebrow.

"Surely people in Rome are the same size as they are here?"

"I didn't mean in *size*!" Julia snapped impatiently.

"Nor did I," said Ethne quietly.

But Julia did not take her meaning. Her heart had been set on Rome since childhood when she was first told that she had been fathered by the Roman general Vespasian. It seems he had been in the district consolidating the Roman position just after the invasion. Since he had become Emperor Julia had become more determined than ever to visit Rome. She had dreams of meeting the Emperor and claiming her rights as his daughter.

"I've thrown more than one gold coin into the Sacred Spring. It's just a matter of time before I go."

"Rome?" Ethne murmured – thinking about the stories she had heard. She could scarcely imagine a city of that vast size, a city yielding such power over so many lives, a city so corrupt and violent, so cruel and arrogant. "They throw people to be torn apart by wild beasts there," she said.

"Only criminals and Christians," Julia said casually.

Ethne looked at her. Her eyes were shining at the thought of Rome – the tall colonnades – the buildings that dwarfed humans – the paved streets and magnificent houses – the banquets – the jewels – the fine clothes...

She could see her in Rome – but she could see her returning embittered and disappointed. She shivered.

"It is not good to gamble too much on dreams," she said softly.

Julia looked at her impatiently, already bored with her company. She stood up, clapped her hands for Sallus the slave, and ordered him to take her guest back to town in the boat.

"But don't be too long," she added coldly. "Don't stop to gossip. The masters and I will be wanting our dinner shortly."

Within moments of leaving the boat Ethne met her aunt Elen, a scrawny, hard working woman with a sharp tongue and a slight limp. Her thin hair was screwed into a tight knot on top of her head and she was dressed in her best clothes though her arms were full of purchases from the market. Elen had never married and she lived alone, tolerating neither servant nor slave to enter her territory, yet she was carrying enough food for a feast.

Ethne greeted her. Her face was flushed and her eyes bright. The girl had never seen her look so young and happy.

"Why, aunt," she said, smiling and indicating the food, "what's the big occasion?"

Elen barely paused and Ethne found herself almost running to keep pace with her.

"I can't stop now," the woman called over her shoulder. "My brother is home at last!"

"Your brother?" Ethne said in surprise. As far as she knew Elen had only one brother and that was her own father.

"You can't mean...?"

"Yes... Yes," Elen replied impatiently. "Your father. And his own father threw him out of his house this morning. Can you imagine that? You would have thought he would be overjoyed to see him after all this time wondering where he was and if he was all right! But no matter – *I'm* looking after him. *I'm* happy to see him."

"My father!" Ethne repeated. She was so shocked by the news she fell behind the hurrying figure of her aunt, and stood in the busy street like a rock in a stream with the crowds washing either side of her. Someone greeted her, but she ignored him. "My father!" she kept repeating to herself. She tried to remember what she had heard about him. Her grandparents hardly ever mentioned him. Friends of the family occasionally let remarks slip but stopped themselves as though they knew the subject was forbidden. She gathered he had been handsome and strong – and strong willed too! She had often dreamed of his return.

She pulled herself together and started to run after her aunt. Was he really back after all this time? What would he be like? Would he take her in his arms and try to make up for all those years he had been away? What would he think of her? She wondered if she should run home and change into her best clothes. She was mud-spattered from the river bank and her dress was covered with burrs. Her hair was tangled. She certainly did not look her best.

But she couldn't wait. Her father! Her father was home!

She caught up and was with her aunt when she entered her small, neat, house. For a moment she could see nothing, for her eyes were dazzled as she left the light for the dim interior, and then a figure

22

moved forward to take a basket from her aunt's arm and the light fell on him. She saw the tall, impressive figure of a Roman centurion.

She caught her breath.

Her first thought was that her father, who had done who knows what in his voluntary exile, had returned home to hide, only to find the authorities were there looking for him. But when she saw the way Elen greeted him, she realized that *he* was her father. No wonder her grandfather had thrown him out!

He was looking over her aunt's shoulder at her. The light from the open door showed her a face strong and lined, with a tendency towards sternness, and yet at this moment his expression was one of affectionate amusement.

Elen was so busy unloading her shopping and fussing to get the meal prepared that she seemed to have forgotten the girl's presence.

The two strangers stared at each other – the man in his military uniform incongruously holding a basket of vegetables, carrot and turnip leaves spilling out over the side; the young woman clutching a pouch of herbs, her auburn hair tumbling over her shoulders, a garland of daisies she had placed there hours before now slipped and at a rakish angle, the flowers drooping and fading.

The man spoke first.

"So," he said. "We meet again."

Ethne looked puzzled. Did he expect her to recognize him after all these years? Did he expect her to fall into his arms and call him "father"? How many times as a child she had envisaged this meeting. Always he had gathered her up, weeping with remorse for having deserted her and her sister, swearing to make up for all the lost years. Never had he said so casually: "So – we meet again."

From his face it seemed he had integrity, honesty and courage. Yet where had those qualities been when he ran out on his two new-born infants?

"Not for sixteen years, sir," she said quietly, but with a hint of accusation. "And in those sixteen years," she thought, "while I was growing up in this valley, in this town... while I was learning to walk and talk and make friends... while I was exploring the hills and finding out about life... all that time were you learning nothing but how to kill people?"

He looked surprised.

"Did we not meet in my father's house this very morning?"

"Ah," Ethne said, "you must have met my sister, sir – your other daughter."

He looked embarrassed.

"I'm sorry," he muttered. He stared at her closely, wonderingly. Could two human beings look so exactly alike?

"We are twins," she said lamely.

"I know. I am sorry. I didn't think..."

Elen came bustling back.

"If you're going to stay for the meal, you must help, girl. If you're not, you must get out of my way."

Ethne looked at the man, her father, the stranger. She wanted to stay, and she wanted to run away.

"I must get back, aunt Elen," Ethne murmured. "Grandfather will be wondering where I am." Then politely, stiffly, awkwardly to the Roman centurion: "Will you be staying in Aquae Sulis, sir," she asked, "or are you just passing through?"

"I will be staying," he replied gravely. "We will meet again."

She bobbed her head shyly to him and started backing towards the door. At that moment the strap on the pouch at her hip broke and all the leaves and flowers she had carefully collected tumbled out on to the floor. She crouched down at once, her cheeks burning. "What will he think of me – clumsy fool – country bumpkin in muddy homespun. I should never have come to see him like this!"

But he was squatting beside her, helping her to gather up the herbs – helping her to put them back in the bag. His large brown hands brushed against hers as he did so. She trembled and tears began to blind her. She wanted to hug him. She wanted him to be proud of her.

"What on earth are you doing, girl?" Elen cried. "Clear up that mess at once. Take the broom to it. There is no time to pick up every leaf."

"There is time, sister. Don't be so impatient."

"Impatient? That's a laugh coming from the most impatient man in the world!"

"Not any more, Elen," he said so quietly that she could not possibly have heard. He gave Ethne a quizzical, conspiratorial look as though he was telling her something about himself that no one else knew.

24

Her heart skipped a beat. He had acknowledged her. They had connected. They would never again be parted.

She stood up, flushed, and watched him as he finished picking up her spilled herbs. When he handed them back to her they looked into each other's eyes and he knew that one at least of his daughters had forgiven him.

Chapter 3

When Decius Brutus left Aquae Sulis sixteen years before, his name had been Kynan. He had stormed off, a young and bitter man, cursing Sul who had let his young and beautiful wife die, leaving him with two ugly and squalling infants he did not know and did not want.

"My life is over," he thought. "I don't care where I go or what I do."

For a while he had drifted aimlessly, half hoping he would be killed in a brawl that would save him from the effort of living.

It was after one fight of many that he was thrown into prison by some Roman soldiers. There he was not allowed to languish, but was forced to exercise frequently and hard, and eventually trained to fight in the disciplined Roman way. The captain of the guard had spotted his potential early on and took a personal interest in his training. It seemed to Kynan that he was singled out for brutal treatment, but gradually the rigors of his situation paid off and he was told that he would enter an arena in Gaul and, if he won three battles, he would be set free.

Packed like a carcass of meat among other prisoners he was transported across the Channel to be delivered to a new set of guards and another stinking prison.

In the arena he fought savagely, determined to free himself from his captors, but his very success told against him. He became famous as the "British Brute" and was much in demand for the shows. When he had won three times his demand for the release that he had been promised was ignored.

In the end he realized there was only one way out and that was through the army. He took the name Decius Brutus and signed on for twenty-five years.

He had not intended to return to his homeland – yet here he was, in his late thirties, back in Britain, assigned to guarding the huge Temple of Claudius the God at Camulodunum.

He and his fellow guards found it something of a joke that the misshapen little Emperor was to be worshipped and a gigantic romanticized statue of him erected. But he knew that there were many locals who looked on it as an insult added to injury that they had to do obeisance and offer sacrifices to the man who had invaded their land and taken away their liberty. That was why, night and day, a guard was mounted on the effigy. Decius Brutus and his fellow officers were well aware that there was still a strong underground resistance to Roman rule despite the apparent outward calm obedience to an efficiently run administration. Though nearly twelve years had passed since Boudicca's bloody revolution, the Governor was taking no chances. The slightest sign of disaffection was stamped on immediately, and, although it was unlikely the Governor really believed Claudius was a god, visible acceptance of his deification was made compulsory as a test of loyalty to the regime.

Decius had entered the army only to escape the arena, and his loyalties at that time were to no one. But over the years he had come to admire the Roman strength, sophistication and order, and to identify with their desire to rule the world. He had been present when Titus devastated Jerusalem, destroyed Herod's magnificent Temple and carried off the sacred symbols of the Jewish religion to Rome. Much of what he saw touched his heart, but his belief that Romanization could bring peace and order to any region if the people would only cooperate, made him accept the massacre of trouble-makers as the necessary sacrifice of the few for the good of the whole.

He was alarmed to learn, when he was sent to Aquae Sulis to erect another statue of Claudius, that his own father's name was on the list of local trouble-makers to be watched.

When Megan arrived home late that summer's day she learned that the centurion she had so fiercely ejected from her home was her own father. It was her grandmother, Olwen, who told her, for her grandfather refused to speak about the matter, but sat in a corner, slumped in his chair, sulking and occasionally muttering imprecations against Romans in general and his son in particular.

"Why has he come back after all these years? What did he want?" Megan asked.

"He came to supervise the erection of a statue of the Emperor Claudius," her grandmother said. "And he came to warn your grandfather not to cause any trouble," Olwen added, looking hard at her husband. This seemed to make the old man even angrier, and his growling and snorting became even more incomprehensible.

"What arrogance!" cried Megan. "*I'll* give him trouble! He will regret coming back here as long as he lives!"

"Hush, child!" warned Olwen quickly. "You don't know what you're saying."

"I'm not a child, grandma, and I know what I'm saying. To come back after all these years in *such* a uniform – threatening *such* things..."

"He didn't threaten. He advised."

"Oh, grandma, you're so innocent! You don't get advice from Romans – you get threats and commands and death if you don't obey!"

"Your father is not a Roman, dear," Olwen protested mildly.

"As good as. Worse in fact. He has turned against his own people."

"Perhaps..." Ethne spoke for the first time, having come in only on the latter part of the conversation but guessing at once the context of her sister's words. "Perhaps he can see that there is no way of getting rid of the Romans now so it is best for all of us if we can learn to live with them."

"And worship their stinking Emperor as a god!" Megan cried bitterly.

Ethne was silent.

Megan turned to her grandfather. "Where are they to put this slab of rubbish?" she asked, her lip curling scornfully.

"In the forecourt of the temple!" Owein snarled. "As though the sacred space is not desecrated enough."

"It won't stand there long!" muttered Megan darkly.

"Megan!" her grandmother said sharply. "Your grandfather has his head in the past and his feet in the grave. I won't have you throwing away your young life to follow his wild schemes."

"I'll not throw my life away, grandma, but what kind of life is it when strangers can come who know nothing of our beliefs and traditions and make us dishonour our gods and honour our enemy on a pedestal."

"You don't have to honour it," Olwen replied firmly. "You just let it be. If they want to play childish games and set up a doll as a god – we can humour them as we would a child – but go on honouring Sul and the others secretly."

"Can you really not see, old woman," Owein said impatiently, "the implications of that damned statue?"

"It will just be a statue, old man," Olwen replied. "A lump of stone. It will have no power."

"It will be a symbol," he said. "And a symbol is more powerful than a whole army of soldiers. Why do you think the Roman legions take such care of their eagle standard? It is, after all, just a bird on a stick. But when it is captured, a disciplined and well-trained army of men becomes a rabble and flees from the battle field."

"Well, all I know," grumbled Olwen, backing down somewhat, "is that if the Governor wants a statue of Claudius here, we will have a statue of Claudius here – and there is nothing we can do about it without getting into trouble. Why don't we just ignore it?"

"They won't let us ignore it, Grandma. They'll make us worship it!"

"No one can ever make you worship something you don't want to worship." Ethne said suddenly. "Worship is a secret of the heart. Words and rituals have nothing to do with *real* worship."

"Quite so!" cried Olwen triumphantly. But when Megan and Owein's eyes met, a tacit agreement passed between them. They would let the matter drop for the moment – but neither intended to let it lie for long.

Chapter 4

When Lucius Sabinus returned home the image of the girl he had met in the forest that morning was still vivid. He had spent most of the day dreaming about her. At the evening meal he learned that a girl fitting her description had been at his home but a few hours before.

"What was she doing here?" he asked, astonished.

"I found her staring at the house."

"Just staring?"

"She was tired and muddy. She had been picking herbs along the river and in the marshes. She's some kind of healer I believe. I sent her to town in the boat. Why the interest?" Julia looked curiously at her step-brother.

"I met her this morning. Was she not the most beautiful woman you have ever seen?"

Julia pursed her lips.

"Well..." she began grudgingly – and then laughed at his expression. "I'll grant you she was beautiful. But she was too quiet and serious – too earnest. Rather dull I thought."

"Did you not notice the spark in her eye, the pride in her step? She had a kind of – a kind of majesty. I felt like falling at her feet. She could have been the handmaiden of a goddess!"

"Not by the time she reached me," Julia laughed. "She looked more like a peasant or a slave."

"You must have been blind!"

"Perhaps a woman sees different things in another woman."

"At any rate – she was here!" Lucius cried joyfully. "Praise be to Orpheus!"

"Speaking of Orpheus – the men finished the mosaic today. They're working on the one on the verandah now."

Without another word Lucius turned and ran towards the new house. The men had finished work for the day and the place was deserted. The pattern on the verandah floor was only half completed. By stepping very carefully Lucius could just avoid the new paving and squeeze through to the door of the Orphic room.

There the newly cemented mosaic gleamed, jewel-like, in brilliant colour.

Lucius stared at the figure of Orpheus himself at the centre of the design. Around him animals of many different kinds circled, giving the impression of power and movement, energy whirling around a still centre. Even the trees between the animals seemed to be in motion, their branches tossed by the wind. Orpheus, in his Phrygian cap, was playing his lyre, controlling all by the sweetness of sound. Further out, signs and symbols of the vortex were depicted suggesting the raw force of nature – nature unmanifest, awaiting the shaping and control of a god.

Lucius and his father, Aulus, had taken to the imported religion with enthusiasm. Everything foreign seemed interesting and exotic to them, while their local traditions and customs seemed primitive and boring. With their rise in fortune they had taken on Roman names and in everything they imitated their conquerors – even to using the family name of the Emperor Vespasian, Sabinus, as their family name. Perhaps if the officer who had seduced his first wife had not become Emperor, Aulus would not have been so ready to publicize the affair, nor Julia to boast of her illegitimacy. As it was, none of the local men seemed good enough for Julia, the Emperor's daughter, and, on her rare trips to town, she scanned all the pilgrims who came to the Sacred Spring in the hope of meeting a suitor worthy and rich enough to take her to Rome.

The Orphic cult had started in Thrace, passed on to Greece and then had been adopted and adapted, like so many other religious cults, by the Romans. Minerva herself, now identified with the Celtic goddess Sul, had been associated in Rome with the Greek goddess Athena, the fierce and wise, the guide, mentor and warrior goddess who had defended the Athenians against their enemies.

Aulus, in rejecting the primitive superstitions of his people in favour of the worldly, sophistication of the Romans, chose Orpheus as his favourite god. Orpheus made sense to him. Orpheus made order out of chaos, like the Romans did. He played his lyre and the lion lay down with the lamb – warring tribes settled down and worked together for the first time under one over-all master. It was unlikely that Aulus, when he made his choice, had any idea of the deeper and more profound implications of the Orphic cult.

He set aside a room in his house for Orpheus and commissioned a mosaic for the floor. A priest was to come when the room was

31

ready, and Aulus hoped his house would become an important centre of influence in the community. Foreigners and Romans might come who could not find satisfaction in the town. Locals, disappointed with the Oracle of Sulis Minerva, might turn to an alternative oracle. Aulus could not wait for the great house to be completed and the priest to arrive. Nor could Lucius. His interest in Orpheus was perhaps slightly different from his father's. Aulus wanted the power that having such a cult centre in his home would bring, while Lucius genuinely believed in Orpheus and secretly hoped that he, himself, through the rituals, would be able to experience the Otherworld as Orpheus had done.

In their youth Aulus and the centurion, Decius Brutus, had been close friends. He had taken it hard when Kynan, as he was then called, had left. But Kynan's father, Owein, was not one of his favourite people. To Aulus he was nothing but a troublesome, meddling fool, and in danger of bringing down the wrath of Rome on their heads and cutting them off from the lucrative trade that kept Aulus and his family so comfortable and wealthy.

Walking back from the market that day Aulus saw Owein holding forth among a small group of men in front of the baths. By his gestures he was very angry and the men, though at present silent, were listening intently.

Aulus had heard Owein speak often enough and knew that in that mood it would not be long before he had roused his listeners to the anger he himself felt.

"Hello, old man," Aulus called out, "what mischief are you up to this time?"

Owein cast him a furious look, but scarcely paused in his oration.

"Don't listen to him," Aulus warned the others, laughing. "He's full of nothing but hot air!"

"Hot air that will burn you to charcoal one day," Owein snapped. "Pass on, Roman lackey – this news is not for you."

"What news, old man?"

"Ask your Roman masters!" Owein's lip curled disdainfully.

"I'm asking you."

Several of the men in the group looked uneasy by this time, and were starting to move off.

"Owein tells us that they are planning to put a huge statue of Claudius in the Temple forecourt," someone told him.

"And we are to sacrifice to it as though it is a god," another added.

"There! What do you say to that?" Owein demanded, looking at him in triumph, sure that even he would be shocked at this.

Aulus was – but would not admit it to Owein. He felt the Romans were making a mistake this time. Had they not noticed that the locals were not rational and pragmatic like themselves? They *liked* things to be mysterious and their gods ineffable and inexplicable. They would never worship an ordinary flesh and blood man – particularly one who had conquered them. The Celts hated defeat and would never lie down quietly under it. The Governor was asking for trouble over this, and would surely get it.

Owein was ranting on.

"There are too many shrines and too many gods here as it is," he grumbled. "Everyone who comes to the town seems to bring his own god and set up a shrine. You can hardly hear yourself speak for the noise of foreign tongues praying to foreign gods, or see for the smoke of sacrificial fires!"

"All the more reason for there to be one god over all," Aulus declared triumphantly, "and that one representing the might of Rome that rules over all the world."

Owein lifted his stick and threatened to strike Aulus.

Aulus stepped back and turned, laughing, to walk away. There, coming towards him, he saw his old childhood friend, Kynan, but Kynan in the uniform of a centurion in the Roman army. He glanced back, astonished, at Owein. The old man, shaking uncontrollably, had fallen back into the arms of one of his companions.

"So, Aulus, old friend," Decius the centurion called out, "you too have fallen foul of my father."

"Kynan!"

"Decius Brutus is my name now," he said, laughing. "I too am a Roman lackey!"

"Decius Brutus!" Aulus could do nothing but repeat the name. The Roman name.

Decius grinned at his astonishment.

"Come, Aulus, let's leave these old men to shake their fists at shadows. We have much serious drinking to do." And he put his arm around his friend's shoulders and led him away. As they turned the corner of the street, they both looked back. Owein, propped up by his friends, was staring after them. When he saw them looking at him he shouted something, but the noise coming from the nearby tavern drowned out his words.

Decius bit his lip and his face shadowed.

"He is a stubborn old man," he muttered. "There's nothing he can do. Why won't he accept it?"

"Many of the older ones cling on to their wounds as though they are afraid to let them go. The war with the Romans was a time of excitement – a time when they did great and heroic deeds. Life has been dull for them since."

"Well, if he keeps this up, he'll find out how exciting life can be in a Roman prison."

Aulus could see the deep concern on his friend's face.

"Don't worry about him," he said soothingly. "He's all bluster. Nothing ever comes of it. He will bow his knee with the rest when the statue is up – or be excused for age and infirmity. He can stride about with the best of men – but when it suits him I have seen him leaning on his granddaughters as though he is a hundred years old."

They had reached the tavern and pushed in through the crowds inside. Shoulder to shoulder they raised their mugs of British ale to the old times when they had been boys together and life seemed much simpler. Aulus looked at the hard lines on his companion's face, the scars on his arms and the side of his neck.

"You've seen some action I see," he said. "Where have you been and what have you been doing while I stayed at home and made money?" Decius noticed the envy in his voice. He laughed.

"Believe me – you would not have wanted to be where I have been or seen what I have seen."

"Have you been to Rome?"

"Yes."

"Have you seen Vespasian, the Emperor?"

Decius grinned. "I have seen Vespasian, the Emperor."

"How close have you been? What does he look like? You know he fathered my step-daughter, Julia, when he was in Britain?"

Decius raised his eyebrows.

"He was not Emperor then of course," Aulus added hastily.

"I heard you married a woman older than yourself already with a child," Decius remarked.

"He didn't rape her. They were lovers while he was here. He

34

gave her a ring and promised to marry her. Julia wants to go to Rome and claim the relationship."

"Discourage her if you can. Rome is not like Aquae Sulis and the Emperor is no longer a lonely soldier on an outpost far from home."

"But he will remember her mother. It was not just a casual affair."

"Not to Julia's mother perhaps – but the man must have had many women in his long career before he became Emperor. There was even a Jewish woman, I remember. But it did not stop him destroying Jerusalem. The world must be full of the illegitimate offspring of Roman soldiers and Roman Emperors. I am sure I have fathered some myself."

Aulus looked annoyed. It had been his ambition ever since Vespasian had become Emperor three years before that he and Julia should go to Rome and bask in some kind of glory reflected from the Emperor's throne. He, himself, had first thought of the plan, and now Julia, unmarried and feeling the years passing her by, had become obsessed by it. He did not know how he could back out of it now. Decius was obviously a man of some influence and power. He had been to Rome. He had met the Emperor. Whatever his first reaction had been Aulus was sure he could call on his help when the time came. But first the man must meet Julia and be convinced by looking at her that she had Vespasian's blood in her veins. Aulus had seen likenesses of the Emperor on coins and statues – but he knew they were idealized. It was difficult to be sure of the accuracy of any detail. Julia certainly looked more Roman than Celt – but that might just be because for so long she had believed herself to be Roman and had affected all the Roman fashions. Her nose was on the aquiline side – and that was a point in favour of her being Roman. But any Roman soldier could have fathered her. He had only his dead wife's word for who it was, and a ring her lover had given her. When this was presented to Vespasian, surely he would remember? A ring of large pearls and lapis lazuli set in gold was surely too valuable for any ordinary Roman soldier to possess. There was no inscription, but the general had said that it was very precious to him because it had once belonged to the grandmother who had brought him up.

"How long will you be in Aquae Sulis?" Aulus asked Decius now. "Will you dine with us tonight?"

The centurion shook his head.

"Sorry. I would like to my friend, but I have to get back to my men. But I will be here for some time to supervise the erection of the statue of Claudius the Governor has ordered. I'll probably have to stay on until the locals have accepted its presence. Which may be longer than I would wish," he added ruefully, "if my father's reaction is anything to go by."

Aulus laughed.

"It's not going to be easy. Do you really have to do this? Have we not enough statues of gods in Aquae Sulis already?"

Decius shrugged. "This one will represent the power of Rome over all the local deities."

"Will it not be like rubbing salt into the wound? Claudius is the one who conquered us. Would it not be better to have another?"

"Who? They are all as corrupt as one another. Perhaps Vespasian is the best of them all."

"Then have a statue of the God Vespasian!" cried Aulus.

"So Mistress Julia could claim she is the offspring of divinity?"

Aulus did not notice the mockery in his voice. His eyes were gleaming, his thoughts racing with this very thought.

Chapter 5

On his way to Britain, the Greek, Demosthenes, broke his journey in Rome. Because he was a priest of Orpheus in his homeland, the Orphic community in Rome, some of whom were Greeks themselves, warmly welcomed him. One, an old friend, Spiros, took him into his own home and prepared a feast for him.

"What makes you go to such a distant and barbaric place?" he asked when told that Demosthenes was on his way to the British Isles. "The people have not been civilized for long and I hear they are quick to rebel most savagely. Besides, the climate is perpetually moist and cold. Stay with us! We have need of more Greeks in Rome."

"I cannot. Orpheus himself has told me to go."

Spiros looked at him in surprise. Like many priests, he told his flock that the god would speak to them – but never really expected it to happen.

"How did he speak? When? Are you sure it was Orpheus himself? You know there are a lot of mischievous spirits around just waiting for a gullible mind."

"I was at Epidaurus. I was ill. So ill I could barely walk, and my friends took me to the sanctuary of Aesculapius. There I slept in the dream cells over the snake pits and there it was that Orpheus came to me."

Spiros, whose first questions had been prompted by scepticism, sat up and looked at his friend's face closely. It was clear that whatever had happened, Demosthenes, who was no gullible fool, truly and deeply believed he had encountered the god Orpheus. It was clear also that he did not want to expand on what he had already said.

Spiros waited expectantly for a few moments and then demanded to know more.

"You mean you saw Orpheus in a dream?"

Demosthenes hesitated before he answered.

"No. I saw him."

"But you were dreaming? You were in the dream cells."

"At first I did dream. I dreamed of hot water springing from the rock. I dreamed of bathing in it and all my aching limbs finding relief. I dreamed of Aquae Sulis in Britain."

"How do you know?"

"I know."

"You thought... you suspected... you didn't *know*. All hot springs look the same!"

"It was the buildings around it – the landscape beyond it. The statue of Sulis Minerva overlooking it."

"Sulis? Who is this Sulis? I've never heard of her!"

"Sul. The ancient Goddess worshiped in that part of Britain. I heard of her just recently from a pilgrim returned from a visit to her oracle and healing sanctuary."

"So the dream was using what you already knew – what was already uppermost in your mind?"

"I don't deny it. The pilgrim told me they were looking for a priest of Orpheus there, and it came into my mind to offer myself."

"You see! Nothing supernatural there."

"The dream was vivid. And when I woke I remembered every detail – and some that were not given to me by the pilgrim."

"You can only know if it was genuine by going there and checking."

"When I first heard about Aquae Sulis I felt a strange compulsion – a strong feeling that I somehow knew the place. I questioned the man repeatedly, hungry for details, never satisfied with what he told me. I kept thinking – no, that is wrong! I felt as though I'd been there long ago."

"When you dreamed about it – did you see it as you thought it used to be – or as it is now – as the pilgrim described it?" In spite of himself, Spiros was becoming fascinated.

"A bit of both. The image kept slipping and sliding from one to the other until I couldn't be sure whether I was seeing it as it is now or as I remembered it from the past. The image of the present had lots of buildings – temples, statues – even a complex of baths on the Roman model. But the image of the past was of a wooden circular building raised above marshland... and then..."

Demosthenes shook his head sadly. "And then I saw the same place – but all that I had seen before was gone. There were new buildings of strange design – one with two huge towers on which ladders were carved in stone reaching to the sky. And there were gods and goddesses – some climbing, some falling. But none of these I knew."

He shivered.

Spiros, watching his friend's face, saw the pain there and waited, patiently at last, for him to continue.

"When I first heard that someone was looking for a priest to officiate at Orphic Ceremonies I knew I ought to go, but I was happy where I was, surrounded by people I loved and who loved me. Life was extremely easy and pleasant for me in Athens."

He paused again.

Spiros waited.

"But I kept dreaming of the place – and the sequence of the images changed every time. I was never sure which of them – the marshland with the hot and bubbling mud, the weird buildings with the stone ladders, or the elegant Roman baths – were in the future, the present, or the past. Often I woke weeping."

Another pause. The silence strong and deep. Bright sunlight falling through a high, small window caused a shaft of light to illuminate a bowl of white lilies. They blazed in sudden glory.

"I began to get ill. I ached in every limb," Demosthenes continued. "But it was not really for this alone I went to Aesculapius at Epidaurus. I wanted to resolve my dilemma. I knew I had to go to Aquae Sulis – and I did not want to. I thought – I suppose I knew – that the pain in my body was a result of this conflict in my soul."

Spiros nodded. "Very likely. Very likely."

"It was after the dream – the same dream I had had so often before – that I saw Orpheus in the dream cell at Epidaurus. He stood at the foot of my bed."

"You were still dreaming?"

"No. I knew I was awake. I could see the chamber quite clearly. I remember the lamp wick was almost burned down. I was trying to decide what was different about the dream I'd just had from the recurring dreams I had been having at home, when I noticed a figure standing in the room. The light was very dim from the lamp, yet there was suddenly light in the room. It was from his face."

"What did he look like?"

"I – I don't know."

"You don't know!" Spiros almost screamed with frustration. "You *saw* Orpheus and you don't know what he looked like!"

Demosthenes shook his head. "I was so startled. I remember it was a beautiful face, a calm and kind face – but I couldn't describe his features. His features were lost in the light."

"Was he fair or dark?"

Demosthenes shook his head.

"Tall or short?"

Again he shook his head.

"How do you know it was Orpheus?"

"Because I had called on him to help me, and he had come."

Spiros took a deep breath. He knew it would do no good to shout at Demosthenes. The man was already looking as though he wished he had not said as much as he had.

"Did he have the Phrygian cap?"

"I didn't notice."

"Did he have animals? The lyre? Birds? What?"

"He had nothing with him. Or if he did, I didn't notice. I was only aware of the light and... I could *feel* his presence. His form was clear and yet not clear. I can't explain."

"Did he speak?"

Demosthenes took his time to reply. At last, he said – dreamily – thoughtfully – as though he were drawing the words back from a long way away: "*It is time to go home.*"

Spiros waited for more, but no more was forthcoming.

"Is that all he said?"

Demosthenes nodded.

"So why are you going to Britain? Why are you not going home to Athens?"

"Because I knew he was not speaking about Athens. I knew he was speaking about Aquae Sulis."

"But how can Aquae Sulis be your home? You have never been there!" Spiros almost shouted.

Demosthenes shrugged. "I don't know. But I have no doubts now."

"Did he say the name out loud? Did you hear the words with your ears?"

"I don't know how I heard them. I just did."

Spiros was angry.

"I've never heard such rubbish. You never met Orpheus at all. And even if you did – you're deliberately going against his instructions. Athens is your home. Athens is where you were born and where you have lived all your life."

Demosthenes was staring into space, not hearing his friend's voice. He was seeing again the calm face of his God and, at his side, a Goddess he knew to be Sul. She was smiling at him as though she had known him a long time.

While Demosthenes was in Rome, like any traveller, he walked about the streets, marvelling at the buildings he saw on every side. Coming from Athens, there was often a slight twist of disdain to his mouth.

"Have the Romans no ideas of their own?" he thought as he passed temple after temple directly copied from the Greek. He recognized the work of Greek sculptors in all the best statues that stood along the way. Often he shook his head at the Roman lack of sensitivity to proportion – columns too squat – distances between them too wide or too narrow, often only fractionally, but that fraction making the difference between true elegance and vulgar ostentation.

The hubbub in the street never seemed to cease. Vendors shouted at him as he passed, orators boomed at him from platforms. "The Romans make up for subtlety of argument by volume of sound," he remarked to himself uncharitably, remembering the teachers in the schools of philosophy in Athens. Demosthenes was a man well advanced in years who had spent most of his life as a student. His greatest pleasure was to learn, coming only recently to the Orphic priesthood.

The crowds flowing up and down the streets seemed never ending – from ragged, brown-clad beggars to rich men in crisp and dazzling white. All seemed as though they were determined to arrive somewhere – yet Demosthenes had the impression that they were all just moving about, passing each other, interweaving in every direction like a vast moving tapestry, ever changing, ever the same, going nowhere.

Suddenly he felt almost dizzy and withdrew between two columns of purple porphyry where he would be safe from being jostled by the crowd.

He shivered – staring in astonishment at what he saw. The great tall buildings were all gone and in their place were broken pieces of stone lying among flowering acanthus and oleander. The beautiful frieze of interlacing leaves he had been gazing at a moment before was smashed at his feet, only one piece still recognisable. The head of Apollo, still smiling, lay in a ditch.

"No," he whispered. "No. I don't want this. I don't want to see this. Take it away." He did not know to whom he was speaking for it seemed to him that not only the people had gone, but also the gods...

Then as suddenly as it had come, the fit passed and the street was busy again and he could smell sweat and garlic and dung, and hear the cries, the laughter – the whole cacophony of a busy living town. He was trembling. It had been like his dream of Aquae Sulis, but he was not asleep. A dog lifted his leg against the column beside him and he moved away quickly. He was not dreaming.

"Am I going mad?"

There had been some incidents in his childhood when he had known things that were about to happen, but as he grew up these had become less and less frequent, until recently he had scarcely thought about them. Now he remembered how frightened and uncomfortable they had made him. If he could know the future, was there any point to the present? Why did we suffer such agonies of choice and decision if all was pre-determined?

He remembered his mother standing over him. "Too much thinking is not good for you, Demo. Run out and play with the other children."

He smiled now, ruefully. He would go out and play with the other children – let the grownups worry about the meaning of it all. He stepped back into the street and followed the crowd, admiring the polished travertine of the walls, the gleaming marble of the columns and statues, the fine and vivid colours all around him – noting here a pretty face and there a child crying for a bauble glimpsed on a stall.

He came at last to the Temple of Venus Genetrix raised by Julius Caesar to honour his ancestors. The Julians believed they were descended from Aeneas of Troy who conquered and married a Latian princess. Aeneas in turn was supposed to have descended directly from Aphrodite, or, as the Romans named her, Venus. Demosthenes paused. More than any other he had passed he felt drawn to enter it. He had heard that here there was a particularly beautiful statue of Venus by the Greek sculptor Archesilaos.

She was indeed exquisite, with cupid on her shoulder and a small child at her side.

"Great Lady," he thought, "I am that child at your side. Lead me. Guide me. Protect me."

He felt a touch on his arm. An ugly priestess with no teeth was indicating that he should follow her.

She led him to a side chamber where, on tables of polished marble, were laid out the treasures of the Goddess. "Offered," the priestess hissed, "by the God Julius Caesar himself – and since his time by many visitors." No doubt she was hinting that he too should leave a generous gift.

He stared at incomparable jewels, at fine crystal goblets, and plates of beaten gold. But the thing that caught his eye and would not let it go was a jewelled breastplate of extraordinary beauty – curled and whorled and interlacing, the design drew him in. He had never seen anything like it – and yet he knew it.

He pointed to it, his eyes speaking the question he could not bring himself to ask.

"That is from Britain," the priestess whispered. "The Great Caesar took it himself from a British chieftain. They say they fought like lions for ten hours before Caesar was victorious."

Britain again. Britain!

Now Demosthenes was off the coast of Britain – tall white cliffs ahead – sea birds swooping and squawking over their wake as the crew threw out the rubbish of the journey. He took a deep breath. He was coming home to the White Island. He had seen these cliffs before.

Chapter 6

The statues for the temples at Aquae Sulis were almost all carved locally of local stone, but the skill to do so was imported. The studio consisted of a rambling series of shacks built on the flat beside the river to the northeast of the town, with easy access to the barges bringing the heavier material. There were two bronze casters from the island of Cyprus, and one master sculptor from Egypt, but locals did most of the hard work.

A huge slab of stone, capable of yielding a statue fifteen feet high, was to be brought by river, and on the day it was expected Decius, the centurion, joined the master sculptor on the quay to await its arrival.

The Egyptian was tall and lean, with a dark and brooding expression. He was a man of few words and many mysteries. Though he had been in the town for many years no one could say that they knew him, and no one called him anything but "the Egyptian". If he had ever given his name it had soon been forgotten or deemed unpronounceable, but his knowledge of his craft was unchallenged. Besides the millennia of stone carving skills he had inherited with his blood, he had spent some time in Rome itself at one of the best and busiest studios before he came to Britain.

Decius glanced sideways at him. What made such a man come to this cold and distant land? His culture was so alien. Everything about him suggested his dislike of being here – yet here he had stayed year after year through bitter winters and wet summers so very different from his own homeland. The statues he carved were of gods that must have meant nothing to him. When he had been told he was to supervise the carving of this huge effigy of the ugly and crippled Emperor Claudius and it was to be so beautiful and perfect that no one would question his deification – his expression had not changed. He had listened as though his own face was carved of stone.

He had visited the quarry, given his instructions, and gone on with his other work until it was ready as though he had no qualms

44

about the magnitude of the task, or the possible local trouble it might stir up.

Decius had travelled enough to know that the Egyptian, though immensely skilled in working stone, was not outstanding as a sculptor. He had seen nothing emerge from his workyard that rivalled the images he had seen in Greece or even in Egypt itself. Indeed, he seemed to take very little part in the shaping of the images. He walked among the workmen, tapping this one on the shoulder and then that one – pointing out a flaw – suggesting a change of line.

Why was he here? Why had he chosen this work? What was he thinking at this very moment? Decius longed to talk to the man, for the Egyptian had travelled as widely as he had and must surely have a more sophisticated turn of mind than those who had never left this sleepy valley. But his stern face, his dark eyes fixed unwaveringly on the distant bend in the river, did not welcome communication. Decius could not find the words to break through his reserve, and so remained silent.

At last the barge appeared, slowly, moving with its heavy load, low in the water. Ropes held the rock firm. A man stood at the front with a long pole guiding the vessel, while a boy sat high on the rock, gazing at the passing scene dreamily. Children ran along the bank keeping pace with it, shouting and laughing. The boy on the barge ignored them, locked into his own world.

The Egyptian spoke at last, issuing orders to his men, several of whom began to prepare the landing stage with pulleys and rollers, while others cleared away every possible impediment.

"I will have to post some of my men here on guard," Decius told the Egyptian. "There may be some trouble from some of the towns-people."

The Egyptian raised an eyebrow.

"Claudius is not a God to them. Many resent him as conqueror."

"I will have no soldiers here," the Egyptian said firmly. "The statue will be safe in my workyard."

"At night when the men have gone home, anyone could break into those sheds."

The Egyptian nodded towards his own house, set back nearer the woods, but nevertheless affording a good view over the sheds and yard.

"I will guard the work."

Decius hesitated. He had already made plans and issued orders. On the other hand, soldiers always seemed to act as an irresistible challenge to the rebel Celts. It would be a matter of pride with them to outwit them. The Egyptian was just one man – but he was no ordinary man. Decius himself was afraid of him, though he could not have explained why. If he were to spread a rumour about magical protection for the statue... that, with the sinister appearance of the Egyptian, might be enough to keep his superstitious countrymen at bay.

"If I do not post guards you will be responsible for the safety of the statue. It may be too heavy a burden for one man to bear."

"I will have no soldiers here," the man repeated. "I will guard the work alone."

"What if many men come?"

"Many men will go," the Egyptian said darkly.

A grim smile passed briefly over the face of Decius, savouring the surprise of Owein and his rebels faced by such a man.

"I don't want bloodshed," he warned.

"And what would your soldiers do – if not shed blood?"

"They have authority from the Emperor to protect his property. You have none. Besides – they would have the force to restrain or to drive off a host of angry men. What could you do alone?"

The Egyptian did not reply, but turned away to supervise the arrival of the barge.

"I want no one harmed," he called after the man's retreating figure.

If the Egyptian heard, he gave no sign.

Decius watched the hectic scene now taking place on the quay. The men scrambling around the gigantic slab of stone seemed dwarfed by its size. Children jumping and dancing around the periphery seemed like so many sand fleas. Only the Egyptian kept his stature, standing apparently aloof, yet directing every movement. At one point the rock slab nearly slipped, threatening to crush a man. Horrified Decius rushed forward, but the Egyptian was already there. Decius did not see what he did, but suddenly the slab was steady again, sturdy wooden logs in place, ropes reinforced.

"The man knows what he is doing," Decius thought. "I'll leave him to it."

The centurion took one last look at the gigantic slab of stone and walked away. It was extraordinary to him how sculptors could draw out of such an object the complex and detailed image of a man. "What if there is one false blow – and the work of months is destroyed in one second?" He was thankful not to be involved in that part of the project.

In fact, he wished he was not involved in any part of it. He had met Vespasian and honoured him as a shrewd and courageous General and a straight talking man. He was probably one of the best of the Roman Emperors. But he was very far from divine. It sickened Decius that statues of murderous and insane men were put up for other men to worship. At least Nero's name on the colossal statue of the sun god in the great square where Vespasian was building his amphitheatre had been chipped away, and all talk of him as a deity was being discouraged. By all accounts Claudius had not been so bad – but still no god. He did not blame his father and the others for resenting the statue being foisted on them in their most sacred place, but if he did nothing about it he would be betraying the vows he had taken as a soldier, and undermining the very system he believed would bring peace, prosperity and stability to the world.

When Aulus told Lucius and Julia about his old friend Kynan returning to Aquae Sulis as a Roman centurion after all these years, Julia instantly pricked up her ears and asked if he had any knowledge of the Emperor Vespasian.

"He has met him," Aulus replied.

Lucius groaned. He was tired of hearing about his half-sister's supposed parentage and was convinced it had no substance in fact, but was a tale fabricated by the adults to give an illegitimate child comfort, and cultivated by Julia to give herself importance.

"I have to meet him," Julia insisted.

"I invited him to dine with us this evening, but there were matters he had to attend to. He is an important man you know, Julia, he cannot just drop everything for us."

"What were you thinking of to invite him here tonight?" Julia cried. "I must have time to prepare. We must give him a feast fit for a friend of the Emperor."

"Father didn't say Decius was a friend of the Emperor. He said he'd met him – once," Lucius pointed out.

"Only once?" Julia looked appealingly at her stepfather.

Aulus, who was almost as excited as Julia, for her status as Emperor's daughter must surely reflect on him – smiled placatingly.

"He didn't say how many times. But even if it were only once..."

"If it were only once, he'd hardly be likely to introduce you," Lucius taunted.

Julia gave him a withering look.

"Give me time and I'll prepare your friend a feast fit for the Emperor himself. If he has been in Rome and moved in Imperial circles he will certainly have advice to give, and friends who will know how things are done in Rome."

"You will never go to Rome, sister," Lucius said. "Why not accept it?"

"I will go!" she replied fiercely. "Aulus promised my mother on her death-bed that he would present me to my father."

Lucius laughed. Aulus looked uneasy. He had always regretted giving that foolish promise, but even more so that he had told Julia about it.

Now he hastily said that he would approach Decius Brutus the next day and invite him to dinner the following evening. Lucius declared he would make sure he was far from the house on that day as he would not be able to stomach the alternate boasting and grovelling that would go on.

"Good!" Julia snapped. "If you were the other side of the ocean it would not be far enough away for me!" This was to be a great moment in her life – and she did not want anything to spoil her chances of making a good impression. She was already thinking about what she would wear.

"The ring, of course," she decided. But she would need something very special in the way of gowns. And her hair? Yes, her hair must be in the latest Roman style.

Megan lay awake deep into the night. In the darkness, the problems that she and her people were facing seemed insurmountable.

She heard the soft and even breathing of her sister beside her. At last she could bear it no more and shook her awake.

"Ethne," she whispered. "Ethne."

Ethne groaned and stirred, and tried to go back to sleep.

"I need you. Wake up!"

Ethne grunted – not opening her eyes.

"We have to talk – now – wake up!" Megan gave her an even more vigorous shake.

Wearily Ethne turned towards her sister. As she opened her eyes she saw that the oil lamp was still burning.

"What are we going to do?" Megan demanded.

"About what?" Ethne murmured.

"About our father! About the statue! About everything!" Megan cried in exasperation.

Ethne looked at her sister. It was clear she was very agitated. Her cheeks were flushed, her eyes feverish.

"I think it wonderful that father has returned to us," she said quietly.

"He hasn't returned to *us*!" Megan said furiously. "He was posted here by the Roman government. It's probably the last place on earth he wanted to come."

"You don't know if he didn't ask for the posting," Ethne replied mildly.

Megan gave an exclamation of disgust.

"I can see I'm going to get no sense out of you. Go back to sleep."

But Ethne was wide awake now.

"Megan – whatever our father has done he is here now and we have a chance to get to know him, maybe to love him."

Megan blew the lamp out angrily.

"Go to sleep," she snapped. "I'll not love a Roman!"

"He's not a Roman," Ethne said firmly. "Neither are you a Dobunni," she added, just as firmly. She could almost feel the heat of Megan's stare through the darkness. "You and he are father and daughter," she continued quietly, "human and human, man and woman. The words Roman and Dobunni are appendages that have nothing to do with the spirit – but only with the very temporary flesh. Why let them run your life?"

"What is this spirit? Have you ever seen it? Have you ever heard it? Felt it? Smelled it? I know who I am. I am Megan, granddaughter of Owein and Olwen, and I am of the tribe of the Dobunni. As Megan, I reject my father as he rejected me. As Dobunni, I reject the Roman as he slaughtered and enslaved my people."

"We are not slaves."

"If we are not enslaved then can we say *no* to the statue of the conqueror Claudius?"

Ethne was momentarily silent.

"There will be ways of saying no without bloodshed," she said at last.

"Show me one! Tell me! I don't want to shed blood – but I will not have that statue in Aquae Sulis."

There was silence in the dark room for a while.

"I will ask the Goddess Sul," Ethne said thoughtfully. "There must be a way. There will be a way. You will see."

And then, very quietly – "Megan?"

There was no reply.

"Megan, are you crying?"

She put her arms round her sister. Ethne could feel the tears on her cheek. She knew how deep Megan's feelings about the Romans went, and held her close.

"I'm afraid," Megan sobbed. "Something terrible is going to happen. I can feel it. We can smash the statue – but not what it represents..." She shuddered.

Ethne rocked her twin sister in her arms as she had often done since their birth. As easily as Megan's heart leapt to anger, it leapt to fear – and Ethne had played mother to her many times.

"Sleep now, little one," she crooned. "Sul will guide us. Sul will help us. Sul will protect us."

Megan finally fell to sleep, but Ethne remained awake long into the night staring into the dark.

The rumour reached Megan that the stone had arrived for the hated statue and that it, when it was finished, would be so tall that it would dominate the temple precinct.

She set off at once for the Egyptian's workyard to see for herself. That Claudius himself had been short and squat brought an irreverent twist to her lips.

"If they are going to make a man a God, let them at least choose someone worthy," she thought. She had heard from her grandfather that Claudius had invaded Britain just so that he could have a triumphal procession through the streets of Rome like his predecessors. He had not been here for the fighting – but allowed his generals to do all the work and then came in for a few days to claim the credit. Rome had enough land. Why bother with this bit so far from home and so difficult to administer? Megan remembered well the excitement in her grandfather's house twelve years ago when the great Queen Boudicca of the Iceni tribe had risen in revolt. The tales of her vengeance against the Romans for the rape of her daughters were told around every hearth fire and at every street corner. The twins, listening with horrified attention, saw in their mind's eye whole cities burning and hordes of screaming warriors bearing down on fleeing refugees – limbs hacked, heads rolling, eyes gouged.

Even at that age Megan had a fierce pride that Boudicca had avenged herself so powerfully – but Ethne turned her face to the wall and wept for all those maimed and slain.

"Not all Romans raped her daughters, you know," she said to her sister, "and not only Romans were killed. People like you and me. How would you like it if someone you'd never heard of and had nothing to do with – a long way away – did something terrible to someone – and then your house was burned and you and your children and everyone you knew and loved were tortured and killed?"

"They shouldn't have come to this country..."

"Our ancestors came to this country from over the sea and conquered the local population just as the Romans have done," Ethne reminded her.

But Megan was stubborn. She did not want to listen. It did not matter to her that the Romans had never done her personally any particular harm, and indeed, in many ways, the quality of her life had been considerably improved by their occupation of her country. She carried her grandfather's hate as though it were her own.

She arrived at a bend in the river and could see the long, low sheds of the sculptor's workyard. She wondered if she would find her father there. Her heart beat a little faster. If she did – how would it be? She both wanted, and did not want, the encounter.

But there was no sign of him. Men were chipping at stone; children were sweeping up the chippings and dust. A blacksmith's fire glared red as he shaped and sharpened tools. A horse tethered nearby to a rickety fence whinnied. Its well-to-do owner had probably come to see how a statue or a tombstone he had commissioned was shaping up.

Most of the sheds were open to the elements and were no more than thatched roofs held up on wooden columns. Some were more elaborate and could be fastened shut. One, the largest of all, had a door locked and barred.

"The Claudius stone must be in there," she thought, scanning the area like an army scout.

There were no Roman guards around.

She sensed someone close behind her and swung round to face the Egyptian.

"Can I help you?" he asked in a deep, strange voice with a foreign accent.

She had only seen the Egyptian from a distance before. Now she was looking into a pair of very penetrating black eyes. She had heard many stories about him – some so fanciful that they could hardly be taken seriously. One was that he could transform himself into a gigantic nighthawk and had been seen flying over the town blotting out the moonlight. No one had ever seen inside his house.

Megan looked at him now and saw a man, probably in this late thirties or early forties, handsome in a craggy, harsh sort of way, with long black hair, straight nose verging on the hawklike, lips thin and tightly closed...

"I was hoping to see the stone you have for the Claudius statue," she said and, as soon as she said it, regretted that she had. What if those piercing eyes could see into her heart and she had now alerted the man to take extra precautions? She hoped he did not know she was the granddaughter of Owein, for the old man had already said too much about the statue, too loudly and in too many places.

The Egyptian gave no hint that he had noticed anything alarming about her.

"Come," he said simply and led the way to the shed she had suspected was the one to house the stone.

He opened the door and led her in. The contrast with the bright sunlight outside made her half blind for a few moments. She stared at the great block ahead of her and was startled. Surely they had not carved it already? Lying before her was the Emperor Claudius in full imperial regalia...

She gasped.

She was aware the Egyptian was standing slightly to the left of her and was watching her face intently.

"How could they...?"

Then she realized she had made a mistake. As her eyes adjusted to the dim light of the shed she saw that there was nothing there but a solid rectangular block of stone, untouched by hammer or chisel.

She began to back out of the place, shivering.

Once outside in the sunlight she recovered and, annoyed at being tricked, spoke haughtily to the man.

"You know the people of the town don't want this statue?" she said, staring boldly straight into those dangerous eyes.

"I know it," he said simply.

"Why, then, do you go ahead?"

He did not reply, but attended to shutting the door and drawing the bolt across. Megan noted that it was wooden and would present no obstacle to anyone determined to enter the shed.

"Do you not fear the consequences?"

He started to walk away and then paused and turned to look at her.

"We can never know the consequences of our actions," he said at last, quietly.

"I don't agree," she cried. "If the Romans foist this on us they will know exactly what the consequences will be!"

"Of whom do you speak when you say 'us'?"

Megan was just about to blurt out the names – but stopped herself in time. His eyes seemed to be drawing them out of her. She bit her lip. "What they say about him is true," she thought, "he is a magician!"

With great difficulty, she withdrew her eyes from his.

"Everyone in the town," she said haughtily.

Then she turned and walked away with as much dignity as she could. She felt him watching her, but she did not look back.

How could an outsider, an Egyptian, whose country had also been conquered by the Romans, be so loyal to them and so stubborn in protecting their interests! He seemed too intelligent to be the kind of man who worked only for payment, caring nothing for the moral implications of what he was doing. The further she strode along the path towards the town, the angrier she became. He knew *precisely* what he was doing!

Chapter 7

When Decius came to dine at the house of Aulus, Julia had her dark hair crimped and curled and piled up on the top of her head and overhanging her forehead in an imitation of a recent elegant Roman visitor to the town. Her gown was of the best and finest Egyptian white cotton, her girdle of gold thread and river pearls, her necklace and ear-rings, again of gold and pearl, imported from Rome, and, on her finger, the large lapis lazuli ring Vespasian was reputed to have given her mother. She was nervous. She had changed through every gown and jewel she possessed, each time asking Aulus and Lucius if it would do, and immediately rejecting the outfit as soon as they said that it would. At last, irritated, they refused to comment, and she had ended up in the simplest garment of them all, looking, in fact, remarkably good. She was not a pretty woman – her features were too stark and her expression often too stern and haughty – but this evening she was handsome and dignified. The centurion taking her hand in his as they were introduced had no idea of the turmoil in her heart, nor of the unreasonable expectations she had of this meeting.

Before dinner was served Aulus and Lucius took their guest to see the new villa they were constructing beside the old. Aulus was sure his old friend could not help but be impressed.

"Centurion you might be," he thought, "but you live in a barracks and have nothing like this to call your own."

"I see being a farmer has its advantages," Decius said with a smile.

"Being a successful farmer!" Aulus corrected.

Decius laughed. "Sorry."

Aulus proudly threw the doors open. Every chamber glowed with floor mosaics in elaborate geometric patterns and wall paintings of nymphs and fountains and birds.

When they reached the largest room of all, the one with the mosaic depicting Orpheus and his beasts, Aulus explained that this was not part of the living quarters but was to be kept as a sacred space for the practice of the Orphic Mysteries.

"A priest is on his way from Greece at this very moment," he boasted.

"Why Orpheus?" Decius looked surprised.

Aulus hesitated and, seeing his father momentarily at a loss, Lucius took it on himself to answer.

"Of all the gods, Orpheus appeals to us most."

"Why?"

"My father has his reasons, but my own are that I have seen him in dreams. I have seen him walking over that hill there, through the orchard, coming to this spot. I have seen a whirl of energy, like wind, coming with him. I have seen it stop here, exactly where we have built this shrine for him."

Decius raised a quizzical eyebrow and looked at Aulus.

Aulus shrugged. "My son believes it – and I see no reason to doubt his word."

"You must forgive me," the centurion said. "I have seen an army tear down the most magnificent temple in the world – and no supernatural whirlwind stopped them. I have no great belief in gods."

Lucius flushed.

"Do you say I lie, sir?"

"No, my boy. But I say you may have mistakenly interpreted what you saw. Could it not have been a common whirlwind?"

"A whirlwind with a face?" Lucius cried indignantly.

"I grant you – a whirlwind with a face is a mighty challenge to common sense!"

The man was laughing! Lucius began to dislike him intensely. Aulus was looking embarrassed.

"People need religion," he said, clearing his throat, smiling deprecatingly. "And Orpheus suits us best."

Lucius turned and walked away. Decius looking after him could see the stiff shoulders and awkward, angry gait. He was sorry to have offended him.

Aulus looked apologetic. "He has had many dreams. He seems very convinced they mean something."

"I'm sorry I laughed. We soldiers are a cynical lot."

"I thought you were more religious than the rest of us. I hear you pray and sacrifice before every battle, and believe your standards have some kind of supernatural power to help you. I heard that if the eagle is captured you believe the gods have deserted you."

"Ah, well – perhaps I should not have generalized. I am cynical. I've heard too many prayers and seen too much carnage in spite of them."

A slave appeared, bowing, announcing that the dinner was ready and that Mistress Julia requested their presence.

As they turned to go Aulus apologized that his friend could not yet be entertained in the large house. "Next time you come, my friend. Next time you'll be entertained more fittingly."

"As long as you don't make me attend your Orphic rituals," laughed Decius.

"I promise," his host replied.

Julia did not wait long after the meal was begun before she raised the subject closest to her heart.

"My father tells me you actually know the Emperor," she began, trying not to sound too eager.

Since his brush with Lucius, Decius had been friendly and civil. She had no idea why her brother was being so sullen and silent, her father so obsequious. "He is a nice man," she thought, "strong, handsome, and a thousand times more interesting than any man I've ever met!"

Decius shook his head. "I can't claim to know the Emperor," he said. "I fought with him in Galilee, and with his son Titus in Jerusalem. I attended their great triumph in Rome for the victory in the Jewish war, and he shook me by the hand and gave me gold – but then he shook the hands of all his officers and rewarded all those who had been with him on that campaign."

"What is he like? What do his men think of him?"

Decius thought for a moment, while Julia waited impatiently.

"When Nero died by his own hand and Rome was plunged into civil war, Vespasian was no more than a general – a brilliant commander of troops getting ready to march on Jerusalem. It was his men on campaign with him in the east who raised him to be Emperor. I was there and shouted his name with the rest. I saw him hesitate to take on such power – but the Empire needed a just and honourable man after the madmen of the past years. If it was to survive it needed him. We knew it and he knew it – and he bowed to the inevitable at last."

"So his men loved him?"

"No General more."

56

"He was just and honourable?"

"But no weakling. He did not hesitate to shed blood when it was necessary – but he was not wantonly cruel like Nero, or Caligula before him. The Empire will be safe with him – and will know peace."

Julia could hardly contain her pleasure at what she was hearing.

"Describe him to me. What does he look like?"

Decius looked momentarily nonplussed. Then he drew out a coin bearing the head of Vespasian on one side, with an image of Mars on the reverse carrying the figure of victory, and put it on the table in front of her.

She saw there a man thick set and jowled – not at all the handsome and dashing man she believed her mother to have loved. She was disappointed – but told herself that the Emperor was now old and her mother had known him nearly thirty years ago when he was young.

"He is square and strong. An old man, but not an inch of him flaps or wobbles. They say you can punch his stomach and break your own fist."

"Who would punch an Emperor's stomach?" laughed Aulus.

"You'd be surprised," Decius replied. "I've seen one of the officers commanded to do so. Vespasian had been wounded in the leg in Judaea, and to prove that he was still fit to fight again he put on this show of strength. It was impressive. He laughed outright to see the officer's alarm. He has quite a sense of humour."

"They say he is fearless in battle?"

"No man is fearless in battle, my lady."

"But he did superhuman feats?"

Decius smiled at her evident desire to worship the man.

"No doubt he'll be made a god one day – like Julius Caesar and Augustus and Claudius."

"Decius doesn't believe in gods," Lucius spoke for the first time, bitterly.

"I don't say he is a god – but he is an extraordinary man," Julia insisted.

"He is worthy to be Emperor – and that cannot be said of all who have held the office."

"They say he is building the biggest amphitheatre in the world in Rome – so that even more poor men and beasts can die for the amusement of the crowd," Lucius said.

"It is the Roman way. He gives the Romans what they want." Decius frowned as he spoke, remembering those hideous years he spent in the arena to please the crowds.

"Orpheus protects life in every form – from the lowliest mouse to the highest king."

"Orpheus is a Greek God – not a Roman."

"The Romans have adopted him."

"Not many. His temples don't adorn the Capitol."

"He is not very well known here either," Aulus said hastily, "but we intend to make him better known."

Julia was impatient that the conversation was drifting away from the subject in which she was most interested.

"They say Vespasian's wife is dead," she said. "Has he married again?"

"Not exactly. He lives with his mistress in Rome as though married to her. It is said she was his mistress even when Flavia was alive – but that may be just an idle rumour." Decius noticed a look pass between Aulus and Julia.

"Do you wonder why we have taken the name Sabinus?" Julia asked, her dark eyes staring into his eagerly.

"Oh no!" muttered Lucius and stood up. Without an apology or another word, he stormed out of the room. Decius looked enquiringly at Aulus. The boy was certainly moody and fretful.

"I apologize for my son's behaviour. You must understand it has nothing to do with you."

"He is angry with me," Julia said sharply.

Decius saw that she was flushed and seemed to be burning to answer her own question.

"Perhaps now is not the time, my dear," Aulus said quietly. "Our visitor has hardly had a moment to eat the food you have so painstakingly prepared."

"But..."

"No, my dear, it is many years since Decius Brutus left this valley. I expect he wants to hear what we have been doing all that time." And to Julia's frustration her father plunged into a long and detailed description of all those Decius had once known – and long since forgotten. It was clear Decius was bored, but he remained polite. "How the trivia of life stay vivid in memory to those whom not much has happened," he was thinking. Occasionally he looked across at Julia. "A handsome and unusual woman," he mused.

She said earlier that she had been all her life in this valley – yet she gave the impression of a much greater sophistication than she could have acquired here. His old friend Aulus had become a bore – a rich bore – but his children were interesting.

As Decius walked along the dark and leafy lanes towards the town that night, the river beside him occasionally yielding a glint of reflected moonlight, he pondered how strange it was that without his lifting a finger to make it happen, Destiny had brought him back to this place. He thought about his youth, playing warriors with Aulus, hiding behind rocks and trees, yelling and ambushing and throwing wooden spears. He smiled wryly to remember how often he had "killed" Aulus, only to have the "corpse" rise again when it was time for dinner. Then he thought about all the men, the many, many men he had really killed both in the arena and on the battlefield who lay there in their blood, and did not ever move again.

He shuddered when he remembered Jerusalem. They had started the siege like the army of professional soldiers they were. This was not their personal fight – but they were under orders and had a job to do. Certain Jewish factions had risen against the Roman overlords in the country. The insurrection had to be punished, for Rome could not allow one of her dominions to get away lest the others followed suit.

He had been at the siege of Jopata before that – month after month supervising the building of ramps and platforms and siege towers, continually harassed by sorties from within the city. He learned then, as his commander did, that these rebels were not to be put down easily. They were wily and courageous and foolhardy and they caused the Roman army heavy casualties before ever the final battle was drawn. He remembered how the soldiers had hated the Jewish leader Josephus, the Governor of Galilee. He had spent some time in Rome and seemed to anticipate their every move. But even the cunning and passionate attacks of his men could not withstand the solid discipline and careful planning of the Romans, and Jopata fell to Vespasian. Josephus was captured hiding in a cave. Vespasian's first thought was to send him to Nero for punishment, but the man managed to persuade Vespasian's son Titus, to keep him prisoner in Galilee.

Decius remembered that Josephus was quick and subtle of mind.

No Greek rhetorician could have outwitted him, or matched the honey of his words. He smiled to think how the prisoner, bleeding and defeated, yet with enough nerve to face up to the conqueror as though they were on equal footing, announced that both he, Vespasian, and his son Titus, would soon be emperors of the greatest empire in the world. Vespasian had laughed, for at that time, born a commoner and knowing nothing but the rigour and discipline of endless campaigning in Germany, Thrace, Crete, Cyrenaica, Britain... and now Judaea – there was no prospect of the prophecy being fulfilled.

By the time the Romans reached Jerusalem, Josephus was no longer a prisoner, but an honoured member of the staff of Titus, supporting the Romans against his own people because he believed their cause was hopeless and it was better to have survival than annihilation.

None of them had thought about Vespasian being Emperor before Josephus prophesied it – but when the year that followed Nero's suicide saw Rome itself in the terrible throes of civil war, Vespasian's troops remembered the words of Josephus and helped the prophecy come true.

Now they were saying that not only was the prophecy of Josephus fulfilled, but another, older and more persistent prophecy of the Jews had come about – that the great ruler of the world would come from the east. Was not Vespasian in the east, in Judaea, when the call came for him to take up the Empire?

Decius paused before he entered the town of Aquae Sulis that night after dining with Aulus and Julia. In this quiet glade beside the gently sliding river, he sat on a boulder and thought back to the momentous events he had witnessed. He remembered the excitement in the camp when Vespasian departed for Rome, via Egypt... the weeks of impatience and uncertainty while they waited... and finally the expression on the face of Titus when the news finally came through that his father had been greeted with overwhelming acclaim on his return to Rome.

Decius was fortunate enough to be chosen to take part in the triumphal parade in Rome to celebrate the end of the Jewish war and the complete crushing of the insurgents. Staring into the dark stream of the river now, he relived that extraordinary day. One of his companions had joked that it was more exhausting than the whole siege of Jerusalem, and Vespasian himself was reported to have said if he had known it was all going to take so long he would not have asked for it.

The parade started at the Temple of Isis and ended at the Temple of Jupiter Capitolinus. It seemed as though everyone in Rome and from all the farms and cities nearby had crowded into the streets that day. In fact, even the night before when the soldiers were being marched out under their commanders by centuries and cohorts to take up their positions, it seemed there was not room for a single other person. Yet still they poured in.

At day-break, Vespasian and Titus emerged clad in crimson and wreathed in bay leaves, and made their way to the Octavian Walks where the Senate and all the other important people were waiting for them. They took their places on ivory chairs raised high on a dais, and from there accepted the rousing cheers and general acclamation. After prayers, Vespasian dismissed the army to a sumptuous breakfast he had provided, and after this the parade began – the victors driving through the city and the theatres to give the people further afield a chance to cheer them. In the parade were moving stages on which the battles of Vespasian and Titus were re-enacted in dramatic form. Behind them came the spoils of war – the fabulous treasures captured in Judaea including the gigantic candelabra, the seven-branched menorah, seized from the very inner sanctuary of the famous temple at Jerusalem. Now, seeing it so clearly in his mind's eye, he remembered Jerusalem itself – the city as he had first seen it with its proud walls of triple strength, one behind the other – the towers, the gleam of gold and white marble, of polished cedar wood, of bronze and silver. He saw the flames consuming everything. He saw the melting silver running from the great cedar doors of the Temple in rivulets, like tears. He saw the devastation. He smelled the death.

When they marched away from that once mighty and beautiful city there was not a building standing, not a person left. Titus had tried to stop short of complete destruction, but his men, filled with a passionate hatred of the Jews who had given them so many months of aggravation, despoiled and killed until they were satiated. In many places they found the Jews themselves had razed their own most sacred places and destroyed their most precious artefacts to save them from falling into the hands of their enemies.

The final act of the Triumph that day in Rome was the public execution of the captured leaders of the revolution who had been dragged about in chains all day.

Decius shuddered, as he so often had in the past, at the crowd's delight in watching people die in agony. For himself – he was sick of it and had thought he would be safe from such scenes now he had been posted to this distant outpost of the Empire. He frowned. Would it not be a cruel twist of Fate if he had returned to his home-town to supervise and carry out the death of his own father? Somehow Owein must be persuaded to bow to the inevitable, as he himself had done, and accept the Roman yoke.

Chapter 8

Some twenty miles across the hills south from Aquae Sulis, on an island in the marshes called Glastonia, two travellers arrived from Rome – a young woman and her grandfather, Martha and Paulus. They were followers of a God who had no statue and no temple, a God whose son had been crucified in Galilee forty years before, and whose followers were still persecuted by the representatives of the Roman Empire, though less under Vespasian than under Nero. Martha's parents and brothers had been thrown to the wild animals to be torn to pieces for the amusement of the vengeful Roman crowds when Nero claimed, without evidence, that it was the Nazarenes who had set fire to Rome. Martha escaped, helped by a family loyal to the State and the state Gods, yet deeply disapproving of what was being done. She joined other followers of the Nazarene Christ meeting in secret. It was at one of their meetings that she met up again with her grandfather, whom she had assumed lost with all the other members of her family.

The two fell on each other with cries of delight, weeping copiously. Those who witnessed the scene wept too, for a reunion after the holocaust of Nero's bloodthirsty reign surely was miraculous.

Paulus had grown up in Galilee. As a youth he had followed the crowd who followed the prophet who claimed to be the Son of God, waiting impatiently for him to stop talking about forgiveness and love and perform some astonishing miracles. The buzz of gossip in all the villages was about so-and-so cured of blindness or so-and-so actually raised from the dead. By the time the man was crucified like a common criminal, Paulus was thoroughly confused. He had seen some extraordinary feats performed. He had also listened to some deep and profound teaching – yet, here was the man who claimed to be the Son of the most powerful God in the universe, hanging from a cross, unable to lift a finger to help himself and dying in extreme agony. It did not make sense.

In those dangerous days after the crucifixion Paulus did not hesitate to deny hotly that he had been a follower of the Nazarene.

Then there was talk that the prophet had been seen alive again after his death.

Little groups began to meet in secret trying to remember what the Master had said. Some of his closest followers who had the skill to write, wrote down what was confirmed by several witnesses, Paulus contributing phrases and sentences he remembered.

When Simon Peter was taken to Rome a prisoner, some of those who now believed implicitly in the divinity of the man Jesus followed him, hoping that they might help him in some way. So it was that Paulus had come to Rome, married, had a family and witnessed the horrors of Nero's persecution of all the Christians the Romans could catch. Helplessly he watched the execution of Peter and of Paul, and became, as time went by, a much sought after speaker in secret Christian circles – for he was one of the few who had actually seen the Christ and listened to his words. There were times when Paulus, seeing the rapt faces of those who hung on his own words, wished he had paid more attention at the time to what the extraordinary young man said. Now he could only remember fragments – but those fragments seemed to be like seeds, for each time he spoke them more and more meaning grew out of them.

He frequently mentioned the moment when it seemed to him that the Master had singled him out from the crowd pressing around him. For years he had tried to forget that look and go on with the ordinary business of living. But he knew he had been "called" and, at last, he could resist no more.

His decision to go to Britain to join the small community of Christians on Glastonia Island was made when he received an invitation. It seemed their founder, no less than Jesus' uncle Joseph of Arimathea, had died leaving them without a leader. Paulus was known as one who had actually been in the presence of the Christ on earth and so would be a powerful inspiration to the struggling community.

It was largely for his granddaughter's sake that he decided to go, taking her away from the constant threat of persecution in Rome.

The journey had been exhausting – by sea to Massillia; overland to Brittany; by sea again to the south coast of Britain; and then finally, like Joseph of Arimathea before them, by river to the island of Glastonia. They disembarked at last to be greeted warmly by the small Christian community established in rough wattle and daub huts at the foot of the Tor.

Although in Rome he had been living among the poor, the conditions at Glastonia seemed primitive indeed. There were no market stalls providing food. If you wanted fish you caught it yourself. If you wanted vegetables, you grew them. If you wanted fowl you rowed out on the marshes and brought it down by arrow. The climate was cold and wet and their clothes never seemed to be dry.

When, on the fourth day after their arrival, they looked out on yet another sleet grey sky and saw the cold rain falling, they despaired of ever being happy in this place. They had thought to escape the Roman yoke, but the long arm of Rome reached even to this remote country. The story of the sack of a hill-top community just south of Glastonia was still fresh in everyone's minds. North, over the hills, lay the Roman town, Aquae Sulis, linked to the Fosse Way, the great road along which troops could move with ease.

Jacob, one of the oldest of the community, told them that in some places the Romans had established amphitheatres and were introducing the locals to spectacular blood sports, though so far no Christians had been sacrificed.

Paulus asked about their work at the mission and how many converts had been made since their establishment on the island.

"Of the original twelve who came with Joseph only myself and one other are still alive – but we have locals who have joined us and they, with their families number sixty three in all."

"The years of my life," Paulus thought. Aloud he said: "Is there much resistance to the new teaching?"

Jacob shook his head. "Some find nothing difficult in our teaching when we are dealing with supernatural matters, for they themselves are familiar with the interplay between the natural and supernatural realms and have experienced miracles and visions of a sort. The most difficult part for them to grasp is our moral teaching. They are a violent people and vengeance is an integral part of their social code. Forgiveness, gentleness and love in a generalized way are very alien concepts to them, and they regard them with the greatest suspicion. The rich ones don't like our teaching that one should give up all our worldly possessions for the good of the community as a whole. When they have done some-thing to please their king, they expect to be rewarded by him with gold and silver here and now, not with vague promises of felicity after death. But the poor welcome the equality we preach and many have come to us for succour."

"They have a strict code of honour," someone else said, "and that is helpful in our teaching. Commitment by vow is sacred to them."

"Rules of hospitality... loyalty to the king and tribe... these things we can draw analogies from," Jacob continued. "But you will see for yourself how best to do your work."

"Should we not tell brother Paulus about this island?" Simon asked, and Paulus sensed the anxiety in his voice.

Jacob pursed his lips and looked hard at the newcomer as though trying to decide whether to speak on the matter Simon had raised or not.

"I would like to know all there is to know about this place and these people before I start," Paulus said quickly.

"You might have wondered why we have established ourselves on an island, remote from the bulk of the population," Jacob said at last, cautiously.

"It did cross my mind."

Jacob paused again, and impatiently Simon burst out: "This island is particularly sacred to the old religions of this country. It is believed that it is the entrance to the Otherworld, and the King of the Otherworld ferries the souls of the dead across the waters and they disembark here."

Paulus looked startled. Martha afraid.

"You mean this island is full of the spirits of the dead?" she cried.

Neither Jacob nor Simon replied at once. There was a pregnant silence.

"If this is so," Paulus said soothingly, putting his hand on his granddaughter's shoulder, "prayers to our Lord will soon set the matter straight."

"We have tried that..." Simon started to say, but Jacob raised his hand to silence him.

"We consider this to be our greatest challenge," he said. "If we can transform this island into a sacred place for our Lord and convert even the dead to his worship – the rest of the country will follow. But if we fail here we will fail everywhere. This island is indeed a portal. And we must take possession of the key."

Martha slipped her hand into her grandfather's. She had been looking for a simple life away from the stresses and strains of Rome. Was there ever such a life, she wondered?

Martha and Paulus settled in to their new life as best they could, trying not to miss the comforts they had known in Rome; trying not to resent the weather.

At the gatherings, when all downed tools and came to the little chamber set aside for the Holy Word, Paulus told them all he knew about the man they called the Master, the Saviour, the Son of God. The community listened intently – every word precious – every word a buffer against the dark and menacing world that surrounded them.

When they were not at worship, they worked hard, shoring up their fields against frequent flooding from the marshes surrounding them. Sowing, reaping, storing. Tending the animals. Hunting and fishing for their food.

Above them rose the Tor – ever present, ever mysterious. At certain times of the year, when the local Celts celebrated their major festivals, Imbolc, Beltain, Lughnasa and Samhain, and believed spirits from other realms could walk freely on the earth, the community fasted and prayed day and night without ceasing.

At such times also Joseph had instituted the custom of lighting two fires at midnight on the top of the Tor believing that if the spirits were to pass between them they would be purified of their old beliefs and ready for baptism into the new. The ceremony always ended with the sprinkling of holy water from the Sacred Spring – the spring at the foot of the Tor that never dried up but yielded clear, pure water at the same volume and speed at every season of the year. The spring had been sacred to the ancient people of the land, but had been claimed for the Christ by Joseph of Arimathea who, some believed, buried in it the cup the Master himself had drunk from at that last supper before he was betrayed. The community dug a well around the spring and lined the walls with stone. They called it the Chalice Well.

Martha did not look forward to these ceremonies. Since she had first set eyes upon it she feared the Tor, possibly even before she heard that it was the place for the gathering of the dead. Paulus had an important and revered position in the community and settled in quickly to his work – but Martha sobbed herself to sleep many a night, longing for her friends in Rome and the old familiar places. There were dangers in Rome she could not deny – but at least they were of this earth which, if you were quick enough you could run from and hide. During her short life she had become adept at avoiding such dangers. But these new ones...

Chapter 9

In Aquae Sulis the work on the colossal statue of Claudius began at last – the Egyptian doing no more at first than supervising his apprentices, reserving his own skills for the fine work later on.

Megan, learning that he was away buying tools in Corinium one day, decided to visit the workyard and try to persuade the workmen themselves to sabotage the project.

"One hard blow in the wrong place will surely break the block open and render it useless," she suggested, after she had been speaking for some time on the reasons why they should resent having such a statue in their town.

But the implications of their work did not interest the men. It was work for which they were well paid and involved a skill they were proud to learn from a master they respected. Nothing Megan could say would sway them and at last, angry at their stubborn resistance, and what she saw as their blind obedience to foreign masters, she prophesied dire retribution from Sul whose temple precincts were to be desecrated. Some looked nervous at her vehement words, but others laughed.

She turned to go, bitterly disappointed – and came face to face with the Egyptian.

She was shocked. Had he heard everything? He must certainly have heard her angry prophecy.

"What makes you think you can speak with the authority of the Goddess Sul?" he asked, watching her closely – reading her every movement, every thought.

"I will sacrifice. She will not deny me," she said defiantly.

"And what will you sacrifice? Your pride? Your arrogance?" His lip curled. She flushed scarlet with anger.

"What if I call on the authority of the Goddess Isis to protect this work?" He was still mocking her.

"By what authority can you speak with the voice of Isis?" she countered haughtily, recovering her self control.

"I am a Priest of Isis," he said. "And you – are you a priestess of Sul?"

She looked surprised. A priest? She did not know this foreign Goddess had a following in Aquae Sulis.

"Well, we shall see who has the greater authority here," she said icily. "Sul who has guarded this land since the beginning of time, or Isis, the interloper, who knows nothing of our hearts, our ways!"

His eyes narrowed, his face grew stern and dark and he gazed over her shoulder as though someone was standing behind her. She felt a presence there and swung round to see who it was. There was no one there.

"One of his tricks!" She thought angrily, and was shocked that she had fallen for it so easily.

She turned back – but he had gone. She looked around to see where he was, but there was no sign of him. "Another trick!" she muttered. If he was trying to unnerve her, he had almost succeeded. Some of the men were coming out of the shed to the left. She glowered at them and turned on her heel.

She scarcely noticed her surroundings on the long walk back to the town. She saw only the sardonic expression of the Egyptian and the stubborn, stupid faces of the workmen. She heard nothing but the continual muttering of her thoughts, going round and round on the treadmill of disappointment and irritation. Her pride! Her arrogance! Indeed! He could talk. She had never met such an arrogant man. She would show him the Celtic Gods were stronger than the Egyptian Isis. She would show him!

Within the hour she purchased a small tablet of lead and a stylus. The vendor offered to inscribe it for her for a few extra coins, but she refused, saying haughtily that she was quite capable of inscribing it herself.

"Be careful," he warned. "A wrong letter, a wrong word, even a wrong punctuation mark could alter the curse."

"Who said I was going to write a curse?" she snapped, slapping the coins down on the counter.

"Your face, lady," he called after her as she strode away. She pretended not to hear, and clutched the small sheet of lead fiercely.

She sat down on the steps leading to the riverbank behind the great complex of temples and baths. The Romans had tamed the waters of Sul and they now flowed docilely down a drain to the river where before they had flowed out to form a marshland of hot mud. Where the drain entered the river, fish gathered in their hundreds to enjoy the warmth.

Megan carved the words carefully on the lead – not in the hated Latin language, but in the language of her ancestors, Ogham, the language the fierce gods of the Celts would understand. She would not call on Sul – for Sul was a healer and a goddess of wisdom. Megan wanted hate and destruction, vengeance and pain. She called on the Morrigan, the ancient Goddess of war, to blast the hated statue and all it stood for out of her land, and added a plea that the fearsome Goddess would pay particular attention to that arrogant priest of Isis, the Egyptian.

"This is not for you, Sul," she whispered as she stood beside the river. "I will not throw it into your Sacred Spring. The river will carry it to its rightful destination."

She lifted it above her head and took a deep breath.

"Morrigan!" she cried aloud. "Lady of Death! Take this. Free our land from foreign foot and fist and spear. Give us back our ancient ways and Gods. Curse the Romans! And curse the Egyptian who does their work!"

She hurled the piece of rolled up lead as far as she could into the swiftly flowing stream. It sank instantly.

That night Ethne was woken by the constant tossing and turning of her sister.

"What is it?" she asked sleepily. "What troubles you now?"

At first Megan would not answer, but growled that there was nothing wrong and commanded her twin to go back to sleep.

Ethne lay wide awake now, feeling the agitation of her sister not only physically in the bed, but psychically in the air around them.

She waited quietly for a while, trying to guess what was wrong. It felt as though her sister was being dragged down by a dark vortex of hate.

"Megan," she whispered in alarm, "tell me who it is you hate so much before it destroys you."

Megan sat up suddenly.

"How did you know?"

"I can feel it – like a dark cloud threatening to overwhelm you."

Megan clung to Ethne.

"I'm frightened," she murmured, shuddering. "It is growing. I can feel it too. And I can't stop it."

"Megan what have you done?" She held her sister's shoulders and pushed her back, peering into her eyes.

"You know those curses people throw into the Sacred Spring?"

"Yes."

"I've always thought they were just nonsense. Do you think they work? Does the Goddess answer them?"

Ethne was silent for a while, now holding her sister tight.

"I don't think the Goddess ever answers them herself," she said at last, thoughtfully. "But the power of hate can give strength to all kinds of dark spirits."

Megan began to sob.

"What have you done?" Ethne cried. "Megan, who have you cursed? Surely not our father?"

It was some time before Megan's sobs died down enough for her to answer.

"I have cursed the Romans in our land – and the Egyptian. But I didn't throw it in the Sacred Spring of Sul. I threw it in the river and called upon the Morrigan."

Ethne gasped. Not much was known about the Morrigan but the dark and fearsome tales told to frighten naughty children. She was thought to be a hideous hag dressed in black, blood-soaked rags, who waited at cross-roads trying to tempt people to follow the wrong path. In ancient days she had been a magnificent warrior galloping on a black horse leading her people to battle. Her name was in many a rousing battle cry, and on the lips of bards telling ancient tales of heroism and victory. But her desire for vengeance fed off the hate of fallen warriors as the carrion crow fed off their flesh, and she grew ever more dangerous and monstrous.

Ethne shuddered. "To call on her! To rouse her! To invite her into your life!"

She held her sister close against her, stroking her hair.

"I hate the Romans. I hate the idea of that statue. I hate the Egyptian who will not give up the carving of it. I wrote the curse on imperishable lead and threw it into the river in a fit of anger. Afterwards when I calmed down I didn't think I'd done anything so terrible because I didn't really believe such curses worked. Now I can't sleep and I keep thinking horrifying murderous thoughts and seeing the people I cursed dying horrible deaths. I feel someone or something is taking over my mind. I am sure these are not my thoughts – I would never imagine such ghastly torment for anyone however much I hated him. Ethne – help me! Tell me it's just imagination and it will pass!"

Ethne was silent. She could feel a dark and menacing presence in the room. She did not feel that either of them had the strength to combat it. She was as afraid as her sister.

Silently and determinedly she prayed to Sul for help while she held her weeping sister in her arms.

Chapter 10

A few days after the centurion had been to dine at the house of
Aulus, Lucius and Decius Brutus chanced to meet at the public
baths. Both men were at the stage of being oiled, massaged and
scraped when they became aware of each other.

Decius greeted the young man cautiously, not forgetting the
antagonism Lucius had shown towards him at their first meeting.
Lucius returned the greeting, somewhat shamefaced. For a while
the slave worked on the bodies of the two men and no words were
spoken. Lucius broke the silence at last.

"I owe you an apology and an explanation, sir," he said humbly.

Decius looked at him enquiringly, but said nothing.

"My sister's belief that she is the daughter of the Emperor is
sometimes hard to bear. I was embarrassed the other night. What
must you have thought?"

Decius grinned and stood up and stretched, feeling good after the
afternoon's pampering at the baths. The place was small and
primitive compared to the baths he had been accustomed to in the
big cities – but it still relaxed him after a hard morning's work.

"If it pleases her to dream – why stop her?" he asked cheerfully.

"But it's not just a dream. She and father really intend to go to
Rome and confront him."

Decius laughed. "Don't worry about it, lad," he said. "The
Emperor can take care of himself."

"You don't know Julia!"

"She struck me as an intelligent woman. She might do well in
Rome. This place is probably too much of a quiet backwater to
hold her interest for long."

Lucius shrugged.

"What about you, Lucius?" Decius asked. "Do you pine to go
travelling too? Will you accompany them when they go?"

"I'd like to – but they'd never take me," Lucius sighed. "I'll have
to stay home and look after the farm."

"And Orpheus?" Lucius could not tell if there was a shade of
mockery in the man's voice.

"If I go anywhere – I'd like to go to Greece," he said.

"A good choice, lad, infinitely preferable to Rome!"

"I'd like to visit Apollo's Oracle at Delphi and the healing sanctuary of Aesculapius at Epidaurus. But most of all I'd like to..." Lucius paused.

"You'd like to visit the great cavern through which Orpheus entered the Underworld," Decius said quietly, with no hint of mockery in his voice.

Lucius looked at him with surprise. He had stopped because he had remembered the scepticism Decius had shown the other night.

"Have you yourself been there, sir?" he asked.

Decius grinned at the young man's eagerness – but not unkindly.

"No, Lucius, I have not been there. Though," he added, suddenly sober, "I have been to the darkest depths of Hades' realm and back many times."

Lucius did not know what to make of this.

"But not the way you mean," Decius added, bringing himself back from his dark memories with an effort. "But enough of that. If you are determined enough Lucius, I am sure you will achieve whatever you set out to achieve." Then, in a lighter tone: "Have you a young woman in mind with whom to share your path?"

Lucius hesitated – and then nodded.

"Aha!" Decius said, with interest. "What's her name, lad?"

"Ethne," Lucius replied and was almost immediately angry with himself for naming her. He had met her once and she had shown no interest in him. It was only in his dreams that their love was passionate and alive.

"Ethne, granddaughter of Owein?" Decius asked at once, eyebrows raised.

Lucius nodded dumbly.

"She is my daughter!" Decius announced proudly. "You could do worse lad."

Lucius looked astonished. There had been no mention of a daughter when Aulus had told them about his old friend.

"I didn't know you had a daughter, sir."

"Two! Twins. Both as beautiful as Venus!"

"Twins?" Lucius gasped.

"Twins," Decius replied. "I've only made their acquaintance myself these past few days. Ethne is the quiet one I believe."

"What is the other called?"

"Megan. She is the fiery one. The man who marries her will not have a moment's peace and quiet. You have chosen the right one."

Lucius was silent. Surely it was the "fiery" one he had met that day on Sul's hill?

Decius clapped him on the back.

"I wish you well, son. I will not be sorry to have the son of my old friend Aulus as son-in-law."

Then he left the chamber before Lucius could put right the misunderstanding.

When Decius next came to dine at the house of Aulus, he brought his daughter Ethne with him. Julia had been warned, but to Lucius it was a surprise. He stepped back when he saw her and almost fled. But it was too late, the slaves were already moving forward to take cloaks and offer drinks.

This time Julia had done her best to arrange an evening of feasting and entertainment to rival those she had heard about in Rome itself. Decius had to repress a smile. The small room, the two inept slaves, Julia herself over-anxious – lamb and chicken instead of peacock and venison... It was hardly what an Emperor was accustomed to – though Vespasian had probably known no better as a boy growing up on his grandmother's farm.

Lucius was persuaded to play the lyre in the intervals between the courses. He protested that he did not feel like it, but Julia would allow no escape.

Aulus settled back to listen with a sigh, expecting to be bored – and so he was at first. A few faltering notes were followed by competent but uninspired playing. Decius' mind wandered to a night in Judaea after a day of violence and killing, sitting beside the camp fire, smarting from the blows he had received, listening to the groans of wounded men... Someone produced a lyre looted from a house before it had been burnt to the ground. He was a young soldier, about the age of Lucius. He had played and played into the night, and Decius listened and wondered what they were doing in this land. Why were they killing these people? If he was to die on the morrow what would he have achieved?

Julia scarcely heard the music her brother was playing. She was thinking how handsome Decius was – though his hair was already greying. She looked at his bronzed hand holding a goblet of wine on the table and noted how strong it was. His face was half turned away from her so she could watch him undetected. Would he be going back to Rome – or was he settled now in Britain forever? She could not believe a hardened warrior such as he was would be content to live in this small town at peace. She had heard that soldiers were causing all kinds of trouble because they were bored and restless with the long years without fighting. They cheered when they were sent off to Gaul or Germany to put down an uprising, and pleaded to be posted to the North or the West of Britain where there was still some chance of a skirmish against the wild Caledonian, Silurian or Ordovician tribes.

Ethne listened intently to the music, then suddenly left her place at the table, and came over to the side of Lucius. She stood for a moment silent and then started to sing. Her voice was high and clear – exquisitely beautiful. It wove into the notes of the lyre as though the instrument and the voice were of one piece. Lucius found himself playing as he had never played before... following her... anticipating her... None of them could understand the words she was singing. The song seemed to be in some language none of them had ever heard – but it brought tears to their eyes. It was as though they were entranced – caught in the sounds as though in a silver net – held there as the world went by without them. Lucius felt the lyre had taken over and was playing without him though he still made the motions of moving his fingers over it. Outside the music there was a profound silence. And in that silence each found him or herself lost deep in a forest – light filtering through a canopy of leaves casting unfamiliar shadows, and illuminating unfamiliar thoughts.

"He is here!" thought Lucius, sensing the presence of Orpheus.

"She is here!" thought Ethne, sensing the presence of Sul.

Decius turned to see his dead wife silhouetted in the doorway and half rose to go to her. But she was gone as suddenly as she had come.

Aulus and Julia felt uneasy. Something was going on they did not understand – and did not want to understand.

Julia clapped her hands loudly for the slaves to enter with the next course.

Bewildered, fingers faltering on the lyre, Lucius stared around as though he had just woken from a deep sleep.

Ethne slipped back to her place at the table. She herself did not know what she had sung, or why she had felt compelled to do so.

77

Decius sank back onto the couch, frowning at the doorway through which the slaves were now passing, carrying dishes of meat and jars of wine.

Aulus cleared his throat. "I'm afraid, my friend, you'll find our entertainment poor after what you've been used to. What was that song, my dear?" He asked Ethne. "It was a pretty tune – but I couldn't catch the words."

"A pretty tune!" thought Lucius indignantly. His father had been privileged to hear Orpheus himself play the most magnificent music ever heard by human ears – and he called it a "pretty tune".

He glanced at Ethne. She did not stir his body as her sister did although she was no less beautiful. But there was something there – some connection between them that went deeper than physical attraction.

While his Romanized son and his granddaughter Ethne were being entertained at the villa of Aulus, Owein, some of his revolutionary friends, and his other granddaughter Megan, were meeting to discuss tactics.

Megan reported the gist of her meetings with the Egyptian and his workforce. They all recognized from what she said that they had a formidable opponent in the foreigner. It was common knowledge that all Egyptians were practitioners of black magic, and this particular man was obviously no exception. Besides, there were so many tales handed down from their own ancestors of dramatic transformations from human to animal or bird, from spirit being to human... that it was not difficult for them to accept that he could do these things if he so wished.

Owein himself had always been a pragmatic man, very much concerned with the things of this world. He had fought the invading Romans for the land he needed for his family and his tribe, and not for the right to believe in certain gods. But the Romans had made the gods a political issue and if the Celts did not take a stand here and now on what gods were set up for them to worship and obey, who knew where it would end.

There was no army garrisoned at Aquae Sulis for it was a peaceful religious centre, but it would be easy to bring soldiers from elsewhere to the town. Owein and his conspirators knew they could no longer fight the Romans with the sword, much as it irked them to admit it. Their only chance was sabotage and disruption.

If the Egyptian sculptor would not willingly join with them and if, as some of them believed, he was a formidable magician, it was suggested that there was only one way to get him on their side. Dylan, almost seventy years old, held the floor as he spoke, pointing out that if she was as passionately dedicated to their cause as she said she was, surely she would consider seducing the Egyptian for their sakes. "No man would be able to resist such beauty," he said. Practitioner of the magical arts he might be – but the cunning of a woman as desirable as Megan could surely, at the very least, confuse and distract him.

There was an instant and vociferous reaction, not least from Owein and his granddaughter.

Megan stormed away from the meeting almost incoherent with rage.

She walked by the river, now darkly sliding away from her, the reflection of the torch in her hand flickering on its surface. In there, somewhere, lay her leaden curse. She would give anything to retrieve it – but there was no way she could. In the old days there had been women warriors in her tribe as formidable as any man. She remembered Boudicca, Queen of the Iceni, who had devastated the south eastern lands of Britain and slaughtered more Romans and Romanized Britons than men could count. Twelve years had passed and still the wounds that had been inflicted were not healed. Megan gripped her torch and held it high above her head.

"These old men are feeble," she thought angrily, remembering the meandering discussion of the group she had just left, "and the young men are mostly lazy and selfish, enervated by the hot baths and the luxuries the Romans have poured into this town." The only man of substance, Brendan, was temporarily away, raising support from the outlying hamlets. "It is up to me," she decided. "If Boudicca could kill. I can kill." Her eyes gleamed in the torchlight. But did she see something stir in the dark waters? Did a shadow pass over it blotting out the reflection of light?

Megan shivered and lowered her arm. She was afraid again. Afraid of what lurked out there. Afraid of herself.

The Egyptian, lying flat on his back on his wooden bed, started and awoke. He lay for a long time staring up at the ceiling – unmoving – listening. It was nearly dawn when at last he shut his eyes. On the underside of his lids blazed the image of a woman warrior, sword raised. He opened his eyes quickly. There was no one there. It was as though he had been staring at a candle flame and the image had stayed with him for a moment as vividly as though he had still been gazing at it.

He no longer felt like sleeping. He rose and stretched and pulled on his garments.

He took a small malachite jar from a shelf at the rear of his chamber and stepped into the tiny room at the back of his house where he had set up a shrine to Isis. There were no windows in this chamber. He lit a lamp, and then a piece of the precious frankincense resin he had brought from Egypt. Speaking the sacred words known to his people since ancient times, he carefully and ritualistically removed the fine linen cloth that covered the tiny statue of the Goddess. Her silver limbs gleamed in the flickering lamplight. Her eyes of lapis lazuli gazed into his. From a golden bowl he splashed holy water on her and then bowed to the ground before her, his forehead held for a long time against the wooden floorboards.

When he rose at last and covered her again, the sun rose with him – and he walked by the river bathed in its light.

Chapter 11

By chance or luck or cosmic design Demosthenes, the Greek, arrived at Aquae Sulis the very day the new villa of Aulus Sabinus, the Roman Celt, was completed and the family were moving in.

The small boat that brought him from the town deposited him as close as it could and he made his way, with his few belongings, up the path Ethne had followed the day she had first met Julia.

The wooden house on its stone foundation that had been home to the family for many years was already standing empty like an abandoned shell washed up by the tide. It would be used for storage and administration. The slaves would be housed there with the farm labourers and the occasional seasonal help.

Julia, in a faded dress with her hair bound up in a scarf to keep dust out, was supervising everything. Tables and chairs were standing about on the grass, while two men heaved a heavy wooden bed onto the new verandah and through a door that was almost too small for it.

"Careful!" she shouted, pressing close behind them and making one young lad on temporary loan from the town so nervous he almost let it slip. His father grinned at him and whispered: "Steady boy. She won't eat you." His son looked at the flushed and agitated face of the mistress of the house and wished he were far away.

Aulus appeared from within the villa and Julia at once turned to him.

"Where is Lucius?" she demanded. "He's never here when he's needed."

"I think he's in the Orphic room," Aulus replied.

"There is hardly any furniture to go in there, yet he never leaves it," she snapped. "Lucius!" she screamed. "Lucius! Come here at once."

Demosthenes put down his bundles. This was not how he imagined his "homecoming" – but it was a long way back to Athens. He wondered if he should keep out of sight until things settled down, or whether he should announce himself right away.

The matter was almost immediately taken out of his hands as Julia spotted him and called out at once that he should not stand idling there but lend a hand. She had hired some men from the town to help with the move and no doubt assumed he was one of them.

He opened his mouth to set the matter right, but shut it again. She had already turned her back on him and Aulus had disappeared into the house.

Demosthenes, the gentle priest, the intellectual, who had never done a day's manual work in his life, found himself lifting and carrying with the rest, slightly amused at the thought of how Julia would feel when she learned the truth about him.

A young man emerged from the house dressed more elegantly than the rest. "This must be Lucius, the son of the house," Demosthenes thought. "I wonder if he will recognize me."

But Lucius was caught up in the excitement of preparing the sanctuary for his God and noticed nothing.

It was nearly nightfall when all the furniture had been moved in and the workmen were lining up before Aulus who was seated at a table on the verandah dispensing wages, when Demosthenes decided to present himself. He waited at the end of the line. Aulus counted out the last batch of coins and prepared to hand them over without an upward glance, when Julia, dusty and exhausted, but still very much in charge, arrived at his side. For the first time she looked Demosthenes in the eye.

"Wait, father," she said, holding up her hand sternly. "I don't remember hiring this man."

Demosthenes smiled.

"You did not, lady, though I have worked to your orders all afternoon."

She frowned. Aulus looked up puzzled. That was not a local accent.

"Demosthenes!" A voice suddenly cried out, and Lucius came running. "The priest, father, the Greek priest for Orpheus!"

Invisible to them before, he suddenly became visible.

Then came the explanations, the apologies, the embarrassment. Only Julia remained unfriendly, for she blamed him for making her look a fool.

And then – at last – sleep in a warm and comfortable bed with the thought that on the morrow he would take up his true calling.

"The idea is," Lucius explained to the Greek the following day, "that we'll introduce people to the mysteries of Orpheus gradually from here, but as soon as we have enough followers we'll set about building a proper temple in the town. I'm afraid there are not many of us yet. I hope you won't think it is not worth your while coming all this way."

Demosthenes smiled reassuringly. "If Orpheus called me to this place," he said, "I believe he must have had a reason."

"There's been too much killing," Lucius said. "Too many animals sacrificed. I feel we need Orpheus to lead us to quieter, kinder ways – to show us the joy of life. We need to be in harmony with each other – like the notes in his music."

"I see I have a student ready and eager to set off on an important journey."

Lucius looked pleased.

"I know I have a long way to go – but at least, now that you are here, I can get started."

Demosthenes looked around him. This was a pleasant place. The river below quietly flowing to the ocean, the hills covered with healthy green wheat, birds perching in the trees, singing.

"Come with me," Lucius said eagerly. "I want to show you something."

He led the Greek around the new house to the field just behind it and up the slope from it. There he stopped. The wheat was knee-high, shimmering in the morning sunlight. Demosthenes looked at Lucius enquiringly.

"It was here I first conceived the idea to send for a priest of Orpheus."

Demosthenes waited.

"It was here I saw – I *felt* – the power of an unseen energy. Something extraordinary. I *felt* the wheat growing – the drive from the seed in the ground to the seedling in the sun. I knew I had taken too many things for granted, for too long. My eyes were opening – but not enough. I needed help. I needed guidance. I kept slipping away from the vision – as though it had never happened. Yet I knew that what I had seen, had felt, was there all the time, but somehow I had just lost the knack of seeing it. Will you help me get it back?"

Demosthenes looked thoughtful.

"We will look for it together," he said humbly.

"But you are an initiate. You are a priest!" Lucius cried.

"Yet I have never felt the wheat growing," Demosthenes said, simply.

Brendan returned to Aquae Sulis. He had been disappointed in the amount of support he had managed to muster for the revolt he was planning. News of the thoroughness with which the Roman army had put down the uprising at his own home town had reached most villages and farms in the area as the Romans had intended. In itself the rebellion of the hill fort had not posed much of a threat to the might of Rome – but as a lesson on what not to do under Roman administration the ruthlessness of the soldiers was most effective.

As Brendan strode back along the road to Aquae Sulis he spat on every Roman tombstone he found along the way. It was as though the stone-cold eyes of the effigies were mocking him. "We are here to stay," the hollow voices called after him. "Even our dead will stay. We rule the Underworld as we rule the Upper. There is no getting rid of us – ever."

Why did the hated conquerors and foreigners put their tombs along the great road that dominated the entrance and exit to the town but to remind all travellers that there was no getting away from them? He had heard the excuse that they wanted to be near the Sacred City in death as well as in life, but he dismissed it.

The Roman idea of an after-life was a gloomy one. Brendan glared at a tombstone of local stone deeply incised with the name of a German merchant.

"Why do you let yourself be buried with *them*?" he muttered. "Do you want to spend eternity wandering aimlessly in Dis as a shadow among shadows? If you had come to us – we would have given you an after-life of feasting and music, of silver bowls and crystal trees and ale as strong as any here on earth."

Then he paused, staring at the stone monument. The German had come a long, long way to die here in this valley. What had drawn him here? As merchant he was more likely to have made his fortune elsewhere. Was he a pilgrim to the Oracle of Sulis Minerva? He must have wanted to ask an exceptional question to have made such a long and hazardous journey to find the answer. Did he find it? Was he given instructions by the Oracle and died before he could carry them out? Where was he now? Was he nothing but a rotting corpse beneath the stone... a ghost wandering the dark forests and mountains of his homeland... a shade in the melancholy regions of Dis? Or was he a happy being among the flowering fields of the Celtic Otherworld awaiting rebirth?

Brendan frowned. He was not accustomed to thinking about death. Poets and bards sang about a rich and shining country much like earth, only better – but to Brendan those tales were nothing more than an attempt to seduce people away from the urgent business of living. Why try to throw the conquerors off and make life tolerable for yourself here and now, when if you just waited until you were dead you would have everything you had ever wished for – plus another chance to walk again on earth? Brendan's own grandfather had died owing a great many cattle to his neighbour. A Druid had brokered an agreement on his deathbed that the debt would be paid back by whoever he became in his next life to whoever his neighbour became. It was perfectly legal and solemnly witnessed by both families.

"If there is rebirth into this world as the Druids say," Brendan thought bitterly, "those the Romans have dispossessed and killed will be waiting for them when they return. There will be no escaping the consequences of their deeds."

He strode on.

"But I'll not look for what I want in some uncertain future," he declared fiercely. "I'll collect my payment *now* for what they owe me!"

He looked neither to the left nor the right on the rest of his journey.

The news that Brendan had returned brought Megan out of the house at once in search of him. With the passing of the night her urge to kill the Egyptian and anyone else who stood in her way had gone like the mist that hung over the river. She pulled on her thick woollen cloak though the sun was well up and warming the land nicely. Somehow the chill she felt came from inside and would not respond to its gentle rays.

Brendan was not at home. She tracked him down to the Temple forecourt where a sacrifice was in progress. She was in time to see the priest raise his knife and to hear the scream of the animal. She watched, without intending to, the Haruspex feeling among the entrails for a message from the Gods. She caught a glimpse of Brendan among the crowds also watching. He had said once that he did not believe the entrails of an animal *could* reveal the gods' intentions – but if the people believed they could, it was worth listening to what the Haruspex said, because that, the belief itself, would influence the actions of the people.

On the opposite side of the crowd from Brendan she saw her father, also watching intently. Two soldiers flanked Decius and the stiffness of their stance told her that a lot hung on what the priest said, both for the Romans and for the local people.

"What question has been asked of the Gods?" Megan whispered to her neighbour. The boy shrugged and shook his head, but the woman standing on the other side of her whispered back: "The centurion wants to know if there is to be peace and prosperity in the town this summer."

"The usual," a man to her left said cynically.

"Hush!" someone else hissed. "I want to hear what he says."

The Haruspex had already started to speak and they had missed his first few words.

"... But the danger can be averted with great sacrifice and effort."

"What danger?" Megan whispered.

"I didn't hear..."

"He didn't say..."

"He meant the statue..."

"He meant the revolt against the statue..."

"Is the danger from *us*, or from the Romans?" Megan thought impatiently. "How I hate these ambiguous divinations!"

She looked at her father's face. It had relaxed. It was clear how he had taken the words.

She heard her name called and Brendan was pushing his way through the now chattering crowds to her side. He looked elated. He too had interpreted the words to his advantage.

"We must call a meeting," he said, his eyes alight. "The gods are on our side."

Megan's heart skipped a beat. No matter what her thoughts might have been before, she could not resist his enthusiasm. He was forceful and handsome. He knew what he wanted and he knew how to get it. He was never made impotent by doubt! He took her arm to lead her away from the crowd and she went with him willingly.

* * *

Ethne chose the same day to visit the Oracle of Sul. One of the priestesses knew her well and admitted her to the old woman's quarters without hesitation. The ancient Oracle was still much respected, although the Romans had changed the rituals that she had once presided over, and introduced the office of male Haruspex who was responsible for the divination of animal entrails in the forecourt. Recently he had been taking more and more of her work away from her. This very day the centurion Decius Brutus had called for the Haruspex, and not the Oracle of Sul, to divine what the next few months in Aquae Sulis would bring.

There was even talk in the town that she might not be replaced when she died, but her office taken over entirely by the Roman diviner. Some were horrified at the thought and would not accept that even the Romans would perpetrate such a sacrilege.

The conquerors had kept her in place, though reducing her powers, knowing that to dismantle such an ancient and yet living part of the local religion would cause more trouble than it saved. People still came from distant countries to consult her. Many Roman provincial towns had the offices of a diviner – but very few had an oracle that was almost as universally accepted as the Pythea of Delphi and the Sibyl of Cumae. Decius Brutus had deliberately chosen to consult the Haruspex on this day for political reasons. He wanted a public proclamation that would serve to warn the people against the uprising he felt was imminent.

Ethne was shown into a small but comfortable chamber where she found her friend, so small and frail with age it seemed as though a strong puff of wind would blow her away. Her face lit up as soon as she saw Ethne. Her life was, and had always been, extremely lonely. Power she might have to shape events, but no one dare befriend her for they feared her insight into their secret, and often shameful, thoughts. The office itself called for isolation from other people – for who would trust a prophet who did her shopping in the market place and haggled like everyone else? But she had met the child Ethne on Sul's hill outside the town and had felt such a strong affinity with her that she dreamed of her taking her place as Oracle one day. Recently she had been too crippled with pains in her joints to make the arduous journey to the hill, but had encouraged Ethne to visit her in her private quarters behind the Temple of Sulis Minerva. Some of the priestesses resented this and muttered jealously about it among themselves, but one or two, who had developed a strong affection for the formidable but lonely old lady, often helped smuggle the girl in to see her.

It was a while before Ethne broached the real subject of her visit this day. She spoke first about her experience in the house of Aulus and how she felt she had been "taken over" by Sul herself and had sung with her voice in the language of the ancients. The old lady listened as Ethne described the whole evening and those who were present. She noted the way the young girl's face glowed when she spoke of Lucius and how he too had seemed possessed by someone greater than himself when he played. She questioned her closely about every detail, coming back time and again to Lucius. The girl's answers confirmed the old woman's suspicions. Ethne was attracted to Lucius. Very attracted. She frowned – the office of oracle demanded chastity and isolation. More than any of her own priestesses Ethne had shown the qualities necessary for a true oracle. There was no doubt that she had the ability to contact supernatural entities easily. There was no doubt the Great Goddess favoured and trusted her. There was no doubt that if she, the outgoing Oracle, could not instate a suitable heir at her departure, the Romans would either dismantle the office, or put in her place someone they could easily manipulate. Ethne must not fall in love, must not marry, must not be distracted...

Ethne talked on and one part of the Oracle's mind listened to her, whilst another was busy with ideas and plans to achieve what she wanted. It was when Ethne spoke of her grandfather and sister's reaction to the statue of Claudius, that the old lady thought of a way to hold Ethne to her calling as heir to the Oracle of Sul.

It was Brendan's idea to wait until the statue was finished before they destroyed it.

"If we sabotage the block of stone before it is carved, they will just get another cut from the quarry. It will be no more than a nuisance to them." He was speaking to his group of dissidents gathered at the house of Owein. Megan bit her lip. She had thought he would praise her for her attempts to subvert the workmen on the site, and her ideas of how they could destroy the block. She had not mentioned her plan to kill the master sculptor – for once daylight had come the passionate urge to draw blood had passed and left her uneasy and unsure.

"But if we wait until the statue is set up – the moment when all eyes are focused on it – and *then* strike! Imagine the effect that will have! The whole population will see that the very thing the Romans have erected to symbolize their might and power over us, can be toppled down under their very noses. It will be an act that will fire rebellion in every corner of the country. The sound of its fall will be heard in Rome itself!" Brendan's eyes shone. He saw himself standing on the shattered hulk, holding up his sword like a statue of Victory he had once seen.

"But will it be possible to topple it?" someone asked anxiously. "The place will be thick with soldiers."

"Of course it will! I didn't say it would be easy. We must train and plan and prepare. We must not make a move until the very moment the statue is put in place. They must think we've given up our opposition, and will relax their vigilance. But I can promise you there will be fighting and some of us will not see the end of that day on earth. Any man here who wants to back out – should back out now. But if he chooses to do so he must swear an oath not to reveal our intention, and that oath will bind him so tight in this world and the next," Brendan emphasized the last words darkly, "that he will *never* escape the consequences!"

Everyone in the room was silent. Several of them would have liked to back out at that moment, but the thought of taking such an oath was almost more frightening than the thought of being killed by a Roman sword.

"I have heard that once a statue is completed, it is as alive as you or I," someone ventured nervously. "I have heard of statues walking..."

"Stone heads have prophesied..." another added.

"Well, this one will *bleed*!" Brendan cried fiercely. "This one will *cry out*. Rome will hear its cry!"

He looked around his motley group of warriors sternly. As he met each eye, he could tell which would be likely to hold steady in a crisis and which would not.

"I have decided we will *all* take an oath of loyalty," he said, "for without it how will we know who we can trust and who we cannot?"

Many shifted uneasily in their seats, some murmured, but Brendan was determined. Who knew who might falter when the stark choice between life and death had to be made?

"*I'll* take an oath!" Megan cried, standing up, her eyes blazing. "An oath that will bind me to this cause no matter what happens!"

All eyes turned to her. Could any of them do less than she had done? Brendan looked at her with surprise and admiration. In sizing up his army he had overlooked her. It was true she had always been at the meetings. It was true she had shown more initiative and enthusiasm than almost any other of the group – but he had never really taken her seriously. She was Owein's daughter and Owein had been the leader before he himself had come to the town. At first it was in respect for the old fire-eater that Brendan had allowed her to stay. Now he could see she was an asset.

He moved to her side and put his hand on her shoulder.

"Megan is ready," he said triumphantly. She flushed, feeling his hand warm on her shoulder. "Who will take the oath beside her? I ask no more of you than that you swear allegiance to our own ancestors and our own gods."

From that moment on they were committed. Not one held back from the oath taking. Every one believed that if they failed to fulfil it, their gods would hunt them down.

Brendan then went on to persuade them to recruit others. "For the more we have, the easier we will find the battle." He hoped none would think beyond the battle to the long arm of Roman retribution.

"Aquae Sulis is a special town," Brendan assured them. "Others may have the strength of walls and weapons – but this one is sacred to the gods and if we defend them, they will defend us. Have no fear. Right is on our side and we will win."

A great cheer went up, for now that they had passed through the oath fire, they were eager for action.

"But remember," Brendan warned them, "until the day – until the very moment I give the signal – all that we do or say regarding it must be in secret. Decius Brutus," and his lip curled as he spoke the name, "must believe all opposition has died down. The more we can convince him of this – the greater our chances of success."

The group dispersed noisily, each bound to each with a new camaraderie.

Only Brendan, Owein and Megan remained.

Brendan looked at the old man closely.

"What do you feel about drawing a sword against your own son?" he asked. "Will your resolve hold?"

"I have no son," Owein said bitterly. "He died when he took an oath to serve the Romans."

"And you?" Brendan turned to Megan.

There was an almost imperceptible hesitation. Then she answered. "I have taken the oath to defend my ancestors and my gods," she said. "I will not break my oath."

Chapter 12

Martha, sent to draw water out of the Sacred Well at Glastonia, filled her jar and then set it down. It was a cold, grey day and a misty rain was drifting down. "How soft," she thought, "compared to the heavy rain of Rome." Her woollen cloak was scarcely damp. Fetching water from the well was one of her favourite chores. The dell in which it lay was green and leafy, jewelled with flowers. Overhanging branches sheltered it from the rain. Although it was at the foot of the mysterious Tor, she never felt threatened there. It was as though there were a charmed circle around it into which no malevolent force could ever penetrate. She wondered if it was true that Joseph of Arimathea had placed the Lord's Chalice there. How she would love to see it! To touch something the Master had touched! Maybe even to drink from it. Would that not give her the strength she knew she lacked for the work her grandfather expected of her? She wanted to spread the word of the Master and live according to His directions but sometimes it was so hard... Even the oldest members of the community, those who had lived and worked with the Master's uncle – even her grandfather who had actually been in His presence – did not always love – did not always forgive... How could they love Nero, for instance? How could they forgive him for the monstrous deeds of cruelty he had perpetrated – the massacre of her parents among so many others? On one terrible night he had used human torches to light the way. As a child she had heard the screams of people burning and seen her mother's face as she held her fast and pretended the danger would never reach *them*. Her mother... tears came to Martha's eyes. Her innocent mother had died in the arena with a thousand jeering voices shrieking for her death. Sometimes the hatred she felt could hardly be contained, and she lay in darkness and felt her thoughts drawn round and round in such a black and bitter whirlpool that she feared for her sanity.

Many a night Martha pulled the woollen blanket up to her chin. She was tired, but she dreaded going to sleep. Would the nightmares come again? The running? The hiding? The sound of screams? Her grandfather told her she must forgive – not the deeds the Romans perpetrated, but the men who perpetrated them. If their Lord Saviour could forgive those who crucified Him surely... But she could not forgive those who led off her friends and family to be slaughtered in the circus. She could not forgive those who caused her abandonment and desolation. As a small child she had not understood the desertion of her parents. As an older child she understood only too well why and where they had gone. Every night in her new home in Britain the mutton fat candle sputtered out before she could reach oblivion.

Sometimes she felt the only way she would learn to forgive was with the supernatural help of the Chalice. Without it she would be doomed and lost forever.

Martha lay down on the damp grass and peered into the depths of the well. Stones, rough-hewn, lined it. Ferns grew from the cracks. She could see the still, dark surface and her own face looking back at her, her eyes deeply troubled.

She leant over as far as she dared and reached down. She could feel the squared stones beneath the water. If the Chalice was in there, it was a long way out of her reach.

She sighed and withdrew her arm from the water, her sleeve soaking wet. Her companions would be waiting for her. She stood up and lifted the heavy jar on to her shoulder.

Ethne stood on the flat top of Sul's sacred hill outside Aquae Sulis. The soft, misty rain dampened her hair but she hardly noticed it. She could not see the panorama of hills and valleys, of forests and fields that she knew lay below her stretching to the far horizon. The mist lay close against the land and visibility was restricted to the immediate circle of the hilltop. Hawthorn smudged the edges, and each tall grass stem against her foot carried a jewelled drop of water, suddenly the focus of her attention.

She stooped and picked a stem and stared into the drop as though into a crystal ball.

The Oracle had placed her in a difficult position and it seemed to her every thought, every feeling in her was in conflict. A few weeks ago she might have welcomed the Oracle's ultimatum. For a long time she had toyed with the idea of becoming the Oracle herself. She knew that many of the townspeople expected and wanted it. A few weeks ago she would have thought no higher honour could have come her way. But recently she had been experiencing thoughts and feelings an oracle should not have. She was beginning to think too much about the young man Lucius. She was beginning to dream of loving him – of his loving her – of children... In her heart she had decided that the hard and dedicated path of the Oracle was not for her. "I can serve Sul just as easily being a mother as a virgin," she thought. "In fact better – for my children will be brought up to love her and respect her..." But the Oracle that day had given her a stark choice – she would prevent the controversial statue of Claudius being raised in the town if Ethne vowed to be her heir and begin the rigorous training for initiation immediately.

"I know I have not long to live," the old lady had said, "and if there is to be a smooth transition we cannot delay."

Ethne's face must have shown her dismay, for the woman frowned. "It is not I who demand this," she said, sternly. "But Sul herself."

For the first time in her life a rebellious thought had flashed through Ethne's mind – a moment of doubt that the Oracle of Sul was speaking the words of the Goddess. It would be so easy for the Oracle to say what *she* wanted to say, and no one could check whether they were the words of Sul or not. But even as she thought it, she checked herself, feeling deeply guilty at the blasphemy. Falteringly she tried to argue her way out of obedience to the command. She was not ready. She was not worthy. She had obligations to her family...

But unblinking, the Oracle had stared into her eyes and the words of protest had frozen on the young girl's lips. Before she left the Oracle's presence Ethne had committed herself.

She walked back blindly to her home that day. Someone greeted her but she did not respond. She longed to talk it through with Megan, but Megan was preoccupied with troubles of her own. She thought of seeking out Lucius. "If Lucius thinks he could come one day to love me as I love him, I will defy the Oracle." But Lucius had given her no indication that he responded to her in the way she wanted, and if she pressed him on the matter too soon he might well be frightened off *ever* loving her.

She knew now she did not want to spend all her time communicating with the supernatural worlds! How strange that she had ever believed that was what she wanted. Why could not things stay as they were? At the moment she had all the pleasures and possibilities of an ordinary, natural life with the great joy of occasional magnificent excursions into the supernatural.

The crystal drop of water she was staring at so desperately trickled down the grass stem and fell to the ground. She felt utterly alone. The Goddess would not come to her. No one would tell her what she wanted to hear. No one would release her from the responsibility she did not want to bear.

With tears running down her cheeks she turned away from the Sacred Hill and made her way slowly and sadly back to the town.

Lucius meanwhile, unaware of the conflict in Ethne's soul, was in town attending to some business for his father. There he saw Megan loading her baskets at the market.

When he first spotted her he held back, watching her closely, wondering which of the twins it was. But he soon decided by the vigorous and argumentative way she was haggling over prices with the stall holders that it had to be Megan, "the fiery one" as her father described her. He moved closer, hesitating to accost her. They had, after all, met only once. She could not know she had become a familiar visitor in his dreams and they had, in that way, shared many an intimate moment.

He watched her for some time, moving when she moved, admiring everything about her. Suddenly she turned and stared straight at him.

"Are you following me, sir?" she demanded, her eyes flashing with anger.

Startled, he longed to melt back into the crowd, but her gaze held him transfixed.

"Only as an admirer..." he stammered.

"Have we met before, sir?" She frowned, seeming less certain of herself.

"Once," he said, becoming more confident. "I mistook you for a Goddess!"

She continued to stare. It was clear she had no memory of the occasion.

Desperately he tried another tack.

"I am a friend of your sister, Ethne," he said.

"Oh, Ethne!" she cried in relief. "We're always being mistaken for one another."

95

"I didn't mistake you," he thought. "I could never mistake you!" But aloud he said mildly: "I'm sorry if I discomfited you."

"No matter!" She was laughing now. "You can carry my baskets if you like. I'm going home and Ethne is probably there."

Silently he picked up her heavy baskets and followed her through the crowd. She walked boldly, as though she owned the town, and was greeted enthusiastically by many a passer by.

"She is treating me like a slave," he fumed inwardly.

At the door of her house she stopped at last and looked back at him.

"Thankyou," she said cheerfully, her hand on the door.

"Will she look into my eyes?" he thought.

But she lifted the baskets from his hands without meeting his eyes and pushed open the door with her foot.

"Ethne!" she called. "Ethne – there's a friend of yours here."

She turned. "What is your name?" she asked impatiently.

Lucius looked at her furiously.

"I have no name. I am nobody," he said with sudden explosive bitterness, and before she could react to this extraordinary remark, he had turned and was striding off down the narrow street.

She stared after him in amazement.

Chapter 13

As the days and weeks passed, the colossal statue of Claudius the God began to take shape. Decius Brutus visited the workyard from time to time to monitor the slow transformation of the featureless block into a shape disturbingly like the body of a man.

Staring fascinated one day as the Egyptian's most skilled apprentice chipped away at what would be the head, he wondered at what moment the inanimate stone would take on the illusion of life. He knew that many people believed statues could hear what was said in their presence, some even believed they could walk and talk. He, in his travels, had seen stones so mimicking life that, rational man as he was, he himself could almost believe this was true.

He had been present once in a Serapeum in Egypt when he could have sworn the God Serapis raised his arm and pointed a stony finger at one of the supplicants. He had seen the man fall down dead before his very eyes. The room was dim, almost black, with flickering lamps throwing gigantic shadows, and priests intoning a weird and hypnotic chant for what seemed like hours beforehand. They were standing in the suffocating heat of an underground chamber, and he for one was shifting from foot to foot wishing the whole thing would end. He could scarcely see the faces of those around him, but he could feel the hysteria building up until, at the moment when it was almost too much to bear, there was a sudden silence. The God lifted his arm.

He did not see anyone douse the lamps, but suddenly they were in total darkness. He heard the rasping intake of every breath. He felt the terror. In vain, he tried to tell himself this was all a theatrical trick of the priesthood, the statue was lifeless stone and could not have moved – but even he was cold with fear in all that heat. He fancied he could hear the heart-beats of all those present.

Then as suddenly as it had gone, the light returned.

Everyone in the room fell to his knees and bowed to the ground before the statue of the God. He tried to resist, but found himself down with the rest.

"You are wondering at what point the statue comes alive?" A

voice beside him said, and he was back in Britain, a thousand miles from the Serapeum in Alexandria, staring at an ordinary block of stone with workmen chipping at it.

He spun round. The Egyptian was there. How had he known that was exactly what he was thinking?

"I'm not one of those who believe a statue ever has life," he said gruffly.

The Egyptian smiled.

The centurion looked at him hard.

"Do you believe it has?"

The Egyptian shrugged. "What I believe does not matter. It is what you believe that does."

"Do you mean if I believe a statue has life, for me it will have. My own mind and imagination gives it the illusion of life?"

The Egyptian did not reply. His attention had been drawn to something on the work floor.

Decius grabbed his arm.

"Answer me," he said roughly.

The Egyptian turned and looked into his eyes.

"The statue has no life of its own," he said slowly, deliberately, each word emphasized as though speaking to a child. "But it can become a channel for life."

Decius had heard this theory. It was supposed that the god or goddess came into the stone from time to time and used the form as our spirits use the bodies of flesh and blood we are given at birth. Both statues and bodies are like the shells hermit crabs use – temporary houses for beings from other dimensions and realms. He had heard the theory – but he did not subscribe to it. He did not believe there were other realms and other dimensions, nor other beings floating around invisibly.

"If the gods need a vehicle to manifest on this earth," he sneered, "why do they need us to carve a life-like representation of them? Surely they can manifest themselves in any form they like, any time they like, anywhere they like."

"They do," said the Egyptian. "They do not need the statue. It is we who need it."

This time he walked away and Decius did not hold him back.

The centurion gazed after him, annoyed. Why had he even entered into such a conversation. Was he becoming as superstitious as the mass of ordinary people? The statue would be a statue – no more. The only thing he had to watch out for was the rebellion of the locals against Rome, using the statue of Claudius as a focal point for disaffection.

He stepped forward and looked more closely at the work of the man carving the stone face. He was working on the left eye and, at that moment, withdrew the chisel and stood back to admire his own handiwork.

Decius leaned forward, interested. The sculptor had outlined the iris and the pupil in charcoal on the blank stone eyeball. It seemed to Decius it was looking directly at him. He moved away uneasily, frowning.

Aulus and Lucius had only the vaguest idea of what Orphism was when they decided to build their Orphic room. Lucius had had his experience with the being he believed to be Orpheus and they had heard the legend of his descent into the Underworld. They had also heard that some of the major Greek philosophers like Plato and Pythagoras were initiates and that it was one of the most persistent and ancient of Greek religions.

Demosthenes told them that it was not Greek in its origins at all, but had come from Thrace and in its early stages had been closely associated with the cult of Dionysus, or as the Romans called him, Bacchus.

Lucius frowned. "But I thought the followers of Dionysus, the Maenads, were supposed to have torn Orpheus to pieces?"

"That is true," Demosthenes said. "It seemed that Orpheus became dissatisfied with the wild frenzies that the Dionysians practised in order to reach a state in which they could communicate with their God, and hated the tearing apart of animals at the height of the frenzy and the eating of their raw flesh... It is said he preached that the sacrifice, or even the eating of animals, was anathema and taught the sacrifice of Self instead – the restraint over one's own flesh – the symbolic, pure state in which communion with the God was possible. It couldn't have been further from the methods the Dionysians used."

Lucius listened wide-eyed.

"But I think the Maenads attack on him might have been more complicated than just vengeance for his insult to Dionysus," Demosthenes continued thoughtfully. "I believe his death and the scattering of the pieces of his body was an act in a wider drama –

necessary to bring about his deification. His story is similar to the story of the great Egyptian God of the Underworld, Osiris. He was a king torn apart by his brother Seth and the pieces scattered across Egypt. His wife Isis gathered the parts and bound them together. It is said that by the energy of love she even brought him to life again and conceived their son Horus by him. These events gave him his power over death and made him the risen God. The head of Osiris is buried at Abydos, the most sacred place in Egypt. The head of Orpheus is buried on the island of Lesbos and to this day still speaks and pronounces words of wisdom and prophecy."

"So Orpheus was an ordinary man who became a god," Lucius cried, his eyes shining. "The last thing his enemies wanted when they killed him so savagely."

"Perhaps not quite an ordinary man," Demosthenes replied, smiling.

There was a long pause – broken at last by the Greek.

"Of course, there may be yet another interpretation of the way Orpheus died."

"What is that?"

"It may be that he offered himself as a willing sacrifice. He gave himself to their homicidal frenzy voluntarily, knowing that his death would shock men into finding a better way of religious ecstasy – a way that was worthy of man's highest and not lowest emotions."

Lucius sat quietly in the room he and his father had created for the God, and felt overwhelmed by the thoughts that crowded into his mind. Hitherto he had a fairly simple grasp of what he wanted to achieve by introducing Orpheus to the local community, but now he realized he knew too little. He felt as though by bringing Demosthenes to the country he had thrown a pebble into a pond and the circles that were only just beginning to travel out from the centre would reach further than any he had anticipated.

He had hoped, through the Orphic ecstasy he had heard about, to visit the outskirts of the Otherworld, as Orpheus himself had done in his search of Eurydice. But what if he was expected to pass through the agony of Orpheus's last moments on earth in an initiative ritual to achieve that end? Would he have the courage and strength of will to endure the ordeal? Demosthenes had hinted earlier that to become an initiate of the Orphic Mysteries was not an easy path to choose. He began to wonder if he really wanted to embark on it. The denial of the flesh and the purity of soul it called for no longer seemed so appealing.

Chapter 14

The Roman Prefect in Aquae Sulis at this time was one Cornelius Sartorus, a man Decius did not much like or respect, and he avoided contact with him as much as possible. But as the growing opposition to the statue of Claudius came to his attention, he forced himself to request a meeting with him.

Although a time had been arranged, Sartorus kept him waiting more than an hour, and even when he was ushered into his presence, the man continued examining papers on his desk as though he was not aware of the centurion's presence.

At last he looked up, raising an enquiring eyebrow.

Decius stated his case briefly.

"It may not have come to your attention, sir," he said politely, curbing his desire to hit the man, "that the statue of Claudius as god that you propose to erect in the precinct of the Temple of Sulis Minerva is most unpopular."

Sartorus snorted.

"Aquae Sulis is not far from the lands not yet conquered by us," Decius pointed out, "and no doubt full of warriors who would be happy to fight us. I would ask you to remember the rebellion of Boudicca."

"That rebellion had been fomenting for some time," Cornelius Sartorus said scornfully, "the rape of that Iceni woman and her daughters was only one of many causes. If we change our policy every time a Celt doesn't like something we do, we might as well pack up and go home."

"Nevertheless, sir, I think..."

"I have noted what you have said, centurion," the Prefect said sharply. "But I do not agree the statue will cause trouble. Even if it does – I am sure you and your men will be able to handle it."

A muscle in Decius' cheek tensed ominously, but he kept his rigid military pose. Only his eyes blazed angrily into those of the official. Sartorus dropped his own eyes to the papers on his desk once more, and waved his hand in dismissal.

* * *

As he walked away, Decius thought about all the places he had been where Rome had made her mark. Not all of them had benefited. He had visited the city of Sela before the Romans had taken it over. He wondered how it would change under their rule. As he walked now under green overhanging branches, his mind slipped back to the deserts of Judah and Moab. He and his friend Aras had taken the caravan route from Damascus to Egypt through the ancient land of Edom. He remembered days of heat and dust... huge desert rocks lying rounded, humped and hollowed until at last, raised in gigantic spines, they became impenetrable mountainous barriers, reaching to the sky. Suddenly they had come upon guard-posts at the entrance to a deep gorge.

"I have been here before," Aras whispered.

They had been allowed to pass and walked their horses between elaborately carved cliffs.

"Tombs," Aras said. "Shrines to their gods."

Obelisks as in Egypt, Decius noted. Greek columns. Syrian stepped decoration. There was a wonderful and burgeoning disorder about the place before the Romans imposed their civilized uniformity. The city was in the kingdom of Nabataea, but through it the world passed, carrying its trade and its influence. Aras had seen slant eyed merchants from a country so far away to the east not even the Romans had penetrated it. He had seen men from Babylon and Jerusalem, from Samarkand and India, from Dalmatia and Scythia and the Black Sea.

"It won't be long before our Emperor turns his attention to this place," Aras said. "I can't believe he won't want to secure this valuable trade route."

Decius was glad the Romans had not yet come in force. Here was one place where at last he could forget the tight military discipline, the politics of power. A column of laden camels began to file past them. Their horses whinnied and backed against the multicoloured rock wall, and the camels snarled, baring filthy and alarming teeth. The camel drivers shouted and the animals fell silent, padding quietly past on cushioned feet, casting only supercilious glances over their shoulders at the strangers with their nervous and inferior beasts.

Aras pointed out the runnels for water cut into the rock walls.

"There are sometimes heavy rains here," he said, "and when they come every drop is saved. It is said that the Nabataeans could teach us a thing or two about water conservation."

Decius laughed. Roman arrogance always implied that they were the teachers and innovators wherever they went, but in fact much of Roman knowledge came from those they had conquered.

High above them a deep blue sky showed between the close high walls of rock. The path in the cleft snaked slowly into the depths of the mountain. Occasionally a wild fig tree, precariously rooted in a crack high above them, leaned down and held its dappled green shadow over them for a moment.

The narrow gorge seemed endless, but suddenly it opened out and they found themselves confronting a magnificent building carved out of a towering red cliff, and a space before it crowded with people in every kind of dress... stall holders shouting their wares, loaded carts trundling by. A child cried and was comforted. A dog lifted its leg.

As the valley floor widened wooden buildings became more frequent, often backing on to the rock walls. Houses and taverns and shops filled every possible space, while the carving of facades on the high cliffs behind them gave them the impression that the city was much larger and mightier than it was.

Aras muttered an obscene imprecation. He had trodden in a mess of camel dung.

They found an inn and a stable for their horses. They ate tough goat meat and drank sour wine that first night, Decius remembered, but the next day they found a tavern that served a meal fit for a king.

Now in Aquae Sulis, on the other side of the world from that place, Decius Brutus sighed. This quiet green town was all very well – but suddenly he missed the buzzing cosmopolitan vigour of that rock bound city. The music, the dancing, the hot blood racing as he took a Nabatean girl to bed. Were those people still there? Were those travellers still crossing the desert – hot, desperate, tired – rejoicing at last in the cool shade of Sela, taking advantage of the deep wells of water, the stacked wine jars from Greece, the roasting meat of animals sacrificed to the gods?

Here in this country, the country of his physical birth, there was no contrast between desert and verdure, between deprivation and plenty. There were no mighty mountains, no endless, scorching plains... there was a smallness, almost a pettiness, that irritated him. A breeze stirred and shook the raindrops from the over-hanging branches.

"We walk in one landscape," he thought, "but we carry with us all the landscapes we have ever known." The desert kingdom of the Nabataeans, the bleeding city of Jerusalem, the slow inexorable flow of the Nile – all were here because he was here. How complex and wonderful the consciousness of man! A pity the Governor of the Province of Britain had thought fit to appoint a Prefect over the town of Aquae Sulis who was not capable of seeing or understanding even the most obvious of matters. A man, as so many others in such positions, who ruled "by the book" and not by observation and intuition.

Having abandoned hope of preventing the statue of Claudius being erected, Decius watched Brendan closely.

The centurion could sense that nothing had changed and yet on the surface it seemed as though everything had changed. He was not greeted with warmth by those he knew to be dissidents – but he was greeted politely. It was as though the whole community had accepted the inevitable with a sigh of resignation. They did not like it – but they had stopped fighting it. The men he had drafted in to help keep the peace began to relax. They were invited into people's houses for meals and looked resentful when Decius warned them to be on their guard.

"I don't trust them," he said. "Most of these people have made a life's work of opposing us. How can they so suddenly change? Brendan himself has known no other life. His hatred of us is deeply rooted. As a child he was throwing stones at Roman soldiers. As a youth he watched his father and elder brother executed, his mother and sisters caught in the fire we set. Since he has been in Aquae Sulis he has done nothing but foment rebellion. That he smiles at us now is reason to double our vigilance, not to halve it."

The soldiers obeyed him because they had to – but it was hard being hostile and wary when everyone else seemed bent on friendliness and forgiveness.

Chapter 15

Not long after this the Governor's wife, the Lady Domitilla, came from Camulodunum to Aquae Sulis to consult the Oracle. She found an apparently peaceful, sleepy town nestling in a hollow between hills. As she stood on the smooth flagstones of the precinct before the Temple of Sulis Minerva, she could almost feel herself in Rome – the tall columns, the pediments, the steps – the feeling of order and control. In the open air there was a great altar, carved with Roman Gods at each corner. She sighed. It might look like Rome, but it was not Rome. She missed her Roman friends and family. She missed the sunshine and the cypress trees. She missed the hubbub of great events surrounding the Emperor. She found the indigenous people of Britain so difficult to get to know. They were either obsequious and trying to profit from their invaders, or resentful and sullen. She never quite trusted them. It was as though their civilized behaviour represented only a thin crust over a savage and untamed nature. The local women she had to invite to her dinner parties were provincial in the worst sense. They had nothing to talk about but their children and their clothes, and aped her in everything she wore. She had been brought up to read and debate, to question and think and explore. She had been happy to come to Britain when her husband was appointed Governor. A new country, a new culture interested her – but everywhere she found she was surrounded by pale and unsatisfactory imitations of Rome.

She had looked forward to this visit, having heard that the Oracle of Sulis was still of the old faith. Here would be a chance to contact something raw and uncorrupted by Roman influence. She had experienced a thrill of anticipation as her cavalcade had climbed the last hill before the town and she had looked down on the silver arc of the river, the honey coloured buildings clustered at its side, the thin wisps of smoke rising from the hearth fires. On the outskirts there were still wooden houses in the old style, many dilapidated and crumbling. But as she drew nearer to the centre she was reminded of Rome in its early days before the mighty

Temple of Jupiter and the great forums were built – before the triumphal arches and the hippodrome... before the Empire.

Her party was greeted by a handsome bronzed centurion.

"He could not have been in this climate long," she thought, and allowed herself to be helped from her carriage. She was stiff and tired, but had to endure the speeches of welcome from the various dignitaries of the town before she was allowed to bathe and rest.

Now she was on the threshold of an adventure. She had an appointment with the Oracle of Sulis. The curious crowds who had gathered to stare at the Governor's wife were being held back by the centurion and his soldiers, and a pale young woman in a long white robe, a handmaiden of the Oracle, was approaching her.

She was led down some steps and along a corridor lit by flares. She remembered her visit to the Pythoness of Delphi – the great cavern – the flickering shadows – the intoxicating smoke that almost choked her. She had been young and impressionable then and so terrified by the weird supernatural atmosphere of the place that she had fled before the Pythoness had appeared. She had always regretted that missed opportunity.

She was ushered into a small, dark chamber, her companion guiding her to a chair before she retreated, closing the door behind her. The place was suffocatingly hot and pitch dark once the door was closed. She felt her heart pounding. She heard the rushing of water beneath the floor. She waited, wondering if she should speak – almost wishing she had not come.

Whether her eyes were gradually adjusting to the dark or whether some faint light was present, she could not decide, but she began to see that columns of steam were rising from a hole in the floor before her and through it she thought she could see a dim shape. As she leaned forward in her chair to see more clearly it seemed she was surrounded by women – all of them immensely tall and thin – their forms as insubstantial as smoke – wavering, dissolving, reforming around her. She told herself that this must surely be an illusion caused by the steam and the positioning of the light source. She tried to keep her critical faculty, her civilized, rational mind in control. She cleared her throat and wiped the sweat from her eyes. She tried to grip the arms of her chair, but her hands were so wet they slid off.

"Who is there?" she demanded in a voice that she could scarcely recognize as her own.

She strained to hear an answer above the roar and rush of the water that rose from the depths of the earth, from the mysterious caverns of Sul, and poured along an underground channel beneath the chamber.

"Speak to me!" she repeated. "Speak!" She was almost in tears. If she wanted to leave she doubted she would have dared put a foot on the slippery floor to try to find the door. In fact, both door and walls seemed to have disappeared.

At last there was a voice – faint and whispering, as though it came from a long way away – or from her own mind.

"You have the power in your hands," were the words she thought she caught. "Use it well... Use it... Use it..."

She frowned. Her husband had power. Her father and uncle had power. What power had she?

The whisper seemed to echo all around her – the sibilance like the hiss of a snake.

"How must I use it? What must I do?" she cried. But the hiss had faded and there was now only the sound of the rushing water. The shadowy figures had gone. The darkness was returning.

"This is not enough!" she shouted, suddenly angry. "I have come all this way to be given a message – to know what I must do with my life. Tell me something more. What must I do with the power? What power? What power do I have?"

She heard a sound behind her; the priestess was there with the door open, her hand on her arm drawing her away.

"No," she said, "that is not enough. This is not what I came for."

But the young woman's grip was firm and strong and Domitilla was drawn out into the corridor, stumbling and protesting.

Why was it so difficult to get worthwhile advice? There was always plenty of advice from well-meaning friends and self-seeking fools, but never from someone who really knew what they were talking about.

Since her mother's death she had become painfully aware of her own mortality and the speed with which life was rushing towards death. There was so much she still wanted to do, but she knew she could not do it all. She must choose – and she must choose well. It was no longer enough for her to be her husband's shadow and carry out the duties that went with his position. Recently a restless longing to achieve something of her own troubled her.

She had hoped the Oracle would tell her what to do. But it had not.

"Use your power."

Indeed!

While Domitilla was in the West Country she stayed with friends of her husband in a villa to the north east of Aquae Sulis, at the foot of an ancient flat topped hill on which the remnants of the earliest town in the district had been built. It was now almost deserted, most of its inhabitants having moved to more comfortable quarters in the valley below. It had been used as a hill fort at a time when the various tribes were continually at war with one another. Under the Pax Romana there was not such a need to live behind fortified ditches and barricades, or to keep watch night and day.

Domitilla expressed a wish to visit the old town. Her hostess, Lavernia, tried to dissuade her, but she insisted that she would not be happy until she had climbed the green slopes and seen the view from the top.

"There are still some people living there," Lavernia said, pulling a face as though she had smelt a bad smell. "People you would rather not meet."

Domitilla laughed. "I have met all sorts of people in my life," she said. "I doubt whether there are any that would surprise me."

And so it was that an eager Domitilla and a reluctant Lavernia, accompanied by two burly slaves as protection, set off towards the summit of the old fortified hill on a day of bright, clear sunlight, not long after Domitilla's visit to the Oracle.

Domitilla longed to talk about the Oracle's enigmatic pronouncement, but she knew her host and hostess would not be sympathetic. They had been shocked that she wanted to consult one of the primitive pagan gods.

"It won't be long before that dreadful old woman is dead," Lavernia said. "Why don't you consult the proper Haruspex from Rome?"

"We can't get rid of her," Lavernia's husband added, "because the locals hold her in such superstitious awe. But no one of substance consults her these days."

They meant, of course, no one of the fashionable Roman set living in villas around the town, for there were still pilgrims coming from distant countries for no other reason than to visit her and throw their prayers and curses into her famous Sacred Spring.

Domitilla wished her hostess had not insisted on accompanying her. Ever since she had come to the valley she had been attracted to the hill. It was as though it was calling to her in some way. Lavernia, with her chatter, was a distraction and an annoyance. But one thing she did say proved to be of importance.

"They say the place is haunted by some ancient hero. Not that he managed to save them when we attacked," she sniffed.

"Was this where they made their last stand against us?"

"If you could call it a stand! There was no sign of discipline. Just a lot of screaming and animal noises and flailing about. We made short work of them."

Domitilla was silent. She had heard enough about the wild, barbaric charges of the Celts not to dismiss them so easily. Her husband was still haunted by nightmares, having faced, and lost to, just such a charge.

Half way up Lavernia was out of breath.

"Truly, Lavernia, I would be most happy to continue on my own," Domitilla said.

"Nonsense," the woman replied. "I would never forgive myself if something happened to you."

"I have protection." Domitilla looked quizzically at the two men waiting patiently, like wooden statues, a few paces from them.

Lavernia snorted. "They are muscular but slow witted. They need me to tell them what to do in a crisis."

Domitilla was embarrassed. The men could not have failed to hear what their mistress said. She suspected the expressions of blank docility they habitually wore in their mistress's presence were assumed, like masks, and only worn when it was to their advantage to do so.

She sighed. She longed to be alone. She was tired of wearing her own mask of grand lady, wife of the Governor. She would like to have kicked off her shoes and run to the top of the grassy hill barefoot as she would have done as a young girl.

They had reached the first of the steep man-made banks that protected the hilltop. Lavernia indicated that they should now walk along the contour for a while to reach a break in the fortifications. There they found the remnants of massive wooden gateposts. Someone had rigged up a makeshift gate to keep the cattle out that were grazing on the slopes. But it was clearly not the original gate which, to fit those posts, must have been huge and heavy and quite capable of keeping out raiding parties and slowing down armies.

One of the men lifted the rickety contraption off the latch and Domitilla passed through. There was another ridge, another gap with a gate, this time better made but still not from the time when the hilltop was in full use. Children ran out of the houses to follow them. Lavernia looked disgusted by their ragged appearance and tried to shoo them away. Domitilla smiled at them. The slaves raised their fists in mock menace and the children laughed and kept just out of range calling out in piping sing-song voices that the ladies were beautiful and kind and could surely spare something for them to eat. Occasionally parents looked out, some calling their offspring back angrily, some joining the considerable crowd that was now following the two women. Lavernia was red in the face and decidedly flustered by the attention they were getting, she never ceased to mutter that they should leave. Domitilla, who was used to crowds following her and her husband whenever they appeared, was determined not to leave before she had seen the whole place.

"People should not live like this," she said to Lavernia. "Look at that shack. Look at the rubbish in the streets!" They were picking their way in their dainty shoes though indescribable filth. "I must see that better houses are built," Domitilla thought. This was one way to use her "power". She could scarcely see the view she had come to see because of the buildings crowding around her, but she began to have a vision of how it could be, and how it probably once was.

Suddenly they came upon a relatively open space and the curious crowds following them, fell back, bunching up among the last of the houses. Up to now every construction had been of wood, which did not surprise her because she knew the Celtic tribes, at heart still nomads, never built in stone.

But here before her at the heart of the town was an open space with the ruins of stone buildings. She looked at Lavernia in surprise. It was clear her companion had not seen the significance of this. All she could see was that they were not being hustled by dirty people any more and there was somewhere to sit and recover her breath in the sunshine on the remnants of an old wall. She plumped down at once with a great sigh.

Further into the ruins Domitilla caught a fleeting glimpse of another figure. He looked as out of place as they did themselves.

"You rest here, my dear," she said to Lavernia. "I want to explore."

Lavernia started to protest, but her own weariness and distaste of the place made it easy for Domitilla to persuade her to accept. She ordered one slave to go with her guest and one to stay with her – but Domitilla refused his company.

"The people seem reluctant to come here," she said. "Keep both with you. If I am in trouble, I will call at once. I will not go far, but I want to be alone."

Lavernia shrugged her shoulders. She had tried to be friend to the Governor's wife, but could sense that the Governor's wife did not want to be a friend to her.

She had done everything to make her stay comfortable – but Domitilla seemed ungrateful and restless, always asking for things, like this expedition, that no one in their right mind would want to undertake. Lavernia had never been to this place before. From below, the hill was green and wooded, beautiful and peaceful looking. She had never wanted to climb to the top and certainly never would again. She was beginning to feel angry at Domitilla's stubbornness. One look at the gate had told them what kind of an unsavoury place it was! They should have turned back there and then.

Meanwhile Domitilla was marvelling at what she saw. The foundations were all that was left of the buildings, with an occasional tumbled block and broken column. Those who had built Aquae Sulis in the valley since the Romans came had probably quarried the rest for their own buildings.

She found the stranger she had glimpsed standing beside a broken column, his hand against the stone, his head bent as though in deep meditation. She thought instinctively "Greek" – though in dress he could just as well have been Roman, or Romanized Celt. He looked up as she approached.

They stared into each other's eyes for a long moment – neither in surprise – both feeling that they knew the other. Then the moment passed and they were two strangers not knowing what to say to each other.

The man was in fact Demosthenes, the Orphic priest Aulus had imported from Athens. The lady, he guessed, was the Governor's

112

wife come to Aquae Sulis to consult the Oracle. But what was she doing here? None of the upper classes ever came up here – although he was intending to bring Lucius.

Since his arrival in Aquae Sulis, scraps of memory or visions about the place in the distant past and in the distant future had haunted him.

Although he had never been told that he would find ancient stone buildings here, he had known they would be here. A persistent dream had shown him a town in its full glory on top of this hill, a town more like one in ancient Greece than one would ever expect to find in Britain.

It was true there was no silk-smooth marble polished to perfection, but local stone had been shaped and worked to a degree that would not have shamed a Roman builder, though perhaps it would not have won him the best contracts.

The local inhabitants of the town shunned this area, claiming that it was haunted, and in his exploration he found many signs around the edges that magical rituals had been performed to keep the ghosts penned up among the ruins.

He knew that only those who could not afford to live in the town in the valley remained up here on this windblown summit, suffering the hardships entailed by having to walk and climb long distances for water. The stone rain-water tanks provided by the mysterious ancient people who had built the stone buildings had long since been cracked and breached and no one had had the sense to repair them. Ghost fear again, he thought.

He longed to meet the ghosts of this place. He heard his home-land singing in the stone. Someone was here who had known his country and tried to recreate something of it here. There was an order in the buildings, in the streets, in everything about the place that was alien to the jumbled haphazard layout of the rest.

In his visions and his dreams he had seen one man who could have had the energy and the knowledge to build this town. A name had come to him repeatedly like a whisper blown in the wind – King Bladud. Aulus, Julia and Lucius had never heard the name, but Lucius had suggested he ask the Oracle.

"She is incredibly old and knows everything about this place before the Romans came," the young man said.

So, Demosthenes had asked the Oracle.

She knew the name. He could see that she did – though she took

113

a long time to admit it. Her gaze withdrew from him and he had to wait patiently while she followed a long and winding path into past memories.

He repeated the name.

Slowly, gradually, her attention came back to him.

"King Bladud," she whispered in a dry, cracked voice, but she spoke the name with reverence and awe, almost as though to pronounce it would be to invoke the man himself.

"Tell me about him," Demosthenes prompted.

"Some say he was a god – Apollo of the Sun himself! Others, that he was only a man."

Again there was silence.

"Whom do you say he was?" Demosthenes asked softly, hardly daring to breathe in case he missed a word spoken in her ashen voice.

"I saw him once in a vision," the Oracle whispered dreamily, as though speaking to herself, as though drawing the long buried memory out from under a stone. Her gaze was far away. Demosthenes had ceased to exist for her. She smiled softly and her ancient skeletal face, her pale skin, her rheumy eyes were suffused with light and for the moment she looked almost young and beautiful.

Demosthenes leaned forward, trying to catch the words, his heart crying out for her to speak, to explain, to inform. But the light faded from her face as suddenly as it had come and it was as though a door had been slammed in his face.

"You must go," she said harshly, and she clapped her hands for her attendant to show him out.

"But..." He started to speak, but was unceremoniously pulled back through the door.

Now, on this hilltop, among these mysterious ruins, he knew without a doubt that the man who had built this town was King Bladud. With his hand on the stone column he was just beginning to receive visions when a woman appeared and interrupted him, dragging him back as suddenly to the present as the Oracle's assistant had dragged him away from the Oracle.

But in the woman's eyes was recognition and for what seemed a timeless moment, they acknowledged each other. Then she spoke and the spell was broken.

"This is a fine day," Domitilla said.

"Indeed," he replied curtly.

"I had not expected to find stone buildings in such a place," she persisted gently. She could see that he was an educated man, a foreigner, and his close attention to the column before him suggested that he was as curious about the place as she was.

Demosthenes now saw a woman past her youth, but still youthful in spirit; eyes alert; her bearing elegant but not effete; strong, but quiet. Her black hair was drawn back from her face and pinned at the nape of her neck, her cloak light and loose. She was Roman, but not arrogant. She was authoritative, but not demanding. She did not, after all, disrupt the atmosphere of the place.

"Have you heard the name 'King Bladud', my lady?" he asked suddenly, looking into her eyes intently. He could have sworn he saw a flicker of recognition there as he said the name, but as suddenly as it was there, it was gone. She shook her head.

"I thought I knew the names of all the Celtic Kings we encountered when we came," she said. "But this I have not heard."

"I believe he built this city."

For a long while they were both silent, gazing around themselves, taking in every detail – the flowers growing out of the old walls, the lichen staining the stone yellow, the wagtail now sitting on the top of the column beside them watching them with one bright and shining eye. The silence became palpable. They were cocooned in it, protected from the outside world, from every distraction, from every other sight and sound and memory. It began to seem to them that they could see the place when it was alive and thriving. The column before them became one of a group gracing a temple to Apollo. Clouds must have gathered though they did not register them – for a single shaft of sunlight beamed down on the ancient city, while all the rest – the hills, the river, the distant landscape – retreated into shadow.

Instinctively the Roman and the Greek reached out for each other, holding hands, like children, in wonder and uncertainty.

They felt the presence of the ancient King. Both turned simultaneously, expecting to see him just behind them. But there was no one there. Both felt their hearts full of admiration for the man – his strength of vision, his courage, his wisdom.

The clouds closed over and the beam of light was snuffed out.

Shocked to find herself holding hands with a strange man, Domitilla pulled away from him, flushed and a little dazed as though waking from a deep sleep. Demosthenes too turned away quickly, clearing his throat.

When they looked back at each other they were no longer strangers, yet no longer children, either.

"You felt his presence?" he asked quickly.

"Yes," she replied.

Question and answer were irrelevant. They both knew what they had shared.

Lavernia's voice calling shattered the moment. She sounded impatient, angry.

Domitilla turned to go, and then, before she hurried away, she looked back. The Greek had not moved.

"I would like to know more about this King Bladud," she said. "I will be in Aquae Sulis a day or two longer. Shall we meet again?"

"Yes," he replied.

"But not in this place," she thought, "not here. It is too strange, too powerful."

Demosthenes might be used to strange visionary experiences – but Domitilla was not.

Domitilla and Demosthenes met again because the Greek encouraged Julia to invite the Governor's wife to dinner, claiming a small acquaintance with her. Since the woman had come to town Julia had been fretting how she could meet her – but Lavernia kept her prize close and fended off any invitations from locals of whom she did not approve. Aulus and Julia, though well-to-do, were not sufficiently wealthy and important to be acknowledged socially. When Domitilla heard that the family who had invited them had a shrine to Orpheus on their property and a Greek priest to officiate, she over-rode Lavernia's protective concern and insisted on accepting the invitation. She tried to persuade the woman to allow her to go by herself, but Lavernia would not hear of it. Her husband was not feeling well so was left behind while Lavernia, protesting every moment that Julia was impossibly vulgar and that the food would be tasteless, accompanied her.

Julia, knowing that Domitilla was related to the Emperor, was beside herself with excitement and anxiety that the evening should go well. The household would not have been more disturbed if a hurricane had hit it. Demosthenes who had sowed the seed, retreated, and it was the rest who bore the brunt of her conflicting orders, her frantic efforts to have everything cleaned and cleaned again; furniture moved and moved again; menu changed and changed again. Aulus, on Julia's instructions, invited Decius Brutus, and was then berated for it.

The greatly anticipated moment came at last. The boatman deposited the two ladies and their attendants at the small landing stage. They were greeted politely by Lucius and shown to the house. Lavernia, who had not known about the new villa Aulus had recently built was somewhat mollified to see that it was more than halfway decent, and a tolerable imitation of a small, but elegant, Roman mansion.

The eyes of the Greek priest standing quietly behind the host met those of Domitilla briefly in recognition of their shared experience in the hill top town, but nothing was said.

Lavernia had met Decius Brutus on several occasions and chose to pay more attention to the handsome centurion than to her host and hostess. Julia had eyes for no one but the Governor's wife and shadowed her every move until the woman felt like screaming. Domitilla had accepted the invitation for one reason only and that was to talk to the Greek priest again – but they had no chance for private conversation because even when Domitilla addressed Demosthenes directly, Julia answered for him. All the information about where he had come from and how long he had been in the area came from her, while he, interrupted time and again as he was about to speak, contented himself with the hint of a smile and an occasional amused glance at the Roman guest.

The food was good enough to satisfy even Lavernia. The oysters, in a sauce of cumin and cinnamon, were as delicious as any she had tasted in Rome, and, cooked nearer to where they had been gathered, were fresher. Domitilla's pearls were commented on during this course but she claimed they had come from the far east rather than from the British channel. The roast duck cooked in a sauce of pepper, lovage, oregano, oil and honey, was delicious, served with fresh green beans grown on the farm and wine from Southern Gaul. The venison was served with a rich nut sauce; the lamb with mint, coriander, fennel, celery seed and pepper, was basted in honey and vinegar.

When the guests were satiated, the attendants withdrew, leaving bowls of fruit and amphorae of wine behind. Aulus and Decius, the two old friends, began to reminisce. Lucius, who, being vegetarian,

117

had only eaten selectively, fetched his lyre and began to pluck its strings – but with nothing like the inspiration of the other night. Lavernia, softer under the influence of the dinner, engaged Julia in conversation about the latest banqueting etiquette in Rome. At last the opportunity arose for Demosthenes and Domitilla to draw together.

"I leave for home tomorrow," she said quietly, "and I had hoped we would talk more about..."

He understood at once.

"I would not have chosen to speak of these matters here," he said in a low voice, "but I cannot let you leave without saying at least something of what is on my mind." He paused.

"Speak," she said softly.

"You will think me presumptuous..."

"Do not waste time..." she breathed.

"It is in the power of your husband to prevent an incident that will surely lead to bloodshed in this town." He paused again, watching her expression closely.

She frowned. This was not what she had wanted to speak about.

"I know. I know," he almost whispered. "It is of King Bladud you wish to speak."

She nodded.

"It is of him I also wish to speak. Would it not be more appropriate for this town to have a representation of him in their most sacred place – than the Emperor Claudius?"

Her face lightened. She understood.

"I do not think my husband has heard of him," she said. "I myself know very little."

Lavernia and Julia had stopped speaking, and Decius and Aulus, laughing heartily over something Decius had said, looked as though they too were about to return to general conversation. The two conspirators, for that is what they both felt they now were, knew that their time of intimate communication was over.

"Write to my husband," Domitilla said hastily. "Tell him about this ancient king and why you think he should be honoured here. But..." She looked at Lavernia already turning towards her, "say nothing against the statue already planned."

"Don't say you two are talking about the statue of Claudius," Lavernia said loudly. "I'm sick of hearing about it! Such a fuss about nothing!"

118

"I look forward to it," Julia said cheerfully, "though I think it would be nicer to have a statue of the Emperor Vespasian instead."

"Why not both!" laughed Lavernia.

The face of Decius had darkened at the mention of the statue. He had temporarily forgotten his worries about the matter.

"Can you not use your influence, my lady," he addressed the Governor's wife directly, "to avert the catastrophe."

"Catastrophe? Rubbish!" snorted Lavernia. "As soon as it is up the locals will accept it. They like having something to protest about. It gives them something to do with their boring little lives."

Domitilla flushed with annoyance and bit her lip. Lucius stopped playing and looked as though he was about to say something, and then stopped himself.

Demosthenes stood up.

"It is time for me to go, Lady Julia," he said. "I thank you for a most delicious meal, and..." he looked pointedly at Domitilla, "pleasant company."

"Oh don't go!" Julia cried. "The evening is not over."

Demosthenes looked at Lavernia, and his expression was cold.

"I think it is – for me at least."

Lucius put his lyre down. "I will come with you Demosthenes," he said. Demosthenes smiled at him – and then sighed. The boy had so many questions!

"Come then," he said and held out his hand.

"May I not see the Orphic mosaic you have?" Domitilla suddenly asked Aulus. "I hear it is most handsome."

"Of course. Of course." Aulus bustled at once to the doorway.

"Demosthenes – what could we have been thinking of not to show the ladies our greatest treasure?"

Julia pursed her lips. She had not broached the subject she most wanted to discuss with Domitilla – the reason for the entire effort of the evening – and she knew it was unlikely she would be able to now that the party's attention was turning towards her father and brother's obsession with Orpheus. Would she be able to get them back to the room to discuss anything sensible at all? Once one guest started showing signs of restlessness the tight and intimate atmosphere of a party could never be the same again. She had never liked Demosthenes and her dislike at this moment was stronger than ever. Everyone was moving towards the door, Lucius and Demosthenes already through it.

"Lady Lavernia," she said desperately. "I'm sure you have seen more mosaics than you can count. Don't go. Stay with me and we'll have some Tuscan wine until the others return. My lady," she called after the Governor's wife. "You will be disappointed. Ours is nothing compared to the others you must have seen in Rome."

But Domitilla had already left.

Lavernia stayed behind – bored at the prospect of looking at yet another provincial mosaic.

"They do these things so much better in Rome," she said. "But Domitilla seems determined to support local efforts." The sneer in the word "local" could not be missed.

Julia was torn between irritation at the implied insult, and delight that the lady stayed behind, thus increasing the possibility of Domitilla's return.

"I am planning to visit Rome," she said, pouring the wine into fine glass goblets and hoping that Lavernia would note their expensive imported quality and honour her for it. "Indeed I am planning to miss the British winter this year."

Lavernia raised an eyebrow.

"Indeed!" she said. "I envy you."

"In fact, I intend calling on the Emperor," Julia continued, watching to see if this would impress her visitor. But Lavernia guarded her expression. She had heard of the woman's absurd claim to be related to Vespasian.

At this moment Decius returned.

"It's getting too intense for me in there," he said laughing. "I think I'll join you ladies in the Tuscan wine."

He glanced shrewdly at their faces and knew that he had entered just in time. With easy familiarity he filled his own goblet and raised it with a quizzical look to Julia.

"A most delicious feast, Lady Julia. You would not be out of place as a hostess in Rome."

Julia raised her glass to his gratefully and then looked triumphantly at Lavernia.

But Lavernia did not meet her eyes.

Extract from a letter to Petilius Cerealis, Governor of the Province of Britain, from Demosthenes the Greek, Priest of Orpheus at Aquae Sulis on the tenth day of the month of June in the third year of the reign of the Emperor Vespasian:

"I would like to draw it to your attention that a great and mighty British King, Bladud, son of Hudibras, worthy of deification and already so deified in the minds of the population, has been for many centuries associated with the town of Aquae Sulis, yet there is no representation of him in this place.

"Recently I had the honour of meeting your wife, the Lady Domitilla, in the town, and she suggested that I write to you with the request that a statue of King Bladud as god should be raised at Aquae Sulis.

"This king was directly descended from the Trojan prince Aeneas, the founder of Rome, through his grandson Brutus who came to this island with his Greek wife many centuries ago. Indeed the name of Britain itself is based on the name of Brutus. Brutus founded a dynasty that ruled this country for many generations – the blood of the great Trojan, Greek and Roman heroes flowing through their veins. The dynasty descended from Aeneas civilized this country and brought many advantages to the savage people. Julius Caesar himself, who first invaded Britain, was related to the dynasty by his descent from Aeneas.

"King Bladud founded the first town at Aquae Sulis, building in stone where before the locals had used only timber and reeds. He was the first to harness the hot waters that flow so forcefully from the earth in the area. He built a healing sanctuary and a temple to the Goddess Sul – now so admirably associated with Minerva. He was a man of wisdom, vision and learning, founding academies for study, honouring both the ancient Druidic tradition and the Greek, and rediscovering the art of flight forgotten since the time of Daedalus.

"I would humbly suggest sir, that this king, descended as he is from Aeneas, and thus closely associated with the might of Rome, would be an appropriate figure to adorn the great temple at Aquae Sulis."

Chapter 16

One night Martha dreamed she found the Sacred Chalice on the summit of the Tor. When the dream recurred on several consecutive nights she felt compelled to face her fears and climb the Tor.

She set off early one morning on a clear, beautiful summer's day when the others were at prayer. At first she could hear their voices chanting the words their Lord had taught his followers, and, as she walked, she whispered the words herself: "Lord forgive us as we forgive others." Her thoughts drifted from the words of the prayer to the cruelties she had witnessed in Rome. Martha shivered. If she did not forgive, would she ever be forgiven?

By the time she had reached the base of the Tor the sky was ribboned with birds winging their way to the distant grain fields. As she rose higher on the slopes, she saw vistas of the water that lay around the island; waterfowl busy among the reeds, the first boats of the fishermen gliding silently out from the shore. She tried to concentrate on the natural beauties around her – the sunlight through the leaves, the rocks covered with moss and lichen, the flowers, pink and white that brushed against her legs – but she found it difficult. The Tor had an atmosphere... She could not have described it, but it was no ordinary hill. She decided more than once to turn back – and indeed twice literally turned around and started to retrace her steps – but after walking for some time found that, strangely, she was further up the hill than she thought she had been before.

She prayed to the angels to help her. The Christ himself, mysteriously manifesting the Mighty Creator and the "Holy Spirit" which, to Martha, was beyond all understanding, was too august a figure, too magnificent for her homely aspirations. Her grandfather described him as a man he had met – one who would listen to his troubles and help – but the practices of the community growing up in his memory seemed to be lifting him out of the sphere of ordinary life into some bewildering metaphysical region beyond her reach. The angels she saw as messengers or intermediaries between the Most High and the world. She had often felt their presence and, though she was somewhat in awe of them, she felt they would surely have more time to deal with her problems than the Christ who had the whole world to care for.

Her steps became more resolute and she no longer felt the urge to return to the village. The dreams she had been having about the Chalice on the Tor had been so vivid she had convinced herself that somehow she would find it there and return in triumph, bearing the Holy Cup. She smiled to think of the excitement she would cause, and the praise she would receive. From being a shy, silent and shadowy figure in the community, known only as the grand-daughter of the man who had met Jesus, she would become an honoured person in her own right, the one who had found the Chalice when all others failed to do so.

These thoughts and images carried her to the top of the Tor. Suddenly the wooded slopes gave way to rock and grass, and a lively breeze tugged strands of her dark hair from the clasp that had held them hitherto so tightly in place.

She took a deep breath and looked around. The landscape of marshland and distant fields and hills was spread out below her to every horizon like an intricate mosaic. As she stared at it, it seemed to revolve slowly as though it were a giant wheel...

The world was turning below as the universe turned above.

She shut her eyes, feeling so dizzy that she nearly fell down. When she opened them again the landscape below was still.

She looked up at the sky and was startled to see that the sun was low to the west. She had reached the summit in the morning. It seemed she had shut her eyes for no more than a moment, and the sun was already near to setting. Hours must have passed.

At first she thought she must have slept – though none of the sensations of awakening were present. And then the conviction began to grow that somehow she had gone somewhere in that time – without her body.

The fear that had accompanied her at the beginning of her ascent returned. Shivering, she looked around her. The summit was bare. There was no sign of the Chalice, or any other feature, natural or contrived, that could house it. What made her think that dreams were anything but dreams! And what had happened to her during those missing hours? Terrified, she turned and ran back down the hill, tearing her clothes and her legs on the brambles, twisting her ankle on the stones. Where were the angels? Why had they not looked after her? Tears streamed down her face, blinding her. The forest grew darker and darker. She lost the path and blundered frantically among the rocks and bushes. At last, exhausted, she sat down on a rock and sobbed outright.

A sound made her look up. In front of her stood a young man with a gentle face.

"Can I help?" he asked.

Could he be an angel, she thought, shocked and awed.

"Are you lost?" he asked quietly when she did not reply.

She nodded, staring at him dumbly.

"It is getting dark. Why did you leave the path?"

"Who... who are you?" she breathed.

"My name is Lucius," he said. "I come from Aquae Sulis."

"Why are you here?" She still could not believe that he had not been miraculously manifested in answer to her prayer.

He smiled. "I don't really know. I heard such strange things about this place. I wanted to see it for myself. But it has taken me longer than I thought to get here. It is too late now to climb the Tor. I don't know why I even thought to try. I'm hoping to stay in the village overnight."

He contemplated her for a while in silence. Her simple clothes were soiled and torn, her face streaked with tears and dust. Her expression was fearful.

"Come" he said, reaching out his hand. "I won't harm you. The path is near here and we are not far from the village."

She hesitated. He looked ordinary enough. He was certainly flesh and blood.

She rose slowly, but did not take his hand. He dropped his own and stood aside for her to move towards the opening in the bushes through which he had come. She passed him and they silently walked down the sloping path to the foot of the Tor, he a step or two behind her.

Soon they could see the hearth fires and lamps of the little community flickering through the leaves. She began to run.

Lucius spent the night in the village, Martha's grandfather taking the youth in at once when he heard how he had found and rescued his granddaughter.

Martha busied herself preparing a meal as soon as she reached home and refused to talk about her experience on the Tor.

124

Lucius had come to Glastonia because he had heard that it was believed to be an entrance to the Otherworld, but he soon found his questions about the ancient traditions of the Tor were unwelcome in the household of Paulus. The old man tried at once to convert him to the new religion away from the old gods, who, he said, were agents of the Dark Forces.

Lucius listened patiently, but none of the old man's words stirred the deep pool of his own convictions. He barely heard what was said for he was watching Martha and the play of emotions on her face as her grandfather spoke. The girl had obviously experienced something dramatic on the Tor and he was very anxious to hear what it was. But even if her grandfather had not so dominated the conversation, he doubted she would have spoken about it. It was as though she clutched the experience to herself with tight fists and would not let anyone else get a glimpse of it. Her eyes never met his. Her lips were closed. Her face was pale and drawn.

"Perhaps in the morning – after sleep," Lucius thought. He was exhausted after his long journey from Aquae Sulis, and he could see that Martha was tired too. But Paulus seemed unwilling to go to bed before he was sure he had driven his point home.

At last, however, the old man gave in, and they retired for the night.

Lucius lay on the old man's cloak and some folded rags on the floor, Martha on the upper bunk of a rickety wooden construction above her grandfather. The wood crackled a while on the fire, but soon grew silent, the red and flickering light of the last meagre flames turning to ash.

Both Lucius and Martha lay awake for a long time staring into the dark. The old man slept instantly, breathing heavily and evenly.

It seemed to Lucius he was awake all night but when first light crept greyly under the ill-fitting door it took him by surprise and he realized he had slept after all. He decided to creep out while the old man was asleep. As he let more light into the single chamber of the house by pushing open the door he looked back at Martha. He would dearly love to talk to her away from her grandfather, but he could not see how it could be arranged. She was lying as still as stone on her back and he could not see if her eyes were open or not. A pity – but he would have to go without hearing her story. Besides, he and she held very different beliefs, and so, whatever events occurred, they would each experience and interpret them in very different ways.

Martha had climbed in fear. He climbed the Tor in eager expectation. It was true there was an element of caution and extra alertness about his every step, for what he hoped would happen to him was extraordinary and dangerous. He had thought long and hard about the matter before setting off, but it seemed to him that he could not bear to live any longer in ignorance of the Otherworld. He could have no joy in this world if it was walled in by mysteries and unanswerable questions. He wanted to *know*. He wanted to see over the wall to the landscape beyond.

As he neared the top of the Tor, he repeated the prayers to Orpheus he had prepared in the safety of his little shrine at home, and spoke them passionately from the heart. In spite of his determination not to be afraid and his conviction that Orpheus would protect him, his heart began to beat fast and the palms of his hands began to sweat. What if he did not return? What if he returned tens of years later as an old, old man to find his family long dead and everything changed? He had heard of this happening to travellers who had entered the magical mounds of the ancient people.

He paused near the top and found he was trembling. Did he really want to go through with it?

He straightened his shoulders and stepped forward.

He stood on top of the Tor and shut his eyes. Every fibre of his being was prepared to surrender itself to whatever miracle or magic was needed to take him from one reality to another.

He did not care if the forces on the Tor were as dark as Paulus said, or as light as he believed them to be. Whatever was there, he wanted to experience it.

He waited.

Nothing happened.

He waited for a long time and then cautiously opened his eyes a crack. A breeze bent the grasses and the stems of flowers. A bird flew overhead emitting a raucous squawk as though mocking him.

Lucius stayed on the Tor during that whole day and the night that followed it. Nothing unusual happened to him. A million, million stars watched him watching them.

At dawn the sky had clouded over and there was no blaze of light – only a grey mist that went well with his sense of disappointment and anti-climax. Demosthenes had warned him that nothing happens unless one is ready for it, "and the readiness I speak of," he had said, "is not under our control."

Stiff and tired, Lucius walked down the path and, without contacting Paulus and Martha again, he set off back over the marshes and hills to Aquae Sulis.

When Lucius arrived home after several days away, he was morose and irritable. He avoided his family and Demosthenes and busied himself about the farm. It was not until he returned to the house for the evening meal that he heard the news that his sister was leaving for Rome almost immediately. He was startled enough by the news to be forced to relinquish his own worries.

"Are you going with her?" he demanded, looking at his father. He knew it had always been Aulus' intention to accompany her – but Julia had announced that "she" was going to Rome. Aulus nodded.

"Of course," he said. "I couldn't let her go alone."

"I could go with her," Lucius said quickly.

"I wouldn't feel safe with you," Julia replied sharply. Aulus had indeed suggested Lucius, but Julia had been vociferous in her rejection of the idea.

"You'll be away for harvest, father – how can I be expected to cope alone?"

Lucius was not surprised his stepsister did not want him with her in Rome, given his attitude to her claim on Vespasian.

"You'll manage," Aulus said unsympathetically.

"Why such a sudden decision? Why now?" the youth demanded resentfully.

He felt himself to be on the threshold of important inner discoveries. The silence on the Tor had taught him one thing – he was not as ready as he had thought to take the big leap. All day, as his body was fully occupied in heavy manual tasks about the farm, his mind had been teasing the problem of why he had not achieved what he had wanted to achieve on the Tor. He needed time to work on his inner journey. The complex responsibilities he would have to face if his father left the farm in his care would make this impossible.

"If we don't go now we will never go," said Julia impatiently. "There is a party of travellers leaving soon for Rome and we will be safer going with them."

"Julia feels she can claim friendship with Domitilla and thus gain access to the presence of the Emperor..."

"Should she not make sure the lady also claims friendship with *her* before she uses her name in Rome?"

Julia flushed angrily.

"Why are you always so spiteful? The Lady Domitilla has visited me in my home and dined with me. We are good friends."

Lucius looked sceptical, but said nothing.

"I know we have things to work out," Aulus said. "I won't leave you without help." He was more excited than he expected about the prospect of the Roman adventure. It is true he had never thought it would happen and, indeed, often dreaded that it would. But with Domitilla's help the whole thing seemed feasible. Whether the Emperor accepted Julia or rejected her the matter would be settled, and Julia would be freed from the obsession that had dominated their lives for so long.

Demosthenes had noticed that Lucius was avoiding him since his return from Glastonia Island, and understood at once that the experience had been disappointing. He said nothing – though he had advised Lucius most earnestly not to go.

It was not until another night had passed that Lucius sought the priest out. He was walking by the river to the west of the homestead, contemplating with pleasure the broad curve of silver water reflecting the wooded slopes of the hill on the far side, when Lucius called his name.

A heron, startled, rose from almost under his feet and flew away low over the fields behind them.

Demosthenes turned to greet Lucius, looking at the young man with sympathy. He knew what it was to be young and impatient.

Lucius stood beside him for some time without speaking. Ducks foraged quietly among the river reeds.

Demosthenes waited.

At last Lucius spoke.

"Nothing happened!" he said bitterly.

The Greek smiled.

"Something always happens," he said quietly.

Lucius looked annoyed. Not even Demosthenes was prepared to understand the depth of his disappointment.

"I am sure you will find that a myriad things were happening to you during the time you shut your mind and decided that "nothing" was happening."

"Nothing *did* happen. I stood there for ages. I even spent the night!"

"What did you see?"

"Nothing."

"Were there no rocks slowly weathering? No grasses growing? No flowers opening... living and dying? Bees working? Butterflies fluttering?"

"Of course!"

"And below the Tor – boatmen and waterfowl? Men chopping wood in the forest? Distant fields with crops growing and ripening – some past their prime while others were sending up new shoots?"

"Yes. Yes – all that! But that was not what I was looking for."

"You were looking for an entry into the Otherworld?"

"You know I was!" Lucius snapped impatiently. He glared at him in frustration. Why was his mentor, of all people, refusing to understand? "It's well known that the souls of the Dead are ferried across those marshes and disappear into the Otherworld through the Tor. It is a threshold between the worlds. Everyone knows it!"

"There are many thresholds. At every moment in our lives we face one – but whether we may pass through is decided in the Otherworld – not in this."

"But Orpheus went to seek Eurydice, and Aeneas went to speak with his father... *They* made the decision. *They* went. *They* came back!"

"We don't know that. What appears to us as our decision, is often not."

Both were silent for a time, Demosthenes calmly staring into the water, Lucius frowning, thinking this through. He did not like it.

Then Demosthenes stooped and picked up a flat pebble.

"Skim it," he said, holding it out to Lucius.

Lucius looked at him, puzzled.

"Skim it across the water," the Greek repeated. Lucius took the stone reluctantly, and turned it over and over in his hand for a moment or two, staring at it. Then he lifted it to the throwing position. What was the point Demosthenes was trying to make?

It did not skim, but sank to the bottom of the river.

The priest already had another stone in his hand – and another. After several unsuccessful attempts, Lucius was determined to have success with the next. It touched the surface of the water lightly and a spark of light flashed up that almost blinded Lucius. In that split second he seemed to experience a clear and precise vision of all the stars he had watched during that long night on the Tor. Invisible but powerful lines were passing between them at unimaginable speed, forming a brilliant net of inter-dependence, of which the world, his world, was part. In that split second he saw all this as though outside himself and then, without realising he had changed focus, within. Was the universe with all its complex magnificence within him, or was he within the universe? It was impossible to tell.

The stone lifted from the water and touched down a few feet further on.

The vision no longer existed. He was standing, shaken, beside the Orphic priest on a mild summer's day, the circle of his attention limited now by the range of his physical senses.

Chapter 17

At about this time, the Egyptian had another visit from Megan. Her nightly dreams of the ways he met his death had become so horrific and so persistent that she began to believe that there was no escape from them but by admitting what she had done and asking for his help in combating the spell. Though her attraction to Brendan and her loyalty to his and her grandfather's cause had not lessened, and she would have killed anyone who opposed her in battle, the ways of torture and death she devised in her nightmares were shameful and degrading to her. She saw herself and her fellow conspirators as "defenders of freedom", performing courageous deeds for the good of their fellow men, not as monsters outdoing the Romans in callous cruelty.

She hesitated to tell these things to her usual confidant and comforter, Ethne, partly because she was too ashamed to admit such images and thoughts had come to her mind, and partly because Ethne seemed more than preoccupied with problems of her own. But one day she did approach Ethne and asked her whether it was possible for "thought forms" from others to enter one's mind unbidden, there strengthen and pass on, without at any stage being expressed openly in words.

"Yes," Ethne had said without hesitation. And then, seeing her sister's alarm, added: "But not if you destroy them when they enter your own mind."

"How can you do that?" Megan asked at once.

Ethne was in a hurry, late for an appointment. "It's not easy to explain Megan," she said. "We'll talk about it another time."

"No. Now!" Megan had almost shouted, seizing her sister's arm and driving her fingers into the flesh until it hurt. Ethne looked astonished.

"I really don't have the time now – it is a big subject. We will talk about it later. It is a matter of transformation. You cannot *kill* a thought, and the more you try to suppress it the stronger it becomes. You have to transform it."

"How? How!"

"There are several ways."

"Give me one."

"You must allow the image that is troubling you to remain in your mind for a while. You must confront it – not avoid it. Say you love someone too much..."

"Or hate someone too much!"

"Or hate someone too much," Ethne agreed. "See them clearly with everything about them that you love, or hate. The image will of necessity be an incomplete one – because you are only seeing what you love – or hate – at first. Fill in the picture. See things you don't love in the one and don't hate in the other. Dangerous, destructive images are usually distorted because they are incomplete, what is known is exaggerated according to one's feelings, and what is unknown is ignored because one doesn't wish to see it. That is why people can kill their 'enemies'. They don't know who they really are."

"But what if it is not just a matter of love and hate? What if you are tormented by an image of terrible cruelty?"

"Transform it. Do not give it strength as it presents itself."

"How?" Megan said desperately.

Ethne looked deep into her eyes. Whether she saw there what was tormenting her twin, Megan could not tell – but her expression became grave and, after a long pause, she said quietly: "See the tormentor and the tormented as I have suggested. Fill out both images. Allow the tormentor to feel pity; the tormented to forgive. Don't cut off the thought-image while the tormenting is still going on – for then it will leave you as it is and may enter another mind in a mood ready to receive it. Keep 'seeing' it until it has changed: until the tormentor has ceased to torment and feels shame and regret. 'See' the tormentor giving the victim water, tending his wounds, asking his forgiveness. 'See' the victim healed and whole again and the two understanding why they have been caught in this situation. Then if the thought-image leaves the mind it will be positive and good, and not dangerous and destructive."

"But what if...?"

But Ethne had to go, and Megan did not have time to ask her what if the Morrigan was powerfully at work in her imagination and controlled her mind so completely that she was incapable of transforming the image.

She began to believe that the only route open to her was to fight magic with magic.

The reputation of the Egyptian as a magician was well known. She knew it was strange that she should go to him of all people for a solution to her problem, but she could see no other way out. At least she would be "confronting" the image as Ethne suggested, and not avoiding it.

As she approached his workyard, the sound of hammering on stone nearly made her change her mind. By daylight the terrors of the night seemed almost ridiculous, while her passionate hatred of the Romans did not.

There was no sign of the statue. The sound of stonemasons at work came from within the largest shed. The Egyptian himself was standing beside a man sharpening tools at the grindstone, and looked up at Megan's approach.

He watched her intently as she drew nearer, noting the drawn lines on her young face, the dark rings under her eyes. She tightened her lips and tried to walk as though she was at ease, though since her eyes had met his, ease was not possible.

"What am I doing here?" she asked herself and tried to turn to leave – but it was as though she had entered an invisible groove and was sliding inexorably towards him.

"Ah, Megan," he said, with satisfaction, as though he had been expecting her. Had he been a conscious partner in those terrifying dreams? Did he know why she had come? And then a thought struck her. Had he in fact fed them to her? She remembered Ethne had been quite certain thoughts could enter one person's mind from another. Was it more logical to believe that he was tampering with her consciousness than that an ancient Celtic goddess of battles should be feeding her images unworthy of the basest of warriors.

She was very pale as she stood before him. At first she could not bring herself to speak. On the way to the workyard she had prepared speech after speech, all in essence the same, some more convincing than others, but in every one she put herself in the wrong and asked for his help, in some cases, quite humbly.

He watched her, his dark eyes taking in every changing expression on her face, however fleeting. He seemed perfectly calm and in control, but if she had been observant she would have noticed that his fingers were gripping the small chisel in his hand until the knuckles showed white.

At last, after clearing her throat several times, she found her voice.

"I have come..." she said, and fell silent again.

He raised one dark eyebrow, but said nothing – watching – waiting...

"Do you know why I have come?"

"There are several reasons," he said, his voice controlled, expressionless. "Most of which you are not aware."

"There is only one reason!" she said hotly.

"And what do you believe that reason to be?"

She was now angry and confused.

"I believe you are influencing my dreams," she said bitterly.

He laughed, suddenly, mirthlessly.

"And why would I be doing that?"

"I don't know," she said, "but I've come to warn you..."

His eyes did not flicker away from her face.

"Warn me?" he said, icily amused.

She bit her lip. It was all going wrong. She was angry enough at that moment to have done any kind of harm to him, but she knew, held in his steady, mocking gaze, that she was powerless. What was worse – she was horrified to realize that she was finding his lean, sunburnt look attractive and that there was something in his expression that had not been there before.

"He is manipulating me!" she told herself desperately. "The sooner I get away from here the better." She hated that she was not in control of herself. She hated that she was beginning to doubt that she knew herself.

She turned her back on him and walked away. She was aware of his eyes following her, but she managed not to turn around. When she reached the shelter of the woods, she ran.

As soon as Megan returned to the town, she sought out Brendan. He rented a room in the house of a lamp-maker, but was not to be found there at that time.

"He's probably at the baths," the lamp-maker's wife suggested. Megan was not so sure. He regarded the baths as a decadent Roman institution, designed to keep the locals so entertained and comfortable that they would not notice they were a conquered people. But he often frequented the forecourt because it was a good place to meet people, all the main temples and the entrance to the baths facing on to it.

She found him chatting to a burly, red bearded man at one of the street stalls. He greeted her cheerfully at once, introducing her to his companion who, he said, had come a long way specifically to help them. She nodded politely but impatiently to the man, distracted and nervous, longing to speak to Brendan alone, and for once, not about the rebellion.

But Brendan was not interested in speaking to her, and turned away almost immediately to greet someone else.

Decius, with his daughter Ethne, walked along the leafy bank of the river on the way to the villa of his friend Aulus. He had given up trying to win the confidence and love of his other daughter, but Ethne was willing to forget the past and eager to experience the novelty of a father-daughter relationship.

At first, they had talked about general matters, but this conversation, satisfactory to neither of them, soon petered out and they walked side by side in silence. The path, still muddy from a recent heavy rain, sometimes forced them to walk single file. The river itself was flowing stronger than usual and occasionally logs floated by. Although the sun was shining now, leaves dripped on them from above and if an arm brushed against a branch or a bush a shower of diamond drops was sent arching into the air. The earth smelled fresh and vibrant. They could almost hear the plant life stretching and growing. Decius, remembering the deserts in which he had spent much of his life wondered why he had ever left this beautiful place. If he believed in gods he would have thanked them for giving him a second chance to enjoy what he had abandoned.

"Father," Ethne said suddenly, coming level with him and slipping her hand under his arm.

He looked down at her thoughtfully. She was hauntingly like, and yet not like, her mother.

"Father," she repeated, "would it not be wise to abandon the statue of the Emperor Claudius? It is clear that there will be trouble."

"You too, my Ethne? I thought you were not interested in matters of this world."

"The worlds are dependent on each other, father. What happens here has an effect there, and what happens there has an effect here."

"What effect will putting up a statue to an Emperor in this world have on the next?" he asked, smiling indulgently, as though humouring a child.

She withdrew her hand and walked silently for a while.

"Each person in this town will have a reaction to the statue, and each reaction will affect that person's journey into eternity."

"Whew!" he laughed. "That is a heavy responsibility for me to carry."

She looked sideways up at him.

"It is not just a matter of the blood that will be shed... though that is bad enough..."

"But surely each person's eternal journey is his or her own responsibility?" he said more seriously. "If they choose to react in a certain way to something, that is *their* responsibility – not the responsibility of the thing itself."

"I cannot argue with that, but I would wish..."

"I would wish too, my daughter," he said almost sadly. "But I am a soldier and soldiers have to obey orders."

"No wonder soldiers can rape and kill without conscience if they take no responsibility for their actions!"

He looked at her in surprise. He had not expected such sarcasm from Ethne, "the quiet one".

"Sometimes it is necessary to give up one's personal wishes for the good of the whole," he said, "though it is not easy to judge what *is* for the good of the whole in a world subject to such constant change. But," he added, "I agree, it can never be right to give up responsibility for one's actions."

Ethne sighed. She was thinking about her own situation. She was expected to give up her own chance of happiness for "the good of the whole".

Suddenly a voice hailed them. It was Lucius rowing along the river towards them. After her first heart-leap of joy, she was disappointed. She had hoped to see him at the villa, but he was heading towards the town. He had manoeuvred his boat to the bank and Decius left the path to be nearer him. Ethne followed closely.

"Hello, Lucius. It must be hard rowing today," Decius grinned.

Lucius laughed, and wiped the back of his hand against his brow.

"Not as hard as staying at home!" he said.

"Why is that? We were both heading that way."

"I wouldn't if I were you. My sister has gone mad preparing for her journey to Rome and you will be grilled unmercifully about what she should take and what she should not. And believe me – whatever you suggest will be instantly dismissed as inappropriate."

"Even *my* suggestions – a confidant of the Emperor!" Decius laughed.

Lucius grinned. "Careful – or she'll expect you to go with her and introduce her."

"She must be very excited," Ethne spoke at last, gently.

Lucius looked at her for the first time since the conversation began.

Already, before he had hailed them, he had ascertained that it must be the quiet one of the twins because of the friendly intimacy between her and her father.

"I wouldn't mind so much if I didn't know that she was going to be rebuffed and disappointed," he said. "I hate to think of how she will be when the sole ambition of her life is taken away from her."

"I think you do your sister an injustice," Decius said lightly. "She is a lot stronger than you think."

"She is certainly strong! That is why I fear the effect of humiliation. She has never had to endure it before." Lucius said with feeling.

Decius grinned. "A strong woman will pick herself up, dust herself off, and go on with life no matter how many disappointments she has."

Lucius looked dubious. "Well – I hope you are right."

"Besides – Vespasian may accept her," Decius added. "Perhaps she *is* his daughter and he will recognize her mother in her."

"Or at least the ring," Ethne added.

Lucius shook his head. "You two are as crazy as she is," he said. "Good luck with your visit!"

Decius looked down at Ethne and saw in her eyes her disappointment that Lucius was preparing to leave them.

"Do you have room for a passenger?" he asked the youth.

Lucius looked surprised.

"My daughter was beginning to regret accompanying me and would be glad to return to town with you."

Ethne flushed scarlet – the more so because Lucius hesitated before answering. But Decius was already pushing her forward, and Lucius was reaching up to help her into the boat.

Heart pounding, she sat where he indicated and looked appealingly back at Decius as they drew away from the bank. He was grinning broadly and waving a hand.

Lucius seemed relaxed about her presence and rowed on towards the town with long, strong strokes. She sat facing him, her copper coloured hair in two long plaits shining in the sunlight.

"I hope you don't mind..." she said at last, timidly.

"Mind what?" Lucius asked cheerfully, ducking under an over-hanging branch.

"My coming with you?"

"Of course not. In fact there are things I have been meaning to talk to you about."

She waited for him to continue. He rowed silently for a while – and then he took a deep breath.

"Have you ever left this world and... and explored the other?" Remembering how she had sung to his inspired playing that night encouraged him to believe that she would understand. She did.

She nodded.

He almost let go of the oars in his excitement, and certainly gave up rowing. The boat began to drift backwards with the current. She pointed this out with a smile and he took control again, but their progress was slower because his attention was no longer fully on the boat.

"How? When?" he asked eagerly.

She laughed. "It is not easy to tell..."

"Try. I have to know. I *need* to know.

She threw up her hands. How could she tell? These experiences were so extraordinary, so private, so inexplicable, so fleeting – no words were adequate – but he was looking at her so earnestly and intently...

"I have thought so once or twice on Sul's hill," she said hesitantly.

"Sul's hill?"

"Where I believe you first met my sister."

He remembered the place and for a moment she thought she had lost him again as Megan's image flared up in his heart.

"The Oracle herself often used to go there to renew herself – but lately..." Here Ethne's voice fell and her expression became sad. "Lately she has not been able to climb – she is too frail." She paused – thinking of the implications of this.

"But how did you reach the Otherworld?" Lucius insisted.

Ethne looked at him, surprised by the passion in his voice. Should he be encouraged in what might be an unhealthy obsession rather than a mystical quest?

"Are the mysteries of this world not enough for you?" she asked mildly.

"The greatest mystery of this world *is* the next!" he replied, almost sharply.

He had stopped rowing again and they were drifting quite quickly back the way they had come. He did not seem to care, and she could not bring herself to point it out again.

"These things are not easily described. They cannot be passed on by words."

"Then take me to Sul's hill. *Show* me!"

"I can take you there," she said reluctantly, "but I cannot *make* things happen for you."

"Just *take* me!"

At that moment a man shouted from the bank, pointing out that the boat was about to drift into the branches of a fallen tree. Lucius became occupied manoeuvring himself clear, and then concentrating on making up lost water. Nothing more was said during the rest of the journey to town.

When he was handing her out of the boat Ethne spoke at last.

"I will take you to the hill tomorrow if you wish," she said in a low voice.

He looked up at her as she stood on the quay – he still in the boat, rocking slightly.

"Truly?"

"Truly."

"What time?"

"We need to be there at sunset."

"I will meet you here – mid-afternoon."

"I'll be here." She turned quickly and walked away, her heart beating faster than usual. Was he aware of her feelings for him?

Ethne was at the meeting place early. She was in her favourite dress – blue, with a blue ribbon uncharacteristically in her shining hair. A light homespun shawl, oatmeal colour, was tied around her waist, for they would not be returning before the chill of the evening.

Lucius had a light step and an eager face when he greeted her.

He believed he was poised on the threshold of a momentous event in his life and he had no doubt the girl before him held the key.

They climbed the Sacred Hill side by side. He felt comfortable – as though they had known each other a long time and did not need to speak.

From the summit they could see the hills shading into blue mist in the distance, the sun still above the horizon, a vast disc of polished gold sliding imperceptibly but inexorably towards the distant and invisible ocean.

At last they spoke and Lucius told Ethne about his experience, or rather lack of experience, on the Tor at Glastonia, and later his experience with Demosthenes when he skimmed a stone on the river.

Ethne listened quietly. She took his arm and pointed south, where she claimed it was just possible to see the Tor from where they were standing. He strained his eyes but could not distinguish it from the other hills that seemed to stretch one behind the other into infinity.

"Never mind," Ethne said gently. "We are here – not there – and we must prepare ourselves to pass through the gates of the Otherworld as they open to admit Sul. If we choose the wrong moment..."

"What will happen?" The spirit of the place was already causing his flesh to tingle.

Ethne was as still as stone staring at the west. She did not reply.

Lucius waited, but her attention seemed far away. He began to be afraid. Should he not be satisfied with the glimpses of Eternity Demosthenes was training him to have? Why was he so persistent in wanting actually, physically, to enter the Otherworld?

Ethne took his hand.

The clear sky in the west was a brilliant gold set at the centre with a red disc still too bright to gaze at directly. His heart beat painfully. Why was she not giving him instructions? What was he supposed to be doing?

He gripped her hand tightly, feeling her warmth and strength. She led him forward like a child to the edge of the flat top of the hill.

The sun as it sank towards the horizon became a deeper and deeper red. Purple shadows gathered on the earth. He could look at the disc directly now though it still made his eyes water.

She tugged at his hand and suddenly he felt as though he had left the solid ground and was flying.

"Don't look down."

He stared straight ahead and through the veil of his tears he saw the crimson disc growing huge until it filled his vision from side to side. There was no heat – only extraordinary pulsating light. His head hurt. His eyes were stinging. He wanted to cry out – but he could not.

"I'm not ready," his heart warned. "What if... what if..."

He clung to her hand desperately.

"I can't stop now... What if I never get another chance..." But he was afraid. Very, very much afraid.

He would never know if it was his fear that made him fail, or whether what Ethne was trying to do was impossible – but suddenly his hand, slippery with sweat, slid out of hers, and it seemed as though he was falling a long, long way and passing through layer after layer of visions as he did so.

From a region where light almost blinded him, he began to notice figures around him. He seemed to be descending in a spiral and, spiralling with him at first, were beings of great variety and beauty. His heart was joyful and he felt he could achieve great things with their help. But the descent continued and the figures that surrounded him later began to grab at him, and cling, and try to pull him down. Somehow he pulled himself free and reached up his arms to the light he could see now only faintly, a million aeons from him...

"Lucius!" He heard a name called. "Lucius!"

Whose name was it?

It was not his.

Was it his?

"Lucius!"

Again and again the name broke through like a melody steadily gaining strength against a disorderly cacophony of sound, until it triumphed over all.

He opened his eyes. He was lying in the grass at the top of Sul's hill with Ethne leaning solicitously over him, her face anxious and pale. There was no sign of anything or anyone else. The sun had set and the first star was shining in a deeply translucent peacock blue sky.

"I thought I had lost you," she said, and her tears fell on his cheek.

"I thought I was lost," he murmured in reply, shuddering.

It seemed to him she was his haven, his anchor, his home. He reached up his arms and drew her to him. He held her as though he would never let her go. She was his life in this world and the next, the love that he had nearly thrown away, but found just in time.

More stars were beginning one by one to prick the darkening sky with points of light.

"Come," she said. "We must go while we can still see the way."

Half-dazed he suffered himself to be raised, and followed her unsteadily towards the path.

Just before they left the summit, they both paused, and something made them look back.

Where they had stood gazing at the setting sun stood a dim figure. Lucius heard Ethne catch her breath. It was difficult to make out features in the fading light, but Ethne seemed to recognize her. She left his side and took a few steps towards what Lucius saw now to be an aged crone. One arm was stretched out and in her hand was a small object that she appeared to be offering to Ethne. The girl reached out her hand to take it – but even as she did so the old woman seemed to become more insubstantial and, as though she were a statue of dust, fell to nothingness before their eyes.

Ethne rushed to where she had been standing and searched the place, weeping. But there was no one there – nor any sign that anyone had been.

It was Lucius' turn to call his companion.

"Ethne, we must go. Come."

"She is dead!" Ethne said wildly. "She is dead!"

"Who? Who is dead?"

"The Oracle of Sul."

"But that woman there was not... she was not flesh and blood... You said yourself she could no longer climb this hill."

"Nevertheless I know that she has gone and my life is over."

"What do you mean?" He looked at her startled.

But Ethne only shook her head, and, weeping uncontrollably, hurried, stumbling away from him, down the darkening path.

Chapter 18

The Oracle of Sul was dead. One of the priestesses found her body slumped on the floor of her bedchamber when she went to take the old lady her usual cup of hot herbal tea at bedtime. It was clear she had been lying there for some hours. In her hand she held a small object. When her stiffened fingers were prized open it was found to be a small and ancient effigy of Sul carved long before the goddess had been associated with Minerva, passed down from Oracle to Oracle as symbol of office. Those closest to her knew that she intended to give it to Ethne as a mark of succession.

All associated with the Temple were summoned at once by Bridget, the High Priestess, the Mother. A messenger was sent into the town to fetch Ethne while the news was broken to the others. Bridget held up her hand for quiet when she deemed there had been enough murmuring and sobbing.

"Sisters, we must hold our sorrow in check for a time. We are in danger not only of losing our beloved, but of losing everything we have." She paused – looking around at the stricken faces. Only one, Gwynedd, showed no shock or sorrow. Gwynedd's expression was cold and calculating. Bridget knew she believed she should be the new Oracle and resented the consensus that it should be Ethne.

The High Priestess sighed. They did not need controversy among themselves at this time.

"You must know the office of oracle is in jeopardy. The Roman administration sees no need for it while they have their Haruspex. Before it is discovered outside these walls that the Oracle is dead, I believe we must inaugurate another. I don't think they will challenge an existing oracle – but they will certainly take the opportunity of a gap in succession to abolish the office."

Gwynedd rose from the bench at the back of the chamber and stepped forward. She was a tall, lean woman, with black hair just turning to grey. Her face was the face of a hawk. The Romans would not find it easy to manipulate or unseat her.

"I am ready, Mother."

All eyes turned to her. She was the most senior of the priestesses and had on several occasions taken the place of the Oracle when the old lady was too ill to attend to her duties. She was not liked and not many wanted to see her in such a powerful position.

"Where is Ethne?" some whispered. "Has she been sent for?"

Bridget looked into the eyes of the woman advancing towards her. She disliked her and she knew that the Oracle who had just died had not trusted her – but she knew that the ancient times were gone and the Romans shaped the future in their small community. Gwynedd, if she were given the prize she wanted so badly, would hold on to it with cunning and passion. Ethne was a more appropriate oracle given her special and extraordinary psychic gifts – but she was a gentle girl and no warrior.

Just at that moment the door opened and Ethne hurried in with the messenger who had been sent to fetch her. She looked drawn and anxious. She had barely arrived home from Sul's hill when she was called to the Temple, surprising the novitiate who knocked on her door by already knowing of the Oracle's death.

"The Mother did not want anyone else to know yet," the girl said.

"Don't worry. No one else knows," Ethne assured her, forgetting about Lucius.

At Ethne's entrance a sigh of relief went round the room, every face turned towards her, most in joyful expectation. Only Gwynedd's expression darkened.

Ethne looked neither to the left nor the right but walked straight to Bridget, and bowed low before her.

"My sorrow is great, Beloved Mother. Accept my sorrow."

The High Priestess put her hand on the girl's head, the red gold of her hair glimmering in the lamplight.

"Your sorrow is understood, my child. Let it go. Our Lady has journeyed to another world and has left us here to continue what needs to be done." She held up the small effigy of Sul the late Oracle had been clutching in her hand when she died, the same small effigy Ethne had seen in the hand of the apparition at the top of Sul's hill as she reached it out towards her. Ethne bowed her head in resignation. If the Oracle had lived, the girl would have done everything she could to persuade her to release her from her vow. But she had died believing Ethne would succeed her and trying to hand her the symbol of succession. Desperate for a way out as she walked through the dark and deserted streets towards the Temple that night she argued that she was under no obligation since the Oracle herself had not yet kept her promise to prevent the statue of Claudius being raised. But she knew this was an unworthy thought. Death would not diminish her power. It was still possible for her to keep her promise.

She looked at the effigy in Bridget's hand. Its eyes seemed to be gazing right into hers. She reached out her own hand to accept it.

But at that moment Gwynedd stepped forward and snatched it.

A gasp of horror went round the room and for a moment that seemed an age the scene in the chamber froze – Ethne with her hand still out to accept, the Mother with her hand out to present, Gwynedd clutching the object to her heart defiantly. To the others in the room it appeared as though lines of energy passed between the three women and they were contained – locked, as it were – in a powerful triangle. And then between them, at the centre of the triangle, a forth figure appeared, transparent, made of light, growing larger and brighter every second until it towered above them – a woman of startling beauty: Sul, the Goddess.

Gwynedd dropped the effigy with a scream and hid her eyes – the figure already too bright for her. Bridget and Ethne fell to their knees and bowed their heads. The rest, in confusion cowered back, some trying to leave the room, others on the floor in attitudes of deep obeisance. For years they had served the Goddess. They had sung hymns to her, prayed to her, petitioned her for help, but most of them had never expected to see her. The figure grew larger at every second and as it did so the light intensified until there was a blinding flash and she was gone. When sight came back to their eyes, the three women looked down at the floor where the effigy now lay. It was shattered into unrecognisable pieces.

Lucius, in fact, met Decius on the quayside when he was untying his boat, and told the centurion all about the strange apparition on the hill and how Ethne had declared that it indicated the death of the old Oracle. Decius watched thoughtfully as Lucius drew away from the quay and set off homewards down the dark river – and then he turned and walked slowly towards the Temple complex at the centre of town. He knew what the Prefect would want him to do, but would it be wise to give the Celts simultaneously two such powerful reasons for rebellion?

He made a decision.

He turned and deliberately walked away.

* * *

By the time it was officially known that the old Oracle was dead, the new Oracle, Ethne, had been formally and secretly inaugurated.

Gwynedd was driven from the Temple in disgrace, leaving the shelter she had known since she was a child of seven with considerable bitterness in her heart. She had no friends in the outside community for her life had been spent within the Temple; rarely venturing out, enjoying the power her position gave her. What she lacked in genuine psychic skill and mystical inclination natural to Ethne, she made up for with cunning and a flair for the dramatic. Those who were guided to the Oracle by her were put in the mood to expect the supernatural in all its fearful grandeur. Bridget knew this and often regretted it, glad that the client had gone away satisfied, but disliking the means by which that satisfaction had been obtained.

Ethne would return a quiet and reliable honesty to the office. It would be interesting to see if this is what people wanted or if they yearned for the flamboyant displays and manipulations of Gwynedd. She knew the old Oracle had preferred Ethne's way, believing that Gwynedd's machinations led people to expect more of her than sometimes she could deliver. She would have liked the people to understand what a delicate and difficult matter the channelling of communications from spirits was, and appreciate that it was not always possible. Gwynedd led them to believe that it was practically automatic, and thus when no genuine message "came through" from the Otherworld, she sometimes made up spurious messages so that the clients would not go away disappointed.

Ethne was given no opportunity to refuse the responsibility. In the mood of excitement and euphoria brought about by the unexpected appearance of the apparition everyone believed to be Sul, her protests were swept aside. She tried to point out that the breaking of the symbolic effigy might mean that Sul herself accepted that the old ways were dead – but no one would listen. Gwynedd had broken the statue because she did not want Ethne to have it. It had no more significance than that. Sul had appeared in anger against Gwynedd. As Ethne was led back into the private rooms of the Temple to pay her respects to the body of her predecessor, she wondered if her own words and wishes would always be ignored and brushed aside as they had just been. She was disturbed and confused. Sul had appeared to them in all her magnificence – of

146

that she had no doubt – but she did not interpret her arrival in the same way as the others. She longed for a quiet place to think it through, but there was no quiet place in the Temple that night, not even in the chamber where the body of the departed Oracle lay.

The secret inauguration ceremony, prepared in unseemly haste, took place just before dawn, Ethne being led in procession to the Sacred Spring.

This hot spring, kept separate from other chambers of the public baths, was never polluted by human flesh except at such a moment. The priestesses in white robes lined the edge of the pool, while Bridget and Ethne stood on the steps at the eastern end. Each priestess carried a flaming torch held high above her head. Ethne, heart pounding, saw fire reflected in the water, and the bubbles that rose from the depths of the earth breaking through it. Steam rose from the surface in the chill pre-dawn air, taking on strange and eerie shapes.

Softly the priestesses began to intone the sacred words as Bridget divested Ethne of all her clothes. When she was as naked as the moment she was first born, she stepped down into the hallowed water. The chant of the women surrounding her grew gradually louder as she lowered herself. When she was totally immersed, the sound became a shriek of triumph.

Ethne emerged, gasping, in dead silence and in darkness, for during the time she was under the surface, each had simultaneously doused her torch in the water.

But it was not long before the first light of dawn came creeping through the high windows surrounding the sacred pool.

In the grey mist caused by the mingling of the smoke and the steam Ethne was ceremoniously clad in the filmy white robes of the Oracle. Her once bright hair, now damp, and dark, was hidden under a veil. All that made her recognisably Ethne was covered. From now on she would be expected to have no personality of her own, but to be solely a vehicle for Otherworld Beings to communicate with the beings of this world.

Silently the women filed out behind Bridget and the Oracle.

A few early worshippers with sacrifices for the various altars in the forecourt stared curiously at the procession – but no one questioned it – for a procession of priests or priestesses was not an uncommon sight in Aquae Sulis.

* * *

Decius was with the Prefect when the latter received a message from the Governor. It seemed the letter from Demosthenes, combined with pressure from Domitilla, had persuaded the Governor to order a head to be carved on the pediment of the Temple of Sulis Minerva representing the local hero, King Bladud. It was his idea to add snakes to suggest simultaneously Aesculapius, the Greco-Roman god of healing.

However, Domitilla had not been able to persuade her husband to abandon the statue of Claudius. He might well have done so had it not become such an explosive issue between the might of Rome and the local population. He believed it would not be good policy to give in to threats.

With his instructions, he sent two skilled stone carvers from Rome to help speed up both projects.

"By August both must be in place," he wrote.

It fell to Decius to introduce the Roman stone carvers to the Egyptian and give him instructions for the new work.

"You understand what is required?" he asked, uncertain as usual what the Egyptian might be thinking.

The man smiled grimly.

"You want a Celtic hero-god to pacify the rebels, but you want it Romanized so that both conquered and conquerors will be satisfied."

Decius grinned. Not for the first time, he appreciated the cynicism of the Egyptian.

"Can you do it in time?" He looked around at the workmen who had stopped work to watch and listen. It was hard to believe any great work could emerge from such a group.

"We will do it," the Egyptian said drily. And Decius knew it would be done.

Preparation for the ceremony that would introduce the new Oracle to the public went ahead urgently.

On the whole the Oracle was never seen out among the people but spent almost her entire life in the inner confines of the Temple buildings, it being important to keep her remote and mysterious from those who might want to consult her as spokeswoman of the Goddess. The previous Oracle had been installed as a child and so was almost unknown in the community, but Ethne and her family were well known and many looked on the gentle young woman as their friend. Bridget knew that because the Roman administration was planning to do away with the office altogether she must move fast to make a very public, and therefore not easily refuted, claim for the continuation of the ancient tradition.

Crowds began gathering in the forecourt of the Temple as soon as the news was out. Some knew the issues at stake, but most hurried to the place out of curiosity, eager for any excitement.

Owein, who remembered his father telling him about the inauguration ceremony of the former Oracle many years before the Romans came, when the place was no more than a rambling village, told how charged with magic the atmosphere had been. Druid priests presided and travellers came from many lands. Two with skins as black as night were there, wearing masks so that no one saw their real faces. "It was said," Owein added, "though this I can't believe – that spirits swelled the crowd – strange beings who appeared and disappeared as though they were made of nothing but coloured air."

Olwen meanwhile had been weeping since she heard the news that her granddaughter had been chosen as Oracle. A small part of her rejoiced and was proud, but by far the largest part feared for the lonely rigours of the life that faced that beautiful and sensitive young girl.

Megan and Owein were pleased that Ethne in her own way was striking a blow for the ancient way of life against the innovations of the Romans, but neither dwelt on what it would mean for her, nor that they would hardly see her again as long as she lived.

When Lucius heard the news it seemed as though his heart stopped beating for an instant. And then he hurried down to the river and embarked at once for the town.

The area near the landing quay was deserted and at first he could run through the streets unimpeded, but as he neared the centre the crowds thickened up and it was only because he was very determined, and unusually for him, very rough, that he managed to push through.

Ethne was in despair as she was being prepared for the moment when she would be presented to the people. The priestesses were fussing round her, requiring her to lift her arms one moment so that a shift of pleated Egyptian cotton could be lowered over her head, and then turn this way and that, as magnificent ceremonial robes were placed one by one on her. She longed to be alone to think.

She knew she did not want this now, though she had wanted it all her life, but she could think of no way out of it. Bridget, motivated by politics rather than by religious fervour, would listen to nothing she said, but dismissed all her protestations as natural temerity in taking on such an awesome office.

She shut her eyes and tried to cut herself off from her surroundings and the ministrations of the Temple women. In the darkness she found within her she summoned up the image of Lucius and with a longing that would surely have melted the hardest heart, she pleaded with him to come to her, to love her and to take her away from all this.

She barely noticed the jewels of office with which she was being adorned. When the golden sun disc was finally set on her forehead, she was led to the portico of the Temple to stand before the crowd.

The people, looking up, were suddenly silent. The sun overhead struck the gold medallion on her forehead, the cipher of itself, and blazed across the forecourt. Lucius, arriving at that moment, felt its shaft penetrating his eyes and involuntarily closed them for a moment. He knew now he loved Ethne and could not live without her. He leapt forward with a cry, but two of the soldiers on duty to keep the peace seized him and dragged him back.

Ethne heard the cry and opened her eyes. She saw nothing of the sea of faces before her. She saw only the distant corner of the forecourt where a man was being dragged away by soldiers. She saw who it was. She saw his eyes seeking hers. She heard his voice calling her name and she took a step forward as though she would go to him.

The High Priestess Bridget close behind her seized her arm and held her back.

Drums and trumpets drowned the name she cried aloud. White doves in hundreds flew overhead, released from dozens of cages. Voices intoned invocations. Priests and priestesses chanted.

Ethne heard none of this but was powerless to break free of Bridget's grip. From then on Bridget guided her every move. She was pushed down to kneel when she was meant to kneel. She was raised up when she was required to stand. The ceremony was magnificent. Only Ethne was left unmoved by it. Nothing on the spiritual or psychic level happened to her. It was as though her body was going through the motions, but her mind, spirit and soul were elsewhere.

Later, when the crowd dispersed, few mentioned the sorrow on her face, but many remarked on the grandeur of her robes, the splendour of the sun disc, the magnificence of the music.

"When they were singing that hymn to Sul," one woman excitedly told her neighbour, "I swear I saw Sul herself standing behind the Oracle with her hand on her head."

"I saw a great light!" Another claimed.

"I saw nothing. I was right at the back. See how my toes are bruised by those who pushed and trampled me!"

The Prefect was not pleased.

He had been out of town, and returned too late to stop these events. He called Decius to him and berated him for not preventing the inauguration of the new Oracle. Decius insisted that he had not known of the previous Oracle's death until it was too late to stop the inauguration of the new one.

Cornelius Sartorus could do nothing but protest and bluster.

Decius, walking away, frowning, pondered whether he would have been quicker to move against it if he had known it was to be his daughter condemned to such a high and lonely life.

Chapter 19

Very soon after these events, Julia and Aulus departed for Rome and Lucius was left in charge of the farm. Day followed day so fast, and by evening he was so exhausted that he fell into sleep as though into a dark pit. There was no time to brood on his feelings for Ethne.

Ethne herself was overwhelmed by her duties as people crowded to consult the new Oracle, no doubt more out of curiosity than need. Her heart ached, but there was nothing she could do about it.

Megan, whose dreams of torturing the Egyptian had been replaced by equally bizarre erotic fantasies involving the same man, realized how lost she was without her twin to comfort and advise her. She went to the Temple expecting to be able to see her, but was told that so many people were waiting to consult the Oracle that her turn would not come for three days.

Angrily she turned on her heel, and with tears pricking at her eyes, strode off across the forecourt. There she encountered Brendan. He noticed, perhaps for the first time, how beautiful she was, and, for a moment, his admiration showed in his eyes.

It was at that moment she made a decision.

That evening those who were most concerned to be in opposition to the Romans met at the house of one of their members on the edge of town. Owein's house had been abandoned for such meetings as it was almost certainly being watched.

The meeting proceeded as usual with several people with grievances stirring the others up to anger, Brendan carefully orchestrating the level of dissatisfaction. The news that an image of King Bladud was being carved had reached them and, for a time, some of them believed this would leave them without a cause; but Brendan soon showed them that their hero's head carved in the Roman way and erected by Romans was as insulting a gesture as any other.

"Besides," he said, "although there have been rumours – who has heard from any reliable source that the statue of Claudius is to be abandoned if this other one is to be erected?" Megan hardly heard a word that passed that evening. She sat unusually silent, with her heart beating so fast with the enormity of her decision that she was surprised no one else heard it. When the meeting broke up, she pushed her way forward to take hold of Brendan's arm. He looked down at her, feeling well satisfied with the way his rhetoric had been received and confident now that he had brought any doubters back to the fold.

"Megan!" he said cheerfully. "It went well don't you think?"

"Very well, Brendan," she said. She could see one of his cronies hovering in the background waiting to walk out with his leader. "I need to see you privately for a moment," she said urgently. "Shall we tell Keith to go on without you?"

Brendan looked surprised but signalled to his friend at once that he would see him later.

"What is it? Have you found out something?"

"Let us walk away from the crowds," she said, "I don't want to be overheard."

A few minutes took them out into the open country. Brendan came willingly.

A full moon lit their way, but the track was uneven and Megan slipped her hand through his arm to steady herself. She was feeling alternately hot and cold and was in great trepidation at the thought of what she was planning to do. But she could see no other way of destroying those disturbing dreams about the Egyptian.

Brendan talked easily about the issues raised at the meeting as they walked and did not at first notice that Megan was leaning more and more heavily against him and that their pace had slowed right down. But by the time they stopped altogether and she reached up her face to be kissed, his monologue had petered out, and his own pulse was behaving erratically. She had no difficulty in drawing him off the path into a safer area and guiding him down beside her on the grass. For a moment he wondered what was happening and then abandoned himself to her passionate caresses, responding with enthusiasm to the stimulus she was providing.

With a kind of desperation Megan encouraged every excess but succeeded in obtaining no satisfaction for herself. At last he pleaded to be given rest and held her off, half laughing at the expression he caught on her face in the moonlight.

She rolled away from him and lay gazing up at the moon. She felt nothing. How could she have felt nothing? Since he had first come to Aquae Sulis she had believed that she loved and desired him. But his touch had given her no pleasure and now she was ashamed and apprehensive. How could she work with him after this? What must he think of her? And the worst of it, because it had left her so untouched, it might not have erased the secret feelings she had for the Egyptian after all.

She sat up and smoothed out her clothes, brushing off twigs and grass impatiently. She looked down at him. His eyes were closed.

She stood up and began to run. How could she ever face him again? She raced along the track back to the town, slowing only when she was in the streets and her breath was coming in short gasps. It would not do to be questioned at home. Owein, she knew, suspected and encouraged her partiality for Brendan – but now that partiality had disappeared completely. She never wanted to see him again. She certainly never wanted him to touch her again.

This was her first experience of the kind and she did not like it.

"I'll never let a man do that to me again!" she vowed. "Ethne has chosen the right life!"

She reached home and washed herself thoroughly, shuddering as she did so.

The following day Olwen commented on the dark rings under Megan's eyes and confessed that for some time she had been worrying about her.

"I wish you would give up listening to your grandfather's nonsense, my dear. Revolutions and war are best left to the men."

"I'm sure Boudicca didn't think that!" retorted her grand-daughter.

Olwen tightened her lips.

"A mother can't stand by and watch her daughters raped – but the erection of a lifeless block of stone doesn't bear comparison!"

"It is not a lifeless block of stone, grandmother. It is a symbol and sometimes symbols are more powerful than armies."

"Well, why can't you make a symbolic protest without getting yourselves killed? Isn't it enough that I have lost Ethne? Why must you leave me too?"

"I am not going to leave you, grandmother. We will make our protest peacefully."

"Oh – are you going to the erection of the statue unarmed?" The sarcasm was evident in the old lady's voice. When would the killing stop? She had witnessed so much of it in her youth and none of it had succeeded in improving the lot of those who indulged in it. The Romans had still come and taken the land – the only difference being that when they took it a large proportion of the population was under the soil instead of on top of it.

"What do you want us to do, grandmother? Give in to every insulting whim of the Romans?"

Olwen sighed. She did not want that. She was glad her own tribe had not been conquered, but she and Owein and the twins had had a good life in spite of the Roman occupation and she dreaded giving it up. If only there could be a compromise between the stark opposites of conquest and submission. If only her husband and her son were not on different sides of this divide.

Later in the day Megan went back to the Temple of Sulis Minerva to try again to persuade them to let her see her sister. She was again repulsed and told she would have to wait her turn. When she claimed that the Oracle was her twin sister, Bridget told her coldly that the Oracle had no family.

Bitterly disappointed Megan turned away from the entrance and set off blindly across the forecourt. She was vaguely aware that there were other people around her, but she took no notice of them.

Suddenly she paused and looked behind her. Something or someone was breaking through into her consciousness.

She knew at once who it was. A tall figure standing among a group of workmen made her draw in her breath sharply. The Egyptian, come no doubt to survey the setting for his latest works, was gazing right at her. The colour rushed to her face and she dropped her own eyes at once – though it was too late – for the expression in his would be with her for a long, long time.

The workyard of the Egyptian that summer was bustling with action. Two major pieces of sculpture had to be completed within a very few weeks and the apprentices were not always as efficient as the Master would like.

As the time went by the Egyptian found himself more and more interested in the giant head of Bladud and less and less in the little strutting Roman emperor – so much so that a mysterious figure he believed to be Bladud himself began to haunt his dreams.

One night he saw the figure standing beside his bed beckoning to him. Believing himself to be fully awake, the Egyptian found himself walking across the room to open the door into the yard. Later, when he thought about it, he was surprised he had not noticed that the inside of the house was heavy with night shadows, while outside the sun was well risen. He stood on the threshold blinking for a few moments, trying to accustom his eyes to the change. When at last his vision cleared, there was no sign of the man who had called him from his bed.

Still weary he was about to turn back when a shadow passed over him and he looked up, puzzled. There above him, soaring in the sky, was a huge bird. The Egyptian frowned and stared intently. What kind of bird could have such an extraordinary wingspan? Was it his own Egyptian god, Horus, manifested in hawk form?

And then he gasped.

It was no bird – but a man flying!

The Egyptian stepped forward, but he had already passed away over the roof of the house and was nowhere to be seen. The sculptor ran out and around the house sure that he would pick up sight of him on the other side, but there was no sign of him.

"This is impossible," the Egyptian told himself. "I must be still asleep and this is a dream like the others I have been having!"

He heard his own voice demanding that he should wake, as though it were outside himself, speaking in his own native tongue and not in the language of his adopted country.

He gazed around himself now sure that he was awake, but found to his astonishment that he was not in his bed as he expected, but on the edge of the woods to which he had pursued the vision. Was the spirit of King Bladud, the winged man, still active in this place?

Brendan did not wait long before he sought the company of Megan again. He found that his thoughts strayed too often from the plotting and planning that had become second nature to him, to the pleasure he had experienced with her by moonlight.

For several days she managed successfully to avoid him, even enlisting Olwen's help to say that she was out when he called. She gave no explanation to her grandmother, but Olwen, who had for some time regretted Megan's attachment to the young revolutionary, was only too pleased to notice a cooling off.

But Megan could not avoid him forever and it was when she was

156

walking down the narrow street of market stalls, baskets laden, that he ran her to ground.

She greeted him coolly, but he did not seem to notice.

"You weren't at the meeting last night?" he accused, gazing into her eyes with a warmth and eagerness that had not been there in the past. "I have been looking everywhere for you."

She shrugged.

"I couldn't come. My grandmother was not well," she said, walking on.

"Owein didn't mention that there was anything wrong with your grandmother."

"Are you saying that I lie?" She stopped and confronted him fiercely.

"N-no. Of course not. But – you would have thought he would have said something. When I asked him where you were he said he didn't know – but he thought you were coming."

Megan started walking again, increasing her pace, and staring straight ahead as though he did not exist.

He grabbed her arm and tried to hold her back. She shook herself free and strode on.

"I know what it is," he called after her. "You are embarrassed to face me after... after..."

She stopped in her tracks and turned, glaring into his eyes.

"After what? After you raped me?"

He was shocked.

"I?" he gasped in indignation, but the awful blaze in her eyes quelled his and he could not continue.

"You expect me to treat you with the respect I once did as though nothing has happened?"

He stared at her dumbly, trying to remember the sequence of events on that night. It seemed to him he had very little to do with the initial moves. But perhaps he was wrong. She looked so outraged – so convinced that she was in the right.

She turned on her heel and walked away quickly. She did not once glance back. She was exultant that she had put doubts into his mind, and was smiling rather grimly when she turned a corner and saw the Temple of Sulis Minerva before her.

Then the smile faded. Her eyes met those of the statue of the Goddess, and she was ashamed.

* * *

It was Decius Brutus who first had news of Julia and Aulus in Rome. Letters from both of them came on the first day of the month named for the Emperor Augustus, but already, of course, the news was several weeks old. Decius had given them letters of introduction to Annaeus, an old friend of his, a retired centurion, who lived on the outskirts of Rome. Annaeus and his plump, hospitable wife had taken the strangers under their wing.

Decius looked at the two letters in his hand, trying to decide which one to read first. He was curious about their reception in Rome and whether they had managed to obtain an audience with the Emperor. He suspected Aulus' letter would be the most concise and factual, but Julia's would give him more of the flavour of their experience.

He opened Julia's first.

His eye passed quickly over her complaints about the discomforts of the journey and settled for her description of Annaeus' delightful "small" house. Decius smiled. It amused him that a woman who had grown up on a farm in a remote and barbaric country like Britain could have such an exaggerated opinion of her own importance that she was disappointed in everything she saw in Rome itself. She had thought it would be grander and spread further afield. The dinner parties she had been invited to, and Decius noted that they had many invitations, thanks to the popularity of his good friends, were not, she said, that much superior to her own at Aquae Sulis.

In the first part of the letter he read a certain impatience with the kindly, but unfashionable, people she had landed among.

Halfway through, however, the tone changed. It seemed there was a break of a week before she wrote again, and in that time she had visited friends of Domitilla, the wife of the Governor of Britain, and the grandeur of her reception there in a villa with terraced gardens overlooking the Tiber, had finally impressed her.

Decius felt a moment of annoyance that she had been so little grateful for the help of his friends, but then shrugged. Julia was Julia, and he should have expected nothing different.

Comparing the two letters he noted that Aulus' impression of their reception at the grand villa was very different from Julia's. He detected there a haughty coldness. Everything was polite and correct but Aulus felt embarrassed and impatient to be away. Julia, on the other hand, waxed effusive over the wonderful marble floors inside the house, the hanging vines of exotic flowers that shaded the verandah and patios, the views over the river to the city. "For the first time Rome looked to me to be as great as it is supposed to be," she wrote. It seemed that at last she had been served a meal she knew she could not easily emulate in Aquae Sulis. Her hosts were "charming" and her request for an introduction to the Emperor, who was personally known to them, was received without demur.

Aulus' description of that same moment was very different. "There was a long and dangerous pause in which even the slaves standing around against the walls seemed to stop breathing. Julia noticed nothing – not even the look that passed between our hosts. I could have died. I have never in my life regretted so much that I had told Julia that foolish story about her parentage. However, the upshot is, that we are to meet the Emperor. I suspect not in private – but at a reception where there will be many others. Julia is ecstatic and believes we will have no problem in drawing him aside and speaking with him alone."

Frustratingly both letters ended before the day of the reception, so Decius still did not know if Julia had achieved her ambition or not, and what had been the Emperor's reaction.

There were messages for Lucius at the end and so Decius set off as soon as he could to visit the lad.

Decius found Lucius skimming flat pebbles on the calm silvered surface of the river. He laughed and accused him of neglecting his chores while his father and sister were away.

Lucius had been frowning discontentedly as the pebbles spun smoothly across the water. He looked up as though relieved to be interrupted.

"I was trying to do something Demosthenes taught me," he said. "But it doesn't work today."

"What did he teach you?"

Lucius shrugged.

"Too much!" He smiled ruefully.

Decius grinned.

"I have letters from your father and Julia."

Lucius flung the last few pebbles he had in his hand into the water, turning away as he did so. There was a sudden commotion and a swan beating its wings powerfully, rose from near where the

159

pebbles had fallen, and, treading water heavily, pounded off downstream.

Lucius turned back and stared after it thoughtfully. Would Demosthenes say there was a message in that?

Decius had scarcely noticed the swan and was anxious to pass on his news to Lucius. He held out the letters.

"Even as we stand here Julia may be with the Emperor," he said.

Lucius brought his attention back from the swan to Decius with an effort.

"Read them," Decius said, smiling.

Lucius held out his hand, but without enthusiasm.

"Don't tell me she has persuaded the Emperor to acknowledge her?" he asked sceptically.

"Well, we know she has an appointment to meet him – but we don't know the outcome yet."

"Believe me – he'll never acknowledge her. He must have hundreds of illegitimate children around the world. If they all came to Rome and claimed…"

"But you must admit Julia is not a woman to be easily ignored or rejected."

Lucius laughed.

"If anyone can corner him, she can," he said, remembering how often he had tried to disobey her commands and how often he had been forced to accede in the end.

"She is a marvellous woman," Decius said appreciatively.

Lucius looked astonished. "I wouldn't say marvellous," he said with feeling. But Decius just laughed, and, having handed the letters over to Lucius, stopped to pick up some pebbles to try his own hand at spinning them across the water.

Lucius glanced at him with interest. Would he experience what he himself had experienced that day with Demosthenes? He noted that Decius, after the first few pebbles, was frowning and concentrating hard as though the activity *had* taken on meaning for him.

Decius saw no blinding flash of transcendent meaning, but he was remembering another time he had skimmed pebbles. It was across the River Jordan. He was with a friend, a very old man, a retired soldier who had been given land in the country he had helped to subdue for Rome. This old man had told him how he had been sent to this very spot many years before to harass and disperse a crowd of Jews who had gathered round one of their holy men. They had been warned to expect an uprising of zealots, but the gathering seemed peaceful enough and he and his men had stood at a little distance, watching developments. The holy man seemed very young, and although Decius' friend could not hear what he was saying, he was raised up on a rock, and so was clearly visible. "He did not pound the air and shout as most rabble rousers did," he said, "but spoke quietly and authoritatively, with clarity and dignity. Even those at the edges of the crowd seemed to hear his words. I have never seen such a stillness in an audience, such complete attention." Some of the soldiers were eager to break up the meeting, bored by waiting, but he, the captain, held them back, straining to hear what the young man was saying. But he was too far away.

"That man, that very man, was the one they crucified as the King of the Jews."

"Do you think he really was the King of the Jews?" Decius remembered asking.

"He was more than that. I'm sure of it," had been the reply.

Decius was brought back to the present in Britain by a snort of laughter from Lucius.

"She'll end up living in the palace and lording it over everyone there, including the legitimate daughters. See if she doesn't!" he cried.

"I wouldn't be surprised," Decius agreed. "More improbable things have happened!"

Not only was Ethne pining for Lucius in her dim little cell that had become her home, but her longing for the hills and forests, the river and the fields to which she had had such easy access before almost made her ill.

Bridget noticed the sorrow in the girl's eyes and the paleness of her cheeks, but told herself that when the period of adjustment was over Ethne would "settle down". She believed the girl's passionate loyalty to the Goddess would eventually win over her very natural homesickness. Believing that Ethne's only real problem was that she felt inadequate to the task, Bridget redoubled her efforts to assure the girl that she was the only one who could possibly uphold the tradition of the Oracle, and that Sul herself had specifically and unequivocally *chosen* her.

This drove Ethne further into despair. Increasingly she felt hunted and trapped. There was no way out. Sul had chosen her. Sul expected her... If she asked to be released she was rebelling against the Goddess herself.

The scene in the forecourt when she saw Lucius struggling with the guards haunted her night after night, however hard she tried to drive it from her mind. Every incident of their brief time together was played repeatedly in vivid imagery even when she was on duty and some petitioner was waiting breathlessly for her pronouncement. Her mind was never wholly on her work. Twisting and turning in her cage, she sought a way of escape. But found none.

Weary from heavy work on the farm all day, and distracted by his feelings for Ethne, Lucius yet made time to listen to Demosthenes trying to familiarize him with the teachings of Orphism.

"One of the prime teachings," Demosthenes told him, "is that men and women can all be immortal, not only the gods themselves."

"We here believe that all go to the Blessed Isles after death," Lucius said, "where everything is beautiful... trees of crystal... flowers that never fade..."

"There is however a difference between the Orphic and the Celtic image of the After-life," Demosthenes pointed out. "To a follower of Orpheus there is an element of judgement, of responsibility. Those who behave with honour in this life are rewarded in the next, while those who have not behaved with honour have to expiate their misdeeds through many trials and tribulations."

Lucius frowned, wondering what actions of his own would be judged honourable or dishonourable.

"The Egyptians also believe in judgement. The heart is weighed against the feather of truth before Osiris, their supreme Lord of the Otherworld, and if it weighs heavier, the deceased is denied a blissful future."

Lucius sighed. Nothing was ever simple. He liked the idea of other worlds to explore. He was even prepared to admit it was fair that people should not get away with evil deeds, and those who stayed honourable through all the suffering and temptations of this world deserved a reward. But *he* did not want to be judged. He wanted to observe – not participate. He wanted to enjoy the elaborate rituals and beautiful imagery... but not take on the burden of duties and responsibilities those rituals imposed on everyday life...

Demosthenes, watching the play of conflicting emotions on the pupil's face, smiled. He too had passed through this phase.

Chapter 20

The evening of the Emperor's reception to which Aulus and Julia had obtained invitations came at last.

Julia spent a fortune on her clothes and would listen to none of Aulus' complaints that they could ill afford such extravagances.

"After the reception money will be no object to us," she insisted confidently. Aulus could not tell whether she really believed Vespasian would welcome her into his family as royal princess on this night or whether this was an instance of the last reckless bluff of the gambler. At any rate he himself felt physically sick as the evening approached and he trailed behind her disconsolately when they finally mounted the marble steps of one of the Emperor's minor palaces.

They were announced but were greeted by court officials and not by Vespasian himself. In vain Julia scanned the throng in the hall for the thickset figure she had seen on so many statues and coins, but there was no sign of him. She would have liked to ask when he would appear, but the line of guests was already pressing at her back and she was propelled into the crowd ahead quickly and forcibly.

Being a tall woman she could gaze over the heads of most of the other guests but still could not spot anyone resembling the Emperor. To her dismay, the vast majority of the people in the room seemed to be of low rank, overdressed, over-excited and vulgar. To her chagrin, she realized she had been invited to a reception of plebeians, no doubt held from time to time to encourage the Emperor's popularity among the common people. She flushed with indignation and tugged at Aulus' arm.

"We will leave," she whispered angrily, "This is not what we were promised at all."

Aulus, remembering the look that had passed between their elegant hosts when Julia said she wanted to meet the Emperor, knew now what that look had meant.

"He isn't even here!" Julia said indignantly.

"Hush," Aulus whispered. "Keep your voice down. He might come later."

Julia snorted and, as eager now to leave the reception as she had been to come to it. She turned on her imperious heel and, dragging Aulus by the arm, pushed her way back through the crowds.

So it was that she was halfway through the entrance chamber, her face flushed and furious, as Vespasian himself strode in and almost collided with her. She might have realized this was about to happen because the crowds that had made it so difficult for her to make progress had suddenly thinned and drawn back, leaving her and Aulus momentarily isolated and exposed.

Vespasian had no entourage but walked in alone, bulky, simply dressed, thick neck, red face, eyes shrewd and amused at the couple who floundered in his way.

Julia recovered her equilibrium in time to make a hasty and rather clumsy curtsy before him and murmur "Emperor" in a hoarse and awe-struck voice. But before the obeisance was completed he was already gone – and without an acknowledgement of her presence or a backward glance.

She stood gazing after him, stunned, as the crowd surged forward again and followed him into the main reception hall.

Julia was in an awkward position. As she had left the reception and demanded the return of her cloak, she had said some scornful things loudly to Aulus intending them to be overheard by the servants. The official who had done so was now looking at her with undisguised amusement, waiting to see what she would do.

She would have liked to go back, but she knew it would be undignified to do so. With cheeks blazing red and tears pricking at the back of her eyes, she swept out of the palace in the grand manner, Aulus trailing in deepest embarrassment behind her.

Julia did not write about this fiasco to Decius, nor did she return immediately to the rich acquaintances who had secured for her the invitation to the reception that she considered so beneath her dignity. Aulus suffered considerably for her chagrin and disappointment, and Annaeus and his wife, Vipsania, who still housed them, believed her to be ill so closely did she confine herself to the house for the next few days,

But on the third day after the reception Julia seemed suddenly to have decided on a new tack and recovered her fighting spirit. She emerged from her room with a letter scroll and announced that she was going to approach the Emperor by letter this time and secure a

165

proper appointment to see him. Aulus could not help pointing out that over the years several letters had been despatched and not one of them had received the slightest acknowledgement.

"This one is different," Julia said confidently.

Since she had been in Rome she had learned that oracles particularly influenced the Emperor. During the year of civil war in Rome when three men, Galba, Omo and Vitellius, vied with each other to rule the Empire, Vespasian, then at war in Judaea, could only be persuaded to put himself forward because of the omens that seemed to indicate he was destined to be Emperor and bring peace and stability to Rome. He had even consulted the Oracle at Carmel, supposedly speaking for the Jewish God Jahweh, and had been told that "however exalted his ambition was, in it he would succeed". Other omens like an ox breaking into the house where he was and falling in obeisance at his feet, and a dog bringing him a severed hand, an emblem of authority, further served to confirm that he was destined to wear the purple. In Alexandria, the Oracle of the god Serapis finally convinced him.

In her letter, Julia fabricated a message she claimed she had received from the famous Oracle at Aquae Sulis.

> "I would not have come to Rome nor sought to appraise your august Majesty of the connection between us had I not been urged to do so by the Oracle of Sulis Minerva in the town of Aquae Sulis in the province of Britain – a province your Majesty knows well.
>
> "During my life I have received many indications from the gods that my destiny is not an ordinary one, but I would never have had the presumption to seek you out had the Oracle I speak of not urged me that it was my duty to do so, and indeed charged me to deliver a secret message to your Majesty."

Having ascertained that the Emperor Vespasian was now in residence at the Golden House of Nero, she insisted on going there at once.

Aulus wondered what further humiliation they would have to suffer before Julia would take his advice, abandon her mission and return home.

Nero had built his Golden House in the broad valley near the end of the route taken by the great triumphal processions. He had claimed his gardens rivalled those of the fabulous hanging gardens of Babylon and certainly they were magnificent and designed to make full use of the terraced hillside. The palace itself was huge and reputed to be the most beautiful in the world. Julia had heard that one great reception hall had a ceiling consisting of ivory panels which, when drawn back during a banquet, allowed thousands of rose petals to drift down upon the guests.

Vespasian still occasionally used the palace itself though, since Nero's suicide and disgrace, some of the gardens had been opened for public enjoyment. The great amphitheatre Vespasian had started building was on the site of the ornamental lake Nero had sailed his pleasure boats upon. The colossus of Nero himself, covered with gold leaf, still stood in its original position, but it was now called a statue of Helios, the sun.

Julia and Aulus had no trouble entering the gardens, but in approaching the main entrance to the residence they encountered guards. Nothing daunted, Julia demanded to see their captain in a tone of such imperious confidence that, to Aulus' surprise, they were indeed approached by the captain.

Aulus could not help but admire the way his stepdaughter handled the situation. She was haughty and dignified, but polite and respectful enough to attract serious attention from the man. He would not allow her to enter the palace, but agreed to deliver her letter personally that very day.

"You understand it must not be brought in with all the petitions and other letters?" she said. "It is not a petition – but a very important message from the great Oracle of Sulis Minerva. He will want to receive it and will be very angry if he finds out that it has been kept from him."

She gazed sternly into the eyes of the young captain.

"You understand? It is very important and very urgent," she repeated.

On receiving his assurances Julia at last turned and walked away.

The captain, knowing his Emperor's habits, waited until the evening meal to deliver the letter from Julia, when Vespasian was invariably relaxed and good humoured. He rarely had occasion to walk through the Golden House and he did so now with interest, following the secretary who had agreed to bring him to the Emperor. Chamber followed chamber decorated in exquisite taste, corridors and stairways of astounding beauty unfolded before him,

He could not imagine how anyone found their way in this labyrinth but people evidently did.

Vespasian had had much of "the clutter", as he called it, removed. In the cultivated Nero's time furniture and ornaments from every country in the far-flung Empire had crowded the rooms so that there was not an empty space anywhere. The bluff old soldier, up from the middle classes, found no pleasure in being surrounded by impediments, no matter how beautiful they were, and ordered the rooms to be cleared of everything but necessities. However, there was enough left for the captain who had not yet travelled abroad to marvel at as he walked through. He wished his guide was not in such a hurry. The wall paintings alone needed much more attention than he could give them. On every wall gods and goddesses disported themselves. The walls of one long corridor alone seemed to be devoted to the God Jove raping various women in different disguises – Europa and the bull, Leda and the swan... The scenes were explicit and erotic and the man found it difficult not to stare, while his companion gazed straight ahead as he hurried him to his destination.

Standing in the doorway as his escort delivered Julia's letter to Vespasian, the captain saw the Emperor bend his head to listen to what the secretary was saying, take the scroll briefly in his hand, and then lay it down on the table before him among the plates of food and goblets of wine. He must have cracked a joke for there was a little burst of laughter around him, and the stiff little secretary bowed and smiled grimly before he returned to the captain.

"Will he read it?"

The secretary nodded, "But not before dessert," he said.

And with that the captain had to be content. He had done his duty – the letter was in the Emperor's possession. More he could not do. All day, having the letter with him, he had longed to break open the seal and see what was so important about the message it contained. But he had not dared. Now he would never know. He had had difficulty in persuading the secretary of the importance of the letter. Evidently, the Emperor was known to have several mistresses and letters from ladies delivered with great urgency were not uncommon.

His cynicism almost shook the captain from his purpose, but, remembering Julia, he decided she was not a courtesan. There was something powerful in the way she fixed him with her gaze – as though she was used to authority and high living. He would not be surprised if the letter was as important as she said. At any rate, he was not going to be the one to keep it from the Emperor.

Julia received her summons the following day.

"You see!" she cried excitedly. "I told you this one would get results!"

"What did you say in that letter?" Aulus looked alarmed. "What lies did you tell? If the Oracle did not…"

"Don't worry! I know what I'm doing," she replied, and he could not persuade her to think seriously about the consequences of lying to an Emperor. He had been uneasy when he heard her speaking to the captain about the contents. When they set off that morning he had had no idea of what she intended. The day had passed as though it were some kind of dream. Afterwards he had consoled himself by telling himself that the young captain would not take the trouble to deliver the letter, or, if he did, Vespasian himself would surely not take it seriously.

But now…!

They returned to Nero's Golden House and, armed with the Emperor's summons, they were ushered respectfully into an ante-chamber where they were instructed to wait.

Julia's eyes were shining and Aulus thought she had never looked so magnificent. He glanced at her time and again and realized she was a stranger. He tried to remember her as a little girl running about the farm, or as a young woman cooking his meals, even as a petulant and arrogant mistress of his household in Aquae Sulis. But the Julia he knew then and the woman sitting so comfortably in one of the Emperor's carved mahogany chairs in the most famous palace in the world seemed to have nothing in common.

They were kept waiting a long time, and as the minutes turned into hours the fine sparkle in Julia's eyes faded and her back was not kept as straight and proud as it had been. The full lips that had been so ready to smile when they arrived set into a thin and bitter line. Conversation between the two ceased and Aulus forced himself to keep silent knowing that the slightest remark might cause an explosion of temper. In one way he longed for them to storm out of there as they had done from the ill-fated reception, but in another, he wanted to get this matter settled. They had come so far this time he could not bear the thought of what Julia might do next if she was frustrated in this.

They had arrived in the morning but the sunlight through the window was already dimming when they were finally called. In all that time they had not seen another soul and Julia had not said a word. When a servant entered at last to ask them to follow him Julia rose immediately and without a backward glance at Aulus stumbling after her, she strode forward, her face an icy mask.

They were ushered in to a comfortable chamber and, apart from a few slaves, found Vespasian alone reclining on a golden couch. The servant who had brought them backed out without announcing them and they were left to wonder whether they should explain who they were or be silent. Julia's curtsey was stiff and slow; the bow of Aulus quick and nervous. Vespasian eyed them penetratingly for some time before he lifted his hand and waved them to seats.

A hundred times she had practised the speech she would make when she finally confronted her father, but during the day it had changed more than once, and when at last she stood before him, she could think of nothing to say.

A slave came forward and poured them wine. Julia's hand trembled as she held an exquisite glass in her hand. They had glass in Aquae Sulis, even a Roman-trained British glass-blower of their own, but never had she seen such a fine vessel, the colour reminding her of the vibrant blue of the sea that washed against these southern shores.

Still with no word spoken, Vespasian raised his own glass to theirs as though saluting them – though whether there was mockery in the gesture they could not be certain.

Aulus again had occasion to admire his stepdaughter as she raised her glass to the Emperor, lifting her chin defiantly, the spark of battle back in her eyes.

"So, you have a message for me from the Oracle of Sulis Minerva?" he asked drily. "I remember I consulted her myself when I was in Britain. She was a formidable lady then. How is she these days?"

"Well, your majesty, and in good form."

Julia was not aware that the old Oracle had died and that Ethne was now in her place.

There was a pause. Should she tell him the fake message now or wait until they had established more of a rapport?

"I am anxious to hear what she has to say to me," the Emperor said quietly, not taking his eyes off Julia's.

Aulus began to sweat and wished himself a thousand miles away back on his familiar farm.

Julia put her glass down on the little Egyptian table of ebony and ivory beside her and gripped the arms of her chair. She appeared at this moment to be tense but calm.

"Certainly my lord."

There was a heavy silence in the room. She took a deep breath.

"She was speaking for the woman you had once loved, sire, my mother."

Vespasian's expression did not flicker. He continued to stare into Julia's eyes.

"She said you would recognize her in me and that you would take comfort in this."

Julia's voice trailed away. Under his gaze she was beginning to doubt that she had chosen the right approach.

"My mother gave me this ring," she said, leaning forward and presenting it to him.

For a moment his gaze left her face as he turned his attention to the ring. He turned it over and over in his hand with no sign of recognition, and then he handed it back to her.

"It is a good ring. You should not part with it."

"Did you... do you remember giving it to her my lord?"

"What was her name?"

"Oonagh, sire. Daughter of Teirnyon. Granddaughter of Naois."

"I do not remember the ring. I do not remember the name."

"Does my appearance stir no memory sire?"

He stared at her steadily.

"No."

She flushed – whether in anger or shame Aulus could not tell.

Vespasian looked at him for the first time and raised an enquiring eyebrow.

"This is the man who brought me up," Julia said. "He married my mother when I was already born. It was she who told him who my father was and it was he who told me."

Vespasian looked amused.

"And you have waited all this time and come all this way to confront me?"

"Not to confront you sire!" Aulus found his voice at last.

"What else?"

"I thought... we thought..." Aulus' voice trailed away.

Julia said nothing, but drew herself up out of her chair and with eyes flashing, met the Emperor's gaze haughtily.

"I see I was wrong to listen to the Oracle," she said at last. "I apologize for wasting your time and will waste no more of it!"

He laughed outright now and held up his hand.

"At least let me provide you with supper!" he said. "It will be my pleasure if you would join my other guests in the peacock room."

"Thankyou, but..." Julia began scornfully.

"What do you think of this palace?" Vespasian interrupted her, rising from his couch and chatting as he led them towards an inner door. "I find it a bit too ornate for my taste, but it's position serves me well. You must come and see my plans for the amphitheatre that I am building at the bottom of the garden. Do you have an amphitheatre in Aquae Sulis?"

He led them into a banqueting hall crowded with other guests, all the time talking as casually as though they were old friends. Julia had gone from ice white to fiery red. Words were hammering in her head to be spoken, but not one was given voice. Aulus followed, bewildered. What game was this?

Back in Aquae Sulis Decius received further letters from Aulus and Julia. It seemed they were having a wonderful time. They were attending the Emperor's banquets; they were surveying the Emperor's building projects at his side; they even went travelling with the Emperor when he went south to visit the magnificent city of Pompeii. There they stayed with friends of his when he returned to Rome.

Decius and Lucius read the letters many times and both noted that in none of them did they say that Vespasian had admitted he was Julia's father and given her princess status. Surely they could not have just forgotten to mention such an important bit of news in their letters.

"Perhaps one of the letters went astray?" Lucius suggested.

But Decius was not so sure. A man did not become Emperor from Vespasian's background unless he was very, very shrewd. He suspected he was playing cat and mouse with them.

Chapter 21

Owein was not so pleased as his wife that Megan seemed to have lost interest in the rebel cause.

"What is the matter with you?" he demanded. "This is the third meeting you have missed. Don't you care that in only a few short weeks now we'll have that monstrosity in our town?"

"Leave the girl alone!" Olwen said. "Can't you see she isn't well?"

The old man looked at his granddaughter closely. He had not noticed before but he could see now that her cheeks were pale and her eyes sunk in shadows.

"What ails you?" he asked in alarm. He realized he had been relying on Megan's fiery enthusiasm and reckless courage to lead the rebels into action. Brendan was good at planning and fighting, but he lacked that spark, that charisma that a leader needed in time of danger and trouble. Increasingly he had assumed that when unexpected things started happening Megan would be at the forefront inspiring them to great deeds.

Megan shrugged.

"Nothing," she said.

Owein frowned, staring anxiously into her face.

"You're not going to let us down are you?"

"Owein!" cried his wife, shocked.

"Well, she is important. We all have our role to play on the day and if any one of us fails, he or she endangers the lives of all the others."

"I'll not fail you," Megan said bitterly. "You need have no fear of that."

"Brendan is anxious for you to return. Things are happening that you don't know about."

"What things?"

"The Prefect has ordered more troops," Owein said.

Megan looked interested and alert for the first time since the conversation began.

"How does Brendan know that?"

"He has his spies."

"Did Decius Brutus ask for them?" Megan never called him "father".

Owein pursed his lips.

"Evidently not. In fact he tried to oppose the order – but the soldiers are coming anyway. They should be here by next week Brendan says."

"This is not good news. We might have to revise our tactics."

"Quite so! Now you see why we are angry with you for not attending the meetings?"

"Is Brendan angry?"

"Of course."

"Did he say so? What did he say?"

"He asked me repeatedly if you could be relied on, and he warned the others how dangerous it is for all of us if one of us leaves the group."

"I have not left the group!"

"Three meetings, granddaughter! Three meetings! What should we think?"

"I'll be there at the next one. Don't worry!" And with that she left the room, and the house.

Owein looked enquiringly at his wife.

"I think she is pining for Ethne," Olwen said quietly. "She has been trying to see her at the Temple but the priestesses seem to be determined to keep her away."

"We all miss Ethne," Owein said brusquely, though in fact he had scarcely noticed her absence, as Megan was and always had been his favourite.

Olwen sighed. "They are so different – but they were very close. When everything was going well Megan ignored Ethne, but as soon as she was in trouble she was the one she turned to."

"Is Megan in trouble?"

Olwen hesitated.

"I wondered if... Have you noticed anything between her and Brendan?"

Owein seemed puzzled. "What sort of thing?"

"Men are so blind!" Olwen exclaimed impatiently. "Go back to your arrows and daggers. You are fit to understand nothing else!"

"You mean Brendan and Megan...?" Owein seemed genuinely astonished. But incidents began to come to mind.

174

"The gods forbid!" he cried. "If that sort of thing starts happening in the group we are lost!"

"Better to find out that you can't rely on your members before you commit yourselves to action."

"If what you say is true, it is a disaster."

"She won't let you down no matter what her feelings are – but young girls and men should not be asked to give up their lives for lost causes."

Olwen was furious.

"Lost causes, madam? Lost causes!"

"You know you cannot win against the might of Rome."

"We may not be able to – but we can make a stand about this to show that we are not puppets! We will make them think twice before they push us around again. Besides, who knows what we will achieve? It only needs one spark to set a whole field alight!"

Olwen bit her lip. She could see how agitated he was becoming and she knew that there was no convincing him. Her only hope was that her son, Decius, would handle the matter with care and good sense and that no one would be seriously hurt. She was dismayed that more soldiers were coming in, for those who had been in the town for some time had become friends with the locals and would be unlikely to put down the small rebellion with the careless brutality for which the Romans were famous.

When Megan left her grandparents that day she went down to the river and walked blindly along the towpath, scarcely noticing anything or anyone she encountered. A barge loaded heavily drifted past her, but she did not even hear the whistles and the shouts of the two young men aboard. A family of ducks waddling almost under her feet making for the water barely made her slow her step. The outside world had almost ceased to exist for her.

Her father, striding towards her, called her name.

She stopped for an instant and looked at him, as bewildered as a sleepwalker suddenly awakened. He smiled. She frowned.

"Where to in such a hurry, Megan?" he asked, his eyes alert and wary though his manner was easy and relaxed. He blocked the path in front of her so that she was forced to stand and face him.

"Are we not free to go where we please under Roman rule?" she said tartly.

He grinned.

"Do all Dobunni daughters resent their fathers?"

"Only when they are traitors to their people."

"That is a harsh word." His expression darkened.

"These are harsh times."

"Only if you make them so."

"I make them so?"

"You and others who resist change. You cannot go back to things as they were, daughter. Even if the Romans leave, nothing will be as it once was. Why not make the most of what the Roman's offer? With Celtic energy and Roman discipline great things could be achieved here. You must admit..."

"Admit? Submit? Never!" Her eyes blazed.

He shrugged and bowed slightly and stepped aside for her to pass.

Head up and shoulders squared, she brushed roughly past him and strode on the way she had been going.

He turned and watched her and wondered if he should follow her.

Why *was* she going to the Egyptian's workyard?

Megan had no conscious awareness of where she was headed. As far as she was concerned she was just walking away from her grandfather's, and now her father's, probing. She wanted to be free. Free! She kept muttering the word to herself as though doing so would bring about the condition of freedom. It was not just the Romans that hedged one about – but one's own family – even one's own self! Was there no such thing as freedom? She was inclined to believe at this moment that the worst tyranny in the world was the tyranny of her own thoughts. Low lying branches brushed her shoulders with green and shimmering leaves, birds flew singing past her out of thickets, swans stretched their wings on the river in graceful arcs of gleaming white – but she saw nothing and longed for nothing but the Egyptian.

Suddenly he was there.

The path opened out to the clearing where he had his workplace.

She gasped. She had not realized... She had not meant...

She blushed. *Had* she realized?

He was gazing straight at her as though he had been expecting her.

She had stopped instantly in her tracks at sight of him, but the look that passed between them was almost tangible.

She wanted to turn and run, but she could not. That gaze held her as surely as a fish is held by a fisherman's line.

She was aware that there was no one else around although her eyes did not leave his. "Where are all the others?" she thought frantically. The workyard was usually crowded with men and activity.

"I must go," she told herself. "I must just turn round and leave."

But she did not.

She found herself walking forward, her heart pounding. There seemed to be a clamouring of words in her ears, a cacophony of conflicting advice, but she ignored it all. Everything about him seemed extraordinarily clear to her – the muscles in his arms, slightly misted with stone dust; his face as chiselled and handsome as that of a god carved by a master sculptor; his height above hers; his thick black hair with the occasional silver streak pulled back from his face and tied behind his neck. His shoulders... His narrow waist … His thighs...

"Megan!"

A voice behind her shattered the moment.

She spun round.

Her father, the centurion, was there.

"Why can't you leave me alone!" she shrieked at him, her face distorted with rage, and, without a backward glance at the Egyptian, she started to run back along the path. She ran until she thought her heart would burst and the town was beginning to close in on her again.

"I hate this place!" she fumed. "One day I will leave and never come back!"

The Romans were very careful not to desecrate the Sacred Spring. The waters of Sul were discretely carried through lead pipes into different bath chambers. At first the citizens of Aquae Sulis could accustom their bodies to warm water in the tepidarium, then luxuriate in the hot healing waters of the calderium, before finally plunging into the cold pool at the end, while the holy of holies, the Sacred Spring, was still kept sacred. There was no bathing there. It was where prayers were said, where offerings were made. Under its bubbling waters lay the evidence of countless dreams and heartaches, disappointments and triumphs. Since ancient times it had been so. Some said the great King Bladud

177

himself had been healed of leprosy by those very waters and built the first sanctuary in gratitude around the source. The mysterious water that came hot from the centre of the earth owed no allegiance to any Roman Emperor – nor indeed to any man. It was an expression of Sul – the waters of life that flowed from the womb of the Goddess – the waters of birth and rebirth, of nourishment and renewal. Some believed that if the waters ever stopped flowing, life itself would disappear from the earth.

Ethne spent much of her free time there, watching the bubbles rise and imagining fantastic shapes and messages in the steam that rose from its surface. She found it a calming, soothing place. Bridget allowed her time there for she saw that it benefited the captive girl. She was becoming increasingly worried about Ethne. She no longer protested and rebelled, but showed a measure of such despairing docility and grew so pale and listless, that the Mother was besieged by murmurings from other priestesses, suggesting that perhaps they should recall Gwynedd, and release Ethne from her vows.

Bridget responded angrily to all such suggestions.

"Who can release her from her vows but the Goddess herself? And until that happens we are powerless to change the situation. Ethne was clearly chosen by the Goddess. You all know that. Who are we to question her commands?"

And with that the subject was closed and no one dared raise it again.

But one compromise Bridget did allow. The former Oracle had conducted her business in a dark cell, specially prepared for maximum dramatic impact, but Ethne requested that her consultations should be conducted at the Sacred Spring itself, and a stone chair was provided for her on the far side from the public entrance. The only concession to theatricality was that the Oracle would be only dimly seen through the rising steam and would be swathed in filmy white robes of Egyptian cotton, thus keeping something of her mystery.

Ethne was much happier here, and for a time Bridget believed they had solved the problem of the reluctant Oracle.

One day Decius Brutus paid a visit to the Oracle.

Decius looked across the water at the slight figure. Her face was veiled, but even so he could see by the droop of her shoulders that she was despondent and unhappy. When she recognized him there was a perceptible lift in her spirits, and she sat forward in her chair alert and eager.

While Bridget was still present he pretended he had come to consult the Oracle officially as the representative of the Roman Governor to find out what the Goddess predicted for the forthcoming ceremony when the new statue would be raised in the forecourt.

Having delivered his speech, he turned to Bridget and insisted they should be left alone. The older woman seemed about to protest, but the centurion indicated that there was no question of her staying. Reluctantly she withdrew with a last anxious look across the water at her protégé. It was not usual for the Romans or the Romanized Celts to consult the Oracle of Sul since they had their own Haruspex. What was the real meaning of his visit? She hovered anxiously at the entrance, but at last moved away as it became clear the centurion would not continue until she did.

After Bridget left, father and daughter remained silent for some time watching each other.

Ethne's heart was beating painfully. There were so many questions she wanted to ask. Dare she? For all her love for him, Decius *was* still the representative of the Roman Governor and he might indeed have come to consult her in his official capacity only. Bridget had drilled into them all the danger the Romans posed to the ancient Mysteries of Sul.

"Remove your veil, daughter, and let me see your face."

"It is not allowed, sir," she answered faintly.

"Nevertheless, put it aside," he said authoritatively.

Slowly, hesitatingly, she pushed aside the fine fabric. Nothing divided them now but the steam that rose from the Sacred Spring.

He could see her sunken, pale cheeks and her dark eyes.

He sighed, remembering his two daughters as he had seen them on his return to Aquae Sulis. Megan had been fiery and vibrant, full of rebellious force and passionate energy; Ethne full of the light of true spiritual power. Now they were both shadowy figures, pale as ghosts, and as listless.

"I have not come to consult you as Oracle, child," he said quietly, compassionately, "but to ask you to intercede with your Goddess for your sister."

Ethne looked concerned.

"Megan!"

"There is something deeply troubling her and she will speak to no one about it."

"I knew it! I felt her pain."

"You must see Megan. She needs you."

"I know... but... but I'm not allowed..."

"I will see to it. You will see Megan."

"Father..."

There seemed to be something else she wanted to ask.

He waited.

But it was too late.

At that moment Bridget returned.

"Sir," said the Temple Mother firmly. "It is time..."

"I know," he said impatiently. "I know."

Decius kept his word and used his position as centurion in charge of the small Roman force at Aquae Sulis to pressure Bridget into letting Ethne see Megan.

On being accused of deliberately keeping the twins apart, the Mother replied: "You must understand the Oracle is very popular with the people and she is very busy. There must be no favourites. No one must have special privileges."

"I am not asking for special privileges. I am asking only for fair treatment. Megan tells me that every time she comes to the Temple to see her sister, her twin, she is refused entrance and told to wait day after day. She says she sees people who petitioned for entrance after her, being admitted,"

Bridget's face was impassive.

"She is mistaken," she said coldly.

"You mean she is lying?"

"She is mistaken."

"You will allow her to see her sister this very day?"

"The Oracle has no family. She has no sister. No twin."

Decius' lips tightened and a dangerous glint came into his eyes.

"You will allow Megan, daughter of Decius Brutus, centurion of the Emperor Vespasian, to consult the Oracle this day?"

It was as though two warriors were sizing each other up before a battle.

"The daughter of Decius Brutus must take her turn as must all who wish to consult the Oracle. There is no time today, but..."

"I am sure you could find time today if you wished."

Bridget bit her lip. She had given in to him once by allowing him access to the Oracle himself without a previous appointment, and she was regretting it. She could feel her power slipping away. The Romans were good at this. They would pretend to honour a local tradition or institution, but somehow the people would find that they had only the empty shell left while all substance had mysteriously disappeared. If she jumped whenever a Roman conqueror snapped his fingers, she might as well give up all pretence of authority in the community.

But she was not ready to do this yet.

"I will make an appointment for Megan, daughter of Decius Brutus, tomorrow."

"I would prefer it today."

"The Oracle can see no one else today."

Decius considered the matter. This was a compromise. At least the old harridan had accepted that Megan could see her sister. "Tomorrow" allowed Bridget to keep something of her authority, while not openly defying the Romans. Bearing in mind the volatile atmosphere in Aquae Sulis at this time, he decided to accept her offer.

"I will come with her," he thought, "and make sure there is no change of plan."

Aloud he said: "The first appointment of the day."

Bridget hesitated.

"The first appointment of the day," she agreed stiffly.

The following morning when Decius had made certain that Megan had been accepted into the presence of her sister, he hurried off along the path to the Egyptian's workyard again.

He had questioned Megan on the way to the Temple that morning about her relationship with the Egyptian, but Megan had been sullen and uncommunicative and given away nothing. She deeply resented the fact that it was the Roman centurion who had secured her appointment with Ethne at last, but was too desperate for such a meeting to refuse his help.

As she plodded beside her father, eyes down, shoulders slumped, her mind was full of questions to ask her twin. How could she escape the tormenting passions she was feeling for a man who was under a fearful curse she herself had devised.

Decius meanwhile had his own questions for the Egyptian. He could not believe that the nubile and desirable Megan, who had every young man in the town pining for her, would settle for such a parched and sour alternative – a man old enough to be her father.

As Decius drew nearer to the workyard, he became increasingly convinced that the man must have tricked her in some way.

Although it was still early, work was in full swing. He scanned the yard for the Egyptian, but could see him nowhere. He asked several of the apprentices but no one seemed to know where he was.

"Have you seen him this morning?"

"Yes. He was here when we arrived."

"Did you see him leave the workyard?"

Most said "no", but one young lad suggested he might be in the woods.

"Should he not be here while you are working?"

"We know what to do. There is a lot we can do without him. He often goes into the woods."

Decius looked thoughtfully at the trees that crowded the edge of the clearing. There was a track leading into them. He decided to take it.

He walked for some way without noticing anything around him, concentrating only on what he would say to the Egyptian when he met him. He had lived so long without the responsibilities of fatherhood he was a little uneasy about how to assert his rights over his daughter at this late stage.

But gradually the forest claimed his attention. The path forked and he had to make a decision. The left hand one was less worn, bracken and brambles in some places leaning right over it. The right hand one was broader and smoother, obviously more frequently trodden.

He stood irresolute for some time, listening intently for any sound that might indicate the presence of the Egyptian, but there was none. A green glimmer indicated the direction of the sun. Beard-like lichen hung from some trees. Others were richly padded with moss and ferns. In the undergrowth there were the various faint creakings and rattlings of small creatures that had resumed movement after the pause occasioned by his noisy approach. Now, as he remained silent, birds sang in the tree tops and flew from branch to branch.

Decius sighed. A pleasant place. It would be a shame to spoil the atmosphere with confrontation and acrimony.

He chose the rougher, narrower path and it was not long before he came upon a still pool covered with water-flowers, and there he found the Egyptian.

The man had heard his footsteps well before he came in sight and was waiting for him, his dark eyes on the path where he expected the intruder to emerge. Whether he was surprised to see that it was the centurion, Decius could not tell. His face certainly showed no surprise.

The two men eyed each other in silence for a few moments and then cautiously and politely greeted each other.

Decius felt awkward. He had been angry when he had set off, knowing exactly what he wanted to say, but the pleasant walk through the woods, reminding him as it did of many happy days of childhood, had distracted him.

The Egyptian spoke first.

"You were looking for me?"

"Yes," he said sternly. "I wanted to speak to you about my daughter."

"The Oracle?"

"You know it is not," snapped Decius, resenting the cold, quizzical smile that accompanied these words.

"Megan?"

"Megan."

"What did you want to say?"

"What game are you playing? She is young enough to be your daughter!"

"I play no games, centurion."

"She will ruin her life if..."

"What she does with her life is her own responsibility."

Decius was silent for a moment, careful to keep his self-control.

"I saw the way you were looking at each other..."

The Egyptian said nothing, his face mask-like.

Decius took a deep breath and his voice had an edge of sharpness to it when he spoke again.

"I believe you are using magic to entice her to your side."

Was that a flicker of amusement in the Egyptian's dark eyes?

"I do not need to use magic to attract a woman to my side, centurion. You insult me."

"Nevertheless…"

"If you are worried about the way your daughter is conducting her life," the Egyptian spoke after another long and powerfully charged pause, "I suggest you examine your own conscience before you accuse others."

Decius stared at him.

"What do you mean?"

But the Egyptian just shrugged and turned away from him to gaze at the calm pool before him.

Decius stared at his back and felt a black rage welling up in him. With a shout he leapt at him. He seized his shoulders and tried to pull him round to face him.

"What do you mean?" he ground out between clenched teeth.

But the Egyptian offered no resistance.

Decius dropped his hands and stared at him, frustrated, breathing heavily.

He had come to accuse the man and now he himself stood accused. Was he implying that Megan was falling so easily under his influence because she had never had a father to love and guide her? No! This was nonsense. The man was twisting his own thoughts just as he must have been twisting Megan's. He did not believe in magic as gullible people did – but he knew the power of suggestion on the mind. He knew the power of belief.

He had been in Alexandria when Vespasian was there and had seen with his own eyes how the General, soon to be Emperor, had healed a cripple of his infirmity as soon as the Oracle of Serapis had told him that he was destined as Emperor to be a great healer. Before, in Judaea, with wounded and dying all around him, his touch had brought no relief.

"A young girl is vulnerable and susceptible – an easy target for a man of your skill."

"It is not I who has seduced the mind of your daughter, Decius. Look elsewhere for the girl's troubles and leave me alone."

The centurion stared at him long and hard. The black eyes gazed back, unwavering,

"If you are not the cause of her distress," Decius said at last in a humbler voice, "will you help me to help her?"

"She has to help herself."

Decius felt his anger rising again, and turned away, bitter and confused.

When Megan first saw her sister swathed in white robes on the other side of the waters of the Sacred Spring, she despaired. How could she talk to this stranger, this icon? How could she shout the secrets of her heart that even she did not understand across such a space? It would have been better had she not come. Tears filled her eyes.

Ethne read all this on her face and was shocked to see the change in her sister since they had last been together. She raised her veil and the twins gazed across the waters at each other, the one the reflection of the other.

No words passed between them, but in the silence that contained them, they communicated. Megan's fear and confusion lifted sufficiently to allow her for a moment to look into the deep well of her sister's loneliness. They reached out their hands across the water and, though there was no way they could physically touch, it seemed to them they were children again in each other's arms, weeping in the night.

Bridget did not leave them alone long. She had given in to the centurion, but she did not intend to allow Ethne's sister to unsettle her Oracle more than she could help. She glided in as soon as she dared and broke the precious thread that was strengthening every moment between them.

Half dazed Megan suffered herself to be led away, but at the entrance she shrugged off the Mother's hold and turned to have one last look at her sister. Like the water rising in the Sacred Spring from deep within the earth, images and thoughts rose in her mind.

Lucius was clearing out the old barn ready to store the harvest when he was startled to receive a visit from Megan.

At first, seeing her silhouetted in the doorway, his heart leapt, thinking it was Ethne. He scrambled down the ladder from the loft immediately, calling her name. But Megan told him at once who she was. She watched his face curiously as he received the information, and she fancied she saw a shade of disappointment in his eyes.

"But I have come from Ethne," she said quickly.

"You saw her? You saw her as Oracle?"

"Yes. Have you not?"

He shook his head. "I tried, but the High Priestess was very unfriendly when I asked to see her. She wanted to know what I wanted to ask her, and when I could not think of anything she was very angry and sent me away. I haven't dared to try again – though I've been thinking of things I could legitimately ask her about."

"I know Ethne longs to see you."

His eyes lit up. "Did she say so?"

Megan hesitated, wondering why she was there. It had seemed so clear when she was with her sister that she had to bring a message to Lucius. She had, as it were, seen an image of him at the centre of the great pool of loneliness in her twin's heart. Now she wondered if she had been mistaken. Had she been projecting thoughts of her own into her sister's mind? Was it her own confused sexual longings making her believe that Ethne's problems had the same root cause?

But Lucius was waiting eagerly for her answer.

"We did not speak," Megan said at last, "but it seemed to me she was trying to convey an image of you to me. I thought, but perhaps I was wrong... I thought I ought to tell you. She looked so sad and lonely." Her voice broke as she remembered her sister's face.

Lucius stood silently, gravely staring at the ground, going over in his mind the implications of what Megan was saying.

"I too have an image of her in my heart," he said at last in a low voice, "haunting me."

He looked up into Megan's eyes – the eyes that had once set him on fire, but now left him cold. The eyes in every physical way exactly like her twin's, but so very different in expression.

"I love her, you know... but I found it out too late..."

Megan reached out and touched his arm.

"I too have discovered many important things – too late."

"What is to be done?"

"I don't know. Maybe I shouldn't have told you."

"Yes. Yes, you should have. I needed to know. I was afraid she did not feel as I felt."

"She loves you."

"I know now. I will find a way... somehow... We *must* be together!"

Megan was silent. She could see no way that this could be. She was afraid that her interference would result in more suffering for her sister. Did everything she touched end in disaster?

186

Chapter 22

In early August heavy rains came to the valley of Aquae Sulis.

Lucius tramped about the farm in the mud trying to get a premature harvest in before it was ruined.

The rain fell day after day, night after night, and so heavily that the normally placid river swelled alarmingly, overwhelming the landing stage by Aulus' farm, and rushing off down to the sea like a great muscular beast, ripping up trees in its path and washing away sheep and cows from neighbouring fields. Soon all low-lying land was waterlogged, and then flooded. Swans and ducks swam where once golden wheat had ripened in the sun.

Aulus' buildings were on high ground and were reasonably safe, but many wooden shacks near the river where the peasants lived were washed away.

Lucius, thoroughly unsettled by Megan's visit, was trapped on the farm and could not follow his inclination to see Ethne and persuade her to run away with him. Demosthenes at first thought the young man's agitation was due to the problems the flooding had brought, but soon realized there was something deeper and more personal that was bothering him.

Lucius was working so hard these days he scarcely had time for his instruction in the Mysteries of Orpheus. But Demosthenes was anxious that he did not forget that life had a spiritual dimension while he did battle on the physical level to save his father's farm. What use was spiritual muscle, he thought, if you did not use it in everyday life?

One evening when Lucius had come in to dinner exhausted and despairing from the day's toil, Demosthenes spoke about the flood of Deucalian famous in Greek history, and the flood of Noah so important to the Jews.

"In both cases all the fields and the cities were destroyed by the wrath of the gods disappointed and disgusted by the human race's inability to obey a few simple but vital moral laws. In both cases only a few humans and animals were saved to start the living world again."

Lucius, gazing out of the window at the river rising ever higher and eating up more of his land every day, listened with half attention. What was the old man saying? Would he be one of the survivors – or one of the lost?

"Think about it,'" Demosthenes said. "If the rain doesn't stop and almost all is destroyed – what things do you think the gods should preserve? What qualities do you have that would make the gods favour *your* survival?"

Lucius was silent.

"Because I love Ethne," he thought, "and she is worth preserving. Because we two together make something more than ourselves."

He could think of no other reason for his own continuing existence.

The Egyptian's workyard was built close to the river bank and the swirling brown waters made short work of the flimsy buildings and the piles of wood stacked around them. The rock was not so easy to shift, but the unfinished statue of Claudius was toppled and lay half submerged, twigs and debris caught in its arms. All work had to cease.

The Egyptian had taken all that was precious to him onto rising ground in the forest and there erected a makeshift tent to house himself while the rains lasted. The workmen and apprentices returned to their homes in the town, many of them, too near the river, with problems of their own.

Decius fretted whether the statue would now be finished in time for the unveiling in late August, when the Governor was planning to visit.

Some took the unusually heavy floods as a sign that Sul herself was angry and wanted to stop the erection of the upstart god in her sacred precincts. The forecourt of the Temple was under a sheet of water, which lapped even at the steps of the building.

Megan wandered beside the flooded river searching ceaselessly among the debris that was thrown up by the turbulent water. Brendan who found her there one day was shocked at her appearance. Her clothes clung to her, soaked through and muddy, her hair, matted and dull, plastered her face and shoulders. She seemed like some mad woman, muttering to herself.

"Megan!" he gasped. But she seemed not to be aware of him though he was close by her.

"Megan!" he repeated, and put out his hand to take her arm.

She rounded on him like a wild animal.

"What are you doing? Come home. It is dangerous here."

"Leave me alone!" she snarled. "I have to find it, I have to find it…"

She pulled away from him and stooped to overturn a dented pewter jug that had been washed down by the floodwater and was caught in some bushes.

"What are you looking for?"

"Nothing… Nothing," she muttered distractedly.

"What have you lost?"

For a moment, she looked directly at him, eyes blazing, and then she pulled away from him, turning back to her search, even to probing the mud right at the edge of the already crumbling bank.

"You might lose your footing. Don't be a fool! Some people have already been drowned."

As she took no notice he made a grab at her. Jerking furiously away from him, she fell. Temporarily paralysed with shock he watched her disappear beneath the turbulent surface and reappear only moments later much further down stream.

Shouting frantically, he ran along the bank, but she was already out of reach when she disappeared under the water again.

Others came running, hearing his cries, but none could see her or save her.

Megan was searching for the leaden curse she had thrown into the river, sure that the disturbance of the mud on the riverbed would have loosened objects that had lain there for years. As the fierce waters closed over her head, she was suddenly calm. She knew now she had to fetch the curse from the riverbed itself. It would not be given to her. She had thrown it. She must retrieve it. She had created the spell, so she must undo it. No one would help her. No one would hinder her. If she did not succeed she would die.

She was strangely unaware of the battering her body was receiving as it was tumbled and buffeted by the flood. The roaring in her ears, the pain in her chest, seemed part of someone else's reality. At one moment she did not care if she died; at another she feared to go into the Otherworld and risk being reborn into this with the curse still active.

But if she had hoped to see the riverbed clearly, she was disappointed. All was murk and gloom below the surface. Blindly she reached out her hands. Blindly she prayed.

She felt strong arms around her. She felt herself being lifted to the surface.

"No!" her mind shrieked. "I haven't found it. I mustn't leave yet."

But she was dragged gasping into the air and thrown roughly down upon the bank.

"Brendan" she thought, but when she looked up it was not he.

The Egyptian stood above her, his harsh black eyes boring into hers.

He held up his hand – and in it she could see a small roll of lead.

It was not long after Brendan had brought the news to Owein and Olwen that their granddaughter, Megan, had been washed away by the river and was surely drowned, that the Egyptian appeared at their door with the limp and unconscious body of Megan in his arms. Without a word he strode past Olwen weeping at the door and laid the girl down on the nearest bed. Brendan and Owein came forward at once to gaze down at what they believed to be Megan's lifeless body.

The Egyptian straightened up and stood for a moment beside her, gazing too, but with a very different expression in his eyes.

"She is not dead," the Egyptian said quietly, turning to Olwen. "Take care of her." And before another word was spoken he had left the house.

The rain had finally ceased.

Meanwhile in far away Pompeii Julia and Aulus were complaining about the blazing heat of the sun day after day, and the dry black dust that seemed to find its way into everything.

"Does it *ever* rain here?" Julia asked her hostess.

"Sometimes, in winter, but rarely at this time of year."

"At least the houses are built sensibly for this climate," Aulus remarked.

They were walking in the shade of a columned ambulatory that surrounded a small garden rich in exotic flowers, a cool fountain playing at the centre. The rooms of the house, behind them, were well protected from the direct sun's heat and glare.

190

Julia and Aulus had been left in the care of Corvinus and Agrippina when Vespasian returned to Rome, and, though they were treated most hospitably, they were beginning to feel restless. Why had he left them there? When would he recall them to his side? One day it was as though they were his closest friends – and the next as though he had forgotten their existence.

Aulus was seriously worried about money. When they had been in the Emperor's entourage everything had been paid for and they had lived like royalty – but if Vespasian did nothing further for them, how were they to get back to Rome and ultimately back to Aquae Sulis in Britain?

As the days passed and they heard nothing from him, Aulus began to wonder if they had said something to offend him and he had decided he had no obligation to Julia after all. Julia took longer to have doubts – but on this day, when the heat was somehow even penetrating the shady walkways of the house, she was beginning to lose confidence. She surprised herself by thinking about the cool green woods of her homeland with nostalgia. A day or two before she had no regrets about the possibility that she would never return to Britain.

"Do you not find that mountain oppressive? It seems to brood over this city."

Agrippina laughed. "The city would not be so prosperous if it were not for that mountain," she said. "The soil on its slopes is particularly rich and the vineyards are the best in the land. When Corvinus goes there next week we'll go with him and picnic while he inspects the vines."

"I hope we will not be imposing on your hospitality much longer," Julia said hastily. "Surely we'll be back in Rome by next week."

Their hostess smiled politely, and bent her head in a slight bow, but said nothing. In truth, she was as anxious to be rid of her rather boring guests as they were to go – but she could not turn them out.

Decius received one last batch of letters from Aulus and Julia before their return.

Julia's described the uncomfortable journey to the mountain called Vesuvius:

"It took us hours to get there and though we left before the sun was up it was blazing fearsomely when we arrived. Corvinus was busy with his vines and we sat in the shade of olive trees and ate bread and cheese with our wine. I have to admit the scenery was beautiful, but I could not relax, seeing the city so far in the distance and thinking of the bumpy ride back before nightfall.

"The air was very still. I cannot quite explain it. But I felt uneasy as though a malevolent force was watching us. I wonder what Lucius would have made of it. As you know I am not prone to the weird fantasies he is, but even I began to wonder if we are not after all surrounded by invisible beings some of which mean us harm.

"Agrippina dismissed all my qualms with a laugh, and insisted that the mountain was benevolent, and wholly responsible for their very comfortable livelihood. Perhaps she is right, Pompeii is certainly a very rich and fortunate city – in many ways preferable to Rome."

Aulus' letter was written later when they were back in Rome.

It seemed the Emperor had not sent for them and finally they had set off themselves, borrowing money from their hosts for the journey. In Rome they had sought out Vespasian, but were not granted an audience with him. It was clear what these rebuffs meant. Julia was devastated and spent most of the time weeping.

As soon as Lucius could send them more money from the farm, they would set off on the return journey.

Megan lay in bed for several days, tossing and turning and muttering to herself. Olwen sat at her bedside a great deal of the time but could not understand a word she was saying. Sometimes the girl would scream and shrink under the blankets as though she had seen some fearful creature standing behind her grandmother. At others, she lay so still and pale Olwen leaned over her to make sure she was still breathing.

Few visitors were allowed. When Owein was away from the house Olwen admitted her son, and Decius stood beside his daughter's bed for a long while gazing thoughtfully down at her. When he heard that it was the Egyptian who had rescued her so far downstream from his own workyard, he frowned, but said nothing.

Brendan came frequently. Olwen, who had held him in disfavour before for his political recklessness and his apparent indifference to Megan, who clearly loved him, noted that he was a changed man.

He knelt beside Megan's bed holding her hand and gazing passionately at her. It was clear it was he who loved her now.

Megan showed no sign of recognizing him.

At last, on the third day, she appeared to recognize her grandmother and where she was for the first time. Olwen herself did not know whether she wept with relief at her recovery, or sorrow that such a vigorous young woman should have been brought so low.

The first coherent words Megan spoke were to enquire after the Egyptian.

Olwen looked surprised.

"He has not been to see you since he brought you here," she said, "but Brendan has been here most of the time."

"Brendan?" Megan asked wonderingly, almost as though she did not remember the name.

Olwen cast a quick and meaningful look at Owein and the door, and the old man set off at once to fetch Brendan.

The rains had stopped three days before, almost to the moment Megan was brought home, but the town's people were still clearing up, mourning their lost possessions and devastated homes.

When Brendan returned with Owein, Megan was sitting up drinking thin gruel out of a bowl of Samian ware – Olwen's finest.

She looked up when Brendan entered, but seemed indifferent. Brendan's eyes however were aglow with feeling.

"I thought you were dead!" he cried. Not only had he realized that he loved Megan, but he had been consumed with guilt that he had not plunged in to save her, while another man had. "What possessed you to go so near the edge?" he scolded.

Megan looked at him coldly.

"To avoid you!" she said.

Olwen and Owein exchanged glances. There was no mistaking the hostility in her voice. What had happened between them to change their relationship so radically?

Megan handed the bowl of half-eaten gruel to Olwen, and lay down again, turning her face to the wall and pulling the covers over her head.

Brendan looked irresolute and embarrassed.

"She is not well," Olwen said soothingly. "She is not herself yet. Give her a few more days Brendan. She has been through a terrible ordeal."

193

He hesitated, staring at the covered figure on the bed.

Olwen took his arm firmly, but sympathetically, and led him from the room.

As soon as she was well enough Megan slipped out of the house and headed towards the Egyptian's workyard. There she found feverish activity. Some were rebuilding the wooden shacks, and others were clearing the pieces of carved stone that had been temporarily submerged in mud and water. Claudius had been raised again, but his right hand had been broken off and the Egyptian himself was standing before him contemplating the damage.

He turned at once as Megan approached and their eyes met.

He said something at once in a low voice to his assistant and walked towards her. No fiery antagonism sparked between them as it had in the past. Megan's expression was humbled, pleading. His was almost gentle and concerned.

He seemed to know at once why she had come, and took her arm to lead her to his house.

As he drew her through the door, she was half-aware that work in the yard had stopped and curious eyes were following them – but she did not care.

Inside it took her some moments to adjust her eyes from the bright light outside, to the dim interior. He led her towards a small curtained alcove. As though sleep walking she allowed herself to be placed in position as he drew aside the veil. She was facing his little shrine to Isis.

He lit a polished porphyry lamp and the exquisite silver statue of the goddess was instantly illuminated.

On the small alter before her lay the roll of lead Megan had seen in his hand as he stood over her on the riverbank.

Involuntarily she reached out for it, but he caught her hand in his own and held it firmly.

"Not so fast, Megan," he said softly. "We do not take from the gods what we are not offered."

She flushed and took a step back.

This brought her body in contact with his, and she was burningly aware of it.

He felt her hand tremble in his own and increased his grip. She dared not look at him. She knew she should move away from him, but she could not. All that she had hoped to feel with Brendan she could feel in her body at this moment.

He released her hand but put his arm around her waist, and they stood before Isis, straight and silent, as a couple, man and woman.

She stared at the shining image and the tears that had risen to her eyes seemed to dissolve the figure until all the features changed and changed again and all the goddesses she had ever heard of passed before her – maiden, mother, wise old woman. In all her aspects the fertile feminine force of the Cosmos appeared to her. As Sul herself gazed down at her, Megan gave a sob, and the Egyptian's arm tightened around her.

Then he began to speak in a deep and distant voice in a language alien to her ears – yet she felt she knew what he was saying.

As he fell silent again it seemed to her the image expanded into a ball of light, growing every moment larger until it totally encompassed them. He bent his head and within the sphere of light, he kissed her. She turned into his arms and gave herself to the kiss, totally and without reservation or fear. "I love this man," she thought. "I love him!"

When he at last withdrew his lips from hers and she opened her eyes to look again, in wonderment, at the statue of Isis, she saw that the scroll of lead had melted and was now a shapeless lump on the altar.

She looked quickly up at him, her eyes glowing with gratitude and relief, but he seemed to have retreated from her already. His arms released her and he moved away to extinguish the lamp.

"Come," he said quietly, in a voice without emotion, and he moved away from the shrine.

She almost stumbled as she followed him out. Her mind was full of questions. Her heart full of pain. What had just happened? What *had* just happened? Surely he was not just going to ignore her now and pretend nothing had occurred between them?

She knew the curse was negated – perhaps only because the hate she had once felt for him had turned to love. But… but… was that all trickery and illusion in there? Did he not, in fact, love her in return at all?

He strode ahead of her out of the house and across the yard to resume his work. He did not cast a single backward glance at her.

She stood for a long moment staring after him, and then pulled herself together enough to walk away towards the town. She was aware that many of the workmen's eyes were on her, curious and amused. She shivered, trying not to think about the bawdy comments they must surely be making about her as she walked out of earshot.

Almost at the town she encountered Brendan. He frowned when he saw from which direction she was coming.

"Where have you been?" he demanded. "Your grandparents have been sick with worry."

"I have been to see the Egyptian," she said coldly. "I needed to thank him for saving my life."

The angry blood rose in Brendan's face and his hands clenched into fists.

Megan noted this, and tossed her head scornfully.

"Are you not pleased I am alive?"

Brendan glowered. "Of course I am, but…"

Every muscle in his body was taut with emotions he could scarcely control. She brushed past him impatiently and continued on her way. He stood for a moment irresolute, and then turned and hurried after her.

"You must be careful of him. He is…"

"What?" She stopped in her tracks and glared challengingly at him.

"He is an evil man. People say…"

Megan snorted. "People say! Since when have you or I listened to what people say?"

"He is a dangerous man."

"You should have thought of that before you sent me to him to try to stop the statue being made!"

She waited for no more words but strode on towards her home.

He had the sense not to follow – but his thoughts were black and bitter against the Egyptian.

So, he had started it?

He would end it!

Chapter 23

The little Christian community at Glastonia had been growing steadily. The rains had raised the level of the marshes surrounding the island to such an extent that the flowering reed beds, so much a feature of the place, were almost submerged. Paulus alluded to the great deluge at the time of Noah and exhorted his little flock to consider the implications. On the final day when the dark clouds were rolling away to the west, a magnificent rainbow spanned the sky and all their spirits lifted.

Martha, weary of plodding about in the mud, with the sky weighing grey and heavy day after day, longed for the warm and sunny climate of her childhood. She pleaded with her grandfather for their return, reminding him that the terrible persecutions of Nero were over, and the new Emperor at least ignored, if he did not approve of, the followers of the Divine Fisherman.

But Paulus felt he had a mission. He was sorry his granddaughter seemed so dissatisfied and restless, but he was not prepared to leave. He felt he owed it to the Christ, whom he had seen, yet not recognized, to pass on his teaching in this remote place.

As soon as the high ground had drained sufficiently for walking to be easier, Martha climbed the Tor again. The missing hours she had experienced there before began to tease her mind. What could be the explanation? Had she been transported to the Celtic Otherworld and returned without memory of anything that had occurred there?

She was less afraid now than she had been.

The sky seemed to have been washed clean by the rains and was a blue that almost rivalled Rome's. Every green thing seemed to have taken on extra life and the path was almost hidden by lush growth.

She paused about two thirds of the way up, because she thought she heard a sound she could not account for. Was it the cry of a baby? Surely not?

She stepped off the path into the woods and followed the sound.

A tree had fallen, its roots, spider like, exposed. On its prone trunk sat a dark haired woman with a baby at her breast. Martha wondered who she could be. The island was not large and she thought she knew everyone on it. The heavy rains had kept away new arrivals all week, though some might be venturing across the waters now.

The woman looked up and met her eyes. Martha thought she had never before seen such a penetrating and gently loving look. It almost seemed as though the woman knew who she was.

"Good morning," Martha said hesitantly.

The woman smiled, but did not reply.

At that moment, from the left, another woman appeared. This one young and lithe, clad all in green with flowers in her light hair. Martha could have sworn her skin had a greenish glow, but dismissed the observation as nonsense. The green maiden smiled at Martha and then joined the other, sitting at her feet, reaching out to play with the baby's toes. The child lifted its head from its mother's breast and gave a gurgle of delight.

A third woman joined the group, leaning heavily on a stick, hair as silver as the young maiden's was gold. She did not look at Martha, but sat beside the mother on the log and took the baby's hand in hers, smiling fondly into its eyes.

Martha stood watching them for several moments, loath to leave the beautiful and peaceful scene, wondering if she dared to join them and play with the baby. She took a step forward and all three women looked at her. There was no hostility in their expressions. In fact, she felt she was being welcomed to join them, but there was something strange about them. She could not decide what it was... something that set them apart... something that was different...

She knelt down in the grass and smiled timidly at the baby. The infant responded with a broad and innocent grin. She wanted to reach out and touch it – but did not. She looked up into the mother's eyes.

"My name is Martha," she said. "What is the baby called?"

The woman laughed – not in mockery, but with a lovely, musical sound as though in sheer delight.

"We call him The Child – The One – The Lord," she said softly. "What do you call him?"

"I meant..." stammered Martha. "I meant... his given name."

"His given name is secret. It is at the bottom of the Chalice. No one may know it until they drink that draft to the last drop."

"The Chalice?" Martha was startled. The very Chalice she had been seeking since she had come to Joseph's island?

The women seemed to know her. Had they been part of her mysterious experience that day on the Tor?

"Where would I find that Chalice?" she asked breathlessly. "I've looked in the holy well and at the top of the Tor..."

The mother was rising from the log, lifting the baby on to her hip. The young maiden was standing too, shaking the grass and twigs from the shimmering green of her skirt. The old woman was watching Martha intently, leaning on her stick.

"Don't go!" Martha cried. "There are so many questions I want to ask. Where will I find the Chalice? Who are you? Have I seen you before...?"

But suddenly they were not there. She did not see them walk away. They just suddenly vanished in a flicker of leaf-light, leaving her with a terrible sense of loneliness and loss.

To Olwen's delight Megan seemed much calmer after her runaway visit to the Egyptian and she submitted to being fed and pampered and made to rest until the colour came back into her cheeks and the light to her eyes. From time to time she seemed to retreat into herself and have periods of quiet and reserve that reminded her grandmother of Ethne.

Megan felt she was free of the curse at last. No dark, cruel, obscene and disturbing images haunted her. She felt indifferent to Brendan, but no longer hostile. As for the Egyptian, the memory of that long moment when he held her in his arms, brought a glowing secret smile to her lips on more than one occasion. She held the memory close as something beautiful and precious, and hardly dared think beyond it or speculate on what it might mean for the future. For a while she seemed to be in a kind of ante-chamber to life and dared not step over the threshold into a place where she would be obliged to think, and plan, and act.

Owein watched her with less satisfaction than his wife did. She was so quiet and docile – so very different from the Megan he knew.

"She needs this fallow time," Olwen insisted. "She will be back to her old self soon."

But how long Megan would have stayed thus had not something happened to jerk her out of her retreat it would be hard to say.

A neighbour brought news that there had been a fight in the forecourt of the Temple.

"Such sacrilege!" she fussed. "Right at the steps of the Temple of Sulis Minerva!"

Owein looked up, shocked.

"Who was fighting? What was it about?" Had the revolt against the Romans started without him?

"That young Brendan and the Egyptian," the woman said. "I've never seen anything like it!"

Megan's attention was now fully caught. She stiffened up and fixed her eyes upon the messenger, but said nothing.

"How did it start? What was it about?" Owein demanded.

"A young man to attack a man old enough to be his father!" the woman continued. "But I must say the Egyptian held his own very well, and it was Brendan who ended up on the paving."

"Is Brendan hurt?" Owein asked, concerned.

"Only a bit bruised. He was lucky he didn't blast him with some foul black magic instead of just knocking him down."

"The Egyptian doesn't use *foul black magic*," Megan heard her own voice insisting indignantly.

Owein cast a sharp look at her. Since when had she defended the magician? She had been one of the foremost to speak against him in the past.

The neighbour looked equally surprised.

"The Egyptian saved Megan's life when she fell into the flooded river," Olwen said hastily. "He cannot be all bad."

"I must say I hate being near him," the neighbour said, shuddering. "I wouldn't be at all surprised if all the stories about him are true."

"Did you hear what the fight was about?" Owein repeated impatiently. "Was it about the statue?"

"I wasn't there when it started, but I hear Brendan just went up to him and started shouting at him. When I arrived, Brendan was hitting him every way he could and the Egyptian was trying to dodge the blows. At first he wasn't fighting back, but Brendan seemed to be in a terrible rage and at last the Egyptian made a fist and just knocked him out with one blow. I can tell you there must have been some magic in it. Just one blow and he flattened that young man!"

"Was the Egyptian hurt?" Megan asked anxiously.

"The Egyptian? No. Not he. It was Brendan got the worst of it."

"Where is he now?" Owein asked. It would be too bad if their leader were incapacitated just when they needed him most.

"I don't know. The centurion came and chased us away. Quite a crowd had gathered as you can imagine."

"Did Decius arrest the Egyptian?" Megan asked.

"I didn't see. But I shouldn't think so because it was Brendan started the fight – though I'm not saying he might not have been provoked. I wonder what the Egyptian had done to him to put him in such a rage."

Megan pressed her lips together to prevent her replying and slipped away – the others too busy debating the cause of the conflict between the two men to notice her departure.

She hurried through the streets. She must see him. She must see that he was all right. She was sure she knew why Brendan had attacked him.

"Stupid. Stupid boy!" she muttered.

She was sure he would not still be on the forecourt, but something made her go there first.

In fact he was – calmly directing his workmen to lay the stone plinth for the statue and cement it into place as though nothing had happened. He broke away from them at once when he saw her coming, and went to meet her. As they approached each other her agitation lessened. He was manifestly unharmed. But she was still anxious about the cause of the fight, and desperate to disclaim any part of Brendan's behaviour.

His eyes caught hers and held them in a strong and tender gaze. Her heart skipped a beat. Surely she was not imagining the meaning in that look?

They did not touch but stood a little apart from each other like distant acquaintances.

"I heard about the fight," she stammered, flushing under the steadiness of his attention.

He smiled.

"As you see – I am not hurt – though I cannot say the same for your – *friend*."

"Brendan is nothing to me. I don't know what he has been saying to you."

His expression was clearly amused.

"He seems to think that you and he..."

201

"We are *not*!" Megan interrupted hotly.

He raised a quizzical eyebrow.

She glared at him in frustration.

A voice spoke close behind her.

"Megan. Its good to see you well again."

It was her father, Decius, the Roman. She swung round on him, annoyed.

"You would think with all the might of Rome you could prevent people brawling on the steps of the Temple of Sul!" she snapped.

He nodded gravely. "You would think so indeed."

She bit her lip. Was he mocking her?

She turned back to the Egyptian, but he was with his workmen once more, his back to her. Nor did he turn again to look at her, though she stayed several minutes hoping that he would.

Decius moved off to join him and the two men became absorbed in arrangements for the erection of the statue. Apparently forgotten and ignored, Megan moved away.

Ethne, in spite of her isolation, was very much aware of these events. The Temple women were gathered in groups whispering and chatting about the fight almost as soon as it had happened, everyone suggesting a different cause, none guessing the real one. It had happened so quickly and unexpectedly no one had paid much attention to the two men until blows were struck.

Bridget had dispersed the groups. Sometimes she wondered at the wisdom of keeping young girls so closeted from the world that they never had the chance to grow up. She herself had entered the community when she was already mature, having suffered marriage to a violent man who had brought about the death of their only child. She sometimes found the company of women who had experienced nothing of the rough complexity of life tedious.

What were they sniggering at now? A few obscene expletives used by Brendan.

She ordered some to wash down the steps of the Temple and that part of the forecourt that had been contaminated by the fight, while others were to perform a ritual of purification.

Ethne retired to her cell, thankful for the quiet.

Dreams and visions of Megan had disturbed her since they had communicated across the Sacred Spring. At the time of her twin's near drowning in the flooded river she had cried aloud – aware of a kind of dark and swirling vortex threatening to overwhelm her sister. She had "seen" the Egyptian as a giant and luminous figure reaching out and plucking her away from it. She had "seen" her sister in his arms and felt the calm that had come to Megan's troubled heart.

Strange as the coupling of these two very different beings would be, Ethne felt there was a strong and important link between them. Would they be able to withstand the many hazards that were still to be overcome? Or would they be lost to each other as she and Lucius were?

Lucius had not accepted that all was lost.

As soon as he could get away from the farm after the floods, he persuaded Decius to use his influence with the Temple Mother to get him an audience with the Oracle.

Bridget, very well aware that her infatuation with Lucius was the greatest threat to Ethne's peace of mind, had refused on several occasions to let him near her. Once again, the centurion tried to assert Roman authority over that of Sulis Minerva. But this time she was prepared for him. She smiled and bowed and seemed all docility, but when Lucius arrived for his audience, and Decius, lulled by Bridget's apparent acquiescence, was nowhere to hand, the young man was told regretfully that the Oracle was ill and could see no one that day. When he requested a specific date for the postponed appointment, the Mother, all smiles and sympathy, told him she could not give him one until she knew how long the Oracle's illness would last.

If he had been certain that Bridget was lying and that Ethne was again deliberately being kept from him, Lucius told himself as he walked away, defeated, he would have stormed the Temple, seized her and carried her away. But he could not be certain that she was not, in fact, ill.

Lucius told Demosthenes about his frustration in not being allowed to see Ethne in spite of Decius' intervention.

The Greek regarded him thoughtfully.

"This young woman," he asked quietly, "How important is she to you?"

"Very," Lucius insisted. "I know we were meant to be together. Do you remember the time she sang with me?"

"I do." Demosthenes said. "But forgive me – since that time I have not seen you together much. You have not spoken of her. Indeed I was under the impression that it was her sister..."

"It was," Lucius admitted. "But only at the beginning."

"You are sure it is not just because you cannot have Megan, that you have turned to her twin who looks so very much like her?"

Lucius flushed.

"Of course not!" he protested. Demosthenes noticed that he hesitated before he continued. "It may have been that Megan attracted me at first." He paused again, "and she still does. But Ethne is attractive to my soul. She understands me. She loves me. If we are to spend a lifetime together, it will be Ethne who will be my other half, my helpmate. Megan would soon destroy everything I believe in."

Demosthenes knew he was right though he was surprised that a man as young as Lucius could be so wise in his choice of lover. He hoped he would not live to regret his choice. The body often rejects what the soul knows. As far as he, Demosthenes, was concerned, Orpheus himself might well bless the coming together of Lucius and Ethne.

"And what do you think the Goddess Sul feels about your love for her Oracle?"

"I'm... I'm sure..."

But he was not sure. It was clear Lucius had not given this a moment's thought. He had believed the High Priestess was his enemy; but Sul herself could be a more formidable opponent. He remembered how the Oracle had appeared to them on Sul's Hill at the moment of her death.

"I know the Oracle herself chose Ethne to be her successor," he said gloomily.

"But that was the Oracle. Not Sul herself," said the Greek.

Lucius seemed surprised. Surely they were the same? The Oracle was the channel through which the Goddess spoke.

"The Oracle is human. Who knows what pressures she was under to find a successor? I hear the Romans would have done away with the office if a successor had not been found immediately."

"Ethne told me she had always believed the old woman intended her to succeed her."

"I am sure that is so. There are very few people in the world so aware of other realms and other realities, so sensitive in spirit to what is beyond our normal senses. It would be wrong of you to take her from the Temple and expect her to waste her great gifts."

Lucius frowned.

"Are you telling me to leave her alone – to live my life without her?"

"No, I am not. But she must only leave the Temple if it is right for her to do so – right in the spiritual sense. Not for selfish reasons on your part or hers."

"But how can I be sure what to do for the best? How can I *know...?*" Lucius cried.

Demosthenes felt his heart ache for the young man.

"She will know," he said gently. "It has to be her decision to leave the Temple, and it has to be your decision to take her into your life if, and when, she does so. It will be up to both of you together to make of it something worthwhile and meaningful."

Bridget sensed no danger in allowing the Greek priest to consult the Oracle – though she was mildly surprised that he wished to do so.

He made his appointment and awaited his turn, but the night before he was to see Ethne he insisted that Lucius and he held a vigil in the Orphic chapel. From sunset to sunrise they were to watch and wait for Orpheus to make his will known to them.

By midnight Lucius was asleep, his body weary from the labours of the day. Demosthenes, more accustomed to sleep deprivation during important rituals, remained awake, praying and meditating, and occasionally tending the one small lamp whose small and flickering light held the night shadows at bay.

It seemed to Lucius that he was entering a great cavern in an unfamiliar land. Thousands of birds flew out around his head, uttering eerie, high, shrill cries. He ducked and held up his arms to protect his face and, though he could feel the breath of their wings against his skin, none touched him.

After this there was silence as he went deeper into the darkness.

He found the ground sloping downwards and stepped cautiously on the uneven surface as the light from the entrance became a pinpoint in the distance and then failed altogether to illuminate his way. Gradually his eyes adjusted to the dark and he penetrated deep into the earth.

His foot found an even place and then another a little lower down. He realized that he was on a rock-hewn stairway. It was narrow, with a solid wall on his right side, but nothing on his left. He could not see how deep the drop was, but he sensed it was immense. The darkness now was absolute and he felt his way along the wall blindly.

When he had entered the cavern, he had not understood why he was doing so. But now he knew that he was seeking Ethne. He believed he would find her somehow, somewhere in this place.

At the bottom of the steps his foot touched ice cold water and he shuddered and withdrew. There seemed to be a glow in this part of the cavern and within moments he could see that he was beside a wide river, its opaque and milky surface giving no indication how deep it was. He knew he had to cross it and he began to feel an agitation, an urgency, as though Ethne would be lost to him forever if he did not reach her quickly.

Silently a boat he had not noticed before glided out from the far side. It came steadily towards him as though being guided by a boatman, though he could see no one.

It came to rest beside him and he could see clearly now that it was empty.

Heart beating faster he climbed in and was taken across the water.

As his foot touched the shore, he hardly felt it. He seemed almost weightless as he glided over crystal pebbles worn smooth by millennia of underground flooding.

He followed a path he found twisting and winding through a narrow chasm. Eventually it became so narrow that it was no more than a crack with two sides meeting low over his head. He crawled through on hands and knees. Suddenly it opened out and before him he saw a great luminous space with what appeared to be a city of tall crystal buildings, glowing and sparkling in a mysterious but brilliant light, and there, coming towards him, he saw Ethne, holding out her hands to him. He rushed forward and took her in his arms, feeling such a rush of relief and love it almost overwhelmed him.

And then it was all gone. He was lying on the mosaic floor of the Orphic chapel in Aquae Sulis and he was stiff and cold.

Half-dazed he clambered to his feet.

Demosthenes was watching him closely and expectantly.

206

"Well?" he asked after he estimated he had given him enough time to pull himself together.

Lucius was bewildered. The experience had seemed so real. Surely it was not only a dream.

Slowly, hesitantly, he began to tell his mentor all that had occurred. It seemed to both of them that this dream confirmed that he and Ethne were meant to be together.

A few nights after Brendan's attack on the Egyptian in the forecourt, the Egyptian's house, repaired since the floods, caught fire and burned to the ground.

The sculptor himself was not at home but in Corinium, and the workmen who had been told to guard the controversial statue of Claudius while he was away were fast asleep. No one saw anyone come or go. The rumour was that the house had burst into flames spontaneously. This surprised no one and many a word was whispered about spells going wrong and magicians getting what they deserved – though in fact the Egyptian's reputation as a magician rested almost entirely on speculation and prejudice and had in no way been proven.

Although all were curious to see what was inside the house and crowds soon gathered to stare, no one dared venture in to the smouldering ruins to see if anything was left intact.

No one, that is, until Decius arrived.

He, as curious as the rest and less superstitious, started sifting through the blackened remains at once. He found the little stone box in which the Egyptian's precious statue of Isis was kept. It was unharmed; a circumstance which in itself convinced the gawping onlookers that magic was involved.

Not much else survived. Beautifully woven wall hangings and rugs brought from Egypt lay in charred shreds. Exquisite furniture of ebony and ivory was virtually unrecognisable. Decius sighed. There was not much of such quality in Britain and now it was gone.

He carried the box of Isis back to town with him to await the return of the Egyptian.

Then he paid a visit to Brendan.

There had been no damage to the statue of Claudius and no trace of foul play around the house, but the centurion remembered Brendan's attack on the Egyptian before the Temple of Sulis Minerva.

Brendan seemed to be expecting him, which, Decius thought, was suspicious, but he hotly denied any involvement when questioned.

"What makes you think it wasn't an accident?" he demanded sulkily as Decius continued to question him closely.

"The Egyptian was in Corinium," Decius replied, watching the young man's face. He was rewarded with a slight start of surprise. Had murder been the intention? "The house was empty. There would have been no lamp lit. Nothing to start a fire."

"Who knows what the man does in there! Sulis Minerva has perpetual fire that never dies in her temple – perhaps Isis demands that too."

Decius shrugged. "It is possible. We won't know until the Egyptian returns. Meanwhile I would like to know where you were in the small hours of last night."

"Asleep in bed of course!" Brendan snapped.

"Of course!" Decius repeated ironically.

"Why this harassment?"

"Why did you attack the Egyptian in the forecourt earlier this week?"

Brendan snorted.

"That! I might have known! You Romans spy on everything. Two men can't have an argument without your interference."

"It seemed to me to be more than an argument."

"Well – it wasn't!"

"What was it about?"

Brendan scowled. "It was a personal matter. Nothing for the great Roman Empire to be concerned about."

"The Roman Empire is great *because* it concerns itself about every little detail that may disturb the peace."

But Brendan would not give any explanation and Decius knew he had not enough evidence to hold him for arson and attempted murder.

He left, but not before he warned Brendan that further investigation might well reveal the cause of the fire.

As he walked away, he could almost feel the heat of Brendan's hatred scorching his back.

Decius asked his sister Elen if she would house the Egyptian for a while, but such was the general fear and prejudice against the man, she would not hear of it. He then detailed some of his own men to construct a makeshift house as best they could close to the site of the old one. He himself was frequently to be seen in the area checking on progress and poking about in the ashes for clues to how the fire had started.

The soldiers, glad to have something to do at last, were more than halfway through when the Egyptian returned. Decius was standing in the ruins of the old house staring thoughtfully at something he had just found, when he noticed that suddenly   everything had gone very quiet. A moment before there had been a steady background noise of hammering wood, chipping stone, whistling, talking and humming.

Now there was nothing.

He glanced up and saw the Egyptian standing a few feet away from him on the blackened threshold of his former home. Everyone on site had ceased to work and was watching him. As though the scene was frozen in time Decius was aware of two soldiers poised holding a heavy log between them as though it were a feather weight. Two others were balanced precariously on a wall not yet fully secured. Beyond them men were standing with hammers raised over chisels, while further away boys drawing water from the river in leather buckets straightened their backs and stared.

To Decius it seemed the Egyptian's eyes were dark wells of black fire as he gazed around him: his face as though carved in stone.

"Your Goddess is safe," the centurion hastily assured him. "I have her in town – safe." He repeated the word to emphasize the point as the Egyptian turned that terrible gaze on him. No flicker of expression crossed the man's face – not even of relief.

"No one knows how the fire was started," Decius continued.

Silence.

"I'm sorry so much has been destroyed. As you can see we've started building you a temporary shelter." He nodded to the right where many of the timbers of the new construction were already in place. The Egyptian glanced briefly at the soldier's work and then back to the shell of his home.

"We'll lend you a hand to rebuild your house when you are ready," Decius added. And then, as the man still said nothing: "I have to know if you had left any lamp burning – any fire – possibly on an altar – anything that could have fallen over and started the blaze."

The Egyptian was scanning the ruins steadily, penetratingly.

"I need to know that. Because if..."

"I left no fire alight." The man spoke at last in a clipped and colourless voice.

Decius took a deep breath. The simple solution to the mystery had been eliminated.

"Have you any idea who might have done this?" he asked.

Decius stood where he was for a while, but it was clear no answer would be forthcoming.

"Well, I'll be going now," he said. "If you need me – or think of anything..."

The Egyptian did not turn his head at his departure and Decius did not linger.

In his hand he still held what he had found among the ash.

When Megan, hearing the Egyptian was back from Corinium, set off along the path to the workyard, Brendan was waiting for her. He appeared suddenly in front of her, wild eyed and dishevelled, having spent long hours in the bushes waiting for her.

"Brendan!" she gasped, and there was no mistaking the dismay in her voice.

"Yes, Brendan!" he repeated savagely. "Remember me?"

"I remember you," she said coldly. Although she now appeared to be in control of herself after the initial shock, she took a step backward.

"Where are you going?"

"Just walking."

"You are going to *him*!" He spat out the last word as though it was venom.

"Him?"

"You and he are lovers. Everyone knows."

"Does everyone know *you* and I were lovers?" Her eyes flashed.

"You don't deny it?"

"What – that you and I made love like rutting animals in a ditch?"

This was too much for Brendan. All the pent up emotion of the past days and nights burst like a red tide against a rocky shore. He leapt at her and brought her to the ground. She was strong, but he was stronger, and he managed to drag her off the path into the bushes where he had lain hidden for so long. She did not scream but she fought desperately to free herself. He was a warrior by nature, held in check too long and frustrated beyond endurance. He would have conquered her if suddenly he had not been seized from behind and dragged off her.

Now, in the iron grip of the Egyptian, it was his turn to struggle. At a disadvantage from the start because of what he had been about to do, Brendan lost ground rapidly and once again, after a brief and savage fight, was knocked out.

Without waiting to see if he were seriously hurt or not, the Egyptian seized Megan's wrist and pulled her to her feet, and then led her back along the path towards town. She was shaking and bruised. It was strange how he always seemed to be there when she needed him. Was he watching over her in some mysterious way?

At last, just before the first houses appeared he stopped, released her wrist and looked into her eyes. She flushed.

"Once again," she murmured, "I have you to thank for..."

"You are safe now. Return to your home."

"What if I don't want to go home?"

"You will do it nevertheless."

"I...I don't even know your name."

It had never bothered her before. In fact, she had never really noticed that no one spoke his name. He was always "the Egyptian". She had never felt the need to know it – but now she did. How could she hold him in her heart if he had no name?

The Egyptian stared into her eyes for a long time, and it seemed to her that his face was not as expressionless as it usually was, and there was a softening of the stern lines around his mouth. There was even a glimpse of the tenderness she had seen in his eyes that other time.

"My name is – Ra-hotep," he said in his deep voice, but very quietly. Somehow she knew that she was the first person to be given his true name in Britain.

"Ra-hotep," she whispered, savouring the sound as though it were a beautiful taste on her tongue.

He lifted her right hand, spread it out palm upward with his fingers, and stooped and kissed it. Then he whispered his name into her palm and shut her fingers over it. She knew by this action that she must not speak his name for others to hear.

* * *

Decius was waiting for Megan when she reached home.

She groaned inwardly when she saw him. Why did her father not leave her alone? Had she not made it clear to him that he was nothing to her? She was exhausted and could think of nothing she wanted more than to be alone to sort out her thoughts and feelings about the desperation in Brendan's face, and the tenderness in Ra-hotep's.

Her father greeted her without a smile, noting silently the dust on her cheek, the tear in her dress, and the bruise on her arm.

"Where have you been, daughter?" he asked sternly.

Her eyes flashed. "Why? Do I have to give an account of everywhere I go these days? Can I not walk about the town without having to be questioned by a Roman?" She always made that word sound like an insult.

Decius did not reply at once but regarded her steadily, and then, without a word, lifted his right hand and held up an object for her to see. It was a bracelet of fine gold chased with an elaborate enamelled design typical of Celtic workmanship.

She reached out her hand for it, but he held it back.

"Not so fast, daughter. Do you recognize this?"

"Of course. It is mine. Where did you find it?"

"Where did you lose it?"

She shrugged – but she was disturbed. Why was he staring at her like that?

"I found it at the Egyptian's house," he said quietly.

She started – and he noticed it. But almost immediately she composed her face into an expression of cold indifference.

"It might not be mine after all," she said. "Ethne has one exactly the same."

"May I see yours then?" he asked.

She glared at him.

"What are you implying?"

"Nothing. I would like to see your bracelet if this is not it."

"Why?"

"Because I want to know how this particular bracelet came to be in the Egyptian's house."

Megan thought rapidly. Did she lose it that day he held her in his arms before Isis? She had not seen it since that day.

"Am I not allowed to visit the Egyptian?" she said at last, with a toss of her head.

Decius' face darkened.

"*Did* you visit the Egyptian?"

"What is it to you if I did?"

"As your father..."

"You are no father of mine," she snapped. "You resigned that office when you ran away."

The conflicting emotions of anger and shame vied for a place in his heart. Since he had returned to Aquae Sulis there had been many times he regretted his youthful decision to leave his family. He longed to be accepted by Megan and his father as he had been by Ethne and his mother. But there seemed no chance of it.

"All right – not as a father then – but as a man who cares about you – I warn you to keep away from the Egyptian."

"Warn me!" she shrieked. "Warn me? Why?"

Decius was silent. He had a certain respect for the man, but there were too many things mysterious and alien about him for a father to trust his young daughter to him. Only a few days before he had left for Corinium, some apprentice returning to pick up something he had left behind at the end of the day, claimed to have seen an amazing glow within the house.

"It was terrifying," he said. "It was as though the house was possessed! I wanted to go nearer and look through the window – but something, some demon, pushed me back. I can tell you I didn't stay. I ran!"

Decius had wondered about this mysterious "glow" when the house had burned down. But if it was a feature of some secret ritual the Egyptian practised it would not have set the house alight when he was away. No, the fire would be more likely to have been caused by one of those superstitious oafs who thought the house was "possessed". Perhaps a gang of them, full of bravado and prejudice when the Egyptian was far away. He hoped not – for he still wanted to pin the guilt on Brendan.

"If you cannot see that the man is old and very strange..."

"He is not as old as you – and as for strange – is there anything stranger than a Celt fighting in the Roman army?"

"You know nothing about him, Megan. You are so young. How can you know what men like that expect of women?"

She snorted.

"And you do, I suppose."

"I have lived in many countries and seen many sights I wish I had not. Beyond this valley you cannot imagine what the world is like."

"The world is in this valley, and this valley is in the world," she said. "Look around. Is there anything different here? There are conquerors and conquered, hate and love, friendship and enmity, kindness and cruelty..."

He raised his hand to stop her.

"All right," he said. "You have made your point. But take care what you do – for nothing is without consequences."

"And nothing is without cause," she replied.

For a moment the two gazed at each other steadily, trying to see into each other's hearts. Decius fancied his hostile daughter was less hostile, but he could not be sure.

He threw the bracelet down on the table, and turned and left the house.

Chapter 24

Almost as soon as Demosthenes entered her presence the Oracle went into a trance and a voice spoke through her, so deep, so familiar, that the Greek was almost moved to tears.

Around him were the forests and marshes of the ancient days, and before him was the man who had been as humble as a swineherd and as mighty as a king; the man who had tried to bring culture to a savage land, and who had died as a Seer beyond his time.

As he spoke of his aspirations and his hopes, Demosthenes remembered. He *had* been to this land before, many centuries before, brought from Greece to found an academy. He remembered strenuous debates with Druid priests. He remembered the stone temple of Apollo and the man who climbed onto the roof. He remembered the great sailing wings, the lift against the sky, the plummeting, the falling, the death … not only of a man rare in any time, but also of a dream for a different world, a better world.

"Bladud!" he whispered. "Great King." And he knelt on the cold stone the Romans had laid down and bowed his head.

The Oracle spoke on, exhorting him to ensure peace in this beautiful and sacred valley. She begged him to persuade the Governor not to raise a statue that symbolized worldly power in the sacred precinct. "If all the places where people look up, become places where people look down, what hope is there?"

"It is too late," Demosthenes thought. "How can I stop it? All the arrangements have been made."

"Sire…"

He raised his eyes half expecting to see the great king before him in the flesh, his heart burning with all the questions he wanted to ask. But in front of him was a young girl swathed in white, dark eyes in a pale face, gazing at him in bewilderment as though she had just woken from a powerful dream.

The King had gone.

Slowly Demosthenes rose to his feet, for the first time feeling his age in the aching of his bones. Slowly he straightened up and met

Ethne's eyes. In them he read her longing to speak with him person to person, not as oracle to supplicant – but he was not yet ready. He was drifting between ages, torn by Time into disparate elements. Like fleeting images at the limits of his vision, fragments of memory teased him from a past life, but disappeared as soon as he tried to make sense of them. The legend of the ancient King Bladud who had tried to bring the culture of Greece to Britain, who had founded the first healing sanctuary in the valley of Sul, and who, like Daedalus, had mastered the art of flight, was well known to him. It had always fascinated him. Was it just the story he had heard that made him believe he heard the voice of Bladud or was the great King himself still in the valley, still trying to make his people worthy of their finest aspirations?

As the days and nights went by Ethne struggled to accept her life as Oracle, and she believed she had almost succeeded in doing so when she had a disturbing dream. It seemed so vivid, so powerful at the time, that when she woke she could not believe that it had been, in fact, a dream. Lucius and she were together in a little wooden house in the middle of a beautiful forest, apparently husband and wife, with a babe at her breast, and two other children playing happily nearby. She felt totally safe, as though she was contained in a cocoon of love.

Then one cold and bitter winter night as they sat snug beside their hearth fire, they heard a knocking at the door.

"Don't open it," was her first thought – not wanting anything or anyone to spoil their idyll – but then she crossed the room herself and flung open the door. As the light from her lamp fell on the stranger outside they saw a gaunt and ragged man, leaning heavily on crutches, so thin with hunger he was almost a skeleton.

For a long moment she stared at him and he at her, and then she invited him in out of the cold. Within moments he was beside their fire, a rug thrown over his shivering shoulders and a bowl of hot soup put before him. Because he was shaking too much to hold the bowl, she herself fed him, while Lucius put more logs on the fire. The children stood at his knee asking questions – but he said nothing in reply. She remembered some bread she had baked that day, unfinished at their evening meal. She turned to fetch it. And when she turned back everything had disappeared, the fire-lit room, the wooden furniture so lovingly made by Lucius, the children, the babe in the crib, Lucius, the starving man – all was gone – and she was alone in her cell at the Temple – weeping.

Who was the man? She could not forget his face. His suffering haunted her.

Gradually an interpretation came to her. She believed she knew the meaning of the dream. She had thought she was following the highest spiritual path available to her – but what if she was wrong? Were repetitive rituals and stern denials of the flesh really necessary for the development of the soul? Would the soul in fact not grow stronger with every-day trials and tribulations to cope with, with the self-denials that came from love, and with the acceptance of responsibility for one's own decisions and actions? Was she not harming the people who consulted her by denying them the chance to make their own decisions?

Suddenly she knew that to leave the Temple would not be a negative act, but a positive one. She would not be turning her back on the spiritual path but stepping on to it.

The new batch of soldiers ordered by the Prefect to help Decius enforce the peace marched into town fresh, vigorous and disciplined with an officer in charge who looked as though he was eager for a battle. He and his men were hard and smart, spending many hours drilling and training, ready for anything.

Decius sighed as he compared them with his own men who had marched into Aquae Sulis in similar fashion but, having enjoyed a relatively quiet and pleasant stay, were now relaxed. Some had expressed a wish to settle in the valley when their years were up and had made friends among the locals. Others, still restless for the world, were yet content to take what they considered a holiday. Most had been fooled by Brendan's apparent abandonment of hostility. Decius was one who had not – yet he was not pleased to see the reinforcements, knowing how ruthless the Roman military machine could be when it was roused. He had witnessed enough in Judaea to have no illusions.

He still had precedence over their officer, but one look at him told him that would not be an easy precedence to maintain. The man, Gaius Agrippa, was tough and would not hesitate to send reports to seniors if Decius did not measure up.

* * *

217

The triangular pediment for the Temple of Minerva was completed in record time, the men working with enthusiasm. Decius took Gaius Agrippa to the Egyptian's workyard the second day he was in town to inspect the work that had been done. They agreed the pediment should be put in place if possible before the Governor's visit.

The day it was raised into position the forecourt was closed to the public, the area being filled with workmen and lifting gear. The soldiers, fit, muscular and skilled at lifting heavy siege apparatus and war machines, lent a hand.

Bridget locked the door of the Temple and she and her priestesses endured as best they could the noise that accompanied the work. No one noticed a slim figure, heavily veiled, slipping out of the back door of the Temple living quarters and gliding away into the busy street of market stalls. The following day had been declared a festival and this day all were looking forward to the excitement, the streets crowded with matrons stocking up with food for the celebratory feasts, stall holders and entrepreneurs of every kind preparing their wares.

Brendan stayed away. He had no interest in the pediment apart from bitterly condemning it as a cynical diversionary tactic by the Romans.

They had brought the pieces by river, wheeled cart and sledge at first light, rousing the town with bustle and noise. They worked hard all day.

At midday, Decius thought the work would never be completed in time for the festival, but before the late summer sunlight failed that night, it was in place. By half-light and flickering torchlight, he surveyed the pediment he had not seen complete before.

He wondered what the priestesses thought about having a male head upon their Temple. When first told, Bridget had strenuously objected but had quietened down when the whole scene had been explained to her.

Demosthenes had instructed the Egyptian well. Minerva's shield was at the centre as expected, but instead of a Gorgon's head to turn all enemies to stone, there was a magnificent male head. It was a combination of the British Bladud, the man who was believed to have mastered the art of flight, both physically and spiritually; and Aesculapius, the Greco-Roman god of healing. Bladud's wings and Aesculapius' snakes emerged from flaming locks that surrounded the mighty face like the burning flames of the sun.

Minerva's handmaids, Winged Victories, held the shield aloft triumphantly, garlanded with flowers and ripening fruits. Beings, half man, half fish, blew trumpets of celebration from the deep ocean, the mysterious realm of spirit in which we all have our being.

Two helmets were depicted, one with Minerva's owl of wisdom perching on its crest. Two spheres bound with thongs puzzled Decius for some time and then he thought they might represent the sun and the moon controlled by a great force beyond human comprehension.

It was a wonderful affirmation of the timeless power of spirit that manifested through forms in time and space but was limited by neither.

Decius gazed and gazed as meaning after meaning came to him. He had no idea when he ordered the head to be carved that he was doing anything more than throwing a bone to the hungry dogs of rebellion to distract them from the statue of Claudius. The Greek Demosthenes and the mysterious Egyptian between them had created a powerful and important symbol that went far beyond the rivalry of Celt and Roman.

People love an "occasion" and the next morning before the sun was up the forecourt was filled to capacity and still they tried to push in from the neighbouring streets.

As the sun rose and shone directly onto the pediment a cry of admiration went up. Even Brendan, standing with arms folded and a glare of disapproval on his face, was awed by the power of the great head. Most could not read the meaning as Decius had the night before, yet nevertheless the symbolic message encoded there, worked subliminally. Like the wind bending the stalks as it blew through corn, the people, one after the other, bowed down before it.

Decius, Demosthenes and the Egyptian standing together were well satisfied.

Meanwhile, within the Temple all was not well. Bridget had planned that she and her priestesses would be ranged on the steps to greet the dawn. Special prayers were to be offered up linking Sul and Bladud, Minerva and Aesculapius and calling on their combined help, male and female, against the dark forces of the Underworld. She planned for Ethne to deliver the prayer, calling on their powers of prophecy and healing.

But Ethne was not to be found,

Instead of an orderly phalanx of priestesses on the steps of the Temple as the sunlight hit the carving, the women were searching frantically behind the scenes. Some were despatched across the forecourt to the Sacred Spring to see if she was there, and had to push their way uncomfortably through the crowds.

She was not there.

"We cannot wait any longer," Bridget said impatiently, a furrow of anxiety and anger between her brows. "Stupid girl!" she muttered under her breath, abandoning her usual respect for the Oracle. "What game is she playing? She knows how important this moment is!"

But the moment had to take place without the Oracle.

One by one the priestesses filed out and took their places on the stairs, their positions echoing the triangle of the pediment, with Bridget in the place of the star at the summit. Ethne should have been at the centre – but the centre was empty.

The crowd did not at first notice her absence, no doubt thinking that she would appear at some more dramatic moment in the proceedings, but Megan, pushing in late from the riverside, wondered. Demosthenes did not, for he alone knew where she was.

Late the previous night a little boat had drawn up at the steps of Aulus farm, and a weary, frightened young woman had hammered at the door of the house. Lucius had found her first and when the Greek reached the place she was already folded in his arms.

It was some time before Ethne could compose herself enough to speak and when she did she tried to convey to them her reasons for leaving the Temple.

"I had a dream," she said with a sob. "I can't tell you … it wouldn't make sense to you, but..."

"You don't have to explain anything now, child," Demosthenes said gently. "Rest a while and then we will talk."

"You must not think I have run away just to be with..." She flushed scarlet, and looked into Lucius' eyes with such desperation and embarrassment that Demosthenes heart ached for her.

Lucius kissed her forehead and murmured incoherently into her hair.

She pulled away from him, trembling, but determined to make the point clear.

"I know it must look as though..." But she could not continue.

"You came to friends you knew would support you," Demosthenes suggested, and she looked at him gratefully through her tears.

"You are safe now," Lucius said. "I'm never going to let you go."

"No. No, Lucius. I didn't mean... you must not... *we* must not..."

She was on the verge of breaking down again.

Demosthenes stepped forward and put his arm around her shoulders, drawing her away from Lucius.

"I think, Lucius, Ethne should be shown a room where she might sleep for a while. We will talk later about what has been done and what should be done. Now is not the time."

He spoke with such quiet authority that Lucius found himself ushering his beloved into Julia's room and leaving her there, curled up like a kitten on the bed.

Demosthenes knew that the Oracle's desertion at this particular moment would cause the maximum furore in the town and perhaps he would not have advised it. But he could see that whatever the deeper reasons she might have had for leaving, she had been driven to it by an overwhelming sense of personal urgency.

"It seems to me," he said to his young pupil, "that Ethne is in no fit state to face up to arguments and persuasion, and indeed, anger, now. She needs time to take control of herself again. If, when she has calmed herself, she believes she has made a mistake in leaving, it will be time enough to go back." He saw the look of alarm on Lucius' face and raised his hand to reassure him. "But if she still believes she made the right decision, then she will have a greater strength with which to stand her ground."

"She must never go back! I'll not let her!" Lucius cried.

"Then you will make her as much a prisoner as the Temple Mother did," Demosthenes said drily. Lucius pouted like a spoiled child. "I suggest you take her right away from here and give her time to think. Did you not say you made friends with some people in the Nazarene community on that island you visited?"

"They are not exactly friends," Lucius said doubtfully.

"Bridget would not think of seeking her there."

"You are right! I'll take her there and we'll stay until Bridget gives up the search."

"It would be better for her if you did not stay with her," Demosthenes said. "It is important that she is clear about what she is doing and why. If you are there she will think only of you."

He knew that Ethne was in the grip of powerful emotions at this time, and that emotions can change as easily as the wind. But this he did not say to Lucius.

At last, unwillingly, because he could think of no alternative, Lucius agreed that he would take Ethne to Glastonia and leave her there.

"But only for a day or two," he insisted.

"Only a short while," the Greek said quietly.

Across the crowd the eyes of Megan and Ra-hotep met – and held.

From her position at the back, Megan could scarcely hear the words that Bridget and her women intoned, nor did she care. She had not seen the Egyptian since he had given her his name, though she longed to do so. Determined to be nearer him, she manoeuvred her way painstakingly through the mass of excited people in the forecourt. He must have had the same thought for she suddenly came upon him edging towards her. Around them, all attention was on the ceremony at the Temple of Sulis Minerva. It was as though they were alone in a thick forest of trees pressing closely around them. He took her hands and held them in his own. She seemed to drown in the dark intensity of his gaze. She murmured his name so low it was scarcely more than a breath, yet he heard it. The pressure on her hands increased. For a blissful moment it seemed he would take her in his arms, but the crowd suddenly surged backwards and they were pushed apart. Frantically Megan strained to reach him again, but the mass of people already between them hid him from her sight. It was as though he had been spirited away.

A voice beside her made her heart sink. It was Brendan.

"Let's get out of here," he said taking her elbow and beginning to tug at it. "There's nothing for us here. It's only Roman cunning at work again."

She tried to pull away, but he held firm and conducted her back towards the open streets. Searching over her shoulder for Ra-hotep, she could see the new officer marshalling the crowd into some kind of order. It may well have been his activities that had caused the wedge to be driven between her and the Egyptian.

She gave up trying to find him. What would be the point anyway with Brendan there?

After the formal ceremony the festivities began in earnest. The crowds broke up into smaller groups and wandered the town, shouting and laughing and wishing each other well. Jugglers, dancers and musicians performed on street corners. Stallholders sold their wares. Friends hugged each other and strangers were welcomed.

Brendan drew Megan down to the river's edge where the boats were tied, and sat with her on a piled coil of rope. After his recent treatment of her, he was surprised that she came with him without a fight. She seemed resigned to his company, although clearly not enjoying it. He kept firm hold of her arm even when they were seated. He was determined not to let her escape before he had some answers. He decided to start with the least personal of the problems between them.

"You have not been to meetings lately. I hope you haven't forgotten your vow."

Megan sighed. That self who had so enthusiastically embraced the movement of rebellion and who had hung on its leader's every word seemed long since dead. She could not believe she was supposed to be the same person. She took her time answering – forcing herself to think about the issues involved and her current attitude to them. It seemed to her she was still against the Roman occupation, but somehow other matters, her feelings for Ra-hotep for instance, had taken precedence over that angry commitment. But she *had* vowed, and she still believed the Romans had to be shown that the local population were not cowed and would not stand by to be insulted and humiliated.

"I'm sorry," she said mildly. "I have not been well."

Brendan glanced sideways at her, surprised. Was this the fire and brimstone Megan he had known, the first and foremost of his lieutenants?

"It is all going to be more difficult now that extra soldiers have been sent. We need to be more committed than ever."

Megan nodded – but listlessly – as though she did not really care.

"Megan!" he cried. "Wake up! What is the matter with you? Don't you realize some of us might lose our lives?"

"I have not forgotten my vow. You needn't worry. I'll be there beside you," she said, but so expressionlessly he could not determine the true feeling behind the words.

"It is too dangerous to have anyone involved whose whole heart is not in it – vow or no vow."

"I will be there. And my heart will be in it."

He sat in irritated silence for a while, watching her impassive face.

"Is it because I was too rough with you that night? A virgin sometimes..."

He stopped in mid-sentence as he met the blaze of her eyes. That was more like the old Megan – but it did not comfort him.

"Forget that night! It was a terrible mistake."

"If you would only..."

She ripped her arm away from his hold and stood up. For a moment she glared down at him as though she was going to say something, and then it seemed she changed her mind and turned to walk away.

When she was some way from him she looked back and called out bitterly: "I'll be there. You can count on it!"

He started to rise to follow her, and then thought better of it and subsided back onto the coil of rope, staring into the river as it flowed strongly past him carrying leaves and twigs and an old discarded sandal down to the sea.

Lucius and Ethne set off at first light on his father's two best horses, and were well on the way to Glastonia by the time the sun rose.

Bridget brooded on what was to be done now that Ethne had disappeared. The girl would not have run away at such an important moment if she had not been driven to it by some uncontrollable passion. The Mother remembered the young man calling out to her so desperately during her first public appearance. She remembered also Ethne's protests at being forced to take on the deprivations and responsibilities of the office. The question was – could she be enticed back? Could she be shamed into coming back? Could Ethne be forced back? And if she could not – how would the Temple's standing in the community be affected? The Oracle had drawn pilgrims from other tribes and other countries for centuries. Just the week before a family from the very south of Iberia had consulted her and gone away content. For a moment, Bridget wished she had accepted Gwynedd as Oracle. She might not have such a reliable link to the Goddess as Ethne, but her sense of duty towards the Temple was unquestionable.

She sent one of the novices to find out where Gwynedd now was, with instructions to report back without alerting her to the problem they were facing.

"If you have to speak to her, make it seem you have come upon her by accident on the way to somewhere else. No one must know the Oracle has left us. No one. Do you understand? If a breath of this gets out the Romans will take away what little remnants of power we have left and the people will have recourse only to divination by slaughtered animals and bloody entrails, the Romans controlling our dialogue with the gods as they control everything else."

Soon after the dawn prayers on the day after the celebrations for the new pediment, the novice set off to find Gwynedd, and Bridget set off to find Ethne. She left behind a group of anxious women, whispering and confused, pessimistic about the future, going about their daily rituals with less attention than usual.

Bridget arrived on the river steps of Aulus' farm as the sun was lifting above the trees. She instructed the boatman to wait for her and strode determinedly up the path towards the house. The farm workers were already out in the fields, the household slaves preparing food in the kitchen. For a moment Bridget herself had a twinge of nostalgia for the time as a child when she had been part of a normal home, with chickens clucking in the yard, and her mother lovingly brushing her hair. In those days her father was not the drunkard he later became and they were a happy family. She almost turned back – understanding why Ethne would want this life instead of the one they offered her, but her own power in the community, depending as it did largely on the famous Oracle, made her continue her pursuit.

She was almost at the house when a voice spoke her name. She spun round and found the old man, the Greek priest, behind her.

She bowed her head politely.

He returned her greeting gravely.

For a moment the two watched each other silently.

Eventually Demosthenes spoke first.

"I'm afraid the family is from home," he said. "Aulus and Julia not yet returned from Rome, and Lucius away visiting friends."

225

Bridget looked at him suspiciously.

"It is Lucius I was hoping to see. How long has he been gone from home?"

"Oh, some time, I believe. The friends live a long way away."

Bridget pursed her lips.

"Would you know if a young girl visited him yesterday?"

"Yesterday I was attending the festivities in town," he replied. "Why do you ask?"

"One of my…" She paused, wondering if she could trust him. "The young Oracle, Ethne, has disappeared."

Demosthenes said nothing, nor, she noted, showed surprise.

"What do you know of this?" she demanded.

"I know that the girl was unhappy at the Temple," he said quietly.

"If she was, sir," Bridget said haughtily, "it was only because she was infatuated with the young man Lucius. I believe she has shamefully abandoned all her duties and responsibilities to run away with him."

"There are always more motives than one behind every action," the Greek said mildly.

Bridget's eyes flashed.

"Where is she, sir?"

"She is not here."

"I can see that. But I suggest you know her whereabouts."

"It is true she is with Lucius – but more I cannot tell you."

"Cannot – or will not?"

"You would be advised to let her be for a while. She needs time to think."

"If I give her time with Lucius – she may not be fit to be an oracle when she returns. You, as a priest, must surely understand that!"

"I do not believe they will do anything to jeopardize…"

"Are you mad! Do you know nothing of young people when the blood is hot?"

"I am sure both are capable of self-control…"

"She has certainly demonstrated *that*!" said Bridget sarcastically.

"I think you underestimate her very real commitment to the spirit world, madam."

"How can you say that when she has just flouted her commitment and for all we know, broken her sacred vows of chastity."

"I do not believe she would do that lightly, madam. Nor would Lucius demand it."

226

Bridget snorted.

"You are naïve, sir, for all your great age."

"And you are determined to believe the worst and shut all doors to understanding."

She stood silently for a while, seething with irritation.

"Can you tell me why she did not have the courtesy to speak to me before she left and explain her reasons?"

Demosthenes sighed.

"I do admit in that she was remiss, and in that she showed her youth. But tell me, madam, was she ever a willing oracle? Did she not on many occasions ask to be released and was refused?"

Bridget bit her lip.

"She knew that Sul had chosen her," she said sullenly.

"I heard that the object of succession was broken at her feet. Might this not have indicated that Sul herself was content for the oracle's role to end?"

Bridget glared at him furiously.

"It is clear you are determined to shield her from the consequences of her action," she said icily. "I trust others will not be so keen."

She turned on her heel and strode with what dignity her rage allowed her back to the boat.

It was unfortunately not Decius Brutus who found out first that Ethne was missing, but Gaius Agrippa. Noticing that a young woman from the Temple of Sulis Minerva was "acting suspiciously" he decided to question her.

The young novice, Corilla, had seen Gwynedd in a crowded street and was following her, hiding behind corners and stalls whenever she stopped, and ducking and diving after her when she was on the move.

When the Roman soldier's hand descended on her shoulder Corilla gave a terrified shriek and it did not take him long to find out what she was doing and why.

Trembling and weeping she returned to the Temple, dreading confrontation with Bridget. Not only had she failed to establish where Gwynedd was living, but she had revealed the very secret Bridget wanted to keep to the very people she most wanted to keep it from.

Bridget was angry, and every woman in the Temple sought to

227

avoid her presence. The young culprit herself was told icily to leave the Temple and never return. Forlornly she obeyed, knowing that the disgrace of being dismissed from the service of Sulis Minerva would follow her all her days.

Ironically, as she turned the corner into the market street, she came face to face with Gwynedd. Startled, she stopped short, gazing wide-eyed at her.

"Do I know you?" Gwynedd asked, noticing the stare.

"No. No. Not at all," mumbled Corilla.

"Why do you look at me like that? Are you from the Temple?"

At this Corilla burst into tears.

"I have seen you before. You *are* from the Temple!"

"Not any more. I've been sent away." Gwynedd could scarcely hear the words accompanied as they were by floods of tears and noisy sobs.

She took the girl's arm and led her away from the forecourt and the busy street, down a quieter side ally.

"Tell me what has happened. Why have you been sent away?"

It was some time before the sobs eased off enough for her to speak, and then she told Gwynedd everything, believing now that secrecy was no longer necessary. Having told the Romans, what harm could it do telling Gwynedd herself?

The older woman listened intently to the young girl's story, an expression on her face of triumph and vindictiveness as she learned of Ethne's defection and Bridget's predicament.

"So she sent you to find me?" she asked silkily.

"She just wanted to know where you were in case she needed you. I was not supposed to talk to you."

"And she expected me to come back after the way she treated me?"

"I … I don't know. She just wanted to…"

"Did she find Ethne?"

The girl shook her head miserably. She wished she was far away from all these troubles and events. Would her mother take her back now she was in disgrace. Would her father forgive her? She hated the thought of returning to the hovel in which they lived with seven other children – but where else was she to go?

Gwynedd was observing her thoughtfully. She was remembering the day she had to leave the Temple and all the problems she had faced then. But there was no time to help another. She needed all her wits for herself at this time.

"You'll be all right. Life outside the Temple is not so bad," she said brusquely, though, in fact, she herself had found it very bad indeed.

She turned and left the girl, not even casting a backward glance at her.

"So Bridget, you need me!" she crowed as she headed for the forecourt. "Well, we'll see how much!"

Ethne and Lucius arrived at the island of Glastonia before the long summer's day was ended. Birds were winging home over calm stretches of water stained gold and rust pink by the setting sun. All day they had ridden close together and after the initial rush to leave Aquae Sulis well behind, the last part of their journey had been more leisurely with many a brief stop to rest the horses and to talk.

Communication between them was easy – every word that welled up to be spoken met with an understanding response from the other. Both were deeply committed to a mystical way of being. Though the gods they adhered to had different names, their deepest aspirations were the same.

They did not touch, though that is what they longed to do.

They passed through glimmering green tunnels of overhanging branches, and up hills that afforded vistas, long before they reached it, of the great Tor dominating the island. Clear streams gave strength to their horses and renewal to themselves.

At last, the marshlands appeared and Lucius left Ethne alone for the first time as he went in search of a boatman to row them over.

Ethne sat on the grass leaning against a rock while the two horses grazed peacefully, and stared thoughtfully over the flat wetlands, the reeds stirring gently in a breeze, all nature quietening down after a busy day, weary before nightfall.

Without Lucius' encouragement to sustain her, she noticed how exhausted she was. She shut her eyes and sank back more comfortably, drifting, without realizing it, into sleep.

When she woke, a punt was drawn up near her, but there was no sign of Lucius. Standing on the craft was a tall man, stern and sombre, holding a long, straight punt pole with leaves sprouting from the top.

He indicated that she should climb on board.

"Lucius must be attending to the horses," she thought. "He'll be here soon."

She found herself stepping on to the punt. But the ferryman did not wait for Lucius. He pushed off from the bank at once and began to weave his way through the reed beds, expertly finding water channels.

"Wait!" she cried, looking back over her shoulder, wondering why Lucius was so slow. But there was no sign of him or the horses, and the punt was making swift progress over the darkening waters.

She remembered Demosthenes had told Lucius to take her to the island community, leave her there and return to Aquae Sulis. But surely he would not have left her thus, without a word?

The boatman was gazing straight ahead, working the punt with long and rhythmic strokes. He paid no attention when she called out – and she began to be afraid. He was like no man she had ever seen – so cold, so unresponsive, so dark.

She had heard that in ancient days Gwyn ab Nudd, a mighty being from the Otherworld, ferried the souls of the dead across these marshlands. It was this belief that drew Lucius to this place before.

It seemed to her that her body was beginning to feel numb. She tried to scream, but she found she could not. Had she died as she lay against that rock?

She was not ready for this! This was not the time!

No! No! This was not the time.

With a tremendous effort she struggled to her feet and the punt rocked dangerously, but the boatman did not glance back.

Somehow she flung herself from the craft and floundered in the sticky, muddy water, weeds impeding her attempts to swim. Ahead the punt continued on its way as though the man had not noticed what had happened.

Clutching at the reeds, she heaved herself on to an island where the fallen vegetation of decades had created a safe nesting place for ducks and moorhens. She heard their squawks of alarm as she clambered up.

"Lucius!" she sobbed. Where was he? Why had he left her alone? And then she remembered she was not alone. For all that there were beings of shadow in the Otherworld, there were also Beings of Light willing and eager to help.

As her heart reached out to them she heard her name called, and looked up. There was Lucius with a small, ragged man and a boat that looked as though it would not keep out the water much longer.

She was where he had left her, awakening from sleep.

She shivered, aware perhaps for the first time in her young life, how swiftly and unexpectedly we can be visited by Death.

Gaius Agrippa lost no time in informing the Prefect that the Temple of Sulis Minerva no longer had a resident oracle.

The day of the Governor's visit was fast approaching and the Prefect decided it would be on that occasion that he would announce the abolition of the office of the traditional Oracle in favour of the Roman Haruspex. Decius, hearing of the matter too late, tried in vain to persuade him that this was not a good idea.

"Gaius Agrippa assures me the office is already virtually dead. Abolishing it will be no more than a formality," the Prefect said.

"You will be surprised, sir, how passionately the local people hold to their traditions. They are very proud of their Oracle. They believe that the Emperor himself consulted her when he was in this area as a young general."

"You speak of the past, centurion. The local people will have to move with the times. This is a Roman town now and we do things the Roman way."

"But…"

"This, I think you will agree, is no concern of yours. Your duty is to keep the peace."

"It will not be easy to keep the peace during the Governor's visit, sir, with two such controversial events taking place.'

"Keeping the peace doesn't mean giving in to every local whim against the better judgement of the government. Gaius Agrippa assures me we have enough well armed soldiers to prevent any unpleasantness. You are dismissed, centurion, and I expect you to do your duty without hesitation."

Decius acknowledged the order with bitter formality, his heart seething with discontent at the stupidity of those in charge of his home town.

Chapter 25

Martha and her grandfather Paulus, noting how tired and pale and anxious she seemed, accepted Ethne into their home at once. Lucius was loath to leave her but Demosthenes had been so sure it would be in her best interest, that he did so after a meal and a night's sleep.

Martha saw how the two gazed at each other in the morning when it came time to part, and she longed to have such a relationship of her own. For a while it seemed as though they would say goodbye without touching, but as Lucius walked down the path Ethne suddenly broke away from her hosts and ran after him. Martha could not hear what they said or if, indeed, they said anything, but she could see the desperation with which they clung together and kissed again and again. And then Martha saw Ethne trying to push him away, and he at last going, but reluctantly.

Ethne stood gazing after him for a long while as though she did not expect to see him again, and then turned back. Martha went to meet her and took her in her arms.

"Don't be sad," she said soothingly. "He promised to be back soon – and he *will*,"

Ethne tried to hold back the tears, but she had done so for too long and abandoned herself now to the sympathetic embrace of her new friend. All the pent up emotions of the past weeks burst out; the enormity of what she had done in running away from the Temple not the least of the reasons for her breakdown.

Not many hours after the Prefect heard of the confusion at the Temple he presented himself and requested a consultation. Bridget, expecting trouble but hoping she was wrong, showed him the chamber where Gwynedd had chosen to install herself. It was the chamber the old Oracle had used, Gwynedd herself as priestess having set up various gadgets to enhance the dramatic atmosphere of the place. Ethne had scorned to use the skilfully regulated lamps and jets of steam from the hot waters that flowed beneath the floor, but Bridget had not dismantled them.

Cornelius Sartorus declined to be seated but stood, arms folded, staring sternly at the Oracle through the rising vapours.

He asked his question: "How can violence be averted at the unveiling of the statue of the God Claudius?"

Gwynedd, her face lit from beneath so that it seemed to rise luminously and eerily from the misty gloom, took her time replying.

When she did, it was in a deep and hollow voice that boomed out across the chamber.

"Violence breeds violence," she said. "The soldiers must withdraw. Sacrifices must be made. Gold must be placed on the Temple steps. Much gold."

The voice thundered and then rumbled away like a storm that had spent its power. The words "much gold" seemed to linger like a whisper long after the other sounds had ceased.

The Prefect bowed his head stiffly in acknowledgement and then withdrew.

He demanded that he be brought immediately to the High Priestess. The woman who had been hovering outside the door when he emerged, said at once that she could not be disturbed.

"Disturb her," he commanded, his voice leaving her in no doubt of his anger.

She hastened away to find others to help her in the difficult situation. Sartorus waited impatiently while the agitated women whispered among themselves.

"Well," he demanded. "Where is she?"

"She is with the Goddess," someone said.

"Good," he replied. "I want the Goddess to hear what I have to say." And he strode past them and entered the sanctuary where no unconsecrated person was permitted to enter.

Bridget was in front of the great gilded image of Sulis Minerva, wafting incense and intoning prayers. She looked up startled, hastily finished her chant and moved with as much dignity as haste would allow to meet him and lead him out of the sacred place. Her anger was certainly a match for his.

"What is the meaning of this profanity?" She asked icily as she led him into the antechamber.

"This concerns the Goddess. Let the Goddess hear what I have to say."

"The Goddess hears!" she snapped.

The two eyed each other with dislike.

Bridget was wondering what Gwynedd had said to make him so angry. She had thought the presence of the Oracle in place would have satisfied him. She suspected he had heard about Ethne and was making a call on the Temple – a thing he rarely did, preferring the Roman way of divination – to check on the truth of the rumours flying around.

"Then let her hear this," the Prefect declared. "She will no longer be served by the Oracle in that chamber of secrets and lies, but by the Haruspex who operates in the open at the great altar in the forecourt."

"How dare you presume to dictate what the Goddess will and will not do!" Bridget gasped; shocked in spite of her foreknowledge that this move was likely, and at the swiftness with which the blow had fallen.

"It is not I but Rome that will not tolerate its citizens being threatened and blackmailed."

"Threatened and blackmailed! What do you mean?"

"Your so-called Oracle," he sneered, "implied that if I gave the Temple much gold there would be no violence at the unveiling of the statue of Claudius the God."

Bridget stared at him, speechless.

"She also suggested I withdraw all my soldiers and leave the town at the mercy of the rebels."

"I'm sure you misunderstood!" Bridget stammered. She had never liked Gwynedd, but she could not believe that even she could be so stupid.

"I am no fool madam. I know what I heard and I know what I saw. Am I a child that you think I will be taken in by such tricks?"

"I assure you, sir..."

"Assure me of one thing only. That that woman will be out of here by noon tomorrow when I make the announcement that the services of the Oracle in this Temple are terminated."

"You must allow me..."

"Good day, madam. If you value your own position in the Temple and this town, you will do as I say." And with this blackmail threat of his own, he was gone, leaving Bridget staring after him in shocked dismay.

* * *

The news that the Romans had forbidden them to have an oracle in the Temple of Sul spread swiftly around the town. Groups of angry people met in the streets, and gathered at the forecourt. Brendan was quick to take advantage of the situation. By the time the Governor arrived, the town was seething with disaffection. Gwynedd, driven from the Temple in disgrace for the second time was a formidable ally. She stood in various public places tearing her clothes and shrieking in voices that purported to be from the Otherworld – prophesying doom and destruction to those who offered this insult to the Goddess and those who supported them. Thus, even those who were not normally likely to protest were forced to support the rebels in fear of supernatural retribution.

On the Prefect's orders, the soldiers stationed in the town began to break up gatherings and threaten arrest if groups persisted in meeting together. This of course, as Decius knew it would, inflamed the people even more. In vain he tried to calm things down, but as fast as he did, Brendan and Gwynedd stirred them up again.

Brendan was clever enough not to be caught, though both Gaius Agrippa and Decius were determined to remove him from the scene.

Gwynedd, shrieking in the market place, was an easier target. It was not long before she was marched away, but it took six soldiers to do it, with others trying to control the crowd that followed her shouting and throwing stones.

When the Governor and his wife arrived they were not greeted as they expected by crowds of cheering citizens pleased to see them, but by lines of soldiers holding back angry crowds.

Decius sought out Demosthenes and together they requested an audience with the Governor. The Prefect, who hated Decius because he had warned him not to ban the Oracle and had been proved right, tried to refuse them access. But Domitilla, remembering Demosthenes, insisted they should be admitted.

Decius, soldier enough not to question the orders of his superiors openly, managed yet to convey the seriousness of the situation and suggest the unveiling of the statue scheduled for the morrow be postponed until the population was calmer.

The Prefect at once raised his voice, protesting that to give in to disaffection was fatal and suggesting that if Decius had done his job properly as keeper of the peace, they would have had none of this trouble.

The Governor listened to both sides gravely, a furrow of care between his eyebrows.

"Why do you believe it is so important to abolish the traditional role of oracle in the Temple?" Domitilla asked the Prefect quietly. "I don't quite understand."

"It is agreed policy, my lady. Where the traditions of the conquered people interfere with the smooth transition to Romanisation, they must go. The Oracle was independent of the Roman administration and was encouraging people in their old ways, their old allegiances, their old superstitions. They will never become truly Roman while they bow to her authority rather than to ours. She could tell them anything and they believed it was from their Goddess. How often have I heard her referred to as the Oracle of Sul – not of Sulis Minerva! We had no control over what she said. I have told you how I myself was ordered to remove my soldiers from the streets and allow the people free access to the statue of Claudius we know they hate."

"It seems to me you could have chosen better timing Sartorus," the Governor spoke at last.

"And allow her to blackmail Rome? She claimed that bringing vast quantities of gold to the Temple would be the only way to avert the trouble we expect, implying that the Temple was in control and that Rome had to dance to its tune."

"I believe the Oracle you saw was a temporary substitute for the genuine one," Decius ventured to say.

"Why was the Prefect of this town, the representative of Rome, fobbed off with a substitute when he asked to see the Oracle? In my opinion, sir, the chief priestess, the Mother as they call her, is a dangerous enemy of Rome and should be replaced at once."

Decius opened his mouth to protest, but the Governor raised his hand to stop him.

"I am grateful to you Decius Brutus for bringing to my attention some of the complexities of the situation. I suggest you leave us now and go about your duties which are, as my friend here says, keeping the peace."

Decius saluted and left, furious and frustrated. Surely the Governor could see what a fool the Prefect was? Surely he was not going to let the situation get worse? Keeping the peace by force had never given long term benefit. It only bred more disaffection.

He looked back over his shoulder at Demosthenes. The Greek had not been asked to leave. Briefly their eyes met. If anything could be done at this late stage, he had hopes that Demosthenes and Domitilla might be the ones to do it.

Ethne found herself drawn into the life of the Christian community at Glastonia very soon. No one there stood outside events and watched. All worked for the common good. After the isolation of the Oracle's life, it took her some effort to adjust to being almost continually with people.

In the early morning the community drew together for prayers and singing, after which they set about their different tasks. Martha's was to tend the vegetable garden and Ethne found herself accompanying her and almost forgetting her problems as she dug and watered and weeded. At midday they gathered for more prayers and teaching, followed by a simple lunch among families. The evening meal was communal, each bringing a contribution to a long table in the refectory. Ethne found the warmth of greeting and friendship offered almost overwhelming and, at first, shrank back from it. But no one pressed her to join in and after a while of sitting silently beside Martha she found herself willing to smile and communicate with others.

Before they ate there was a silent time while Paulus gave thanks for the food and drink on their table, and the love of God that surrounded them. Then there followed a simple but solemn ceremony when bread was broken and passed around reverently, and wine was sipped from a cup that was passed around, each recipient murmuring thanks as he or she received it from the hand of Paulus.

Formalities over, the community settled down to a hearty meal, hungry and tired after the day's labours. There was much laughing and talking.

On the third evening that Ethne shared this meal a thin and ragged stranger came to the door and was offered food and drink at the table. She stared at him, remembering her dream. Another day she asked Martha what the commotion was about when she saw people gathered around a man who had obviously been badly beaten and was clad only in tattered blood-soaked rags.

"He is a runaway slave," Martha replied, "and has come to us for sanctuary."

Ethne, knowing how the Romans punished people who harboured runaway slaves, was surprised to see the community take him in without hesitation.

"Several of our number were once slaves," Martha said comfortably. "We don't recognize such distinctions in people."

Ethne looked at her in surprise. It was not said in a heroic or defiant way, but quite simply as a statement of fact.

Sometimes Martha and Ethne wandered away from the others, usually towards the Tor.

Ethne felt comfortable with Martha and began to tell her something of her life as Oracle as they walked the leafy winding path to the top. She spoke also of the guilt she felt in running away from her vows and her duties. Martha listened quietly and, in her turn, confided in her new friend her own feelings of guilt that she could not forgive the Romans for what they had done to her family. She even told Ethne about her mysterious missing day and subsequent encounter on the Tor. Ethne listened, fascinated, remembering her own experience with the tall dark man in the punt she believed was the ferryman of Death, and Lucius' disappointment that nothing at all had appeared to happen to him on the Tor.

"Paulus and the others don't like me coming here on my own," Martha said. "They believe the place is full of demons. We're supposed only to come when we come together sprinkling holy water from the well and praying."

Ethne smiled at her. "But you come alone anyway."

Martha nodded. "I know something or someone is here – but I don't believe they are necessarily demons. Those women I met and the baby…"

"It seems to me you met the Goddess, the Great One who manifests as three, the Virgin, the Mother, the Grandmother…"

Martha looked astonished. "Paulus says our God should be thought of as three and yet as one. There is the Father, who is the Almighty, His Son whom he sent to earth to teach us and lead us, and the Spirit that He left among us as He departed from this earth to guide us and keep us company. He says they are not separate from each other, but all aspects of the same One. I must say I find it hard to grasp."

238

"I don't find it so," Ethne said. "We ourselves grow and change through life and yet are always the same being who entered the world at birth. The old woman I will be at death is not recognisable as the baby who left my mother's womb – yet both are me. The gods, being outside Time, are capable of all the different phases simultaneously."

They walked in silence for a while, steadily approaching the summit of the Tor.

"What do you think those women meant about the baby's name being at the bottom of the Chalice, and that I would only find it when I had drunk the liquid contained in it?"

"I would think," Ethne said thoughtfully, "that the Chalice you seek is not an object, but life itself. The name – that is, the meaning – only appears in its true form when you have completed all that life requires of you."

"You don't think there is an actual Chalice Joseph of Arimathea brought with him and buried here?"

"If he did – it will not be the one you are really seeking."

Martha frowned.

"I don't want to wait until I am dying! I need help *now*!"

"We believe in a secret Cauldron very like your Chalice, that contains all wisdom and even brings the dead to life again."

"Can it be found? Does it exist?"

"Yes, it can be found and it does exist – but not in the physical sense."

Martha sighed. Ethne took her hand.

"Don't despair," she said softly. "In the seeking of it we are learning all the time. The name we discover at the end is only the confirmation of what we have already come to know."

When they reached the top of the Tor they found it shrouded in a strange mist, and the landscape below invisible.

Martha shivered and drew nearer to Ethne.

"Shall we go down?" she whispered, slipping her arm through that of her friend.

Ethne was gazing around searchingly. They had had no hint of this mist further down the hill, but she seemed to Martha to be unafraid.

A slight swirling movement in the uniform whiteness around them revealed a shadowy form ahead. Martha tried to pull back at once, but Ethne led her forward.

The mist lifted sufficiently for them to see before them a structure, or building. Martha knew it had not been there before in all the many times she had climbed this far.

"Let us go down!" she whispered urgently.

But Ethne, holding her hand firmly, stepped forward yet again and led her through an open door.

They found themselves in a huge hall lit by brazen lamps swinging on large chains from a ceiling so high it disappeared into darkness.

Around a long table, not unlike the one the community used at the base of the Tor, sat a host of men and women watching the door expectantly as though they had been waiting for Ethne and Martha to appear. The table was laid with rich vessels of gold and silver, exotic fruit contained in ebony and ivory bowls, rock crystal goblets filled with glowing wine…

The two young women gazed at everything displayed, the one in fear, the other in calm curiosity.

At the head of the table sat the tall, gaunt man dressed all in black that Ethne had last seen as the ghostly ferryman.

Martha noticed the three women she had encountered before.

She found herself walking with Ethne around the table, surveying all who were there. Some she recognized from dreams, but some were strange to her. All seemed to change shape even as her eyes met theirs.

"These are angels," she thought, "those demons." But even as she named them they changed into their opposites. She became ever more frightened and confused.

She saw images of pagan gods and goddesses she had only seen as statues before – now apparently flesh and blood beside figures she recognized from her grandfather's teaching.

"Who are they?" she whispered to her companion, clinging to her hand as though to a life-line in a stormy sea.

"They are ourselves," Ethne said. "Do you not recognize them?"

And as Martha did so, all disappeared – the hall, the lamps, the gold and silver and crystal, the watching, expectant figures…

They were alone on a bare hilltop in the sunlight.

"How did you know?" Martha asked, awed by her companion.

But Ethne shook her head.

"I didn't," she replied.

* * *

Lucius found that, with his father away and the responsibilities of the farm on his shoulders, he could not return to Ethne as soon as he had hoped.

During this time he had a visit from Megan.

When she arrived she went first to the house, but was directed to the fields. There she found him alone, staring thoughtfully into the distance, leaning on a long-handled scythe. She called his name and he turned to look at her.

"Where is Ethne?" she demanded. "I must see her."

"She is not here."

"I beg of you – let me see her!"

"I cannot. She is not here."

"Where is she?"

"That I cannot tell you," Lucius said firmly. Seeing Megan now he wondered how he could ever have preferred this fierce, restless woman to her twin.

Megan bit her lip, tears beginning to fill her eyes.

"I'm sorry," he said. "I really cannot take you to her. She is far away and she needs time to think about what she has done and what she will do. Even I am not allowed to disturb her at this time."

Megan suddenly sat down on the stump of a tree near her and buried her face in her hands.

"I don't know what to do," she sobbed. "I need her to tell me what to do!"

"That is one of the reasons she gave for leaving," Lucius said. "She said she had come to believe that people should not listen to voices from the Otherworld – but to their own hearts."

"But what if my heart gives me conflicting advice?" cried Megan.

Lucius sighed. What, indeed? But he noticed that he himself was much clearer in his thinking now than at any time since Ethne had gone away. Perhaps it was because he had been so busy with practical things he had not been able to pay attention to the frantic clamour of his heart, and one voice over the others had naturally gained precedence.

Chapter 26

Taking advantage of the rage in the town Brendan led his now considerable dissident troops to the workyard of the Egyptian. He had decided that to wait for the official unveiling as he had intended would be foolhardy. Not only were the numbers of soldiers to be guarding the statue while the Governor made his speech formidable, but he had no illusions about the fickleness of the main body of the crowd.

Owein was there, armed with the very dagger and spear he had used to fight the Romans so many years before. But there was no sign of Megan.

"I haven't seen her all day," Owein replied when Brendan questioned him.

Brendan frowned. In all the planning she was to be by his side, her fierce vigour and popularity with the people to be a strong factor in their expected victory. He had sensed recently that though he commanded loyalty – he was not much loved. But Megan was. Many who had joined the group had done so because of her, and now, when he was using the anger roused by the Roman treatment of her sister, it was more important than ever to have her with him.

Megan was unaware of the change of plans. All day she had wrestled with herself to discover the true message of her heart, and before sunset she made her decision. She would go to Ra-hotep.

Finding the place around the workyard thick with soldiers, she retreated into the woods to ponder what she should do. Having brought her courage to this point, she could not bear to go back without seeing him.

There was moonlight on the path and gleaming on the river, but under the trees it was dark. She stumbled more than once and paused, heart pounding, worried that the soldiers might have heard her. But some of them were playing a dice game by flare and firelight and their guffaws of laughter must have disguised the cracking of twigs in the wood. She circled cautiously until she came upon the path that led directly from the Egyptian's house into the woods. There was light indicating that he was present and awake. She wondered if the soldiers would care if she walked boldly to the door. One lone woman would not constitute a threat, but she shuddered to think of the interpretation they would put on it, the ribald remarks, the winks, the obscene jokes.

What would Ra-hotep himself think?

She was crazy! What was she doing there?

She was about to turn back, her cheeks burning with shame, when the door opened and Ra-hotep himself came out. He said something to one of the guards, who laughed and waved him on, and then he walked towards her.

She froze where she was, incapable of retreating or advancing, her eyes staring and bright like those of a hare startled by torchlight. He greeted her calmly, almost as though they had had an assignation to meet in this place. She could not see his face, but she felt his presence so powerfully that it was almost as though he was touching her.

For a long moment they stood thus, silently.

Then he stepped forward and took her arm, gently but firmly turning her away from the house and leading her further into the woods, away from the guards. She went with him willingly, amazed at how surely he walked over the stony ground – almost as though he could see in the dark.

When they were well away from the workyard he drew her down beside him on a fallen log and they sat close, slivers of moonlight sifting through the leaf canopy above them, dappling the darkness around with eerie magic.

It seemed a long time before he took her in his arms.

At first, she wept against his shoulder, pouring out all that was troubling her and he listened quietly. Then he began to kiss away the tears, and, before she was aware of it, the comforter had become the lover.

How very differently her body responded to his than to Brendan's. Every part of her seemed to be suffused with exquisite pleasure and when at last they drew apart, spent and satisfied, the world seemed a most beautiful and precious place.

But not for long.

Suddenly from the direction of the workyard harsh sounds erupted. The lovers sat up at once, listening. Crashing and thudding, shouting and screaming were only some of the noises they distinguished. Shocked out of her euphoria, Megan scrambled to her feet. Surely Brendan had not... The plan was for when the statue was erected in full view of the Governor... There were no plans for... But she could not mistake the evidence of her ears. Frantically she ran from Ra-hotep towards the noise. What she thought she could do, unarmed as she was, she had no idea. But she knew she had to *be* there.

As soon as she neared the place, she could see a major battle was in progress. Some of the wooden sheds were on fire and by that light she could see hordes of townspeople, throwing stones, grappling with soldiers, while a group of Brendan's strongest followers were smashing up the statue of Claudius with sledgehammers and uttering roars of triumph, throwing the pieces into the river.

For a brief moment she glimpsed the white hair of her grand-father brandishing a dagger before he went down from a blow to the head.

Suddenly she was grabbed from behind and dragged back into the woods.

"No!" she shrieked. "NO. NO. NO!" But the Egyptian would not release her. She fought him as though *he* was the enemy, but he was too strong for her and managed to get her away safe from the riot.

"I must help!" she cried.

"You cannot," he replied. "A rabble like that has no chance against Roman soldiers."

"I must go. You don't understand."

"I do understand."

"Then let me go."

He did not reply, but lifted her struggling body, and took her further and further away.

"Owein!" she sobbed. "I saw my grandfather..."

"You cannot help him. He chose his way to die."

"Is he dead? Oh no! Is he dead?"

The fearsome hag, the Morrigan, seemed to spread her dark wings over the forest. Megan could hear the creatures of the undergrowth running away from her fell presence in terror. Birds were flapping through the air, uttering shrill cries.

Everything seemed on the move.

But where was there to go?

* * *

The Egyptian was right. A rabble, no matter how angry, was no match for well disciplined Roman soldiers.

Brendan had a hard core of dedicated revolutionaries who took the guards by surprise, while a picked group attacked the hated statue. But the ordinary citizens who had followed his lead, roused to action by no more than his rhetoric and a temporary sense of grievance, were easily put down. At the end, many had been wounded and three had been killed.

Decius received news of the riot only after it was over. He hurried to the scene to find Gaius Agrippa's soldiers in control, the dead neatly laid out on the ground, a bunch of prisoners tied up, several sheds smouldering, and no sign of the statue that had been wrapped and ready for transport on the morrow. Gaius Agrippa himself was stalking about barking out orders and looking well pleased with himself.

A swift and anxious glance round told Decius that there was no sign of Megan, but among those laid out on the ground, he saw his father. With a heartfelt exclamation of dismay, he knelt down beside him at once, feeling for a pulse in his neck. There was none.

Angrily he looked up at Gaius Agrippa now standing over him.

"Was it necessary to kill these people?" he snapped. "They were ordinary citizens – not trained soldiers."

"You weren't here," Gaius said with a sneer. "They fought like wild animals with every intention of killing *us*! This old buck speared one of my best men and I only just managed to stop him cutting another open."

"*You* killed him?"

Gaius Agrippa shrugged.

The blood rushed to Decius' head and he sprang at the man. His hands were reaching for his throat when a firm hand on his shoulder pulled him back. He just had time to register the expression on the Roman's face – a mixture of shock, fear and hate – before he swung round to glare at who was restraining him. It was the Egyptian.

The mood in Aquae Sulis the next day was very different from the one in the town the day the carved pediment had been raised on the Temple of Sulis Minerva.

245

As grey light crept down the narrow alleys and over the flagstones of the forecourt, Aquae Sulis seemed like a ghost town, haunted only by grim faced soldiers patrolling the streets. Those who had escaped from the fight brought back exaggerated tales of a massacre in which dozens of locals and soldiers were killed. Occasionally, between patrols, grey figures darted from house to house carrying rumours, while the rest of the population stayed close indoors, peeping anxiously out of the windows, reshaping the incident into heroic proportions as they picked endlessly over what scraps of information they had.

Brendan had disappeared. No one knew it yet but he was well on his way to the west, to the mountains of the Silures and the Ordovices to which the Romans had not yet penetrated.

The first thing Decius did on his return to the town was to hurry to his parent's house. There he found the news of Owein's death had preceded him. His mother was weeping, but Megan, dry-eyed, flew at him in a rage, screeching like a banshee that he was a vicious, heartless, father-killer. She seized the knife she had not had with her in the woods and tried to make up for all her frustration at not being there at the battle, by attacking the hated Roman centurion now. He seized her wrists and held her at bay, yet was almost overpowered by the sheer force of her anger and hate.

"I didn't kill him," he kept repeating, but she would not listen. Romans had killed him. He was Roman. He had been responsible for Owein's death as surely as if he had actually struck the fatal blow. She would not acknowledge the truth of the Egyptian's words: "He has chosen his own death."

Blood flowed from Decius' cheek before, spent and weeping, Megan at last sank back exhausted. Decius had taken possession of her knife and put it in his belt. Olwen, seeing her son wounded, at once started ministering to him. She carried no blind hatreds or twisted resentments. Owein had chosen his path and would have been proud to die in battle against his old enemies.

"Is it true," she asked, more for Megan's benefit than her own, as she dabbed clean water on Decius' wound, "that the statue is totally destroyed?"

"It is," he answered, and she could hear the satisfaction in his voice if Megan could not.

"What will they do now?" she asked.

"I don't know. I would hope not much. There will have to be a show of power of course – some punishment. But I trust they will have the sense not to insist on another statue of Claudius. In fact, mother, I must go to see the Governor right away." Decius rose, suddenly agitated, regretting that he had not gone straight to the Governor and the Prefect before Gaius Agrippa put in his report. Torn, as ever, between his family and childhood loyalties, and his current friends and masters, he left the house and hurried towards the Prefect's domain, frowning.

Decius found Gaius Agrippa already with the Prefect and the Governor.

It seemed he had done his best to talk them into punitive measures against the Celts who, he claimed, were by nature so bloodthirsty and violent, that they would respect nothing less than violent retribution.

Decius put it to the Governor that the rebellion could have been avoided if a little more good sense had prevailed. He suggested that a mistake had been made in abolishing the traditional and prestigious office of oracle at the same time as the much hated statue of Claudius was to be raised.

"The people are proud of their culture and tradition, sir," he said, "and two such blows to their dignity falling at once was bound to cause trouble. Is it not the policy of Rome to keep local traditions alive where possible?"

"Where possible!" Cornelius Sartorus interrupted sharply. "But in this case it was not possible."

The Governor looked at him thoughtfully.

"The timing certainly seems to have been unfortunate," he said mildly.

"It was perfect timing, sir," the Prefect said. "The old Oracle had died and there was confusion about who was to be the new Oracle."

"I still think..." Decius started, but was stopped in mid-sentence by the Governor's raised hand.

"I have noted your thoughts Decius Brutus, but we are not here to discuss what might or might not have been. We have to deal with the *fact* of the riot now."

"I say we get another statue of Claudius carved at once," the Prefect said, "and execute the ring leaders to teach the people a lesson they won't forget."

"Would it not be better if *we* learned a lesson from this sorry

247

incident?" Decius asked. "If we must have a statue to assert the might of Rome let us at least have a more acceptable one."

"And who do you mean by 'we', centurion?" Agrippa parried. "I believe your own father was one of the rebels."

"Is this true, Decius Brutus?" the Governor asked, regarding him intently. He liked and respected the centurion and would be sorry if he could no longer rely on him.

"It is true my father was among the rebels, sir, an old man remembering the battles of his youth. For this he has paid with his life. I believe you will find nothing in my past to concern you about my loyalty to Rome. I served with the Emperor's son Titus in Judaea and the Emperor Vespasian himself in Egypt. If you were to consult the records of my service…"

"Enough! I do not suspect you, centurion. My wife told me you warned from the start that the erection of the statue of Claudius here would cause trouble. I wish I had paid more attention. I fear my Prefect has not been sensitive enough to local public opinion. We Romans are not monsters. We do not rule without consideration of local traditions and requirements. The mark of a good ruler, sir," he said, looking directly at the Prefect, "is to listen to the needs of all sides and produce a compromise that will keep the peace – or…"

"Such compromise is surely not for mighty Rome!" the Prefect exclaimed indignantly.

"Or," the Governor continued patiently, "at least to make it *look* as though a compromise has been reached if it is indeed not possible to do so. The town must have a Roman god looking over them, but it will not, at this time, be identified with Claudius, the conqueror. I will instruct the sculptor to produce a statue of Jupiter. It would be appropriate as we all know Minerva sprang fully formed from Jupiter's head. Besides," and here he gave a slight smile in the direction of Decius, "the threat of his thunderbolts might help to keep the peace."

Annoyed, Sartorus seemed about to speak, but Gaius Agrippa raised the question of punishment for the town.

"Ah, yes, retribution," the Governor said with a sigh. It was clear to Decius he would have liked to forgo this, but Rome must not be seen to be defied.

"All those who are waiting for their applications for Roman citizenship to be ratified, should have their applications rejected –

or at least postponed. The city must pay a communal fine, levied on every household whether they were involved in the riot or not. This will make the innocent resent the guilty."

"And the prisoners?" Gaius Agrippa prompted.

"The ordinary rebels must stay in prison here, but the leaders must be sent to Gaul, to the amphitheatres."

"Too lenient!" interjected the Prefect.

"The leaders have escaped," complained Gaius Agrippa.

Decius was silent, remembering his own years in a stinking gaol and his eventual "escape" to do bloody battle for the pleasure of sadistic audiences in the amphitheatres of Gaul. He was glad his father was dead and would escape this fate.

"What of those we know to have been part of the rebel organisation, but were not captured that night?" Gaius Agrippa asked smoothly, glancing at Decius' face, knowing that one of his daughters was suspected of being part of this organisation.

"They will be watched and warned," the Governor said wearily.

"I believe they should be rounded up," the Prefect said viciously, "and subjected to a thrashing."

The Governor sighed and stood up – indicating that the meeting was at an end.

"My dear," murmured Domitilla. "If you do not give clear instructions on this matter, there may be unfortunate consequences."

Her husband stood still. Then he looked directly into the eyes of Cornelius Sartorus. "I appoint the centurion, Decius Brutus, as acting Prefect" he said. "He has a most sensible understanding of the people here, and I suspect a considerable influence. I will leave it to him to make decisions about the immediate future."

Shocked, the Prefect and Gaius Agrippa opened their mouths to protest, but the Governor dismissed them coldly.

"You will stay behind, Decius," he said to the astonished centurion. "We have much to discuss."

"Yes, sir," said Decius.

Decius returned to his mother's house anxious to have a word with Megan before the officious Gaius Agrippa took it upon himself to pay her a visit.

He counted it as some improvement in their relationship that she did not actually attack him as he entered, but continued to sit at the table where she was helping her grandmother cut vegetables for the evening meal.

After kissing Olwen, who seemed considerably older than when Owein was alive, he greeted his daughter. He did not expect a reply, nor did he receive one.

"I know you don't want to speak to me, Megan," he said quietly, "but I fear you must. Someone much less sympathetic than I will be questioning you if I don't."

"Another Roman?" she asked bitterly.

"He is not a Roman," Olwen said desperately. "He is my son."

Decius raised his hand to indicate that he was grateful for her attempt to help, but that she should say no more.

"Your association with the rebels is known," he said, watching the young woman's face intently. "It surprised me that you were not present at the attack on the statue."

"How do you know I was not?" she challenged, looking up and meeting his eyes boldly.

"I know," he said simply.

Megan dropped her eyes, and he could see that she was distressed. She gave up all pretence of preparing food.

"Where were you?" he asked with surprising gentleness. Perhaps it was this unexpected gentleness that broke her resolution. She buried her face in her hands and shuddered.

"Where?" he repeated.

"I should have been there," she said, a catch in her voice. "I should have."

He waited. He could sense the words building up behind the dam of her resistance, and expected them to burst through at any moment. He was not wrong.

"I tried. I tried! But he dragged me back. He would not let go."

"Who? Who dragged you back?"

"The Egyptian!" She almost shouted, pent up fury and shame in the plosive sound. "He took it on himself to make me break my vow. I would have been there! I *should* have been there…"

"No, you shouldn't," Decius said sternly. "He did right to stop you."

"I hate him!" she screamed.

Decius remembered how the Egyptian had rescued her from the river – and now this. He remembered also how the Egyptian had prevented his killing Gaius Agrippa. He had much to thank him for. A strange and enigmatic man, harsh and mysterious, and yet…

"Pull yourself together," he said sternly. "Gaius Agrippa will be here soon and you don't want to spend the rest of your life rotting in gaol. Believe me, you will thank the Egyptian one day for keeping you out of this sorry escapade."

"Is that all it is to you? An escapade!" she asked bitterly. "Your father gave his life for an *escapade*?"

"I didn't mean it like that," he replied, exasperated. "You know I did not. But we have so little time. Owein would not want you to waste your young life. He gave his life that you may live in freedom – not in gaol."

"Listen to him, Megan," urged Olwen. "No purpose will be served now by your arrest."

"If I am to be arrested – why do *you* not arrest me, Roman?" she said defiantly. "Is it not treasonable that you do not?"

His face darkened.

"I risk much for you, daughter."

She stared at him, and for a moment, he fancied she understood.

A loud knocking at the door shattered the tense silence.

Olwen looked at him, a startled enquiry in her eyes.

He nodded. "You must open it," he said.

Gaius Agrippa strode in. Behind him, two soldiers took up positions at the door. He was obviously surprised and annoyed to find Decius present, and he stared at him with suspicion.

Decius greeted him coolly and introduced him to his mother and daughter as though this was some ordinary social call.

"And what is the meaning of this?" He jerked his head in the direction of the soldiers at the door.

"It is believed the woman Megan, your daughter," Gaius Agrippa said with pointed emphasis on the last two words, "is one of the leaders of the rebels who attacked my soldiers. I believe you already know this."

"I know no such thing," Decius replied haughtily. "My father was involved certainly, and is dead. A house in mourning needs no harassment from you."

Gaius Agrippa strode across the room to stand glowering down at Megan who was meekly cutting beans again with eyes lowered.

"Look at me, madam," he commanded. "I will have some answers."

251

Megan glanced up, and Decius, holding his breath, noted with relief that there was little in her expression to confirm Gaius Agrippa's suspicions. Her eyes seemed hooded in some way to hide the natural fiery hatred she had for everything Roman.

"What answers do you require, sir?" she asked politely.

"Are you, as they say, a member of..."

"Who says, sir?" Decius interrupted.

Gaius Agrippa bit his lip. He had his informants and spies but he did not want to reveal their names, particularly to Decius.

"That is no concern of yours."

"On the contrary," Decius said, "it is of every concern, and until you have enough evidence to take before a properly constituted tribunal I would suggest you disregard rumour and slander – a great deal of which is flying loosely around this town these days."

Gaius Agrippa glared at Decius.

"I will get the evidence, sir, and then it will not only be the girl who stands trial," he snarled.

Decius acknowledged his words with an icy bow of the head.

"Until that time," he said, "take yourself and your men away from here."

Gaius Agrippa looked back at Megan. Her head was bent over the beans again and he could not see her expression. He had to admit she seemed an ordinary enough young girl, and he could not imagine her leading a troop of bloodthirsty rebels. He had been told that she was a wildcat, dangerous and violent, and he must not question her unarmed and unprotected. He would be sorry if he had been misinformed for it would give him great satisfaction to wrong-foot that arrogant centurion, and indeed, if the girl proved guilty, to overthrow him completely.

But he could see that there was nothing to be gained by pursuing the matter at this time.

With a salute, he withdrew.

Decius, after a penetrating glance at Megan, stayed no more than a moment after him.

The next day Cornelius Sartorus packed up his bags and his family and departed for Corinium where the Governor had directed him to a new, less responsible, but not much less remunerative, post. He went with a bad grace muttering that the town of Aquae

Sulis would be a festering sore forever if the Governor did not take his advice on how to deal with malcontents.

Before the Governor prepared to leave he spent some time with Decius, discussing his new, if temporary, role.

Domitilla and Demosthenes visited the ruins of the ancient hill town overlooking the modern city once more, conversing comfortably on the prospect of Jupiter taking the place of Claudius, and Bladud where he should be, overlooking the healing sanctuary of the Goddess Sul. Domitilla had plans for another temple, a lunar one, and they spoke about this.

"My husband will not reinstate the Oracle," she said. "He regrets the Prefect's precipitate action, but cannot be seen to give in to too many popular demands. It seems her great days were over anyway. I am told the Oracle with real power herself rejected the office."

"The old Oracle had the gift," the Greek said, "but on her death I believe there was an unseemly jostling for power. The young girl who was installed, though having a truly remarkable link with Otherworld Beings, found the rigorous rules of the Temple confining and inhibiting. She was too much herself to become nothing but the empty shell for others to inhabit, and began to question the wisdom of the whole system. In fact, she made me question it myself. She made me see how important it is to take responsibility for one's own decisions – for it is through one's decisions that one's soul progresses."

Domitilla was thoughtful.

"I consulted your Oracle once," she said. "Her pronouncement was so vague and ambiguous I can't say it made my decision for me, though perhaps it gave me confidence to assert myself more."

"A good oracle should not deal in specifics. Her pronouncements should make you think, but leave you free to make up your own mind. Gwynedd, the latest Oracle, and not, I fear, a good one, made the mistake of telling the Prefect to withdraw his troops and pay the Temple handsomely for protection."

Domitilla laughed. "That was indeed a mistake!"

"I have to admit I have my regrets that Ethne doesn't feel she should continue. I believe she was to be trusted, and it seems to me the Haruspex with his animal entrails will do far more harm than she would."

"Well, we have no power between us to change that situation."

They began to walk away from the ruined town, the river running silver below them, a lone heron winging over their heads towards it.

"If Decius is wise," Domitilla said, "he will start building the moon temple and replacing Claudius with Jupiter as soon as possible. He must turn the minds of the people away from what they have lost towards what they have gained."

"I think he will handle his new power well. He has the interests of his own people and the Romans both at heart."

"Not always an easy position to be in, but, in this case, probably very necessary."

The first decision Decius made was to send Gaius Agrippa and a group of the men Decius least trusted away from Aquae Sulis to track down Brendan.

It was a clever move, for Agrippa was preparing to cause trouble in the town, and perhaps no other commission would have drawn his fire so effectively. There was nothing he liked more than an actively dangerous foray into hostile territory. Decius suggested Brendan would have more than likely gone north-west to the wilds beyond Roman jurisdiction.

"When you reach the last fort in the line," he said. "It will be up to you whether you go on or turn back. There will be no shame in not venturing beyond our lines. I hear the tribe's people in the mountains are formidable savages."

"I will bring him back," Agrippa promised grimly. "You can count on that."

Decius nodded, and the man left.

In the next few days after his and the Governor's departure, Decius was very busy. He was determined to cool the resentment of the people and, on his own initiative, pronounced an amnesty for those captured in the raid on the Egyptian's workyard, though they were still denied rights to Roman citizenship for the foreseeable future. Also, the fine imposed by the Governor was not to be rescinded.

He announced the erection of the new Temple and described its prospective magnificence with enthusiasm. They already knew of the substitution of Jupiter for Claudius.

The town gradually settled down to normality again. With the unpopular Prefect, the trouble-stirrer Brendan, and the worst of the soldiers gone, and with new projects to attract their attention underway, most people were content.

Chapter 27

Megan determined not to seek out the Egyptian again and several days passed in discomfort as the conflicting emotions of love and hate wrestled for mastery of her heart – not only with regard to Ra-hotep himself, but with regard to her father as well. She wanted to hate them both and to blame them for all that she regretted in herself, but found to her dismay that she was finding it more and more difficult to do so. If she was not careful the hate would fade away like a miasma and she would be left exposed with only herself to blame for all that had happened to her. On several occasions she listened to praise of Decius and the competent, fair way he was administering the town in the absence of a Prefect, and found herself agreeing. She even found a tear in her eye one day when she remembered what he had done for her, and how much he had risked. In vain she tried to recapture the bitterness she had nursed towards him all her life, but it was becoming harder to do so, as he appeared more and more human to her, and less and less Roman.

As for Ra-hotep, she longed for him incessantly – but wanted more than anything in the world for him to come and seek *her* out. She recalled that in every instance it had been *her* initiative, *her* call for help, however subconscious, that had brought them together. What was it about him? Were they bound together in some inexplicable way? She had cursed him and endangered her soul by doing so, yet now she found she could not live without him. Was it some devious trick of the Otherworld, that overshadowed this world, that repulsion and attraction, hate and love, should be rendered thus interchangeable?

Day followed day without motive or meaning. Having lost the one emotion, and keeping the other at bay, she felt lost, drifting and rudderless, a state she had never before experienced. If only Owein were with her to stir her heart against the Romans. If only Ethne were with her to understand her and help her to understand herself. Olwen had always been a provider of food and shelter to her, nothing more. She expected no help from her.

Olwen was saddened by the death of her husband as was to be

expected, for they had been together for almost half a century, but she conducted the daily business of living with great courage. She went to market and returned with a laden basket on her hips as she had before. She quietly and competently managed the house, entertained visitors who came to commiserate, with calm fortitude. Never once did she break down and rail against fate or those who had killed him. Never once did she cease to be what she had always been, the anchor that kept her family riding steady on the billows of a stormy sea.

Now, observing that day after day Megan stayed listlessly indoors, growing steadily paler, Olwen decided to speak to her son, Decius Brutus, to see if he could locate Ethne and bring her back to them.

Decius sent for Lucius, but found that he had left the farm as soon as his father had returned from Rome. The messenger questioned Aulus and Julia, and even the farm hands, but no one admitted to knowing where he was. He would be gone a few days at least.

"Did you question the Greek priest?" Decius asked. The boy's face fell. He had not seen him and had indeed forgotten his existence.

"Never mind, you did well," Decius said kindly, but there was a worried frown between his brows as he dismissed the youth.

He had no fear for Ethne. He knew Lucius loved her and would let no harm come to her. But he was worried about Megan.

He told his staff that he would be unavailable for a few hours, and set off along the river path to the Egyptian's workyard.

When Lucius arrived at the village of Glastonia he was told that Ethne was on the Tor. Martha at once suggested he should rest and take some refreshment while he waited for her return.

"Thank you," he said, "but I think I'll go to meet her."

"She likes to be alone when she goes there," Martha warned.

But he was impatient to be with Ethne. He wolfed down the bread and honey Martha provided and drank the milk as quickly as he could, and then set off for the narrow path that led, spiralling, up the Tor. It was good to be walking again. He had ridden from Aquae Sulis with very few stops and appreciated the firm earth under his feet at last.

It was clear from his conversation with Martha that the little community had not heard of the upheaval in Aquae Sulis. He wondered how best to break the news to Ethne. He could try to hide the fact that her defection had caused the rebellion to be much larger and probably more violent than it might have been, but he could not hide the fact from her that her grandfather was dead, killed as a rebel and given no honourable burial.

He found her at the very top, sitting on the grass with her knees drawn up to her chin, gazing out over the plains beyond the marshes, a light breeze stirring her copper coloured hair around her, one strand across her lips. She seemed so utterly at peace that he stood for some moments watching her, unwilling to disturb her.

But she must have sensed his presence for she turned and looked directly at him, a wonderful smile of joyful greeting on her face as soon as her eyes met his.

In an instant she was in his arms and there were no doubts in his heart that she had made the choice to stay with him. But he still had to tell her what had happened.

"Not yet," he thought. "Not yet."

Neither spoke, though both had much to tell. For the moment, the bliss of being together, woven in love as close as any warp and weft, occupied them completely.

How long they lay thus on the top of the world, the sky arched in blue magnificence above them, they could not tell – but eventually the breeze strengthened and a slight chill touched their skin. They looked up and noticed where they were and remembered what they had to say to each other.

Lucius spoke first and watched the glow fade from her face and the shadows of sorrow take its place. It was as though the sun no longer shone nor light shimmered on the landscape of field and forest and water as it had a moment before. Nothing had in fact changed in the natural world around them – but their perception of it was now very different.

He played down as best he could her own part in the disaster that had taken place, but she was no fool. She sat for a long while in silence, turned from him, staring into the distance. When he tried to take her in his arms again, she shrugged away from him.

After a long, long silence she turned towards him again.

"My love," she said quietly. "A lot has happened to me since I have been here."

He was surprised at her calm after what she had just learned, but he remained still, allowing her to speak.

"I have watched the people here, how they live, and listened to what they have to say. Much of it you would appreciate. Some of it you would not."

She paused, turning away again and gazing out over the landscape without seeing it.

"I have always known our lives are only a part of a great pattern and are so puzzling to us because we can only see such a very small part of the whole. An infant lying on the ground outside a temple sees only its own hand reaching out to grasp the nearest stone, and nothing of the vast edifice behind and all that it contains – let alone the meaning and purpose of it."

Lucius watched her profile, the fine lines of her nose and chin, the long lashes, the shining hair curling against her neck. He longed to reach out and hold her again, but he knew that this was not the moment to do so.

"I have always known this," she repeated thoughtfully. "But now it seems to me that I have had a glimpse that, for a moment, lit up the whole pattern."

The sudden fire in her eyes caught his attention as she turned towards him again. He listened to her words closely now.

"I cannot say what I saw in that moment – for already the vision has faded. It seemed to me that Sul and Orpheus, Jupiter, Apollo and the rest of the gods people believe in are no more than beings in the service of the Creator of the great pattern, the One Beyond All Other. They are the workers at the loom, not the Designer."

Lucius sat quietly, listening, trying to grasp the implications of what she was saying. It was not so very different from his own intuitive understanding of things.

"Does the Creator, the Designer, have a name?" he asked.

"Names limit."

"But we need a name to give substance to our thoughts."

She did not reply directly, but tried to explain how she had come to believe that the "One Beyond All Other" was in fact the God her new friends worshipped and that she did not reject Sul, Orpheus and the others but saw them now in a new perspective.

"Does this mean you have decided to stay with this community?" he asked anxiously.

Ethne took both his hands in hers.

258

"No, my love. I have decided to come back with you. Together we will reconcile the old religions and the new – seeking what is true in either, and rejecting what is not, in both."

"You will have no regrets about giving up your place as Oracle?"

"I will not speak with the voices of others," she said, "until I am sure for whom I speak."

They rose together and started to walk back down the Tor path. The light was fading and the first star came out in the deepening blue – a beacon in the immeasurable depths of space.

When Decius reached the sculptor's workyard, there was no sign of the Egyptian. Men, in no great hurry, were rebuilding the sheds, while others sat on blocks of stone in the sunshine chatting. As soon as the centurion was spotted several leapt up and started to look busy, while others stayed where they were, blatantly idle, waiting for him to approach.

"Nothing is the same," Decius thought. Blood had been spilled... months of hard work had come to nothing... there was a sense of anti-climax, of purposelessness, of waiting...

He learned that the Egyptian had gone into the woods. One man, a sullen fellow, indicated the path Megan knew so well.

"Why have you not started on the statue of Jupiter?" Decius asked sternly.

"The stone has not arrived from the quarry," he was told.

"Has it been ordered?"

It evidently had, and there was nothing they could do, they said, until it arrived.

Decius looked disapprovingly around the yard. There were several half-worked tombstones and a great deal of mess left over from the riot.

"I should think there is plenty for you to do," he said. "Is the Egyptian so rich he pays you to sit around doing nothing?"

Several others stood up guiltily and busied themselves, but the sullen man who had directed Decius to the path, remained seated staring at him defiantly. The centurion had had enough confrontation lately and did not relish more. He stared back into the man's eyes for a moment and then asked his name. There was no reply.

Decius frowned, trying to remember. And then he smiled grimly.

"No matter. I have your name, and I shall not forget it again."

For the first time, the man appeared uncomfortable. The Egyptian had once said to him: "To possess a man's name is to possess power over him."

The man stood up slowly, trying not to lose dignity, and slowly walked towards a slab of rock intended for a tombstone.

As Decius left he saw him picking up a hammer and chisel.

The woods were full of birdsong that late summer afternoon and Decius soon put the irritation of the workyard behind him.

He found the Egyptian sitting on a fallen log in a small clearing, deep in thought. Startled, he glanced up quickly as Decius approached. The centurion wondered what he had been brooding on with such deep sorrow. He had always seemed so aloof from the troubles of the town. Surely he was not regretting the destruction of the Claudius statue? Perhaps he was ashamed because he had been so sure he could protect it, and he had not. But already, within moments of his spotting the intruder, all evidence of the deep emotions he had been experiencing before was gone. Hooded and wary as ever, his eyes met those of Decius.

After a brief word of greeting, Decius sat down beside him. Neither spoke for some time.

"I have come," the centurion said at last, "to thank you."

The Egyptian raised an enquiring eyebrow, but said nothing.

"Not only did you save my daughter from drowning, and from being embroiled in the riot..." Decius studied the face beside him. He could read nothing there. The dark eyes regarded him steadily. "But..." he continued, "you stopped me from committing a crime for which my life would have been forfeit."

The Egyptian shrugged slightly, and turned away as though he had lost interest in the conversation.

"You puzzle me," Decius said slowly, picking his words with difficulty. "You seem so ... so detached from everything going on here ... yet ... everything you do affects us."

There was a long silence while the Egyptian who had been holding a twig, broke it up into pieces and began to throw them idly, abstractedly, at a certain pebble. At a loss to know how to continue Decius stooped and picked up a twig himself and joined the game. None of the twigs reached the pebble. It was too far away and the twigs were too light, but the activity served to fill the gap left by the words that could not be spoken.

After a while even this form of communication ceased and they sat quite still and in silence. Decius was struggling to find a way to say what he had come to say. The Egyptian did nothing to help him.

At last Decius spoke.

"I want to speak about my daughter Megan..."

He did not look at the Egyptian, but he sensed the man tensing up.

He waited, hoping he would speak. But he did not.

"Once I wanted you to leave her alone," Decius continued hesitantly, "and she to have nothing to do with you."

Still no reaction. No word. He tried to see his eyes but the lids were lowered and he was staring at the ground.

"I told her you were too old for her and that we knew nothing about you..." Decius fumbled to a stop, acutely embarrassed by the silence of the man beside him. He began to wish he had not come. But the image of Megan's pale and despairing face came to him.

"I don't know what is between you. I don't know indeed if anything is between you, but... but I have to ask you..."

"I will go to her," the Egyptian said suddenly and stood up.

He towered above Decius, looking down at him for a long moment and then, without another word, strode away.

Decius sat on alone in the woods for a long time. He no longer heard the birdsong. He heard only his own thoughts of fear and hope struggling for mastery, one over the other.

When the Egyptian reached Megan's house he was told by Olwen that Megan was not at home.

"She has gone to Sul's Hill," her grandmother said, surprised at herself for volunteering this information to someone who made her so uneasy. Was it because she remembered he had brought her granddaughter back from the river, or because his gaze was so compelling?

He found her at the summit of the Sacred Hill, seated in the long grass, gazing out over the open country away from Aquae Sulis. Forests covered most of the hills, but occasionally farmers had cleared them and the great road the Romans had built from the south coast, the Fosse Way, could be clearly seen.

Megan had come because she knew it was Ethne's favourite place and hoped, somehow, her sister, wherever she was, would sense her presence there and give her advice and comfort. How many times had Ethne told her about the sacred nature of the hill and how the Goddess herself had appeared to her there?

But Megan felt nothing supernatural about the place. Try as she might she could not project her spirit out of her body, nor draw another in. She felt the earth, smelled the seeding grass, stared at the distant hills, the dark green forests now with long shadows as the sun slowly stained the sky red in the west over a thin line of shining copper that was the distant sea. She even heard a boy calling to his cows in the valley below. Every natural sight and sound was experienced, but these were not what she was seeking. She felt as though her body were made of lead, anchored securely to the ground. How was it that her twin, born of the same mother at the same time, could fly with ease into the Otherworld, while she was so clumsy and inept?

She heard a sound close behind and turned to see who or what it was.

Her heart lurched. It was Ra-hotep.

Her first impulse was to fling herself into his arms, but she turned away instead, remembering it was he who had made her forswear herself and leave her companion rebels unaided.

He came no nearer, but stood behind her, waiting. He had noticed the joy that had flashed in her eyes for an instant when she first saw him.

She felt his presence overpoweringly, but would not turn.

"Ethne," her heart cried. "Ethne, help me. What shall I do? Shall I ever be forgiven? Shall I ever forgive?"

The dying sunlight seemed to glint one last time off something at the top of a hill a long way away to the south – the Tor at Glastonia – a spark of light that penetrated the darkness of her heart.

She turned and looked up at him.

He drew her to her feet and held her close.

She forgave – and was forgiven.

Later, they sat together on the sacred hill and talked long and intimately for the first time since they had met.

Megan asked why he had left his home country and come to Aquae Sulis.

He did not reply at once, but stared into the distance as though he was seeing right back into the country he had left behind.

"My land was once mighty," he said at last, "the greatest civilisation in the world. Its kings conquered other lands. Its gods

262

took precedence over other gods. All that the Greeks know they learned from Egypt. All that the Romans know they learned from the Greeks."

Megan watched and listened intently. She knew very little about his land.

"Then we were conquered as you have been conquered – but many times and by many different nations. Our kings had become less mighty. Our gods debased. Each time the conquerors pushed aside the royal dynasty and crowned their own people kings in our land. But..." and here he turned to look deeply into Megan's eyes. She was held as though entranced, breathless for what he would say next. "But," he continued, "our royal blood-line remained intact, and..." he paused again, "I am of that blood-line."

"You are a king?" she gasped.

He shook his head. "Not in the eyes of the Romans – but in the eyes of my people."

"Were you crowned by your people?" she asked in awe.

"No," he said. "Not yet. But I believe I will be one day when the time is right."

"How will you know when the time is right?"

"When you and I, my love, have re-established the power of the ancient gods."

"You and I?" breathed Megan.

His gaze was strange and penetrating. Her heart was beating fast.

"When I was a young man eager to overturn the Romans – just as you are now," he added, and for a moment a half-smile flitted across his face, "I was imprisoned and flogged. I would have been executed but I managed to escape." Another, but grimmer, smile touched the corner of his lips. "I had a reputation for being a master of magic," he said. "And, playing on this, I broke free from my superstitious guards. I hid in the tomb of one of my ancestors, which had been broken into and left desecrated. As I slept exhausted after my trials, I saw a vision. Isis herself came to me and told me that I had a mission to restore the proper worship of our gods and the sacred blood-line to the throne. She also told me that I would not succeed without the help of the woman who was destined to be my helpmate. When I asked how I would find her, she described a land far to the north west where a goddess who heated the waters under the earth was worshipped."

They sat in silence together for a while. Then he continued:

"I left Egypt and sought a land where hot waters sprang from the earth. I lived several years on an island off the Roman mainland, and then, when no one I could recognize as the woman who was destined to work with me appeared, I travelled on. I stayed awhile in several other places, but knew in my heart each time they were not right."

"So you came to Aquae Sulis?" whispered Megan.

"I came to Aquae Sulis."

"And – have you found her?"

Ra-hotep looked deeply into her eyes.

"I believe so," he said.

It seemed to Megan that Time had stopped and she was contained in an eerie and invisible sphere. She knew with great clarity that this was meant to be. She had run through fire – and had found her destiny.

"Will you come with me to Egypt?" he asked.

"I will," she replied.

It would be wrong to say that Ethne had any clear idea of what was happening to her twin, but she felt a nagging anxiety about her. Before she and Lucius came down from the Tor, she sent out a fervent prayer to the "One Beyond All Other" that Megan would be helped, guided and protected. It seemed to her that briefly the darkening sky lightened, and her anxiety lifted.

Lucius and Ethne walked hand in hand down the spiralling path to the village, but when they reached Martha's house, they found all in confusion. Paulus had died, suddenly, without illness or warning. A momentary surge of pain in his chest had felled him, and he lay now on his bed, his face peaceful and resigned, many of the community gathered round him praying for his soul's journey and its acceptance into the shining kingdom beyond death.

He had seen Jesus, the Christ. He had been touched by God in the world. His loss to the community was incalculable, but their sorrow was tempered by the joy of knowing he would be safe with their God.

Martha could not see it so philosophically. She was weeping inconsolably, remembering the many times she had been impatient with him, the many times they had argued. He was gone, uprooted out of her life, leaving it disturbed and damaged.

Ethne took her into her arms at once to comfort her. Together they mourned the grandfathers they had lost – comfortable links with the past broken, the future to be faced alarmingly different.

Lucius watched the two women thoughtfully, wondering how he and Ethne were to do what she proposed. He had seen enough of the community to know that it did not like compromise. Paulus had said to him: "Orpheus, Apollo and the rest are myths – meaningful stories dreamed up by men to explain the inexplicable – but Christ is real. He was the actual son of God walking upon the earth – not an insubstantial vision – but in flesh and blood – bringing real and incontrovertible truths from the Otherworld to this." If they accepted any part of the new religion, they would be expected to embrace the whole. Would he be prepared to do this? And if he did not – would his relationship with Ethne be damaged? He sighed. Was nothing *ever* straightforward and easy?

On her return to Aquae Sulis Julia found it very difficult to settle down. There had been talk of her staying behind in Rome, but she soon noticed that once the Emperor ceased to invite her to attend him, others did also. She decided in the end it would suit her better to return to where she was appreciated than stay where she was not.

Those who listened to the report of their adventures received the impression that she had been entertained royally by the Emperor and had been accepted as his daughter. When pressed as to why, with such an exciting life in the capital, she had returned to the provincial backwater of Aquae Sulis, she said she had been homesick. The more cynical among her acquaintances did not believe this for a moment, and Julia, in some circles, became a figure of fun. But in others her friendship was cultivated. Few successful dinner parties among the wealthier citizens did not have her as star guest.

Decius did not see her or Aulus for some time after their return. He was busier than he had ever been encouraging a state of peaceful co-existence between the local and the immigrant community. There were still mutterings against the Romans and wounds to be healed, but on the whole Decius was liked and respected. Owein was dead, Brendan had disappeared, and Megan had given up the struggle. The townspeople sank back into a comfortable state of passivity.

There were soon two startling pieces of news to keep them happily gossiping in marketplace and baths.

"Have you heard that Megan and the Egyptian have been seen together?"

The rumour spread swiftly around the town, causing amazed speculation wherever it reached, shortly followed by another, perhaps not quite so surprising piece of news, that the former Oracle, Ethne, was to settle down as a farmer's wife in the valley west of the town with Lucius, son of Aulus.

Decius heard both of these reports from strangers and hurried to his mother's house as soon as he could.

There he found the twins quietly talking together, a rare sight in former days. He saw at once the change in the two young women. Shadows had lifted and the light had come back to their beautiful eyes. Both looked up when he entered, Ethne standing at once and reaching out her arms to him, Megan remaining seated but regarding him with a not unwelcoming smile.

"What is this I hear," he asked Ethne cheerfully. "Are you to marry Lucius?"

Ethne laughed and flushed.

"Yes, I am," she said. "Do you approve, father?"

"I do most certainly," he replied, hugging her.

When he released her, her face shadowed again for a moment. "I'm sorry I ran away like that. Lucius told me the trouble it brought about for everyone."

"Nonsense," he said gruffly. "Trouble would not have occurred if it had not already been brewing. But are you sure, Ethne, that this is what you want?" he added more seriously. "You have a great and rare gift and ordinary domestic life might stifle it."

"Not with Lucius as my husband," she said with confidence, her eyes alight again. "We have plans for our home to be a centre of real spiritual transformation to which all will be welcome."

Decius smiled, content to believe that nothing in her new life would make her abandon her marvellous gifts. Lucius was young and intelligent enough to grow with her – not to hold her back.

He turned from Ethne to Megan. Her liaison was more problematic. The Egyptian puzzled and disturbed him, but he had grown to respect and admire him. Megan's headstrong nature would not be able to tolerate a weaker man. He believed she could meet the Egyptian strength for strength. Together they would exert a considerable force over those who encountered them. If only he could be sure it would be a force for good...

"And you, daughter," a frown between his brows. "Is it true that you and the Egyptian..."

"He is leaving Aquae Sulis," she said calmly, meeting his eyes steadily, "and I am going with him."

This was not expected and Decius showed his surprise.

"Where will you go?" he asked when he had recovered his breath. It seemed this was a surprise to Ethne as well, and she joined her father in the question.

"To Egypt," Megan replied calmly.

And more than that she would not say.

Epilogue

One winter, many years later, Demosthenes found himself rowing towards the town on an icy river. The valley was deep in fog and he would not have chosen to leave the comfort of Aulus' villa that morning if he had not been driven by a strange impulse.

He could scarcely see the banks on either side. Ghostly branches, dark, twisted and bare, reached out through the miasma as though to catch him as he passed. Several times he thought to turn back, but the same compulsion that had set him on his journey drove him on.

His mind drifted comfortably – sometimes remembering his early years in Athens, sometimes remembering his arrival in Aquae Sulis and all the events of that first summer and since.

Lucius and Ethne had married not long after their return from Glastonia and now had three children. Lucius had almost entirely taken over the working of his father's farm, for after his journey to Rome Aulus seemed to lose enthusiasm for everything except comfort and pleasure, and spent much of his time at the baths in Aquae Sulis gossiping with friends. The drive that had made him so successful in those early years of Roman occupation had withered and died.

Ethne had rejected the office of Oracle, but she could not escape her own nature and, as time went by, their home had become a natural focus for people needing physical or spiritual help. She remained true to her belief that each should find his or her own path, but those who came to her in despair usually left in hope, confident and capable of facing their problems. She had not become a fully dedicated Christian, as her friend Martha would have wished, but there were some who left her presence who went to Glastonia to join the growing community there, having heard of it first from her.

The Orphic temple had not been built in the town, and Demosthenes still presided over gatherings in the villa's little shrine. It may not have been large and impressive as a temple would have been, but it was certainly an active and intense centre of light for those who were drawn to it.

After the birth of their first child, Lucius almost died in an accident on the farm. He lay in a coma for many days. What he experienced then he would never talk about, but from that time on he made the most of this life and no longer hankered to experience the Other.

Martha had married a retired Roman soldier. She came to terms with the problem of forgiveness at last through him. In his youth he had done many bloody deeds, some in Rome against the Christians, but now, bitterly regretting them, he sought absolution. Martha grew to love him and in that love understood what Jesus had meant by forgiveness. For a long time she had resisted connecting the words he was reputed to have said on the cross about his persecutors: "Forgive them for they know not what they do", with her own feelings about the persecution of her family and friends by Nero. Suddenly she saw the connection and the significance. She told Ethne she was free of bitterness at last – free of the parasite of hate that was suffocating her. For was not Nero blind, as Saul of Tarsus had been when he set off from Damascus to torment and punish Christians and ended up giving his life for them? And did we not all have something to regret from our past when we saw less clearly than we do now?

Decius had recently retired from the army and built himself a villa close to the town. He was now an influential member of the civil administration, married to Julia Sabinus. Demosthenes sensed no great love between them, as between Lucius and Ethne, but the marriage seemed to work well enough, each pursuing his or her own agenda without interfering with the other.

He wondered what had happened to Megan and the Egyptian. Nothing had been heard directly from them since they left Aquae Sulis early that autumn. Three years after their departure a traveller had told him of a Temple of Isis he had visited on an island in the far southern reaches of the Nile, where the power and presence of the Goddess was so strongly felt that people were flocking to it from far and wide. Demosthenes wondered when he heard a description of the High Priest and Priestess of this place if they were in fact Megan and her lover. There could not be many Egyptians with flaming auburn hair.

Brendan was never caught. Some said he joined the Ordovicians in their fight to keep the Romans out of their country. He certainly never returned to Aquae Sulis. Gaius Agrippa was rumoured to have died doing battle with some tribesmen in the mountains during the first few weeks of his pursuit.

Suddenly Demosthenes was brought back to the moment by the sound of rushing water. He frowned. Something was wrong. He would have thought he would have reached the landing stage at the town by now and could not understand why there were no boats drawn up. Surely no other fool was venturing on the river in this weather? He guessed he must have misjudged the distance. With visibility so low, time and space seemed out of focus. And what was this sound? There was no waterfall so close to the town.

The fog lifted slightly and he uttered an exclamation. Directly in front of him the river rushed down the curved steps of a weir, churning up the water into a rough and wild pool. His frail boat was caught and whirled around, narrowly escaping splintering against a stone wall. Somehow, he pulled back enough to see what was ahead. Beyond the weir there was the broad arch of a stone bridge. The bridge supported buildings along its whole length. It was as though the town continued – ignoring the river in its way altogether. But what town? Where was he? Everything was different.

The sun struggled through the fog and even as he stared in amazement, his surroundings became clear. On the bank to the left a huge building with a colonnade of columns rose. To the right he saw trees and people walking. They stared at him curiously for a moment and then walked on. He gasped at their strange clothes, mothers pushing babies in little chariots, fathers in tight clothes with writing and pictures on their chests. Some of the buildings had writing on their walls.

He looked back the way he had come and another city stood in the place of the one he had known. Buildings crowded upon buildings, tall spires pointed at the sky. The hills were the same shape as he remembered but now were covered with houses. Could it be? Was it possible? He remembered the flashes of vision he had had from time to time when he had seen a place as it was in the distant past or in the distant future. Could he be seeing the future of Aquae Sulis?

He pulled the boat up to the bank and scrambled ashore. He walked the streets, trembling with excitement, astonished at the vehicles that rushed past him. Everything he had known had gone. A huge temple-like building loomed before him. He stared up and up at its carved and decorated façade. Two towers with stone ladders intrigued him. Stone figures were struggling up towards a figure dominating the whole at the top.

He searched for the temples he had known, but he could not see them. He noticed people pushing in great crowds through an open doorway. A sign read: "To the Roman Baths". He listened to what people were saying as he followed the crowd. It seemed that the Roman baths had lain forgotten and unknown, buried under the earth, for centuries. He was shocked to learn that almost twenty centuries had gone by since he had bathed in those waters. Now all was in ruin and in place of the friendly arguments between bathers, the sweet songs of musicians from the perambulatory, there was only the sound of the shuffling of the crowd and the murmur of hundreds of voices speaking a dozen different languages.

It seemed the Romans had ruled Britain for more than three centuries. During that time, Aquae Sulis had been important and prosperous with its fertile valley, hot waters and temples. He wondered why the Romans had left.

The Temple of Sulis Minerva had disappeared completely. There were signs pointing to where it had been, and in another place the broken pediment had been pieced together in an attempt to show how it once was. The great head was labelled: "The Gorgon's Head"!

After the first excitement of seeing what was before him, Demosthenes began to feel lost and lonely. Where were his friends?

He was perturbed that his vision was lasting so long and that it felt so solid. He wanted to go back. He did not like the crush and push of staring people, the feeling of loss and bewilderment. Someone grabbed his arm.

"There you are!" A cheerful voice said close beside him. "I've been looking everywhere for you."

He turned and examined the face close to his. It was that of a stranger – but a stranger grinning at him as though he was known.

"What's the matter, Jack?" the voice continued. "You look as though you've seen a ghost!"

He looked down at the hand on his arm. He saw his own clothes, his own body. He was no longer an aged Greek priest in flowing robes, but dressed in unfamiliar trousers and shirt like everyone around him, his body firm and young…

He knew, this time, there would be no going back.

Notes

Chapter 1

Page 13 – Cadbury Castle, a Celtic hill fort approximately twelve miles south east of Glastonbury, Somerset, was occupied briefly by the Romans who put down an insurrection there in 70 AD.

Page 16 – The Pythea, or Pythoness, the famous Oracle of Apollo at Delphi in Greece. On the seventh day of each month she underwent ritual purification and then, seated on a tripod over a chasm out of which billowed fumes from the Underworld, and chewing bay leaves to invoke a hallucinogenic state, she prophesied. Priests interpreted her enigmatic pronouncements before they were given to the client.

The Sibyl of Cumae. A famous Oracle inhabiting underground caves and tunnels near Naples in Italy. In the fifth century BC the Sibyl of Cumae, a priestess of Apollo, offered to sell King Tarquin nine books of prophecy. The King refused, saying the price was too high. She threw three of them on the fire, and demanded a higher price for the remaining six. Again he refused, so she threw another three on the fire. The king bought the last three and they were kept in the capitol in Rome. They were known as the Sibylline Books and gave instruction for gaining the favours of the gods.

Page 16 – Sul's Sacred Hill. It is known that the goddess Sul was worshipped on several hills around Bath in Celtic times. One, now simply called Round Hill, off Mount Road in the district of Southdown, Bath, rising above the southern ridge that rims the town, has always seemed to me a likely sacred hill. The view from the top is extraordinary. Glastonbury Tor, almost 20 miles away, is visible on a clear day, and I cannot believe that it has not been used as a special place since prehistoric times. It has more recently been used as a beacon hill, and sometimes, on Good Friday at Easter, three crosses in imitation of Golgotha are erected on the summit. Kelston, on the opposite ridge, was probably similarly sacred.

Later in this story I mention Solsbury. Please note this is not the same hill, but a much larger iron age hill fort to the north east of Bath, near Batheaston and Swainswick, now in the care of the National Trust.

Chapter 3

Page 27 – On the death of Prasutagus, the king of the Iceni, the Roman administrators acted as though the tribal lands had become the property of Rome though he had left them to his wife Boudicca, in trust for his daughters. Corrupt officials tyrannized the population. Boudicca herself was flogged for flouting their authority, and her daughters raped.

The Trinovants, a neighbouring tribe, also thoroughly disenchanted by Roman rule, joined the Iceni in a violent uprising c.60 AD.

The Celtic forces swept through the country with tremendous speed, burning and slaughtering indiscriminately, but were finally stopped and, in their turn, massacred.

Chapter 4

Page 30 – Orpheus was originally a great hero of Thrace, possibly a king, distinguished for his wisdom and his musical talents, rather than for his warrior exploits. He was believed to be the son of Apollo, playing the lyre with such skill that beasts of the fields and forests, and even trees, gathered round him to listen.

When his great love, Eurydice, died from the bite of a snake, he journeyed to the Underworld and persuaded Hades and Persephone to allow him to take her back to earth. The only stipulation was that he was not to look back until they were safely out of the Underworld. Anxious to know if she was following, he looked over his shoulder – and lost her forever.

A Mystery Religion grew up around his name – featuring love and harmony between all beings. Texts believed to be songs and poems by him were closely studied. One of his most famous followers was Pythagoras (c.570-470 BC), a sage from Samos, who performed miracles and founded a centre at Crotona in southern Italy teaching Chaldean, Egyptian and Orphic wisdom. The Pythagoreans believed in reincarnation, and were vegetarian. They also believed with other followers of Orphism that mankind had inherited the guilt of their ancestors, the Titans, for which they were being punished by being kept prisoners in the flesh until they were "redeemed". They believed all, and not just "the gods", had immortality, but blessedness had to be earned. Pythagoras, like Orpheus, was believed to have completed a journey to the Otherworld while still in the body. The possibility of such a journey was therefore an acceptable tenet of their belief system.

Certain "golden leaflets" were found in third century BC tombs at Thurii, near Crotona, the centre for Orphism in Southern Italy, describing the Otherworld in vivid and beautiful detail.

Great philosophers who gained from and contributed to Orphism, such as Pythagoras, Heraclitus and Plato, broke away from the anthropomorphism of Greek religion and spoke of God as a spiritual power or

276

energy. It was the mysticism of Orphism that led easily into the mysticism of Christianity and it was likely that St. Paul, succeeding with the Greeks where he failed with the Jews, was familiar with this mysticism.

There are several instances of floor mosaics throughout the Roman Empire that depict Orpheus, and behind him the chi-rho symbol which is made up of the Greek initials for Christ's name.

Page 30 – In chapter 9 of *Bristol and Avon Archaeology 1990/91* there is an article by James Russell on the remains of a Roman villa at Newton St. Loe, near Bath, which inspired me to place the villa of Aulus Sabinus in this area. It seems the villa was discovered during the building of the Great Western Railway in 1837. It was destroyed, but luckily a young engineer, T. E. M. Marsh, working on the railway, recorded all he could of it. One of the finest features was a mosaic of Orpheus surrounded by animals and trees. Parts of this mosaic are in the City Museum at Bristol, England.

Page 31 – When the Romans found that the Celts in this area worshipped a goddess called Sul, they "Romanized" her by associating her with their own goddess Minerva. Actually, Minerva had first appeared in Etruria associated with lightning and thunder, where she was depicted with wings, holding an owl in her hand. Later, the Roman Minerva, believed to have sprung fully formed from Jupiter's head, was associated with work and wisdom. Later still, she became a warrior goddess with spear, helmet, and shield decorated with a fearsome Gorgon's head.

Chapter 5

Page 38, and Epilogue – Bath Abbey has carvings of angels ascending and descending stone ladders carved on the two west towers. The Biblical reference is to Jacob's dream: Genesis chap.28, v.12.

Pages 38ff – Plato's concept of "the periodic creation and destruction of civilisations" must have been well known to the Demosthenes of this novel (*Mystery Religions in the Ancient World*, Joscelyn Godwin, Thames & Hudson, 1981, p.119). Also, the concept of continuous and inexorable change so vividly described by Heraclitus. He has no illusions that what he sees around him is immutable and witnesses, in visionary form, the changes that are to come with calm acceptance.

Chapter 7

Page 58 – Sabinus is the family name of Vespasian. In the year following Nero's suicide in 68 AD Rome was virtually in the throes of civil war. Three men became emperor: Galba, Otho and Vitellius, each overthrown within months of taking power. Stability returned only when the commoner Vespasian (the first of the Flavian emperors) took over in 70 AD.

Pages 56, 59ff – An uprising of Jews against the Romans in Judaea was crushed by Vespasian and his eldest son Titus.

The utter destruction of the Temple of Jerusalem by the Romans occurred in 70 AD, closely followed by the siege of the mountain of Masada and subsequent suicide of all the defenders, men, women and children, just before the Romans reached the summit in 73 AD.

Joseph ben Matthias (later known as Flavius Josephus) was born 37 AD, the year Caligula became emperor. He visited Rome in 64, the year Rome burned under Nero. He died c.100. He began as a leader of the Jewish rebels and ended as a fervent Roman supporter. He wrote a vivid contemporary account of these events in *The Jewish War*.

The temple the Romans destroyed in Jerusalem was the Third Temple. The *First Temple* built by Solomon c.966 BC was to house the mysterious and powerful Ark of the Covenant containing the very tablets of stone Moses brought from Sinai inscribed with the Ten Commandments. It was of legendary magnificence... polished paving stones of intricate geometric design... two huge columns at the entrance inscribed with secret and symbolic names... a huge bronze bowl standing on the backs of twelve brazen oxen... walls of gold richly decorated with images of angels with wings outspread... fine curtains of blue and purple and crimson embroidered with pomegranates... ten gigantic seven-branched candle-sticks in two rows of five glimmering in the darkness of an inner sanctum leading to the Holy of Holies where the Ark of the Covenant lay... (2 Chronicles: 3-7). An Egyptian pharaoh attacked Jerusalem and carried away much of the treasure from the Temple (c.925 BC) after Solomon's death. (1 Kings: 14 v.25,26). Joash repaired the Temple. (2 Chronicles: 24). Nebuchadnezzar II, the Chaldean king, attacked Jerusalem c.597 BC and deported the Jewish population to Babylon. (2 Kings: 24,25. 2 Chronicles: 36. Jeremiah: 37-39,52. Dan 1:1).

The *Second Temple* was built by the Israelites after their return from captivity in Babylon at the time of Cyrus and Darius c.520 BC. (2 Chronicles: 36, v.22. Ezra: 6,3).

The *Third Temple* was built by Herod "the Great" c.19 BC, and it was this one that Jesus must have known as a youth. Although magnificent it had only one gigantic seven-branched candlestick (menorah), which is the one taken back to Rome by Titus and Vespasian, displayed at their triumphant procession, and represented on a victory column still extant among the ruins of ancient Rome today.

Ezekiel's vision of Jerusalem and the Temple can be found in the Bible (Ezekiel: 40-48).

(The above dates are taken from *Chronology of the Ancient World* by H. E. L. Mellersh, Book Club Associates, London (from the Barrie and Jenkins edition 1976.)

Chapter 8

Pages 63 and 64 – Glastonbury in Somerset, England is no longer an island. It is a place rich in legend, one of the most persistent being that the uncle of Jesus, Joseph of Arimathea, came there and established the first Christian spear-head in Britain.

Some believe that he brought the boy Jesus on one at least of his expeditions to the tin mines of Cornwall, when he was a wealthy merchant. See William Blake's famous hymn *Jerusalem*: "And did those feet in ancient times walk upon England's mountains green?"

Glastonbury was already a powerful sacred place for the ancient peoples. The Celts believed it was an entrance to the Otherworld, and a gigantic magical figure, Gwyn ab Nudd, stood upon the Tor and welcomed the dead as they were ferried across the marshes.

In Roman times it was known as "Glastonia", and in Saxon times "Ynys Gwidrin" meaning "glassy isle". Centuries later it became known as Avalon because of its many apple orchards (from the British word "aval" for apple), and was associated with the heroic stories of King Arthur. Before Henry VIII destroyed the great Christian abbey there in the 16th century, it had been for centuries a centre of holiness and scholarship renowned throughout Europe.

Page 64 – Here follows a brief chronology relevant to the apostles Peter and Paul, based on information in the book *Chronology of the Ancient World* by H. E. L. Mellersh, pub. Barrie and Jenkins, London, 1976:

AD 26	Pontius Pilate became Prefect of Galilee.
AD 30	Traditional date for the crucifixion of the man known as Jesus, the Christ.
AD 33	Saul of Tarsus is converted to Christianity on his way to Damascus to persecute the Christians, and takes the name "Paul".
AD 36	Paul meets Peter in Jerusalem.
AD 39	Caligula declares himself a god. Caligula dismisses Herod Antipas from the Tetrarchy of Galilee and appoints Herod Agrippa (grandson of Herod the Great who built the Third Temple) in his place. Caligula cancels his proposed invasion of Britain.
AD 41	Caligula murdered.
AD 43	Romans invade Britain under Claudius.

AD 44	Herod Agrippa kills James the Apostle and puts Peter in prison. Herod Agrippa dies.
AD 45/7	Paul on missionary journey. Annoys the Jews by preaching to the Gentiles (heathen/pagans). Peter stays at home.
AD 50	Paul's second journey.
AD 51/2	Paul in Athens and Corinth.
AD 53/7	Paul's third journey. Ephesus. (Note: the letters and writings of Paul were probably all the Christian scriptures available at that time. Other Gospels written later.)
AD 58	Paul arrested in Jerusalem by Romans on the advice of angry Jews. House arrest for two years.
AD 60	Paul appeals to be tried in Rome as he is a Roman citizen. (This is the year of Boudicca's revolt in Britain and the end of the power of the Druids.)
AD 61	Paul shipwrecked off Malta. Reaches Rome. Is under house arrest but goes on preaching.
AD 64	Great fire in Rome which Nero blames on the Christians. Dreadful persecution. Peter in prison in Rome is crucified upside down.
AD 65	Paul is decapitated.
AD 66	Revolt in Judaea against corrupt Roman procurators.
AD 67	Vespasian and his son Titus forcibly restore order in Judaea.
AD 69	Vespasian declared Emperor at Alexandria and returns to Rome.
AD 71	Triumphal procession in Rome to celebrate Judaean victory.

Page 65 – The Fosse Way. The Roman invaders set about building roads as soon as they could, to transport troops and provisions. We know the three major ones as Watling Street, Ermine Street, and the Fosse Way. The Fosse Way, which became a major trade link, runs from the south-west coast near Seaton, not far from Exeter, to Lincoln in the north east, passing through Bath on the way and hardly deviating from a straight line along the whole length of 200 miles. Today much of the Fosse Way lies beneath fields, but parts of it are still in use, for example, in sections of the A358, A37, A429, A46.

Page 67 – The Celtic year was divided into four parts with a great festival marking the beginning of each part:

Samhain	1st November. The first in the Celtic year. When the beings of the Otherworld became visible to the beings of this world. Present day "Halloween".

Imbolc	1st February. A pastoral festival. Honouring the Female Trinity: Maid, Mother, Grandmother.

Imbolc   1st February. A pastoral festival. Honouring the Female Trinity: Maid, Mother, Grandmother.

Beltain   1st May. Distinguished by magical rites to promote growth and fertility. Cattle were driven through bonfires to purify them. (This custom suggested to me the ceremony of fire to purify the Tor and its ghosts.)

Lughnasa   1st August. Harvest festival. Honouring the god Lugh – Wisdom and Light.

Chapter 9

Page 69 – Isis. An extremely important ancient Egyptian goddess. Wife and sister of Osiris. Mother of Horus, the far-seeing, hawk-headed god. She was a powerful magician who even dared to trick the Mightiest God of all into revealing his secret name, which she then used against him.

Apuleius, the 2nd century author of the book *The Golden Ass*, points out that she is, and has always been, the ultimate and universal Goddess, though in different cultures she has appeared under different names. See *The Golden Ass*, Lucius Apuleius, trans. Robert Graves, Penguin, 1969, p.271.

Page 71 – The Morrigan. The triple raven war-goddess of the Celts: the Three Morrigana – sexually potent as well as mighty controllers of battles. Noted for skill in prophecy and in cunning shape-changing. In one Irish legend the Morrigan, while punishing the hero Cuchulainn for rejecting her sexual advances, changes from a slippery black eel coiling around his legs to a russet-coloured she-wolf to distract him so that his human enemy might have a better chance of killing him.

Page 72– Many curses inscribed on thin pieces of lead and then rolled up, were found in the sacred spring at Bath when the archaeologists investigated. For example:

"Decimedis has lost two gloves. He asks that the person who has stolen them should lose his mind and his eyes in the temple where she appears."

"I curse him who has stolen, who has robbed Deomioris from this house. Whoever stole his property, the god is to find him. Let him buy it back with his blood and his own life."

"Uricalus, Docilosa his wife, Ducilis his son and Docilima, Decentinus his brother, Agoliosa: the names of these who have sworn at the Spring of the Goddess Sulis on April 12th. Whosoever has perjured himself there you are to make him pay for it to the Goddess Sula in his own blood."

Chapter 11

Page 84 – Many inscriptions from Roman times are still to be seen in the Bath area:

"Lucius Vitellius Tancinus, son of Martalus, a tribesman of Caurium in Spain, trooper of the Cavalry Regiment of Vettones, Roman citizen, aged 46, of 26 years service, lies buried here."

Statue base: "To Suleviae Sulinus, a sculptor, son of Brucetius, gladly and deservedly made this offering."

Altar: "This holy spot, wrecked by insolent hands and cleansed afresh, Gaius Severius Emeritus, centurion in charge of the region, has restored to the virtue and Deity of the Emperor."

"Peregrinus, son of Secundus, a Treveran, to Loucetius mars and Nemetona willingly and deservedly fulfilled his vow."

Dedication block: "… son of Novantus set this up for himself and his family as the result of a vision."

Page 89, and chapter 13 page 97 – It was not only the Egyptians who believed that a statue could be "taken over" by the spirit of the god it represented. The Greek Porphyry spoke of the "divine power" of a statue and the fact that it could have a life of its own. There were many tales circulating around the Classic world about such miraculous happenings. Lucian (Philoseudes,18) tells of a statue walking about a town at night. Others that were taken from their original sites, returning there by themselves. "At Hierapolis statues were worshipped which perspired, moved and gave oracular answers." (Lucian De Syria dea,10). We may mock such superstitions today but it is interesting that whenever a hated government is overturned the rioting people attack and destroy the statues of the oppressors almost before they do anything else. Witness recent attacks on the statues of Lenin and Stalin in the former Soviet Union. In recent times there have been claims that statues of the Virgin Mary have wept, and Christ on the cross bled. In 1995, the statues of a Hindu god were believed to drink milk put before them. In the Middle Ages the Knights Templar were reputed to have a stone head in their possession that prophesied. Certainly, the ancient Celts believed that stone heads gave oracular pronouncements.

282

Chapter 13

Page 97 – Serapis: a hybrid god worshipped in Egypt probably not before the Greek pharaoh Ptolomy I (c.304-282 BC). Serapis is a combination of the ancient Egyptian Lord of the Otherworld, Osiris, and the sacred Apis bull of Memphis.

Page 100 – Osiris: the husband and brother of Isis who was dismembered by his brother Seth. Isis bound the parts of him together again and, taking the form of a bird, fanned him with her wings until he came alive again long enough to father a son on her (Horus). Because of this he became the symbol for resurrection and new life and was set up as King of the Underworld before whom we must all go to be judged worthy of eternal life.

Chapter 14

Page 103 – Sela: today known as Petra in Jordan. Dean Burgen, the Victorian traveller and poet, called it the "rose-red city, half as old as time." It was a city of the independent Nabataean kingdom until 106 AD when it was annexed by the Roman emperor Trajan. After the fall of Rome in the fifth century it was deserted, and fell into ruin. It was rediscovered in the early 19th century for Europeans by a German traveller, Buckhardt, and is now an exciting and popular destination for travellers.

Chapter 15

Page 109 – Overlooking present day Bath to the northeast, near Batheaston and St. Catherine's, is a flat topped hill, with the remains of an ancient Celtic hill fort called Solsbury Hill. Some say it is where King Bladud built his town in imitation of the cities he had seen in Greece. No stone ruins were found in this century, but that does not necessarily mean that there were none in 72 AD. He built his healing sanctuary in the valley, for it was there he discovered by personal experience that the hot waters bubbling up from deep underground had healing properties.

Page 113 – King Bladud. There is a persistent legend in the northeast Somerset area around the City of Bath in England, that in the ancient days a wise king, descended from Aeneas of Troy, lived and died. His dynasty was reputedly founded by Brutus, the grandson of Aeneas, and his Greek wife, who came to Britain, landing at Totnes in Devon. Hudibras was his father, and Lear was his son (later immortalized by Shakespeare in his play *King Lear*). Many wonders were attributed to him – notably the ability to fly like Daedalus, and to heal, like Aesculapius. He was believed to have founded the first academy in Britain to study philosophy, having brought back four philosophers from Greece. Dates attributed to him vary between 800 and 500 BC. For further information see my novel *The Winged Man* published by Headline in 1993. Also *Histories of the Kings of Britain* by Geoffrey of Monmouth, trans. Lewis Thorpe, Penguin, 1996; and *Bladud of Bath* by Howard C. Levis, Chiswick Press, 1919, and Pitman Press, Bath, 1973.

Chapter 16

Page 122 – To find the Chalice, the sacred cup, that Jesus reputedly drank from at the last Passover supper he attended before his arrest, became a major quest in later years, the object itself becoming a potent symbol for the Quest of the Soul for its mystic origins. In the Middle Ages Chrétien de Troyes in France in 1185, Wolfram von Eschenbach in Germany in 1211, and many other writers, composed major poetic narratives on the search for the Holy Grail (as it became known) and in Britain it became linked with the King Arthur legends.

As mythic material ebbed and flowed through the original story of the man, the cup and the supper, the story grew richer and more complex. It became associated with the classic Horn of Plenty out of which food endlessly poured to nourish the multitudes, and the cup of the Celtic goddess Ceridwen that contained all knowledge and wisdom. Even the cauldron of Bran, which gave life back to soldiers who died in battle, became part of its tradition. The Grail, mysterious, hidden, still haunts the imagination of writers and readers – always beckoning, yet just out of reach to those who are not worthy. To become worthy, even to glimpse it, leads us to strive to be better than we are.

For more about the Grail see my own book *Mythical Journeys: Legendary Quests*, published by Cassells in 1996. Also:

Eschenbach, Wolfram von, *Parzival*, trans. Helen M. Mustard and Charles E. Passage, Vintage Books, New York, 1961; another translation is by A. T. Hatto, Penguin Books, Harmondsworth, 1980.

Jung, Emma and Marie-Louise von Franz, *The Grail Legend*, trans. Andrea Dykes, Sigo Press, Boston; Coventure, London, 1986.

Matthews, John (ed.), *At the Table of the Grail*, RKP, London, 1984.

——, *King Arthur and the Grail Quest: Myth and Vision from Celtic Times to the Present*, Blandford, London, 1994.

——, *The Grail: The Quest for the Eternal*, Thames and Hudson, London, 1981.

——, and Marion Green, *The Grail Seeker's Companion: A Grail Guide to the Grail Quest in the Aquarian Age*, The Aquarian Press, Wellingborough, 1986.

Page 123 – Martha's "lost" day. There are many myths and legends about humans straying into "Otherworld" territory and finding that they have "lost" time as this world knows it. There is a Welsh story of an unhappy boy who is taken underwater to the kingdom of the Tylwyth Teg where he plays a game with a golden ball. He becomes restless and finds his way home. He believes he has only been away two weeks, but his mother tells him he has been away for two years. There is another Welsh story of a shepherd boy being taken to the Otherworld where he finds a fine wooded country, a palace, and beautiful singing birds. He finds he cannot speak until a young maiden kisses him. He lives there among these happy people for a year and a day. But when he returns home he finds that he has been away for years. He has not aged, but his family and friends have. See *The Fairy-Faith in Celtic Countries* by Y. W. Evans-Wentz, pub. Colin Smythe, Gerrards Cross, 1977, pp. 148-149 and 161-162.

Chapter 17

Page 131 – The ability to enter another's "mind space" is well known in certain circles. Paul Brunton, on page 275 of *A Search in Secret Egypt*, pub. Rider, 1980 (first published 1935) describes meeting an Adept who could exchange thoughts with another no matter how far they were apart, and could even temporarily take over the body of another in a process called "over-shadowing".

Chapter 18

Page 156 – The desire to fly has ever been the aspiration of the human race. In legend there are many instances of humans achieving flight, and I see no reason why para-gliding and hang-gliding might not have been within the skill of certain enterprising men in ancient times. It is known, for instance, that manned kites were flown in China. From Crete, we have the powerful story of Daedalus and Icarus. From the ancient Celts we get the legend of the Druid Mog Ruith, a sorcerer who could create tempests. In the story of "The Siege of Druim Damhghaire" he put on a speckled bird-dress and "rose up, in company with the fire, into the air and the heavens" (Anne Ross: *The Pagan Celts*, pp. 114,115).

For the flight of King Bladud see Geoffrey of Monmouth, *The History of the Kings of Britain* II xx, Penguin, p.81.

Chapter 20

Page 167 – The Colosseum in Rome was started by Vespasian in 72 AD, continued by his son Titus (Emperor from 79 to 81 AD), and finished by Domitian (Vespasian's younger son, Emperor from 81 to 96 AD).

Chapter 22

Page 191 – In AD 79 the volcano Vesuvius erupted and destroyed Pompeii. The city, buried almost instantaneously by ash and pumice was rediscovered only in 1750 in a remarkable state of preservation. Excavation continues today while millions of travellers marvel at the ruins. In 1834 Lord Bulmer Lytton wrote his classic novel *The Last Days of Pompeii* (pub. George Routledge & Sons, London).

Chapter 23

Page 198 – Martha's meeting with the three mysterious women on the Tor is suggestive not only of Mary and her son, The Saviour, but of the Celtic Triple Goddess and the mysterious infant known in Welsh myth as The Mabon. A book that deals most interestingly with the Mabon and the Modron (The Son and The Mother) as it appears in the *Mabinogion* (a collection of ancient Welsh tales) is *Mabon and the Mysteries of Britain: An Exploration of the Mabinogion,* by Caitlin Matthews, Arkana, London 1987. On page 152 Matthews asks "And if he is without a personal name, what might that name be?" On pages 167, 168, and 172, she examines the Mabon archetype – the hero who is born with Otherworld connections, is rejected and hidden, comes into his own at last and takes on a redemptive role.

Page 198 – The idea of a revelation at the bottom of the cup I adapted from an ancient Irish story about Cuchulain. Three men argued as to whom was the greatest hero amongst them. Queen Maeve, who had been asked to arbitrate, gave each a cup. One a bronze Chalice with a bird of silver at the bottom. One a silver Chalice with a bird of red gold at the bottom. The third, the one she intended for the greatest hero, a Chalice of red gold with a bird of precious crystal at the bottom. (See *Early Irish Myths and Sagas* by Jeffrey Gantz, Penguin Classics, 1981; *Crystal Legends* by Moyra Caldecott, Aquarian Press/HarperCollins, 1990).

Page 198 – The name at the bottom of the Chalice. Not only did the ancient Egyptians believe that names have a particular magical significance and consequently destroyed the names of those pharaohs who became anathema (e.g. Akhenaten and Hatshepsut) so that they would have no power over future generations, but many other cultures, including the Celts, had similar beliefs. In magical rituals, naming invokes the power of those named, as does prayer. "Do not take the name of the Lord thy God in vain," is an awesome commandment. From the last book of the Christian Bible we get the following:

"His eyes are like a flame of fire, and on his head are many diadems: and he has a name inscribed, which no one knows but himself." (Revelations, chap.19, v.12).

"To him that overcometh will I give to eat of a hidden manna, and will give him a white stone, and in the stone a new name written, which no man knoweth saving he that receiveth it." (Revelations, chap.2, v.17).

Chapter 24

Page 219 – "Two spheres bound with thongs…" Note that the ancients knew many things that were later forgotten or denied by Medieval scholars. Example: Anaxagoras the Greek, who lived before Socrates, knew that the moon's light was derived from the sun and that eclipses of the moon were due to its being screened by the earth. He taught that the heavenly bodies were red hot stones – not gods – and that the true god was an abstract force – not in human form. (Richard Olson, *Science Deified, and Science Defied*, pub. Univ. of California Press, 1982, p.79).

Aristarchus of Samos knew the earth went round the sun – yet more than a millennia later people were being burned at the stake for suggesting this "heresy".

Chapter 25

Page 240 – Of the many legends that are centred on Glastonbury, Somerset, there is one that involves a confrontation between the 6th century Saint Collen and Gwyn ab Nudd, a powerful and magical being of the Celtic Otherworld. To Collen, a Christian hermit, living at the base of the Tor, Gwyn ab Nudd was a demon. He received three invitations to meet with Gwyn at the top of the Tor, but the first two he refused. The third time, taking some holy water with him, he went. "And when he came there he saw the fairest castle he had ever beheld" surrounded by comely youths and maidens. On entering, he saw Gwyn "sitting in a golden chair" before a banquet. He was invited to eat and offered anything his heart could desire. But he refused and threw holy water over everything he saw. "Whereupon they vanished from his sight, so that there was neither castle, nor troops, nor men, nor maidens, nor music, nor song, nor steeds, nor youths, nor banquet, nor the appearance of any thing whatever, but the green hillocks." This legend may be found in the following books:

The Green Lady and the King of Shadows, Moyra Caldecott, Gothic Image, Glastonbury, 1989.

Lives of the British Saints (Saint Collen), S. Baring Gould, John Hodges, London, 1875.

The Mabinogion, trans. Lady Charlotte Guest, J.M. Dent & Co., 1906, p.310, note to p.100.

In fact, stories of humans stumbling into the presence of Otherworld beings and witnessing sumptuous banquets of which they are invited to partake are very common. In past times they were thought to be encounters with gods, fairies, angels or demons. Now they are thought to be encounters with beings from other planets: "extra-terrestrials."

From the book *The Fairy Mythology* by Thomas Keightley (pub. George Bell, 1892 and Wildwood House, 1981, p.283) we get the Yorkshire story about a peasant returning home late at night from a neighbouring town who heard singing from a burial mound. He went to investigate ... found a door open ... and entered. There he saw a great hall full of people enjoying a banquet. An attendant offered him a cup but he poured out the liquid without drinking it and ran away with the cup. The legend has it that this cup of unknown material and unusual form and colour was presented to the king and possibly still exists in some royal treasury.

The implication of most of these stories is that if one actually eats the Otherworld food one is trapped in that world and cannot return to one's own – or not for a very long time. One is *committed*. Note that Persephone in the Greek myth had to stay with Hades in the Underworld because she bit into a pomegranate in his kingdom. The eating and drinking of the bread and wine at the Christian Eucharist is also a commitment.